He could see Tanya, but she was not alone.
A tall man was with her, a man with a dark,
hawk-like face, and Luke knew at once that
he was no customer. They were standing intimately close. Tanya was looking up at him
with a light in her face that he had never seen
before. He could not hear what she said, but
her companion bent his head and kissed her,
her arms went round him and they melted together into a long embrace that was oblivious
of anyone around them.

Luke stood staring at them, filled with a deep
and passionate anger that seemed to well up
and choke him so that he could not bear to
watch a moment longer. He turned and went
blindly down the stairs.

Constance Heaven

★ ★ ★

THE FIRE STILL BURNS

Mandarin

A Mandarin Paperback

THE FIRE STILL BURNS

First published 1989
by William Heinemann Ltd
This edition published 1990
Reprinted 1991
by Mandarin Paperbacks
Michelin House, 81 Fulham Road, London SW3 6RB

Mandarin is an imprint of the Octopus Publishing Group

Copyright © Constance Heaven 1989

A CIP catalogue record for this title
is available from the British Library
ISBN 0 7493 0296 8

Printed in Great Britain
by Cox & Wyman Ltd, Reading

For SIMON and JEAN
with Pippa, Joe and Toby

From my youth upwards
My spirit walk'd not with the souls of men
Nor look'd upon the earth with human eyes;
The thirst of their ambition was not mine,
The aim of their existence was not mine,
My joys, my griefs, my passions, and my powers
Made me a stranger.

Byron, *Manfred*

Part One

LUKE
1930

1

Years later Luke was to think of that Wednesday morning in May
as a turning point in his life simply because nothing was the same
afterwards, but at the time all he remembered was the small red
car and the furiously barking dog that tripped him up so that the
banner he was carrying flew one way and he was flung the other,
skidding across the bonnet of the car and hitting his head so hard
against the kerb that he temporarily blacked out. When he opened
his eyes he was dimly aware of a vision with pale gold hair under
a scarlet tam o'shanter glaring down at him furiously while a small
crowd gathered round all loudly voicing different views as to what
had happened.

'You knocked me down,' he muttered groggily.

'No, I did not,' exclaimed the vision in high indignation. 'It was
you who knocked into me. Are you hurt? You'd better take this.'

A handkerchief was thrust into his hand only just in time. Blood
from the long split above his left eyebrow was running freely down
his cheek and dripping on to the jacket of his one good suit. He
dabbed at it ineffectively.

'Your forehead needs stitching,' said the vision crossly. 'I'd
better drive you to hospital.'

'I'm all right,' he murmured feebly and tried to sit up.

'No, you're not. You look ghastly.' She glanced about her.
'Someone help me get him into the car.'

'I will,' said a stocky young man who had picked up the fallen
banner, the only one of the small group of demonstrators who had
not discreetly melted away just in case the majesty of the law
should appear. Crudely written letters on the large cardboard sheet
screamed a flaming message about starving children and Welsh
miners.

'I'll give you a hand,' went on the young man. 'It's all my fault
really.' That was true, thought Luke muzzily, considering he had

3

never really wanted to take part in this idiotic demonstration. It was Colin who had persuaded him – which was odd, since *his* name wasn't Luke Llewellyn Jones and he'd never set foot in Wales, let alone gone down a coal mine.

A small boy obligingly offered to hold the banner while Luke was hauled to his feet and pushed into the little car. His ankle appeared to be badly bruised, and he uttered a yelp of pain when he tried to stand on it.

'Are you a friend of his?' demanded the vision.

'Yes, I am,' said the young man. 'We share digs. Will you be all right, old boy?' he went on anxiously. 'Shall I come with you?'

'No room,' announced the vision decisively, squeezing into the driver's seat beside Luke. She took the blood-stained handkerchief out of his hand, replacing it with a clean duster. 'I'd better hurry before he bleeds to death.'

'Where are you taking him?' shouted Colin above the sudden roar of the engine.

'Guy's,' she yelled back, sounding her horn imperiously just as a large policeman bore down upon them. The little crowd fell back reluctantly and she shot off down the road.

To Luke, unused to motor cars and his head throbbing, they seemed to dash through the busy city streets and across London Bridge at an alarming speed, horn blowing madly, and to avoid oncoming traffic by a miracle. They pulled up with a jerk in front of the hospital building. The vision got out and materialized into an extremely pretty girl in a short, pleated white skirt and scarlet jacket, with long, beautiful, silk-clad legs that even in his sick and sorry state Luke couldn't help appreciating.

'Come on.' She hauled him out of the car and, despite his protests, took him firmly by the arm as he limped up the steps and through a door marked Casualty.

There were a number of people there already huddled on the long row of benches looking depressed while a young nurse went from one to the other checking them off on a list.

'You'd better sit down,' said his guide, pushing him on to the end of one of the benches and grabbing the arm of the nurse as she came towards them enquiringly.

'My friend has been seriously injured. Would you go and fetch Dr Aylsham to look at him?'

4

She had a faint foreign accent, a precise manner of speech which intrigued Luke even through the sick pounding in his head. He frowned as he tried to concentrate. What on earth was she? French – German – Italian?

The nurse was staring at her in horror, rather as if she had been asked to go and fetch God.

'Oh no, I couldn't, miss, I couldn't really. There's a doctor in Casualty. Your friend will be examined in a few minutes.'

'A few minutes won't do. I want someone *now*. You tell Dr Aylsham that his daughter has had an accident. He'll come.'

'His daughter?' The nurse seemed taken aback. 'I'm sorry, miss, I didn't realize . . .'

'Well, don't just stand there with your mouth open. Go and fetch him,' said the girl impatiently. 'Can't you see how he's bleeding?'

'Yes, yes, of course . . .' The nurse gulped and fled while the other patients turned round to stare, curiosity mingled with indignation, much to Luke's embarrassment.

'You needn't have made such a fuss,' he protested, 'I could have waited.' Resentment at her high-handed manner was beginning to burn inside him.

'No, you couldn't. It might be very serious – how do you think I'd feel then?'

He might have made a sharp answer to the effect that surely it was *his* feelings that mattered rather than hers, but he was trying to combat an alarming wave of giddiness. He shut his eyes for a moment and opened them again to see a tall lean man in a white coat come briskly across to them.

'What's wrong this time, Tanya?' he was saying a trifle brusquely. 'Nurse Fisher said you had been hurt in an accident. Is it that wretched car again? Are you hurt?'

'Not me, Papa. I'm all right. It's this young man.'

'I'm beginning to regret that I ever allowed you to have a car, let alone drive it. Did you knock him down?'

'No, I didn't. He ran into me.'

'And what did the police have to say about it this time?' enquired the doctor drily. He sat down on the bench beside Luke and removed the hand that was still clutching the blood-soaked duster

5

to his forehead. 'M-m-m, very nasty. That needs stitching. Could be concussion too. How do you feel? Sick? Giddy?'

'Yes, a bit,' Luke confessed.

'I thought you might. We'll have to keep you in for a day or two under observation.'

'Oh no, I couldn't possibly stay. I have work to do. Couldn't you just stitch me up and stop this bleeding?'

'I could *and* let you walk out only to have you fall flat on your face in an hour or so. I'm afraid that won't do. There is such a thing as delayed concussion. You don't want to end up under another car, do you? We must keep you here for a while just to make sure.' He beckoned to the young nurse who had been hovering beside them. 'Take this young man up to Ward Seven and ask Sister to see him into bed. I'll be up in a few minutes.'

Luke opened his mouth to protest and the doctor held up an imperious hand. 'Now don't argue with me, boy. If my daughter knocked you down, then you're my responsibility. If there is someone who ought to know where you are, tell Sister and she will see that they are informed.'

If he hadn't felt so sick he might have fought against it, but as he got to his feet he came over so dizzy he began to think the doctor might be right. As he was led away he heard the girl ask anxiously, 'He won't die, will he?'

'Of course he won't, silly child.'

'Thank goodness. I must fly. I ought to have been at the gallery hours ago.'

'Very well, but don't rush, Tanya – drive slowly, for heaven's sake. I can't go on putting your victims together after you've knocked them apart.'

'Don't be beastly. There've only been two.'

'Two too many.'

'Look after him for me, Papa.'

The doctor laughed and patted his daughter's cheek. 'What else am I here for, puss?'

Then Luke was being bundled into the antiquated lift and heard no more as it slowly creaked up to the top floor.

A little later he had been efficiently put to bed in a hospital nightshirt and his blood-spattered jacket had been taken away by a ward maid who clucked disapprovingly over it. His forehead had been stitched, a light plaster fixed into place and he had been given an injection.

'Don't worry,' said the doctor as Luke looked alarmed. 'It's only against infection. There could be dirt in that injury of yours.'

His ankle was examined, pronounced bruised and strapped up, his blood pressure was taken, a thermometer was stuck in his mouth and cool fingers were on his pulse. Anyone would think he was really ill, he thought disgustedly.

The doctor wrote something on the chart that would hang at the end of his bed, handed it to the hovering nurse and looked down at him dispassionately.

'Well now,' he said, 'it doesn't seem too bad. Do you want us to inform your family in case they are wondering where you are?'

'They don't live in London,' Luke muttered.

'I see. My daughter told me you were carrying a banner. What was the burning cause? Welsh miners?'

Luke looked up, startled. 'How did you guess?'

Simon Aylsham smiled. The lilt in the boy's speech had been unmistakable. 'It wasn't very difficult. What about your employers?'

'I haven't any.'

'Looking for work?'

'No. I'm a student . . . at King's.'

'University of London, eh? What are you reading?'

'English,' Luke said reluctantly, resenting the note of surprise he had detected in the doctor's pleasant voice. He pushed himself up in the bed. 'That's why I can't possibly stay here. The finals are in June, only a few weeks away.'

The doctor's keen eye had already observed that this tall, rangy young man was a great deal too thin for his height. Starving himself, probably, on some tiny grant. He had an impression of pent-up energy, a spirit fired by burning ambition in grave danger of wearing away a naturally good physique.

'A few days away from your books won't make much difference. Take it easy, lad.' A hand eased him back against the pillow. 'Don't worry. That dizziness will pass sooner than you think,' went on the doctor reassuringly. 'Carry on, Nurse.'

He walked away and Luke watched him go, a handsome man in his way, lean aquiline features, dark brown hair lightly silvered,

7

about fifty perhaps, and speaking perfect English – so why did his daughter have that intriguing accent? His random thoughts were interrupted by another nurse, who seated herself by his bed: starched apron, starched cap, starched manner.

'A few details,' she said briskly, paper and pen in hand. 'Name, address, next of kin.'

Did they think he was on the point of death?

When she had done she handed him two pills and a glass of water.

'Swallow those and you'll soon be feeling a lot better. You're a very fortunate young man to be here in Dr Aylsham's private ward. I hope you feel properly grateful to be attended by one of the hospital's leading surgeons.'

'I didn't choose to be here at all,' he said indignantly.

'Well, you couldn't have arranged it better if you'd deliberately chosen to fall under his daughter's motor car,' she said tartly, taking the glass from him and tucking in his blankets. 'Now try to sleep before the tea trolley comes round.'

But he couldn't sleep, not immediately. He looked around the ward. There were expensive flowers by some of the beds, curtains were drawn around others. Nurses moved quietly about in their spotless white uniforms with their soft-soled shoes. This kind of treatment must cost a fortune. They wouldn't expect him to pay for it, would they? He was suddenly panic-stricken. He could never afford it, never! He had won a State Scholarship with an additional bursary but the tiny grants were barely enough to live on. He supplemented them where he could, doing all kinds of odd jobs and working four evenings a week in a Soho restaurant, peeling potatoes, washing up, anything that would bring in a few extra shillings and save him buying an evening meal, even though sometimes the heat and the constant smell of spicy food sickened him. But he hated to accept the small postal orders his mother sent to him regularly out of her scanty earnings when she needed every penny at home with his two young sisters still at school and Dai, his elder brother, out of work and married already with one baby and another on the way.

He thought of the overcrowded ward in the infirmary where, two years ago, his father had lain, slowly dying of the dreaded tuberculosis that afflicted so many miners – the cough that racked

8

his frail body, the bloodied towel, the plate of food slowly congealing by the bed because he was too weak to feed himself. The overworked doctors and nurses did their best, but the place was hopelessly old-fashioned, urgently needing new equipment, only kept going by the pitifully small subscriptions from the men's scanty wages. When his father died, he had offered to give up his scholarship, to go down the pit with his brother, to help alleviate the family's sorely straitened circumstances, but his mother wouldn't hear of it.

'It would break your dada's heart, Luke love,' she had said to him. 'He'd be crying out to me from the grave. Hasn't he been set on it ever since you won the place in the grammar school? Didn't he work night and day to keep you there? "Our Luke's going to be a fine scholar one day, Mary girl," he used to say. "He's not going down any old pit like his dada, coughing his lungs away." Right at the very last he spoke of it. "Remember now," he said, "wherever it is I'm going, I'll be watching and it's proud I'll be, you mark my words!"'

The tears had been in her eyes and she had shamefacedly dabbed at them with her apron.

His mind blurred as the drug took effect. What a queer result of the chance impulse that had brought him out with Colin Tait, who had a passion for lost causes and the well-meant zeal of the comfortably off who'd never trudged through the snow in leaking boots, had never gone hungry, never known the torment of watching someone you love slowly die because the treatment he needed was beyond your wildest dreams. Anyone could have told him that, four years after the General Strike and its dismal failure, any demonstration only aroused derision even if it wasn't broken up by the police. He drifted off to sleep at last and dreamed of enormous eyes shadowed by dark lashes, of pale golden hair and lovely bewitching legs – only they were not for him, never had been for him. He could not afford girls of any kind, not even Megan, who wrote him pathetically ill-spelled letters and was always stiflingly there when he saved enough money for the train fare home. He had known her since he was six. They had been snotty-nosed infants together at the council school; Megan with her long plaits and snub nose whom he had once dragged out of the muddy, stinking rivulet that ran along behind the row of

9

miners' black cottages and unwittingly earned her lifelong adoration.

The following day brought Dr Aylsham, making the rounds of his private patients. He paused by Luke's bed.

'So far, so good. No giddiness, no feeling as if the room is turning somersaults around you?'

'Only for a minute when I first stand up, then it goes off.'

'Excellent. If this goes on, we'll let you go home tomorrow, but you'll have to keep that ankle bound up.'

'I'd rather go today, sir. I'm grateful to you, but I'm all right now, really I am. I don't need any of this,' and he made a sweeping gesture around the ward.

'That's for me to decide.' He looked down at the boy's troubled face. 'Want something to read?'

'Oh yes, please.'

'I'll see what I can find.'

To Luke's surprise he was as good as his word, and later in the morning some magazines were dumped on his bed by Nurse Fisher.

'Aren't you the lucky one, treated like a prince,' she exclaimed breathlessly.

He caught at her hand. 'Why, nurse, why do you think?'

'Ask me another. I mustn't stop or Sister'll be after my blood.'

The magazines were mostly literary, except for one which at any other time he would never have dreamed of opening. He flipped idly through the pages of the *Tatler*, which seemed to be devoted exclusively to the gilded young amusing themselves, playing polo at Windsor, or chasing after the harmless fox, or eating at the Café de Paris or dancing cheek to cheek at fashionable night clubs. Then he stopped abruptly. One photograph had caught his eye. 'Lord and Lady Aylsham taking a day off from the hospital,' he read, and there was the man who had stitched up his head, in morning coat and grey topper, with a woman whose calm, beautiful face and simple, elegant dress even he could see had nothing in common with the bejewelled, befrilled and overdressed company surrounding her.

'Golly!' he said to himself. 'Golly! What the devil have I gone and got myself mixed up in?'

He suddenly had a mental picture of his father on that painful last visit before he died, stretching out a skeletal hand and gripping his arm.

'Never forget, son, however high you rise – and you will – I've never doubted it though I'll not be there to see it – never forget your roots are here in the good black earth of Wales.'

'And the good black coal too,' he had said, trying to joke in an attempt to hide the tears in his voice.

'Aye, that too. Don't despise it, Luke boy. It's served us well enough, your grandfather and me and Dai. Your brother's never looked further, more's the pity, but you have and it's for you to move on, speak out, tell the rest of the world about us, about Wales.'

He caught his breath in a painful cough and Luke put his arm around the thin shoulders till the spasm eased.

'But Dada,' he said gently, 'I'm going to be a teacher, not a politician.'

'A teacher can put the right ideas into the heads of children. He guides those who come after,' his father said hoarsely. 'And what about those exercise books you fill up with your writing, what about those, lad?' The eyes in the ravaged face burned with fever, the hot fingers gripped his hand painfully. 'D'you think I've not seen them up there hidden away among the schoolbooks?'

'Oh, they're nothing, just a lot of old scribbles while I'm thinking.'

He'd never confessed to anyone, not to Dai, not even to Megan, his burning ambition to write, create his own world, tell the story of the Welsh valleys, the warmth, the cruel poverty, the pride, the history and the rich poetry, put it on the literary map as Arnold Bennett had once put the five pottery towns. A laughable dream, they would call it, as yet only hovering in his mind, something he was afraid to speak of in case the bloom should vanish.

He was deep in one of the magazines when lunch came: chicken in a cream sauce, a fruit pudding. It was eaten and cleared away, and with the afternoon came Colin Tait, looking around him appreciatively, a huge grin on his pleasant, irregular features. He pulled up a chair and dropped into it.

'Well, you've struck it lucky, old chap, I must say, enjoying all

11

this VIP treatment. I could scarcely believe my ears when they directed me up here. You'll never have the nerve to sue his daughter for damages, not after this, will you now?'

'What on earth are you talking about? I don't want to sue anyone. It was my fault, or rather it was that blasted dog that tripped me up.'

'You could still make out a case and it won't be for the first time. She's a bit of a caution by all accounts, and her father has had to come to the rescue more than once so my pa tells me.'

Colin's father, James Tait, was a distinguished journalist on one of the more important dailies, a man who knew everyone, whose assignments had taken him all over Europe and the Near East, a man who viewed his world with an air of good-humoured cynicism.

'That's a beastly thing to say.' To his own considerable surprise Luke was suddenly up in arms against Colin's airy dismissal of the generous treatment he had received.

'Have it your own way, but doesn't it strike you as a bit peculiar for the most eminent surgeon at Guy's to be rushing to treat the cut forehead of a little whipper-snapper who happens to fall under the wheels of his daughter's car?'

'Oh, shut up!' Luke growled, the little glow of wellbeing in which he had been basking suddenly threatening to vanish.

'You know who they are, don't you?' his friend asked.

'No, why should I? I don't move in such exalted circles as you do.'

'Put a sock in it. Don't you ever read newspapers in the streets of the Rhondda?'

'Only those wrapped round the fish and chips.'

'It was a few years ago now,' went on Colin imperturbably. Like his father he had a nose for a good story. 'It seems Simon Aylsham was a very successful doctor in St Petersburg – or Leningrad, as they are calling the place nowadays – oh, for years and years, and he married a Russian princess. Then his elder brother was killed on the Western Front, so he inherited the title whether he wanted to or not, the Bolsheviki moved in and things became damned uncomfortable. He was obliged to get himself and his family out pretty quickly before they nobbled him. His wife was murdered by the Red Guards on the train journey, and there he was with three

12

children plus a young baby and their nurse, governess or whatever.'

'How do you know all this?' asked Luke curiously.

'My pa had to write it up, so I gave him a ring last night and got the facts. I thought you'd like to know. It was quite a drama. It seems one of the Russians had it in for them, and when they reached the Crimea, the only way our Dr A. could get the governess out was to swear before God that he had married her! He blackmailed the British Consul into supporting his claim and they escaped by a hair's breadth, the British cruiser picking them up just before the Red Guards came galloping down to the Black Sea. Mind you, once they got back to England they were decently married, but there was the inevitable crop of scandal. Plenty of people ready to hint that she'd been his mistress all along and his wife was knocked off just in time. But who knows? Might be all moonshine.'

Luke thought of the photograph he'd seen. It could be true, of course, or at least part of it, and it did explain Tanya's intriguing accent. Not that he was likely to see her again, or any of them come to that, nor did he want to – or did he? He sighed and turned back to his friend.

'When are they going to let you out of here?' Colin was asking.

'Tomorrow, and I'll have to work like stink over the weekend to make up.'

'Rubbish, you're okay. I wish I was as sure of a First as you are. At least you don't have anything to live up to,' went on Colin gloomily. 'My father won everything in sight at Cambridge including the poetry prize, and he expects me to do the same or he'll know the reason why.'

Colin liked to grumble, but his father was indulgent and not short of money and influence. Any son of his could be sure of a place in the world. He didn't have to justify his mother getting up at five on raw winter mornings to clean the mine manager's offices and make the few extra shillings that helped to keep him at the grammar school when other boys of his age were already working down the pit and earning. There had been times when he had resented the unfair burden it had laid on his shoulders.

Tea came, Colin was given a cup, and presently he left promising to let their landlady know that Luke would be coming home the

13

next day. The other visitors departed and the ward had settled into the usual evening routine when suddenly the calm was broken by a clear young voice demanding entrance.

'But I must come in, Sister. I know it's after visiting hours, but I couldn't get here before. I do work, you know. I'll only be a few minutes.'

'We have our rules, Miss Aylsham,' said Sister in her most starchy voice.

'I know, and I do understand, and I won't be more than five minutes, I promise.'

'Very well, just this once, but only five minutes now,' and to Luke's surprise, and it must be said to his pleasure, Tanya herself came running down the ward, the bobbed hair curling deliciously around her ears, pleated skirt flying around those long slim legs.

Against all the rules she perched herself on his bed and said breathlessly, 'I had to see you. I've just had the most wonderful idea.'

Gazing at her, quite bemused, Luke asked, 'An idea about what?'

'About you actually.' She leaned forward. 'I was talking to my father, and he happened to say that in his opinion you were much too thin and probably worked too hard, and I suddenly thought that, since in a way it is all my fault that you are laid up here, why don't I drive you down to Ravensley so that you can spend the weekend with us in the country?'

It was all so sudden and unexpected that Luke couldn't think what to say for a moment.

'But I couldn't, I couldn't possibly,' he said at last, rather lamely. 'I don't really know you, it would be imposing – and where is Ravensley anyway?'

'It's in the Fen country, near Ely, and we go there most weekends when Papa can get away. Do come. I'm sure you'd like it, and I'd feel less guilty about doing such an awful thing to you.'

'You didn't do anything, not really, and what would your father say and the rest of your family?'

'Papa said I could ask you if I liked but he didn't think you would come, and there's only my little sister at home and my stepmother, but she doesn't count as she always agrees with Papa.'

Of course the idea was ridiculous. He couldn't possibly go with her. These were people with whom he had absolutely nothing in common, living in a world totally unfamiliar to him. He would be like a fish out of water, hopelessly ill at ease, wrong clothes, wrong accent, wrong everything. And yet – for years and years, it seemed, he had done nothing but work, never daring to look beyond or step outside his small world, his one aim to fulfil the trust, the devoted love, that was so determinedly pushing him forward, and now suddenly that world had become a desert, dry, without human contact, without the warmth and fun and joy of friendship.

He said, 'I shouldn't – I ought to spend the next few days working extra hard for my finals.'

'You can work down there if you like. Papa has loads of books, or you could bring some with you.'

'I suppose I could,' he said slowly, beginning to weaken.

'Of course you could.' She stood up. 'I'll come and fetch you tomorrow evening after I leave the gallery. It's Whitsun so I have Saturday off and Monday too. Papa usually drives down in the Mercedes. He likes it because he had one in Russia, but it's dreadfully old-fashioned. He bought me the Sports for my birthday.' She glanced over her shoulder and lowered her voice. 'Sister is giving me one of her dirty looks. I'd better go before she gets ratty. Don't forget, will you? See you tomorrow. Bye for now.'

She was gone before he had time to protest or change his mind. Now he was committed. He began to think desperately about what he ought to take with him. He must ring up Colin and ask him to pack a bag. It was crazy. He was mad even to think about such a thing, but all the same he scrambled out of bed asking the nurse if he could telephone and was led along the passage to wait while she got the number for him. The telephone in his digs was in the hall and there was a long pause before the landlady located Colin.

'I say, aren't you going it?' he remarked after Luke's breathless explanation. 'Ravensley is very grand, you know, ancestral home and all that. They may be a bit unconventional, but the girl was presented at Court a year or so ago and all that jazz. Her aunt, the former Lady Aylsham, is married to one Nicholas Blake, who is a very big noise in the City.'

'They can't eat me,' retorted Luke, 'and for once I'll find out how the rich live. Good material for the book.'

15

'Oh, that!' Colin knew something of his friend's nightly scrib- blings, though he'd never been permitted to read any of it. 'They're not altogether typical, you know. Want to borrow anything?'

'A clean shirt if you have one, otherwise I'll manage.'

He went back to bed with a feeling of 'do or die'. If the weekend turned out to be an unmitigated disaster, put it down to experience, and if not – it was like a door opening, and he was possessed with a sudden guilty feeling of excitement, of adventure, something that had been suppressed for a very long time and had suddenly burst into flower.

The next morning Dr Aylsham took off the plaster. 'You don't need it now,' he told Luke, 'it's healing nicely. The scar will soon fade. It won't spoil your manly beauty. I understand my daughter has invited you to spend the weekend with us.'

There was a dryness in his voice and Luke looked up at him quickly.

'Would you rather I didn't come?'

'Not at all. Tanya may invite whoever she pleases within reason, but don't expect too much. We each go our own way when we're lucky enough to have a few days free, and guests must fall in with us.'

'I shan't mind that.'

'Good. Try and prevent Tanya knocking anyone else down and we shall all be grateful.'

Was he behaving like a prize idiot? Luke was still not sure. All the same, he was up and waiting for Colin when he arrived that afternoon with the suitcase, and he changed quickly into his only other respectable outfit, a pair of grey flannels, a white shirt and a navy college blazer which he had bought second-hand from a third-year student who was going down and was horribly hard-up.

'I've put in a pair of my pyjamas, revolting scarlet stripes, I'm sorry to say, a gift from one of my more dotty aunts,' Colin said. 'Did you realize that yours had a split just where it shouldn't be?'

'You're a pal,' said Luke fervently.

'I still think you're crackers to go off like this. Country weekends can be the very devil. I know, I have had some. Anyone for tennis, tea on the lawn all togged up in white flannels, church on Sunday, and settling down to listen to the detestable young playing its only piece excruciatingly on the pianoforte. You'll be screaming with boredom in no time at all.'

'Shall I?' Luke grinned. 'I've never experienced it so I might find it intriguing.'

'Intriguing, my foot! It's the bright eyes of the Princess Tanya that've got you in thrall, my lad, so beware –

> '"I met a lady in the meads
> Full beautiful – a fairy's child . . ."'

'Don't be an ass!'

> '"She took me to her elfin grot
> And there she wept and sighed full sore . . ."'

'Shut up, you fool! Hop it before I bash you!'

'Don't say I didn't warn you.'

Colin departed still grinning infuriatingly and bumped into Tanya as she came through the doorway. He waved to her and she waved back.

'Was that your friend?' she asked Luke.

'Yes.'

'He looks as if he might be fun.'

'He is.'

But he was not really listening. It was as if he were seeing her for the first time, and it knocked him sideways. She had tied a bandeau of green chiffon round her bright hair and the ends floated behind her. Her dress, of some expensive golden silk, clung to the slender figure, and a light cream jacket was draped carelessly round her shoulders. She looked good enough to eat, a being from another world, and he could scarcely believe that this glamorous girl was to be his for a weekend at least.

'Come on,' she said, 'let's get started,' and he followed her meekly down the stairs and into the car, feeling quite idiotically happy, and with absolutely no idea that he was embarking on a course that was going to change and bedevil his whole life.

They arrived late that night because a few miles beyond Cambridge they ran out of petrol. Garages were few and far between, and at Tanya's look of comical dismay there was nothing Luke

17

could do but offer to trudge the two miles back to the filling station they had passed, knock up the owner, who had closed for the night, and bargain for a two-gallon can. Then, when he had got it into the tank with some difficulty and a good deal of splashing, the car absolutely refused to start. He nearly broke his back pushing it, and when that didn't work, almost dislocated his shoulder trying to crank it up, until Tanya got out, pushed him aside, swung the starting handle with a practised flick of the wrist, and the engine immediately sprang into life. She grinned at him triumphantly. It took a second or two before he could grin back, then the absurdity struck him and they were both roaring with laughter.

They reached Ely, passed the cathedral with its exquisite lantern tower and turned off down a long country road through flat fields stretching to a limitless horizon still streaked with gold by the setting sun. Presently they drove between a pair of handsome gates and wound their way through woods and a flower garden. It was growing dark by then, but he could see that the house was huge and old and rambling, a house that had been home to many generations, all of whom had stamped their mark upon it.

There were dogs, two large and one small, barking madly, bumping into him and leaping up at Tanya until a manservant called them to order.

'Shall I put the car away for you, miss?'

'Yes, please, Jake. Is my father here?'

'Hours ago, Miss Tanya. You're very late.'

'Yes, I know. Come on, Luke. Don't bother about the bags. Jake will bring those.'

He followed her up wide shallow steps into a spacious hall, the dogs running ahead, then she opened a door and they were in a drawing room. His first impression was how shabby it was and then how lovely and how elegant. Chinese wallpaper a little faded, furniture worn but antique and beautiful, mellow lamplight, logs glowing on the hearth against the chill of the May night and filling the air with an aromatic scent.

Dr Aylsham looked up from the depths of his armchair to smile at them.

'Here you are at last. We were just thinking of sending out search parties. What happened?'

'I ran out of petrol, and don't tell me I should carry a spare can, because I know I should and I forgot,' said Tanya ruefully. 'Luke had to tramp a couple of miles to fetch it.'

'Wasn't that a little hard on your guest, Tanya?' said her stepmother mildly, smiling up at Luke from the sofa. The smallest of the dogs, which looked rather like a woolly hearthrug crossed with a tea cosy, had leaped up beside her and stared at him with round black eyes. 'You must be Luke,' she went on, holding out her hand. 'How are you feeling? My husband told me about the accident.'

'I'm fine,' he muttered, suddenly confused. Did you say 'my lady', did you bow or kiss her hand or what? This was obviously the woman in the picture he had seen, the Russian governess who had escaped capture and death by a romantic expedient and later married in haste. Her hair, parted in the middle and caught up in a loose knot, had a reddish sheen in the lamplight. Colin might be right, of course, but Luke was aware of some rare quality, and her voice had the same faint accent he had already noticed in Tanya.

'You must be hungry, both of you,' she was saying. 'I'm afraid we have eaten already. I'll ring and ask them to bring you some food.'

'Don't bother, Galina,' said Tanya quickly. 'We'll forage for ourselves.'

'You know Cook doesn't like her kitchen to be invaded.'

'She doesn't mind me. Come on, Luke, let's go and see what we can find.'

She took him by the hand, pulling him after her down a series of passages and into a huge kitchen with a dresser along one wall stacked with more copper pans and pottery dishes than he had seen in his whole life, a table scrubbed to white perfection and a stove that simmered and bubbled, filling the room with warmth and a faint aroma of delicious food.

'We'll explore,' said Tanya, opening the door into a larder like a small room and peeping into the dishes on the well-stacked shelves.

'And what do you think you're doing, miss, poking your saucy nose into my pantry at this time o'night?' said a sharp voice, and they both spun round guiltily.

'I wouldn't touch anything I shouldn't, Cookie darling,' said Tanya coaxingly, 'but we did miss our dinner and we're starving.'

'And whose fault is that, I'd like to know?'

'Mine, of course, but you wouldn't let Luke suffer for it, now would you?'

Cook was small and thin, her skimpy hair screwed into a knot on top of her head. She glared at them forbiddingly through spectacles perched unsteadily on her pointed nose, but she proved no match for Tanya, who had slipped an arm round her waist.

'Haven't I always been your special girl, Betsy?' she whispered. 'You couldn't let us go hungry, could you?'

'Oh, give over, do, the pair of ye!' said Cook, putting Tanya aside and marching towards the larder. 'I had a nice spring chicken roasted and your favourite sherry trifle with charlotte russe for her ladyship and more than half of it wasted,' she scolded, but she was already bringing out dishes, carving thick slices of the chicken, putting out butter and crisp bread and filling bowls with some rich creamy pudding.

'We'll eat it out here,' said Tanya placatingly.

'You'll do no such thing. You'll take your gentleman into the dining room and eat your supper like decent folk.'

'He's not my gentleman, he's just Luke.'

'That's as may be. We do things properly at Ravensley. We always have, and we always will while I'm in the kitchen. You take the tray, sir,' she commanded Luke, 'and Miss Tanya will show you the way.'

So they ate their supper companionably at a large refectory table in the oak-panelled dining room.

'She's a poppet actually,' said Tanya with her mouth full of chicken. 'She scared us all to death at first, even Father, but then I think she took pity on us. Orphans of the storm, I suppose we must have seemed, refugees from some barbarous land where people were murdering each other. She ended up letting Andy and Paul and me do just as we liked, even to stealing her hot cakes as soon as she brought them out of the oven. I dare say Nicola does the same. She was only a baby then, now she's twelve. You'll see her tomorrow.'

She had brought wine from the sideboard and filled two large glasses. He sipped it cautiously while she went on talking and a picture of the household slowly grew in his mind.

'Andy is my elder brother,' Tanya explained. 'He's a doctor too but only just, that's why he isn't here today. He's on duty at the hospital. Paul has gone up to Cambridge reading Modern Languages, but what he really wants to do is to farm, only he's rather delicate so Papa is against it. I expect you'll think we're all a bit peculiar, most people do. Have you had enough? I always eat so much when I'm down here that I have to starve for the rest of the week.' She leaned back in her chair and gave a prodigious yawn. 'I'm dead beat, aren't you?'

'Oughtn't we to wash up?' asked Luke, conscientiously piling the dishes on the tray.

'Lord no, the servants will do that.'

Lady Aylsham came in just as they were getting to their feet.

'Luke is in the Indian room, Tanya, will you show him the way?' she said.

'All right. I'll just say goodnight to Papa first.'

She pushed past her stepmother so rudely that Luke felt obliged to stop.

'I'm so grateful to be asked down here,' he said awkwardly.

'Any friend of Tanya is welcome. That place on your forehead still looks a little angry. Are you in pain? Would you like me to give you a sleeping pill?'

'No, I'm fine, thank you.'

'Goodnight then. Sleep well.'

The only things Indian about his bedroom were an exquisitely carved lacquer screen and a two-foot-high idol carved out of some kind of black stone.

'I think it's hideous,' said Tanya. 'It makes me feel creepy.'

Luke looked at the idol with interest. The inscrutable oriental face was filled with secrets. It was very old, he thought, and had probably come from some temple.

'I think it's Shiva,' he said slowly, 'goddess of life – and of death. How did it come to be here?'

'One of Papa's ancestors had an Indian servant. It belonged to him. This was his room. He was drowned in some ghastly accident on the Fens.' She took a step nearer and whispered, 'The servants say they can still hear Ram Lall muttering to himself and padding along the corridors, his bare feet leaving wet footprints.'

He caught her hand and swung her round to face him. 'Are you trying to frighten me?'

21

She giggled. 'Perhaps.' She put up a hand and touched the raw place on his forehead. 'Poor Luke, what a beast I am to you.'

She reached up on tiptoe, kissed his cheek lightly, and then was gone, the door slamming behind her.

Someone had unpacked his meagre luggage, and had hung up his only decent suit and laid out his toilet articles with Colin's glaringly striped pyjamas. At another time he might have felt a little disconcerted, but his mind was full of Tanya as he undressed – quick, flashing, so vividly alive and as elusive as the moonlight that flickered across the floor when he drew back one of the curtains. Not at all like the earnest girl students he had danced with at the Commem Ball; not like Megan, honest and plain as good bread. She was exotic, brilliant, utterly different.

He lay in the big comfortable bed, enjoying the smooth touch of sweet-smelling linen sheets, so different from the lumpy mattress in his digs, and tried to sort out his impressions, which so far were not much like Colin's gloomy predictions.

He had only once before been in a great house like this, and that was Penhale, a mile or two outside Tredegar. He thought of it now and of how much he had hated it. Even to his unformed taste, it had had a lavish vulgar richness that had offended him. He had been a skinny thirteen-year-old dragged there by Isaac Morgan, the gamekeeper, who had caught him red-handed in the woods, a rabbit in one hand and a pheasant in the other. Both his companions had fled, leaving him to face retribution alone.

Lady Penhale's husband was a Member of Parliament who owned most of the land outside the town and had a large share in the pit where Luke's father and grandfather worked. She was a big high-coloured woman tightly corseted into a handsome gown of purple silk. Eyes like chips of grey granite had looked him over coldly.

'I know this boy. He's one of the miners' brats aping his betters,' she said.

She had been on the school governing board when he had been brought up before them for his scholarship, and he shivered at the rasp in her voice. Poaching was frowned upon by the headmaster of the grammar school, but *he* didn't have a brother and two baby sisters who never tasted meat from one week's end to another. It had been a daring exploit, an act of rebellion, and now he was to

22

suffer for it. As if they didn't have enough game in their woods to feed a multitude of hungry miners! It was enough to make anyone turn Bolshie! Down at the Working Men's Club the Russian Revolution, only two years old, had been chewed over with fascinated interest and excitement. If she got him thrown out of the school he didn't know what he would do. He could never face his mother's tears, his father's grave disappointment. He stared back defiantly at the stony face. Whether she was moved by some faint glimmer of pity or whether, far more likely, she could hear the coarse jests of her fellow governors, red-faced sportsmen out with a gun or riding to hounds most days of the week, he did not know, but she stood up abruptly.

'You can go this time, boy, but don't forget we can take back a gift as quickly as we can award it.'

A gift! Is that what they called it? By God, he'd worked hard enough to earn it, slaving at his books night after night, freezing cold or burning hot in the tiny room under the roof that he shared with Dai.

'You can set him free, Isaac, but make sure he has learned his lesson.'

'Oh, I'll do that, my lady, never you fear. He won't come after my pheasants again, not when I've done with him.'

So he escaped with a beating, that filled him with a shamed rage almost worse than the pain – the brutal pulling down of his trousers, Isaac Morgan's obvious enjoyment as he brought down the leather strap on his bare buttocks. It hadn't been easy to march down the drive with a jaunty step when pain burned like fire at every movement but he managed it somehow, and at the end, perched on his pony, sat Edmund Penhale, only a few years older than himself, home from his public school, grinning like an ape from ear to ear.

'Scum!' Edmund had shouted. 'Miner's dirty scum!' and he laughed as he urged his pony against him, crowding Luke into the dirt and mud at the side of the track. For a long time he had dreamed of the revenge he would take one day, until his father's recurrent illness, his mother's valiant struggle to keep them afloat, his own fight for the university scholarship that he sometimes despaired of winning, had taken all his energy and made such thoughts seem childishly futile.

He turned over restlessly. Why was his mind running on that old rubbish when it was so far behind him? He fell asleep at last, undisturbed by the sound of Ram Lall's ghostly bare feet padding along the passages, and slept soundly without dreaming till someone came knocking at the door.

2

'Good morning, sir, it's eight-thirty. Shall I run a bath for you?' asked Jake, coming in and crossing to the window.

It was not like Luke to sleep so late. He struggled to sit up in the big bed.

'Thank you, but I think I can manage.'

'Very good.' The manservant drew back the heavy curtain so that light flooded into the room. 'It's a rare fine morning, sir, and I've taken the liberty of borrowing Master Andrew's dressing gown, seeing as you no doubt forgot to pack one.'

He placed the dark blue silk dressing gown across the chair, and Luke bit his lip, uncomfortably aware that Jake must have guessed that a dressing gown was a luxury he didn't possess.

Then as the door closed he began to laugh at himself. This was the high life, he thought, and he leaped out of bed determined to make the most of it. The bathroom at the end of the corridor must have been installed in Victorian times. The bath with its mahogany surround was immense, and it was a delight to plunge into hot water gushing from brass taps and not in spasmodic jerks from an antediluvian geyser that threatened to blow up every time Colin or he put a match to it.

Bathed, shaved and dressed he made his way down to the dining room, which was empty, though the table was laid and a row of tempting silver dishes stood on the sideboard. He peeped into them, and was wondering whether he should help himself or wait for the rest of the family to appear, when a small maidservant put her head round the door, gave a squeak on seeing him and quickly straightened up.

She gave him a shy grin, bobbed a curtsy and asked, 'Tea or coffee, sir?'

'Coffee, please.'

It had been quite beyond their means in Tredegar and not to

25

their taste either, but he had developed a liking for it in the last few years.

He had helped himself lavishly and rather guiltily to an egg with rashers of crisp bacon and a fat sausage when she reappeared with a silver pot on a tray and a rack of freshly made toast.

He had hardly begun to tackle it when Lady Aylsham came in. He struggled to stand up but she put a hand on his shoulder.

'Do not disturb yourself. Have you everything you want? I am afraid you will find us rather – how do you say? – forgetful of our guests at weekends.'

'Dr Aylsham did warn me.'

'Did he? You see, because of his work he is not often here, so he likes to ride round the estate with his brother-in-law, who manages it for him. They were out very early this morning and Tanya went with them. She loves to ride with her father. I expect they will be back by lunchtime. Jake is going to drive me into Ely in a few minutes, if you would like to spend the morning there. The cathedral is very fine.'

'Don't worry about me, Lady Aylsham. I'm very happy to explore on my own, really I am.'

'The library is along the hall at the back of the house, and Nicola is about somewhere.' She put a cool hand on his forehead, lifting the heavy lock of hair that fell across the stitched wound. 'No headache this morning? No ill effects?'

'No, none at all.'

'Good. The place is healing well. There is still a good deal of bruising. It will be a few days before we can take the stitches out.'

'Are you a doctor too?' he asked curiously.

'Yes.' She gave him her rare, sweet smile. 'But a very humble one, not at all like my husband and my son. There is a clinic for children in Ely that I like to visit whenever I am here. Have a quiet morning. It will be best for you.'

He watched her go and then attacked his breakfast with renewed zest. An hour later he found his way to the library and was entranced by what he found there. It was a large room that looked out on to a stretch of lawn. At the far end there was a silver gleam that he thought might be a river or a lake. That would be something to explore with Tanya. His spirits rose at the thought of it.

Books had been such a rarity in his life, so desperately expensive, so highly valued, so treasured, that to be let loose among such a vast and mixed selection was intoxicating. He was filled with envy. The fruits of a couple of hundred years of collecting lay here. Some of the volumes, finely bound in leather with gold tooling, had never been opened, while others, worn and falling apart, had been read and reread. They were hopelessly out of order, many of them piled up, or pulled out and replaced at random. There were rare first editions of old favourites that he had struggled through in the university library: Richardson's *Clarissa*, all seven volumes through which the heroine battled against her handsome seducer only to fall into his bed in the last few pages – he smiled and handled them with reverence. There was one whole shelf of modern classics cheek by jowl with bestsellers like Evelyn Waugh and D. H. Lawrence, with Eliot's poetry and Edith Sitwell and a pirated copy of Joyce's *Ulysses*, and tumbled among them popular potboilers (who on earth reads those? he wondered) Michael Arlen's *The Green Hat*, Elinor Glyn, *The Sheik* – he picked it up and opened it at random.

'The shamed blood surged slowly into her cheeks,' he read, 'his dark passionate eyes burned into her like a hot flame. His touch was torture . . .'

'You must be Luke.' The fresh young voice startled him and he looked up. A slim, elflike child with dark hair cut into a heavy fringe across her forehead stood in the doorway. Large brown eyes frowned at him.

'Tanya bought that one for a lark and I got caned for reading it in the dorm under the blankets,' she remarked. 'It's the most awful tosh.'

'Is it?' He smiled. 'I'm glad you warned me.'

She came further into the room. She was wearing a very grubby pair of jodhpurs and a huge canary-coloured pullover.

'You've got a terrible black eye,' she said, looking him over critically.

'I know. I saw it when I was shaving.'

'Are you one of Tanya's lame ducks?'

'I hope not. What are they?'

'Oh, she's always bringing people down, and some of them are very peculiar. I don't mean that you are,' she went on quickly. 'You look clean at least.'

'Thank you,' he said drily. 'I'm relieved to hear it.'

'Galina told me I ought to look after you as Tanya has gone off with Papa, so here I am. I'm Nicola, by the way. What would you like to do?'

'What do you suggest?'

He moved towards her and she put up a hand, warding him off.

'Better not come too near. I might still be infectious.'

'What kind of infectious?' he asked teasingly. 'Plague?'

'Oh no, measles. It broke out at school and Papa whisked me away. He says I'm all right now, but it would be awful if you broke out in spots, wouldn't it?'

'Terrible, but you needn't worry. I've had it. Now what about showing me Ravensley?'

'All right, if you think you'd like it. Can we go to the stables first? My pony has sprung a limp and Jake has been dealing with it.'

'Isn't Jake the butler?'

'I suppose he is – sort of,' she said doubtfully, 'but Jake can do everything. You see, he was with my father in Russia, Siberia and everywhere. I don't remember that but the others do.'

The stables were almost a village in themselves with room for a great many horses, though at present the stalls only held Nicola's pony, an elderly donkey called Jacob and one other horse.

'That's Blackie. Andy rides him when he's here. We don't have many horses now,' Nicola told Luke sadly. 'Jake says my Uncle Robert, who was killed in the war, had as many as twenty at one time and once owned a racehorse, but now Papa doesn't hunt, and anyway we can't afford it. You see, we really are rather poor.'

'Poor?' exclaimed Luke gesturing around him. 'Poor, with all this?'

'But that's just it,' went on this knowledgeable child. 'It costs an awful lot of money to keep it up, and Papa lost all his private fortune in Russia, and the house and everything he owned there, and so did my mamma.' She perched herself on the stone mounting block. 'My Uncle Niki, who is really Prince Nicolai Malinsky, had huge estates and thousands of servants, but now he's only a farmer in the South of France and he had to sell his wife's jewellery to buy the farm. My cousins have to act as chauffeurs to rich Americans in the holidays to help pay their university fees. Yuri hates it but

Boris says it's tremendous fun. He is very handsome, you know, and the American girls are so thrilled at having a prince to drive them about that they all fall in love with him and want to give him expensive presents – a gold cigarette case and things like that – but Aunt Sonia found out and made him send them all back. He was furious. He wanted to sell them and buy a taxi for himself.'

It was a side of the Revolution that had never occurred to Luke when he had gone with Dai to the first meeting of the Communist Party held in deadly secret in a disused hut some way out of Tredegar.

'Why do you dislike your sister so much?' he asked curiously later that morning as they continued their little tour.

'Oh, I don't exactly dislike her,' Nicola said, rather shocked, and wrinkling her nose, 'but you never know where you are with her. She can be sweet as sugar one minute and a perfect pig the next. I expect you'll soon find that out, everyone does. Andy says she is schizo – schizo something – '

'Schizophrenic?'

'That's right. How clever of you to know.'

'Isn't that rather hard on her?'

'I don't suppose he really meant it. They were having one of their flaming rows at the time. Andy is our half-brother, you know.'

He didn't know but supposed he would very soon find out.

'Andy came with Papa to one of our school sports days and all the girls went dotty about them both. Doctors are so whizzo, aren't they? My status went up no end.'

They met the riding party when they came back to the house for luncheon, Tanya looking like a slim and lovely boy in her trim riding breeches and pale yellow shirt. She was talking animatedly with an impeccably dressed young man with silky fair hair, a small moustache and a high-bred voice. Introduced as Cecil Harcourt, he gave Luke a cool stare and a limp handshake.

'That's the gorgeous Cecil,' whispered Nicola wickedly in his ear. 'He's an absolute drip and runs after Tanya like a puppy on a string.'

'Does he now?'

Luke hated him instantly, and then forgot him when Tanya slipped her arm through his.

'Has my kid sister been giving you a frightful time?' she asked.

'I felt awful about deserting you, but I don't often get the opportunity of exercising Rags nowadays and it *was* such a lovely morning.'

'I've just acquired a new MG Sports,' drawled the gorgeous Cecil. 'So what about coming for a spin this afternoon, old girl? She runs sweet as a dream.'

'Sorry,' said Tanya with her flashing smile. 'Luke is going to take me on the river, aren't you, darling?' and she gave his arm a little squeeze.

'Yes, rather, I'd love to.'

'Then that's settled. Now let's have some food. I'm starving. Nicola, do go and change out of that filthy pullover. You can't sit down to table looking like that.'

'It's *not* filthy. It was Andy's and he gave it to me,' the child said indignantly, and then appealed to her stepmother. 'I needn't change, need I, Galina?'

'Not if you don't want to, darling, but perhaps you ought to wash your hands.'

'Sucks to you!' muttered Nicola under her breath and gave her sister a dirty look as she slipped out of the room. She returned five minutes later with a scrubbed face and smelling pleasantly of scented soap.

There was quite a crowd round the luncheon table, where a cold buffet had been laid out and everyone helped themselves. Paul had arrived from Cambridge for the weekend, a neat compact boy of medium height, with something of his father's good looks and a faint suggestion of delicacy. There was Lord Aylsham's sister Margaret in a well-cut tweed coat and skirt, brisk and kindly, the typical country lady, thought Luke, who sits on a dozen committees and runs the village and everyone in it. Her husband, Frank Carroll, a well-built man of about fifty, was still deep in discussion with his brother-in-law over some knotty agricultural problem.

Imperceptibly Luke's long-cherished resentment against the English upper classes had begun to melt away, and he did not realize yet how very untypical they all were. In how many country houses would two of the younger members of the family suddenly burst into a flood of Russian with loud bursts of laughter, to be sternly called to order by their father in the same language?

'Forgive my brats,' he said, glancing round the table. 'They are still inclined to forget they are in England, even after all these years.'

'Do you speak Russian too?' whispered Luke to Nicola as they helped themselves to the food.

'Oh yes, I had to because the others did. Papa told them they must all speak English all the time, but they didn't, so I grew up with it.'

The family scattered after luncheon. Cecil Harcourt took himself off, much to Luke's relief. He hated to admit it, but he found that supercilious stare slightly disconcerting. Nicola and Paul went off to the stables arm in arm. Margaret was earnestly trying to persuade her reluctant sister-in-law to take an active part in the grand Fête to be held on Whit Monday. Tanya had gone upstairs to change out of her riding clothes, and Luke was hanging about in the hall waiting for her when Simon Aylsham came through.

He paused and ran an expert eye over the boy. 'Are you feeling all right, not overdoing it?' he asked. 'I'm afraid we neglected you shamefully this morning.'

'Oh, you needn't worry about me. I had a wonderful time looking round your library before Nicola took me in hand.'

'I'm afraid it's in a pretty sorry state. My brother was not at all a bookish man. I know for a fact that there are some quite valuable and interesting editions tucked away there somewhere, but I simply haven't the time to take it in hand. One of these days I shall have to get someone to do something about it, but do feel free to browse there as much as you like.'

'Aren't you afraid of unscrupulous guests making off with some of your treasures?'

'It has crossed my mind, but if there is one thing my life has taught me it is not to put too much value on personal possessions. They can vanish all too quickly,' Dr Aylsham said wryly. 'Besides, I can't help thinking that a Welshman with a taste for literature is going to be a man to value books as much as I do.'

Luke was vividly aware of the warmth, the charm, and was about to respond to it, when Tanya came running down the stairs and took her father's arm.

'What were you two talking about? Me?'

'Certainly not,' said the doctor. 'Something a great deal more solid and dependable than my flibbertigibbet of a daughter. What part are you playing this afternoon, puss, a dryad or a water nymph?'

'Neither, I hope. We're going on the river. Come on, Luke.'

He took up the picnic basket that stood ready in the hall and followed after her.

'Take care you don't drown him,' called her father as they ran down the steps.

At some time in the nineteenth century a tributary of the river had been diverted into the park to form a small lake. Luke eyed the punt moored at the water's edge with considerable misgivings, not at all sure if he could manage the pole with any degree of skill. The abominable Cecil, fresh from punting down the Cambridge Backs, was probably an expert, but he himself was far more likely to end up ignominiously in the water. It was Tanya who mercifully saved him from that disaster.

'Let's take the paddles, shall we, then we can talk. It's much more cosy.'

So he found himself sitting close beside her on the cushioned seat, very aware of the slim body in the thin silk dress, the chiffon scarf she had wound negligently round her throat blowing in his face and bringing with it a faint fresh perfume.

It was a fine day in late May, a little hazy but very warm, with a light breeze, as they glided across the lake and presently entered the narrow tributary that wound its way through tall reeds and clumps of sedge under the overhanging branches of willow and the green of bog myrtle. The air was filled with the tang of water mint and the scent of the meadowsweet just coming into bloom. It was that hushed time in the afternoon when even the birds have fallen silent, and they did not speak much at first, paddling along in a kind of dreamy peace until they came in sight of a huge windmill, black and gaunt now, its wrecked sails creaking eerily as they swayed in the wind, the once strong wooden door gaping open, the iron catwalk hanging in broken and rusty struts.

'They say that's the place from which Ram Lall fell to his death,' said Tanya with a shudder. 'Silly, isn't it, but every time I come here, I remember terrible things I want to forget.'

For a moment a dank chill seemed to flow out and all around them, then they were past and into the sunshine once again.

Presently they drew into the side where there was a stretch of mossy bank, and while Luke tethered the boat to a stout willow branch Tanya unpacked the picnic basket Betsy had thoughtfully provided.

'Nicola told me you worked in an art gallery,' he said, watching Tanya unscrew the Thermos flask and begin to pour the tea.

'Yes, I have been there for a year now. There was an awful row about it. Aunt Hester, who is my Uncle Robert's widow, was furious. She told Papa that no Aylsham had ever served in a shop, and if I did I was ruining any chance I might have of making a good marriage, as if that was all I was thinking about. She hates us because my father is alive and is now Lord Aylsham and her nose has been pushed out of joint, though I don't know why she should mind now she has married again. Nicholas Blake is ever so much richer than Papa.'

'Where is the gallery?'

'Just off Bond Street. Giovanni Ricci is an Italian. He used to run a gallery in St Petersburg, fine pictures and *objets d'art*, you know the kind of thing, all very exclusive. My mother took me there once to choose a present for Papa. Those brutes of revolutionaries burnt the shop to the ground but he escaped and started up again in London. It took ages but he's quite successful now. Lots of Russians over here are having to sell their treasures bit by bit in order to live, so it's useful for him to have an assistant who can speak Russian, and I enjoy it. I'm learning all about antiques because Giovanni takes me to important auctions with him. He says I have a flair for the real thing. Father disapproved at first, but I can usually get round him if I try. Now, that's quite enough about me. Have a piece of Betsy's chocolate sponge and tell me about yourself.'

'What do you want to know?'

'Everything. Tell me about where you live and what made you want to study and come to university.'

He took the piece of cake she offered him but did not eat immediately. Instead he looked down the little river where the sunlight coming through the branches dappled the water with moving light and dark. How describe to her that black little house

33

that his mother strove so hard to keep immaculate, the small stifling rooms which had once been home and now seemed only to choke him? He had never been very successful talking to girls and sometimes wished he was more like Colin, who could come up with a stream of amusing small talk, but somehow this was different. She was looking at him expectantly and he took the plunge.

'I think it was my grandfather who started me off. My grandmother was dead so he lived with us. It was he who taught me to read when I was about four. I remember how he used to come home from the pit, his face all black from the coal dust, and he had his bath in front of the kitchen fire. I used to watch my mother scrub his back, and afterwards he would have his tea and bring out his books. Sometimes he would read to me and Dai, and then later he used to tell me about the history of Wales, filling it with grandeur, making me proud to be Welsh – wonderful stories of Llewellyn the Great, who lived in the twelfth century, and of his grandson, another Llewellyn, who after years of struggle and betrayal died at last in an obscure skirmish, killed by an English soldier who did not even know who he was. Grandfather took me once to the very place where it happened. I remember Grandfather standing there, tears in his eyes, saying, "They paraded his head round the streets, they stuck it up on the Tower of London with a crown of ivy, Llewellyn, our lost leader –

Och hyd atat-ti, Dduw, na ddaw – môr dros dir!"'

'What does that mean?' she whispered.

'It's from the lament they wrote, a whole people's anguish – Oh God, why are we left to mourn? I used to feel proud that my name too was Llewellyn.'

Then suddenly it was as if he woke up. What on earth was he thinking of, pouring all this out to the girl beside him? What could it possibly mean to her? She must think him crazy going on and on like that. He turned to look at her apologetically.

'I'm sorry. I must be boring you terribly.'

'No,' she said, 'no, you're not. Go on. What else did he talk to you about?'

But the spell was broken.

'Oh, he knew all the old legends, ballads of King Arthur, Merlin the magician, dragons that still live in the mountains. My father used to say, "You're filling the child's head with rubbish," but to me it was wonderful, far more thrilling than anything I learned about at school.'

'I know exactly what you mean. My nurse used to tell me tales like that. Marina was a peasant and she knew all about Baba Yega, the witch who flies through the air, about the Wood Demons whose skin is blue and who imitate the song of birds, and the Rusalki who lure young men to their death in their black icy lakes. Your grandfather must be very proud of you now.'

'He never really knew. He died in a pit accident when I was twelve.' He had not meant to go on, but then it was as if he couldn't stop, and the words came pouring out. 'That was a terrible day. I was at the grammar school then, and during the afternoon we heard the hooters. They are always sounded if there is an accident. Nearly all of us had someone working there, so we were let out of class and I ran to the pithead. My mother was there with the other women, not weeping, not saying anything, just standing quite still, waiting and waiting. It was hours before the first lot came up and she saw Dai and my father. She burst into tears then because they were alive, but it was far into the night before the rest of the men were brought out, and they were all dead. I remember looking at my grandfather and I couldn't believe it. He didn't look any different, and yet the light had gone out of him, and I felt a huge emptiness inside me as if some vital part had been taken away and nothing would ever take its place.'

'I know that feeling,' she said, very quietly. 'I felt like that when they killed my mother. Sometimes I dream of it still. It was a dirty station waiting room that smelled horrible. It was bitterly cold, and we'd been waiting for hours and hours, stiff and frozen and very hungry. Then a doctor came who knew Papa and he spoke to the soldiers. Andy whispered, "It's all right, Tanya, it's going to be all right," but it wasn't. One of those Red Guards grabbed hold of me, and I was so frightened I screamed. Papa was angry and hit him. He raised his gun, my mother threw herself between them, and he shot her. After that it was like a nightmare that goes on and on because you can't wake up. I hated the Bolsheviki for that, and I hate them now. They have spoiled everything.'

She was staring in front of her and he guessed that this was a Tanya not many people saw. It was as if she was still trapped in

35

that terrible moment, and he took her hand in his and after a moment felt her fingers curl into his. Something seemed to fuse between them. She turned to look at him, and he saw the lovely heart-shaped face, broad of brow, eyes set well apart, the delicate nose and trembling mouth. Is it ever possible to know for sure the magical moment when one falls in love? Afterwards Luke was certain it was then that it struck him with a disturbing swiftness that took his breath away, and because of it, perhaps because of the confusion that rose within him, he blundered badly.

He said gently, 'You must not say things like that. To hate can only be destructive, and after all didn't they have cause? Isn't there something grand and noble about a people who after years of oppression can still do battle with the tyranny that has beaten them down?' He was quite unprepared for the storm he provoked.

She snatched her hand away.

'How can you speak like that? You weren't there, you don't know, you can't guess how hateful it was. My Uncle Niki had looked after his peasants, built them a school, cared for them when they were sick, and for that they killed his dogs, they stole his horses, plundered his house, that lovely, lovely house where we had been so happy. They drove out his wife and children and would have killed him too if my father had not hidden him. They wrecked our house, they arrested Papa when he tried to help the wounded and dying in the streets, and they brutally murdered my mother. Is that what you call grand and noble? It's bestial, and I hate them for what they did to our Russia – nothing has ever been the same since.'

She choked and turned away from him, and began to put the tea things together, her hands trembling so much she could not screw the top on the Thermos flask. After a second he took it from her.

'Let me do that. I'm sorry, Tanya, I didn't mean it personally. I know how you and your family must feel. I am only trying to be fair.'

'You're like my father,' she said shakily; 'he is always so calm, so just, he can always see both sides of a question, and so can Galina. It makes me angry. I don't want to accept. I don't want to be fair. I want to fight. I want my revenge.'

'Revenge for what?'

'I don't know, injustice, cruelty, the blind hate that destroys all that is beautiful and fine and old – for nothing.'

'Perhaps it's not for nothing.' He repacked the picnic basket and then took both her hands in his. 'Don't count me among the savages, will you?' he said. 'It's been such a marvellous afternoon. We have confided our inmost secrets to each other, we've quarrelled and made it up – what better basis for friendship? We are friends, aren't we?'

'I don't know – perhaps.'

She looked up into his face, that was still a little bruised, and saw the hair that flopped across his forehead, the cheeks slightly hollowed and the tiny smile that lurked about the firm mouth. It was a face of character, with a strength lacking in many of the young men who cirled round her.

He leaned forward suddenly and kissed her gently on the lips, and to his surprise she didn't turn away or push him off or say anything, but for the space of a heartbeat their eyes locked together, then she withdrew her hands and stood up.

'We must be getting back or Father will think we've come to grief somewhere.'

And he picked up the picnic basket and followed her into the boat.

That evening he saw another side of Tanya – restless, brittle, even a little cruel. They dined rather late because Jake had driven the car into Ely to fetch Andy from the railway station.

'We don't change for dinner,' said Galina, who had seen Luke looking faintly uneasy. 'We like to relax as much as we can when we are down here.'

It was a family party that sat down at the table, with the addition of Margaret and Frank Carroll, and Andy, who had travelled down from London. He came in with his arm round Nicola, who had gone with Jake to collect him, a tall young man very like his father, with something of his quiet charm, but also with a quality of his own, a certain toughness that Luke could sense in his firm handshake, in the quick appraising look Andy gave him, and the slight sharpness with which he quelled some of Tanya's exuberance.

After the meal was over Nicola was packed off to bed, much to her disgust, coffee was served in the drawing room, and Tanya suggested they might dance.

'Must we?' complained her father. 'Wouldn't it be rather delightful just to be quiet for once?'

'Oh, don't be so stuffy, darling. It only means rolling up the rugs. Paul, come and help me with the gramophone.'

She began to hunt through the records while Andy and Luke obediently pulled the rugs aside and pushed back the sofa and chairs. The two larger dogs eyed them apprehensively from the fireplace while Buttons, the tiny one, took refuge under Lady Aylsham's chair.

Tanya found what she wanted and put it on the turntable before she turned round with an air of suppressed excitement.

'I've had a wonderful idea. Luke and I were talking about Russia this afternoon. If I play the Polonaise, Papa and I could show him just what it was like when the Tsar opened one of the court balls at the Winter Palace.'

'I don't think that's a very good idea,' said her stepmother quickly.

'Neither do I,' agreed her husband firmly. 'It's all over and done with. We don't want to go delving into the past.'

But Tanya would not be denied. She seized her father's hands, crying, 'Don't be such a spoilsport. I remember Mamma telling me about the first time she went there with you after you were married. She even showed me the dress she wore, it was organza over white satin and all sewn with crystals and pearls. I thought it was gorgeous. Please, Papa, dance it with me as you did with her.' Reluctantly he let her pull him to his feet. 'Start the gramophone, Luke,' she commanded, and he moved the tone arm into position.

The music, rich, triumphant, flooded into the room, and hand in hand they moved into the stately measure. With a quick, angry frown at his sister Andy took his mother's hand, and the two couples moved round the room so that for a second in the mellow lamplight Luke seemed to see and hear a faint echo of something long past that would never come again, something that had already gone into legend. It was more than ten years since the Tsar and his family had been brutally murdered at Ekaterinburg.

The dancers circled the room with a slow grace until suddenly Simon Aylsham stopped.

'Turn it off. This is ridiculous,' he said abruptly.

'No, it isn't, it isn't, it's lovely. Don't you want to remember?'

'No, Tanya, no, I don't.'

'I do. I used to dream of the day when I would be old enough to go with you and Mamma. Am I very like her?'

He cupped her face between his two hands. 'Yes, Tanya, you are, very like,' he said huskily. Then he left her, striding across to the gramophone and taking off the record, but not before Luke had seen the shadow of pain that crossed Lady Aylsham's face. Tanya did that deliberately, he thought, she wanted to hurt, and he wondered why.

Then it was all over.

'Put on something lively,' said Dr Aylsham, and Andy came over and started to rummage through the records.

'Show us the charleston, Tanya, isn't that your latest craze?' Andy said.

'Heavens, no. That's old-fashioned already,' replied his sister scornfully.

'Such a pity,' sighed Aunt Margaret placidly. 'I was rather enjoying that. I always regretted that I never got to Petersburg, Simon. It must have been glorious in those days.'

The Savoy Orpheans burst into a lively rhythm and Tanya took Luke's hand.

'Come and charleston with me.'

'I don't know that I can. I'm not very good at this kind of thing.'

'Of course you are. Anyone can do the charleston,' she said, and in no time, under her direction, he got the hang of it and they were circling the room, kicking high, and to his own surprise he was doing pretty well.

Paul said, 'Come on, Aunt Margaret. I'll show you how it's done,' and the evening ended in a great deal of noise and laughter with Nicola appearing in her nightgown and demanding to know why everyone else but her should be having fun. Nevertheless Luke was left with the strong feeling that even in this close and united family there were inexplicable stresses and tensions, and that already, by some freak of chance and the whim of this lovely girl who moved so rapidly from one mood to another, he was caught up in it.

'You still spoil Tanya,' said Lady Aylsham to her husband that night as she took the pins from her hair and shook it out so that it hung, still shining and lustrous, around her shoulders.

'Did that prank of hers upset you this evening?' He had come up behind her, his arms round her waist drawing her back against him.

'Only because it proved to me that after all these years you still feel guilty about Nina.' She twisted round to look up into his face. 'I'm right, aren't I?'

'No, you're not.' He moved away, a little impatiently. 'That was over long ago. I should feel grateful because what she did have given me these years with you.' He sighed. 'It's only that now and again Tanya is so extraordinarily like her, with that same lack of balance, that same wildness. It touches me on the raw and I worry about her.'

'Is that why you let her bring this Welsh boy down here this weekend?'

'Partly. At Giovanni's gallery she meets too many wilting Russians, all of them devastatingly charming and feckless, yearning after a past that has gone and will never return. I sensed something sturdy, something strongly independent about Luke. He has fought his way up through hardship, and under that shyness I guess that he is intensely proud of it and healthily ambitious.'

'Supposing he falls in love with her. She is very attractive, you know.'

'Let him. Young men of his age fall in and out of love and come to no harm,' he said easily.

She gave him a quick look of amusement. He had loved unwisely in his own youth and suffered badly from it, but men forget such agonies while women somehow treasure them.

'I could wish she trusted me a little more,' she said slowly.

'You fret too much about it.'

'Only because I think it does her harm. She is still jealous, you know – jealous because after her mother's death you turned to me for comfort and not to her. She has never forgiven me for that.'

'She was only a child, Galina.'

'But a child with a great deal of her mother's wilful, passionate temperament. If Nina wanted something she went all out to get it and hold on to it. Until the very end she never found out how to give, only to take, and that is something Tanya may find difficult and painful to learn.'

'My God, there are times when I could wish them babies again,' exclaimed Simon. 'It was simple then. All they needed was food and warmth and love. Now it's becoming a battle. Paul rushing into all kinds of dangerous activities, refusing to listen to me, forgetting that he is not fit and never will be. Andy head over heels in love with a young woman who delights in tormenting him. And as for Tanya – ' He shook his head and sighed. 'Nicola is the only one I feel happy about.'

'And she is not yours,' said his wife drily. 'When are you going to tell her who her real father was?'

'Certainly not now. She is a child still. Why upset her safe world to no purpose?' He stretched out an arm and pulled her against him. 'Thank God you don't change, Galina. How many years have I loved you – twenty-four, twenty-five? It must be a record.'

'Don't be so smugly self-satisfied. I could still take a lover,' she said teasingly.

'Don't you dare, not unless you want to see murder done.'

She laughed as she tied back her hair and slipped off her dressing gown. Later, lying in the close shelter of his arms, she thought how fortunate she was – the heartache, the long years of frustration, the sharp pain of love denied, now far behind her, her one passionate regret that she had not been able to give the man she loved another child. A year after their marriage, to her joy, she had become pregnant, but it had ended disastrously, the baby lost and her own life in danger. Torn with anxiety for her he had said never again. She wished she could in some way teach the children how to deal with the traps that life would inevitably set for them, and knew it was impossible. All of them, Andy, Paul, Nicola and Tanya – most particularly Tanya – must find it out for themselves.

At the same time the cause of so much of her father's anxiety was standing in her bedroom staring into the mirror and not liking

41

herself very much. She knew she had behaved badly, had in fact done it deliberately to hurt her stepmother, and had known a moment of triumph before the inevitable reaction. She was given to sudden wild moods which often ended badly for others as well as for herself. She was hitting out at a world that she felt in so many ways was proving disappointing.

She looked disgustedly at the revealing black silk nightgown and knew it had been a mistake. She had bought it in a mood of rebellion against the white-trimmed lawn Galina considered suitable for a young girl barely out of her teens. The same garment on one of her friends had looked marvellously sexy, but Tanya's shoulders were too thin, her bosom too slender, and the black extinguished her delicate colouring. She decided to give it to the parlourmaid tomorrow. Alice would be thrilled and a little shocked. With her strict Methodist upbringing she would never dare to show it, off or on, to the under-gardener who had taken to haunting the kitchen quarters all this past year.

She giggled over it as she climbed into bed, and then lay thinking about Luke. Inviting him down had been one of her sudden whims that more often than not had ended in boredom if not in disaster, as when the charming Russian aristocrat had been caught by Jake just in time decamping with most of the silver. That afternoon on the river had possessed a magic of its own. Luke had touched a chord deep inside her that none of the other young men pressing attentions on her had ever reached. Her father had been right. She possessed in no small degree her mother's beauty and enchantment and her wayward ways, but there was something else too, a strength she had inherited from him and his sturdy British ancestors, a quality as yet untapped.

The transition from Russia to England with the war still raging throughout Europe had not been easy for any of them. After a long and exhausting journey through Spain and weeks of waiting in uncomfortable lodgings for passage on a ship, they had arrived in a Britain still shrouded in black-out and suffering from acute food shortages. In her self-absorption Tanya had never realized how difficult it had been for her father to leave everything behind and make a new home on the estate which his sister's husband had struggled to keep going despite wartime exigencies. His brother's widow was still in residence and not at all anxious to make way for this new half-Russian family. She had looked with the deepest resentment and dislike at the beautiful Russian woman whom her brother-in-law was obstinately determined to make his second wife just as soon as it could be conveniently arranged.

In that first, troubled year, with a young family, a shortage of ready money, and at the age of forty-one obliged to make a new career as physician and surgeon in a country he had deliberately turned his back on some fifteen years before, it was little wonder that he listened to his sister-in-law and sent Tanya off to the school where her own daughters had been educated. Tanya had hated every single minute of the traumatic two years she had spent there.

That her beloved father was willing to send her away from him had seemed to her like a betrayal. Late one evening in those first few weeks she had come from the bathroom and seen him come up the stairs with the woman who had taken her mother's place. She shrank back as they paused outside the bedroom door. She watched him take her in his arms, saw their bodies melt into one another, and shut her eyes fiercely against it. How could he! How dare he! Later she fled back to her own room and flung herself on the bed in a rage of sick disgust and jealousy. She sulked at home when they were married in the Russian Church in London, and after they had gone she ran out of the house in a torment of misery, taking refuge for some reason she could not explain in that ruined, desolate mill that had once spelled tragedy.

She had achieved her object. They could not ignore her. When they returned and she could not be found in the house or gardens there was considerable anxiety. Search parties spread out across the Fens, the quiet evening party with friends was irretrievably ruined. It was her father who found her, shivering and forlorn, crouched among the reeds on the muddy riverbank. He had said little, merely putting his coat round her and guiding her into the boat, but his sternness, his anger, was worse than anything she had ever experienced. At the house there were no hugs and kisses, only Paul looking at her reproachfully and Andy saying disgust-edly, 'When are you going to stop making a spectacle of yourself, Tanya?' and Galina, whom she had hated and humiliated, quietly undressing her and putting her to bed with hot water bottles and warm milk and then leaving her alone to cry herself to sleep.

School, that should have been a refuge, in fact turned into a purgatory.

It was not really anyone's fault. It was a famous institution with an excellent reputation, but Tanya had never been subjected to discipline of that kind. She had grown up in a luxurious household, had run free with her cousins on her uncle's vast estates, and she badly missed her beloved *nianya* and her English governess. She hated sleeping in a dormitory with a dozen other girls, loathed being obliged to wear uniform, and to undress, wash, bathe and perform all such private functions in their company. She detested all forms of sport and took part in them unwillingly and badly, and though in some respects, in languages, for instance, and literature, she was a long way ahead of her contemporaries, in mathematics and subjects she despised she was woefully and obstinately ignorant.

She took refuge in a haughty silence and occasionally, when goaded, would round on her persecutors with an eloquence that to English ears sounded very like boasting. At thirteen she was horribly vulnerable and girls of that age can be merciless. They made fun of her precise English, mockingly called her Princess, laughed at her instinctive modesty, and resented the way she chattered blithely to the French mistress, leaving them far behind. She stuck it for two years then crisis came. A valuable bracelet disappeared, and for some reason, perhaps out of spite, blame fell on her. She hotly denied any knowledge of the wretched bauble and, inflamed beyond reason, hurled herself on her tormentors, biting, kicking, punching. Horrified teachers dragged them apart. Tanya was isolated as if she were a moral leper while her father was informed, but before he could get there, sick with misery and with the connivance of the gardener's boy, who ought to have known better, she had escaped through a window.

Frantic about its good name the school wanted to keep the matter as quiet as possible. After two days Dr Aylsham, furious at the slur on his daughter and racked with anxiety, called in the police. They found her in the waiting room at Euston Station, starving, penniless, and huddled in a corner terrified of the men who, tempted by her frail beauty, were only too ready to proposition her. In some ghastly way it had become the station at Kiev all over again, and she fell into her father's arms sobbing wildly and incoherently. He took her home and kept her there for a year, petted and spoiled, and then on the advice of friendly neighbours who also had a daughter he sent her to a finishing school in Switzerland where the girls were treated as individuals and where she made a friend.

Diana Harcourt was the sister of Nicola's gorgeous Cecil, a year older than Tanya and far more experienced and self-confident, very sure of herself and of her beauty. Unlikely as it was, the two girls became firm friends, and since their families lived so near each other they were not even parted in the holidays.

It had seemed a joke at first that Andy, sensible, down-to-earth Andy, working his way steadily through medical school and hospital, should fall hopelessly in love with Diana. They all teased him about it at first, till suddenly it wasn't funny any longer but just another tangle in their lives which would at some time have to be straightened out.

Sometimes she envied Diana, who had known exactly what she wanted to do, had clung to it steadily all through the year when they were presented at Court and endured those madly boring debutante parties. She seemed to possess the happy knack of persuading her family and those close to her to fall in with her plans. Lucky, lucky Diana!

In all that vast house Tanya was the only one lying awake, all her senses tinglingly alive, wishing that something stupendous would happen, that life would flower for her in some wonderful way and carry her along with it, not yet realizing that what she longed for did not exist, that joy is fleeting and happiness does not come as a gift. It has to be worked for and sometimes a price must be paid. It was near dawn before she fell asleep.

3

'Must we go to this dreary Fête?' asked Tanya plaintively over breakfast on Monday morning. 'It's going to be the most dreadful bore.'

'Yes, we must,' said her father. 'I don't often play Lord of the Manor, but this time it is expected of me and I rely on my family to support me. We can't let the Harcourts down. It's being held in their grounds, and it is for charity after all.'

'The funds are to go to the starving millions in Russia,' said Nicola thickly through a mouthful of toast, 'so it's up to us to help, isn't it, Papa?'

'If that's true, I suppose it is,' he replied doubtfully. 'Where on earth did you find that out, Nicola?'

'Jake told me. He always knows everything. Paul and I are going to take the horses over and Jacob too so that we can give children rides. They love the donkey. Would you like to come and help, Luke?'

'I was about to suggest that if our guest prefers to stay quietly here instead of joining the merry throng, we shall quite understand,' said the doctor with a glance at his wife.

'Yes, of course, you must do what you prefer,' added Lady Aylsham. 'Our housekeeper is away this weekend, but Cook will give you luncheon and Alice will look after you.'

'I wouldn't dream of it,' said Luke. 'I'd like to help with the horses so long as I'm not expected to ride one.'

'Oh no.' Nicola was very serious. 'All you have to do is lead the children up and down the field and make sure the little ones don't fall off. They nearly always do if you don't watch out.'

'And what am I supposed to do?' complained Tanya.

'You can help me judge the cakes and home-made wine,' said her stepmother. 'Your Aunt Margaret seems to think I'm an

46

expert, I can't think why. Do I have to *taste* everything?' she asked her husband anxiously.

'I hope not,' he replied, grinning heartlessly. 'Parsnip wine can be very potent. I remember getting very tight on it when I was a boy. I don't want to bring you both home reeling drunk.'

'It's all right for you. All you have to do is to declare the Fête open, make an amusing little speech, and retire to the library for brandy and cigars with General Harcourt.'

'I shall do nothing of the kind. I shall go and watch the village cricket team. People always expect a doctor to hand out free advice on their lumbago or their arthritis or little Willie's persistent cough. I shall take care to make myself scarce and leave them all to you, Andy.'

'No fear,' said his son. 'I intend to take Diana on the swings and roundabouts.'

'Lucky beast,' grumbled his sister. 'Catch Diana letting herself in for anything like hard work.'

'I've not been to that kind of fair since I was a child,' said Luke. 'I used to be a dab hand at a coconut shy. Will you have a go with me, Tanya?'

'Done!' She clapped her hand on his. 'We'll do that just as soon as we've judged the cakes and ale!'

The gardens at Chalfont Manor were very extensive. A huge marquee had been set up on the lawn where entries for the competitions for flowers, fruit, vegetables, and home-made cakes, jams and wines were set out, and round it were grouped stalls with fancy goods, guessing games, raffles, with a giant tombola presided over by sturdy farmers' wives and their daughters, all wearing their flowery best despite fugitive sunshine and a chill little wind. The jingle-jangle of the fair came faintly on the breeze from a distant meadow far enough away so as not to disturb the lavish luncheon laid out in the dining room for privileged guests. Here Luke experienced for the first time this weekend the cool brush-off of the English upper classes who sensed at once that he was an outsider, not one of them. He found himself stiffening against it.

He had come with Tanya in her little red car but lost her almost immediately to a group of acquaintances including Cecil Harcourt, young men in impeccable white flannels, straw boaters and a variety of dashingly striped blazers. A striking young woman whose dark red hair had been shaped to her small head like a copper helmet seized upon Tanya with a shriek of welcome and turned out to be Diana Harcourt.

Most of the guests when introduced looked Luke up and down, smiled emptily, uttered a few patronizing words, and afterwards totally ignored him. Dr Aylsham and his wife had been engulfed in an older group. It amused Luke for a few minutes to look them over with what he thought of as his novelist's eye. General Sir Harry Harcourt was a big man, red-faced, white-haired, with a bristling moustache, and so much like the cartoons that it was almost laughable, while Grace Harcourt, slim, self-effacing, gentle-voiced and dowdy, was the General's wife down to the tips of her fingers encased in lady-like white gloves.

Luke was given a glass of champagne by one of the footmen and was just wondering how soon he could slip discreetly away when Nicola tugged at his sleeve.

'Aunt Hester says I can't possibly show my face in these togs,' she whispered, 'which is daft. You can't ride a horse in a summer frock. I did put on my best too.' She was in fact looking remarkably clean and elegant in brand new jodhpurs and an expensive cashmere pullover. 'Paul and I are going to take our lunch and have a picnic in the meadow. Would you like to come with us?'

'Yes, I would.'

'Good-oh. You can help carry it. The cook here is a treasure and Di says we can collect it from the kitchen. There's salmon and cold duck and she's found us some simply spiffing trifle. The only thing is we'll have to make do with ginger pop, do you mind? I don't think I dare steal a bottle of champagne.'

'Ginger pop will do me fine,' said Luke. 'Lead the way.'

It was late afternoon by the time Tanya came in search of him, and they had been doing a roaring trade, long queues of boys and girls from four to fourteen lining up and holding out their sixpences.

Diana had taken Tanya's arm as the two girls came out of the giant marquee and they walked together across the lawns.

48

'I've something to tell you,' she said. 'I've got the part. It's only small but I'm to understudy the lead. We have one week at the Brighton Royal and then open in London.'

'Oh, Di, that's marvellous. What do the parents say?'

'Daddy threw a fit at first but he's getting over it. Mother is still convinced I'm going straight to the devil, but I expect she'll come round eventually. They just don't realize that I'm not just playing around. I'm deadly serious.'

Ever since Diana had been taken to her first real play at the age of ten she had known that she wanted to be an actress, had felt the power burn within her, was quite certain that one day she would be moving audiences to tears or laughter, and since then she had pursued her aim with a single-minded determination that rode above argument, objections and strong disapproval.

She and her brother Cecil were the children of elderly parents, old-fashioned, set in their ways, to whom the stage was anathema. Despite the years of war her father was still largely Edwardian in his tastes. You might have a bit of a lark with a girl from a musical comedy, take her to supper at Romano's, even go a step further, but as a career for your only daughter, carefully brought up and presented to their Majesties – never, never! thundered the General.

She had adored *The Scarlet Pimpernel*, cried her eyes out over Martin Harvey in *The Only Way*, was shocked and enthralled by *The Garden of Allah*. Now she was beyond all that, but to persuade him to let her go to drama school had been uphill work. Diana was far too clever to shout him down or rebel openly; instead she worked with a slow, insidious determination to wear him down. The war was long over. In between Ascot, Wimbledon and Henley even debutantes were getting down to work.

'Everyone's doing a job nowadays, Daddy,' she pointed out to him. 'Think of Ollie Winter, she's a model showing off her legs – you wouldn't like me to do that, would you? Look at Tanya working in Giovanni's gallery . . .'

'Aylsham's a good fellow, one of the best,' the General grumbled, 'but he's got that Russian wife, not quite the thing, y'know,' but he had weakened.

'What do you think?' Diana went on to Tanya. 'I'm even being allowed to stay in the family flat in Curzon Street during the week with Nanny Gibbons to look after me and keep me out of mischief.

49

You will be able to come and spend a night any time you like. We might have some fun, Tanya.'

'May I?' Visions of enticing freedom danced before the younger girl's eyes. Indulgent though her father was, he was still strict about knowing exactly who was taking his daughter out, and except on very special occasions insisted on her being returned safe and sound by eleven o'clock at the latest.

'Who is the new young man?' asked Diana, eyeing Luke appreciatively as they came up to the field.

It had been warm work sweating up and down the meadow all that afternoon, and he had taken off his jacket and rolled up his shirt sleeves. For the first time Tanya noticed the breadth of his shoulders, narrowing to a slim waist. He had a kind of whipcord strength despite his leanness. She watched as he swung the child easily into the saddle and then stood hands on hips, laughing as the pony broke unexpectedly into a canter across the grass.

'He's a distinct improvement on some of your weedy protégés,' went on Diana. 'Where did you pick him up?'

'I didn't pick him up. As a matter of fact I knocked him down. Papa had to stitch him up.'

'And you brought him down here to recuperate.' Diana laughed. 'Well, that's one way to start a romance.'

'It's not a romance. He's Welsh and he's reading English at King's.'

'Is he? Intellectual type but with plenty of muscle and brawn, I'm glad to see. I'll leave you to him. I must go and find Andy.'

'Di, what are you going to do about Andy?'

'What do you mean? Why should I do anything about him?'

'You know exactly what I mean. He's crazy about you. Don't you like him – just a little?'

Diana looked at her friend and then away. 'Oh yes, I like him. As a matter of fact I like him far too much,' and with that enigmatic statement she walked away, leaving Tanya frowning and for once at a loss for words.

The queues were shortening by now. Tea was being served and parents were collecting children.

'You'd better go and get yourself some food, Paul, you look fagged out,' said his sister.

'Don't fuss, Tanya,' he snapped, 'I'm perfectly all right. You go off with Luke. Nicola and I can finish up here.'

'If you're sure . . .' said Luke uncertainly.

'Of course I'm sure.'

'Right then.' Luke picked up his jacket, slung it across his shoulders, and took Tanya's arm. 'How did the judging go?'

'Awful. All those who had won prizes went around with smug faces, and the others were simply glowering at us. You could positively feel them breathing fire and fury and saying, "Of course they're only foreigners!" I hate the English!' she exclaimed vehemently. 'Come on, let's have a bash at the coconuts.'

Half an hour later, strolling back across the grass, each of them carrying a fat hairy coconut, they ran full tilt into Aunt Hester.

'Damn,' muttered Tanya under her breath then abruptly switched on her sweetest smile.

'I don't think you've met my Aunt Hester, Luke, Lady Aylsham that was, now she's Mrs Nicholas Blake. May I introduce Luke Llewellyn Jones?'

She was looking him over through the lorgnette that hung round her neck on a gold chain and reminded him irresistibly of Lady Penhale, the same high colour, the same tightly corseted figure in the rich flowered silk. The old childish rebellion against everything she stood for rose up inside him.

'And where do you come from, young man?' she asked, her eyes taking in everything mercilessly, the dusty blazer, the rolled up sleeves, the loosened tie.

'From South Wales, Mrs Blake. My father was a miner and so was my grandfather,' he said coolly. He nearly added, 'And my mother scrubs the mine manager's floors,' but bit it back just in time.

'Indeed,' she said icily, 'and what are you doing here, may I ask?'

'Enjoying himself, I hope,' put in Tanya quickly. 'Luke has been helping Paul with the horses.'

'I saw Nicola – that wretched child dressing herself up like a kennel maid! After all, she *is* an Aylsham. I will have to say something to your stepmother. Being a foreigner she can hardly be expected to understand English ways.'

'I wouldn't if I were you, Aunt Hester. Father doesn't like

Galina to be criticized,' said Tanya maliciously, closing family ranks against the enemy. 'And now if you will excuse us Luke is going to take me on the roundabout.'

'Slumming it, are you, Tanya?'

'Yes, Mrs Blake, she is slumming it with me as it happens,' said Luke, suddenly so angry he didn't care what she or anyone else thought of him. 'Tanya wants to know how the other half of the world lives, and that's something I can teach her.'

Aunt Hester seemed to swell with indignation. 'Don't be impudent with me, young man. I don't know what you think you're doing, Tanya, running around in company such as this, but I shall certainly speak to your father.'

'Oh, Papa, knows all about Luke. It was partly his idea to invite him for the weekend. We really must go now or we shall be too late.'

She dragged Luke away, and beyond the lawn stopped to look up at him breathlessly.

'I love the way you stood up to her. My father is the only one who does. She is furious because she can't crush us all as she does my poor cousin Penny, who's rather plain, poor darling, and hasn't found a husband yet.'

They spent a mad, merry hour on the roundabout, on the dodgem cars, on swings that flew out so high that Tanya shrieked and clung to him, and then came back to the roundabout in which Tanya took a childish delight.

'I think I was about seven when Papa took me and Andy for the first time,' she said. 'I thought it was wonderful, all those prancing horses in gorgeous colours. I wanted one for my very own.'

It was then that Luke caught sight of Cecil Harcourt. He was standing with two other young men like himself. They moved closer and called out to Tanya, beckoning her to join them. She shook her head, laughing at them and letting Luke lift her on to the roundabout as it slowed down. This time it was crowded and only one horse was available. He lifted her on to it and leaped up behind her. It was a tight fit and his arms went round her waist. He could feel the slim body within the thin silk pressed hard

52

against him, the blonde hair blew against his mouth, the flower-like perfume made his senses swim. The carousel gathered speed. As it swept round again he caught a brief glimpse of Cecil's frowning face and deliberately pushed aside the soft curls, dropped a kiss on Tanya's neck, and felt the tiny shiver that ran through her. Next time they pranced by the young men had vanished.

The garden party was beginning to break up by now, but coloured lights had sprung up throughout the fair and the villagers would be making merry until very late. Nicola came racing up as Luke and Tanya jumped off the roundabout.

'Paul and I are just going home and Papa is looking for you, Tanya.'

'What for?'

'Something about presenting prizes.'

'Oh Lord, I had forgotten. I suppose I'd better find them.'

Luke was conscious of looking dusty and dishevelled, not at all fit for aristocratic company.

'You go,' he said, 'and I'll come later.'

'We'll all be leaving soon, I expect. You know where the cars are.'

'Yes, I'll meet you there.'

He saw Nicola and Paul leave with the horses and then strolled across the park, glad to be alone for a while. A belt of sparse woodland surrounded a large lake, the water overgrown with thick reeds and a little desolate. Now that the sun had gone down there was a kind of green twilight under the trees. He walked along the path and paused where there was a wooden platform jutting out into the water. A boat must have been moored here at some time and an old rotting oar was still lying half in and half out of the lake. He stood there thinking of the whole weekend, of the family who in an entirely unexpected way had gripped his interest, and of Tanya in particular, so different, so unpredictable and yet so very lovely. He'd known her for only a few days and already she had seized upon his imagination. Once he had been content to think soberly of his future, a good teaching post possibly in Wales, a decent salary so that he could repay in some measure the debt he owed to his mother. Now other mad, soaring ideas raced through his mind. If he obtained his First, if in some magical way he finished his novel and it got somewhere – if – if – He was lost in his impossible dream and did not realize he was surrounded until Cecil spoke, his high-bred voice thin and malicious.

'Go back to your valleys, Welsh boy. You're not wanted here.'

Startled, Luke looked up, saw the three grinning faces in the greenish half-light. They moved in on him chanting softly.

> 'Taffy was a Welshman, Taffy was a thief,
> Taffy came to my house and stole a piece of beef – '

'Shut up!' he said.

But they didn't shut up, they went on chanting louder and louder. He was gripped by the arms.

'A cold bath, that's what is needed!'

'Cool his ardour – '

'Teach him a lesson – '

'Send him back where he belongs!'

The jibes, the laughter, were all around him. They were forcing him towards the lake, and in a sudden burst of rage he tore himself free. He hit out wildly and felt his fist meet with a target, but they were three against one. He was fighting a battle now. He knew he had already done damage and was glad of it, but it was growing dark under the trees. One of them reeled back with a bloody nose, but another was on him forcing him back and back.

'You keep your filthy paws off Tanya,' hissed Cecil suddenly and viciously.

He picked up the half-rotted oar and swung it dangerously. Luke saw it coming and dodged, but the wood planking under his feet was slippery with green slime. He tried to recover his balance, but someone punched him in the stomach and he went over backwards into the water. It filled his mouth as he came up. He spat it out and made a grab at the edge of the platform, but the wood gave way under his groping fingers. Cecil still had the oar. It hit Luke hard in the chest, sending him sprawling into the bed of reeds, the stinking water closing over his head. He came up spluttering and dazed by the blow. The oar made another deadly swing and he ducked just in time.

'That's enough, Cecil,' said a frightened voice. 'Leave him now.'

'I'd like to kill the bastard!'

'Don't be a damned fool! Leave it, come away.'

There was a confused babble of voices, the sound of running feet, and then silence.

The last swing of the oar had hit him a glancing blow on the cheek. Blood was running into his mouth. It should have been easy to climb out, but was proving unexpectedly difficult. The wooden platform had been built up a foot or so and was so rotten that he could not get any kind of grip on it. A thick wedge of tangled reeds had knotted themselves about his feet. It was ridiculous, he must be able to hoist himself up on to the bank, he thought despairingly, as the wood broke away into splinters under his hands and his ankles sank deeper into the soggy mud.

The two coming along the bank had been too engrossed in their argument to notice anything except a muddled sound of voices.

'I don't want to marry anyone, not yet,' Diana was saying firmly. 'We've got so much to do. You must see that, Andy. You want to be a surgeon like your father, and that's going to take years, and I've only got the merest toehold in the theatre. Are we going to give all that up?'

'Of course we're not. I'm not suggesting we get married right away, only that we commit ourselves to each other. We can keep it to ourselves if that's what you want, something just between us.'

'No, it's wrong. I must be free and so must you. Making a promise is too binding, and if a time comes when you have to break it you feel so wretchedly guilty.'

'Why should we break it?'

'Who knows what is going to happen to either of us?'

'You don't care enough,' said Andy moodily; 'that's the real truth, isn't it?'

'No, it's not. It's unfair of you to say that. Oh, Andy, why can't you be sensible? Why can't we go on as we are? What are you afraid of?'

'That I shall lose you – and I can't bear the thought.'

'Now you're just being silly.'

'Am I? Am I, Diana?'

He swung her round to face him, and before she could resist was kissing her with such violence that she gasped for breath when at last he released her.

55

'Wow! I didn't bargain for that!' she said, smiling rather shakily.

'You shouldn't be so damnably beautiful,' he said huskily, and would have reached for her again.

'No, Andy, no, not now, please not now.' She held him off and then suddenly lifted her head. 'Listen, do you hear something? That splashing. It sounds as if someone has fallen into the lake.'

'Probably one of those confounded children.'

'I'm always telling Daddy the old boat jetty is dangerous.'

'Oh Lord, better go and investigate, I suppose.'

They both raced along the bank, peering into the water as they came out from under the trees.

'Good God, it's Luke,' exclaimed Andy. He leaned over. 'Here, give me your hands.'

'It's these damned reeds – '

'Move along a bit if you can. That's better. Come on now, heave!'

With some difficulty and with Diana lending a helping hand Luke at last managed to scramble up on to the bank and stood shaking himself like a dog, green scummy water streaming off him.

'How the devil did that happen?' asked Andy.

'I slipped and fell in,' was the curt reply.

'Are you all right?' asked Diana with concern. 'You're bleeding.'

'It's nothing. A few grazes, that's all.'

'You'd better come up to the house. We'll find you some dry clothes.'

'No,' Luke said fiercely. 'No, I'd rather not.'

'But you can't just stay like that. You'll catch your death of cold.'

'I know what we'll do,' said Andy, who had made a shrewd guess that was pretty close to the truth. 'I'll take Tanya's car and drive Luke home. You go up to the house, Di, and tell Father – but quietly, don't make a fuss about it. Tanya can come back with him and Mother. Come on, Luke, it's blowing up cold. We'd better hurry.'

By the time they reached where the cars were parked, Luke was shivering violently and beginning to feel the effect of his cuts and bruises.

Andy found his father's Mercedes, pulled a couple of rugs out of the boot, and handed them over.

'Wrap those round you. It won't take us long to reach Ravensley.'

He had noticed with interest that three young men looking decidedly the worse for wear were grouped around one of the cars and Cecil Harcourt was holding a blood-soaked handkerchief to his nose. One of them made a movement as if he would have spoken, but Andy turned his back on him and got into the driver's seat. The little car started with its usual explosive roar and they were off at a spanking pace.

'Have a bath,' Andy advised, taking charge as soon as they reached the house and were climbing up the steps, 'as hot as you can bear it, and then I'll take a look at the damage.'

'I'm afraid I stink to high heaven,' muttered Luke ruefully as he stripped off in the bathroom.

'Never mind about that. Throw in some of Tanya's bath salts.' Andy picked up the sodden clothes. 'I'll give these to Mrs Alison, our housekeeper. She's been away for the weekend, but she'll be back by now. She'll know how to deal with them. I'll lend you something of mine. We're about the same size.'

An hour later, warmed through and wearing a pair of borrowed flannels and a thick woollen pullover, Luke was in the drawing room close to a blazing fire, a tray of tea and toasted scones between him and his rescuer.

'Contrary to what most people believe, in moments of stress Russians fly to tea and not to vodka,' said Andy cheerfully. 'Our old nurse used to keep the samovar on the go from morning till night. Are you feeling all right? Would you like some brandy?'

'Tea will do me fine.'

His hands were smarting badly from the splinters which Andy had carefully extracted with tweezers. He had frowned over the bruises where the oar had struck. 'Dashed lucky it didn't crack a rib,' he muttered, prodding cautiously at Luke's chest. He had cleansed the bleeding cut on his cheek and put on something that made it sting. 'Thank goodness you didn't split your head open again and spoilt Papa's beautiful stitching.'

But none of the pain or the aching stiffness really mattered beside the humiliation at being made to look a fool, and the wretched conviction that Tanya had been deliberately playing a game, using him merely to spite the young men who were all so

57

much closer to her in every way than he was or was ever likely to be.

Andy poured more tea for them both and offered the box of cigarettes.

'Want to tell me what really happened?' he asked quietly.

Luke shot him a quick glance. 'You've guessed, haven't you?'

Andy grinned. 'I'm pretty sure you inflicted quite a bit of damage before you went overboard.'

'I hope I did,' Luke said savagely. 'Who are they, those three?'

'Cecil is Di's brother, of course, revolting little pipsqueak. He tried that sort of thing on me once when we first came here. The other two are pals of his. They all live round here.'

'What do they do?'

'Nothing except make themselves obnoxious. Too much money and too little brain,' said Andy drily.

'My father and my grandfather worked all their lives down the pit, as my brother did until he was laid off. My mother speaks Welsh better than she speaks English, and so did I once. What of it? I'm not ashamed of it. In fact I'm bloody proud, if you really want to know,' said Luke fiercely.

'And so you ought to be, but there is another side of the picture too,' said Andy ruefully. 'If it's any comfort to you, you're not the only one to suffer. I'm at their mercy the other way round. Because my father is Lord Aylsham, and I suppose it's what I shall be one day unless I turn it down in favour of Paul, how can I possibly be a good doctor?'

Luke stared. 'They don't say that about you, surely?'

'Oh, don't they just, at school, at medical college, at the hospital, even though my mother was the illegitimate daughter of a Russian peasant who washed her master's shirts and shared his bed,' said Andy savagely. 'Sometimes I feel like hanging it on a placard round my neck. I have to be twice as good as anyone else to make up for my aristocratic ancestors. Father suffers from it too. You see, in Russia nobody thought about who he was, only that he was a very good surgeon, but when he came back to England he had to start all over again, and it was not easy. He did think of renouncing the title, except that would be giving in to stupid prejudice and there are people who depend on him here at Ravensley. My Aunt Hester thinks he should give up medicine and go into politics, take his seat in the House of Lords, but he won't. He is a doctor first and foremost, everything else comes a very long way after, and quite apart from all that we're horribly hard up.'

Luke looked around him. 'I find that difficult to believe.'

'You try keeping this place going with Aunt Hester and her brood grabbing everything they can lay their hands on.' Andy grinned suddenly. 'She had a furious row with Pa a few years ago because he sold the family mansion in Belgravia. It was an absolute monster, cost a fortune to maintain and needed a load of servants to run it. Now we have a small house in Wimpole Street where he can have his consulting room and where we can all sleep and eat when we are in London. Part of the money he got for it went to funding Mamma's clinic for children. Aunt Hester blew her top about that and said we would probably all die from some disgusting disease. Luckily Pa's fairly resilient to attacks of that kind and told her if he didn't object, he didn't see why she should, and if she was afraid of infection she had better not visit us too often. That shut her up. She can't bear not to know everything that's going on.' He sighed and stubbed out his cigarette. 'All the same I can't tell you how maddening it is to be regarded as a playboy like Cecil. So you see, from different points of view you and I are in the same boat, and it can be a damned rocky one.'

'Are you just saying all this to make me feel better about it?'

'No, I'm not. It's fellow feeling. I mean it. You're a Celt and I'm a Russian, both of us what they would call bloody foreigners.'

Luke smiled. 'I suppose you're right. I hadn't seen it like that.' He glanced at the other's lean, handsome face. 'May I ask you something?'

'Fire away.'

'If Lady Aylsham is your mother, why does Nicola call you her half-brother?'

Andy laughed. 'We must seem a frightful muddle to outsiders, I suppose. You see, my mother was Pa's mistress before they decided to get married. Then he had to leave Russia rather suddenly because his father was dying, and during the months he was away something happened to her. What it was I don't know. They have neither of them ever told us. Maybe it was because she found herself pregnant and was afraid of the scandal. You see, he was rather stepping out of line by marrying his mistress, who was also

59

the daughter of a peasant. When he came back she had vanished, gone completely out of his life, and after a time he married the Princess Nina. Tanya and Paul were born, then after five years he met my mother again. She was working in a pharmacy in Kiev and on the point of being condemned to Siberia for complicity in the assassination of the Prime Minister.'

'Was she guilty?'

'All she had done was to try and save the life of the man she worked for, who had been good to her, but they exiled her all the same, and my father took me into his own home.'

'That must have caused problems.'

'It did. I was five, but I can still remember how lost I felt. I clung to Pa like a limpet, and Tanya resented me like hell and so did her mother. We fought like cat and dog, but in the end we settled down. Then there was the war. Father was at the Front with a medical team, and my mother was a nurse with the Red Cross. Neither of them was free. He could not abandon his family, and though they were still in love they were parted till the Revolution came and the Bolsheviki drove us all out of Russia.'

'And murdered Tanya's mother?'

'Yes, that too. Quite a saga, isn't it? But they did survive, and so did their love. You can't be with them and not be aware of it.'

It was true, thought Luke – not in the least obvious, and yet it was there at the very centre of the family.

Andy lit another cigarette and stared thoughtfully into the fire.

'Sometimes I envy them,' he said.

'Because you're in love with Diana?'

'Is it that obvious?' he said wryly. 'What about you and Tanya?'

Luke shrugged and they grinned at one another, a quick bond of fellow feeling springing unexpectedly between them, something that was to grow and endure in the difficult years ahead. Then they heard the car drive up outside and the sound of voices mingled with the barking of the dogs. A few minutes later the others were coming into the drawing room.

'We've been worried about you,' said Dr Aylsham. 'Diana told us you fell in the lake. Are you hurt?'

'Nothing to speak of.'

'I've taken care of him, Pa. A few nasty bruises and grazes, that's all.'

Tanya was frowning at him. 'What happened? I saw Cecil. He was covered in mud and his nose was bleeding. Did he try to pull you out?'

'No, he did not, very far from it,' said her brother shortly.

'Better let me take a look at that forehead of yours,' said Dr Aylsham. 'And what on earth have you done to your face?'

'I hit it against something as I fell.'

'Mrs Alison's back, Mamma,' interrupted Andy. 'Shall I tell her we're ready for supper?'

'Please do, dear,' said his mother. 'Speaking for myself, I'm quite worn out with smiling and trying to look interested. Where are Paul and Nicola?'

'They're having supper in bed.'

'Good idea.' The doctor straightened up from making a quick examination of Luke's face. 'I can't really say I'm sorry that's over. Andy, tell Alice to bring in the drinks trolley. We'll all have a relaxing glass of sherry. None of Tanya's disgusting cocktails.'

'Oh, Papa, that's not fair. My Russian Special has been highly praised.'

'It's a knockout, certainly,' commented her father drily, 'guaranteed to put you under the table in no time at all. Luke, you are given fair warning.'

Supper was a light-hearted affair, and some time later when they had eaten and everyone had settled for an early night Luke went to the library to pick up some books he had left there and was cornered by Tanya.

'I wish you'd tell me what really happened this afternoon. It was those beasts of boys, wasn't it? Did they push you in?'

'It's over and I don't want to talk about it,' he said gruffly.

'But it was so hateful. How dare they do that to you? Next time I see them I shall tell them exactly what I think of them.'

'Please don't fight my battles for me. I'm quite capable of looking after myself.'

'It's only because they have more money than sense. It's so unfair.'

'Don't patronize me, Tanya. I don't want it and I don't like it.'

'That's a horrible thing to say.'

'Is it? You must have enjoyed using me to annoy your bunch of rich admirers.'

'I didn't do any such thing.'

'Didn't you? I thought it was fairly obvious. Cecil and his crew were pretty clear about it.' He picked up the books. 'Now if you'll excuse me I'm going to bed. Your father has to make an early start tomorrow and has offered to drive me up with him.'

'Of course if you prefer to go with him instead of with me – '

'It's not that I prefer it, it's just that I must get back to work as soon as possible.'

'I see. Well, if that's how you feel – '

'Tanya, I – '

'We'll meet again some time, I expect. Goodnight.'

She turned away and went out of the room before he could stop her, leaving him regretting that he had let the feeling of hurt and disappointment carry him away. He wanted to see her again desperately and had thrown away his chances simply because of his stupid jealousy of young men whom he despised.

In his bedroom Mrs Alison had hung up his flannel trousers and blazer. She had done her best to clean off the mud and green slime as well as pressing them dry with a hot iron, but they would never be the same again. He had offered to return Andy's pullover and slacks and had been told to keep them if they were of any use. Pride fought with necessity and the battle was lost, but only after a struggle. This brief foray into an alien world was over now, and it was back to his books, to a hard grind, in a fortnight's time he would be put to the test, to win or lose all. He had never thought of himself as a gambler, but perhaps he was after all. Slowly he began to pack his bag ready for the early start.

In her own room Tanya had stormily kicked off her shoes, pulled her dress over her head, tossed it into a corner, and then stared angrily at herself. Luke, who had sparked off her interest, who had seemed so different, so excitingly new, had dared to reject her, had proved as disappointing as all the others. Why? she asked herself as she got into bed. What was wrong with her? Why does nothing ever go right? She thumped her pillow, switched off the lamp, and lay staring into the darkness unable to find a ready answer.

4

Outside Imperial College in Kensington, where the examinations were being held, the students eddied up and down the pavement in awkward, uneasy groups.

'Won't be long now,' said Colin with a determined cheerfulness. 'Lambs to the slaughter, that's what we are.'

'Oh, shut up!' growled Luke. He was not looking forward to the days of torture and then the agonizing wait for the results. What the hell was it all for?

Ever since he had come back from Ravensley he had given himself up to a day and night revision, suddenly convinced that he knew nothing, that faced with a battery of questions his mind would go completely blank leaving him staring down hopelessly at empty sheets of paper. A hectic rush through poetry, drama and fiction was not the best antidote for a young man who had most unwisely fallen in love. Time after time his thoughts scattered wildly. He was seeing Tanya as Shakespeare's Rosalind filled with laughter and flashing wit, as Browning's 'Lyric love, half angel and half bird, and all a wonder and a wild desire', as Eliot's Italian girl, 'Weave, weave the sunlight in your hair'.

Memories jostled one another as he stared through the grimy window into the dusty Bloomsbury street – Tanya's hand in his, her provoking smile, the fragrance of her perfume, the lovely curve of her neck when he had kissed it, the ice in her voice when she walked away from him that last night. Then he cursed himself for a damned fool and plunged back into his work.

The doors of the college were already opening when a small red car drew up at the kerb with a jerk, causing a taxi to swerve so suddenly that it skidded, and out of the car came his own particular delight, her hair an impossible gold in the June sun, her eyes glancing swiftly over the boys and girls who had turned to stare. She came running towards him, one white rose in her hand.

'From all of us, just to wish you luck,' she whispered.

She put it into his buttonhole, stood on tiptoe to kiss his cheek, and then was gone again before he had time even to thank her. The car roared away.

'You sly dog!' exclaimed Colin. 'Keeping mum all this time, not a word out of you.'

They were laughing at him, teasing him, not a few of them envious. What's a dull chap like Luke Jones doing with a gorgeous girl like that? they asked one another.

But he didn't care. He marched into the examination hall with a new step, a mounting certainty, a feeling that now nothing could stop him, he was going in to win.

Of course the exhilaration didn't last. How could it? There were times when he felt like a god who could do no wrong, and other times when he faced grim despair. Then it was over, and there were only the grinding weeks to wait for the results. He should have gone home to Wales, but he knew he couldn't have endured it, his mother's loving belief in him, Megan's cloying affection, Dai proud of his little brother but just a shade contemptuous. All that studying, all those years with his nose stuck in his old books, that wasn't *real* work, that wasn't hacking at the coal face, sweating in the damp stuffy darkness, always on the alert for danger, coming up with face grimed with the black dust, every muscle aching viciously. They loved one another, but it had always been there ever since the first day he went to the grammar school, wearing the green cap with its badge and a pair of new boots his father had starved himself to buy.

Colin had left to spend a few weeks with his father, who was on a special assignment in Paris, so Luke was alone in his tiny room, working every night in the Soho café to keep himself alive and sweating away day after day at the novel, an unwieldy collection of exercise books that seemed suddenly to have become a huge mass of indigestible material that, try as he might, he could not bring to life.

The day of reckoning came at last. The heat wave had broken. The sky was a leaden grey, the rain came down in a slow drizzle, and there was a distinct chill in the entrance hall of the college as the students waited for that ominous list.

'It ought to come out with a flourish of trumpets, not with old

Prof. Thompson, who's forgotten what it feels like if he ever knew,' muttered Colin, who had arrived home unbearably cocky after his weeks in Paris but was now as much on edge as any of them.

It certainly seemed absurd, thought Luke, as the Senior Tutor in the English Department came tottering out. A few names typed on a sheet of paper that could ensure the future or damn you for ever. The old man pinned it up on the board, beamed round at them, and trotted back. They crowded forward to look, jostling one another, calling out names in a meaningless jumble. Luke suddenly couldn't move. It was all over, win or lose, his mouth had gone dry. Then Colin was thumping him on the back.

'You've done it, old boy. Oh, glorious day! Ring out the bells!'

Unbelievably, his name was there, heading the list. For a second he felt quite weak, then he was laughing with the others.

'What about you, Col?'

'An Upper Second – Pa will have something to say, but, damn it, it's respectable. I'd been dreading a Third. The old man said he'd throw us a party if I made the grade. Let's keep him to it.'

And a party they had, about a dozen of them, with James Tait sportingly providing the champagne, and during that evening Luke found an opportunity to telephone. He couldn't reach his mother directly, of course, but he could get through to Eli Pritchard, who had been his English teacher at the grammar school.

'I'll send one of the boys up to her,' said the old man, 'I will indeed, Luke boy. A First, think of it, splendid news it is, not that I ever doubted that you had it in you, *and* there's something else. There could be a post coming up here in a few months when I go.'

'You're not sick, sir?'

'No, never, hearty as ever, but I'm getting on and I fancy a few years in retirement. Shall I be putting in a word for you?'

Once might have been the height of his ambition, an assured post in a good school at a decent salary, but not now. It felt like prison gates closing in on him.

'I don't know yet, Mr Pritchard, but thank you all the same for the kind thought.'

The old man was eager to talk, but he cut him short.

'I must go now, no more money for the phone and we're having a party. I'll be home soon.'

Colin glanced at him as he came back into the room. 'Everything all right?'

'Yes, fine.'

'Come on, me boyo, drink up before the others scoff the lot.'

Luke tossed aside the momentary depression and threw himself enthusiastically into the rejoicing, reeling home to his digs late that night with his arm round Colin's neck, drunk with the unaccustomed champagne but even more with the sense of achievement. The first step into the future had been taken, though he was not yet sure where he was going.

The next day Andy telephoned congratulations. 'Pa is delighted for you, so is Mamma. Tanya says she's coming to your graduation come what may, so you'd better look out!'

His mother was coming up from Tredegar too, even though it meant getting up before six o'clock to catch the early train, and Megan was coming with her. His two sisters had just begun to work – Bron apprenticed to a dress shop in Cardiff, and Nesta typing in the coal merchant's office. Dai, who had a job at last after two years on the dole, didn't dare to take a day off to share in his little brother's triumph.

The day had its surprises. In addition to the degrees there were the prizes and exhibitions and bursaries, and that was what left him breathless. There had been hints, but he had never allowed himself to hope, never dared, but that morning when the list was read out he knew he had won it, an extra award granted to a student of distinction in the English school which would give him two additional years to prepare a thesis and take his MA. There were a dozen reasons why he should not accept it, not the least that it was scarcely enough to keep him for that extra time, but he still hugged it to himself. Somehow he must find a way round it; he could not give it up now, he could not. Surely no one could expect it of him.

When it was all over he joined his mother and Megan, and they exclaimed delightedly over his hired gown with its russet hood, the mortar board cocked over one eye.

He grinned self-consciously. 'I'll take this lot off, then we'll go and have a good lunch somewhere if you're not too tired.'

'Oh no, how could I be tired on a day like this?' said his mother, her lined face pink with excitement and pleasure. 'I just wish your dada could have been here, Luke boy, he would have been so proud. His son with the right to put BA after his name! Makes a man feel twelve feet tall, he would have been saying to me.'

'There's plenty of others who can do the same.'

'Ah, but not like you, not right at the top. I wanted to say to everyone "That's my boy up there" and you'll be coming home soon. I've missed you, Luke, we've all missed you. Mr Pritchard came up himself to tell me, he was that proud, you'd have thought it was his own boy, and soon, he says, there will be a vacancy coming up at the school. He's a sly one, but I knew what he was hinting – there could be a fine job waiting for you.'

'Well, perhaps not just yet, Ma, later on maybe.'

He took her arm, and as they moved towards the door they ran into a tall man with a girl in a cream silk suit coming in search of him.

He paused uncertainly, and Tanya ran to him, taking his hands, kissing him on both cheeks in her foreign way that both delighted and embarrassed him.

'I knew you'd do it,' she said. 'I told Papa and made him come with me. My wonderful, clever Luke!'

He had not expected it. His mother was staring, Megan was all eyes.

He stammered a little over the introductions.

'My mother – Lord Aylsham and his daughter Tanya.'

He was suddenly conscious of how they looked. His mother's grey coat and skirt, neatly pressed, but at least ten years old, the little black straw hat, the cotton gloves. The doctor with his easy charm had taken her hand in his.

'You must be very proud of your son, Mrs Jones.'

She was flustered by these grand people but still retained her dignity. 'I am indeed, my lord, and he's such a good boy, the best in the world.'

'I'm sure of it, and he is going to have a splendid future.'

The two girls were eyeing one another. Megan's round pleasant face was obscured by an unbecoming mustard-coloured hat. She smoothed down the skirts of her cheap summer dress and looked defiantly at the wisp of straw with one cream rose on the blonde head of the other girl.

'Is this your sister?' asked Tanya sweetly.

'No,' he said hurriedly. 'No, Megan is a friend, a very old friend.'

Impulsively Tanya had taken her hand. 'Isn't it splendid? There's nothing to stop him now, is there? Luke is going up and up.'

'If that's where he wants to go,' said Megan coldly and pushed away the hand.

'Don't let us detain you,' said Dr Aylsham. 'You must have so much to say to one another. Do you stay in London for a day or two?'

'Oh no, we must go home to Wales this evening.'

'I'm taking them to lunch,' interrupted Luke, 'and it is getting rather late.'

'Yes, of course. Enjoy your day, Mrs Jones.'

'Oh, I shall, my lord, I shall indeed, no fear of that.'

Luke resolutely took his mother's arm, and Megan tagged along behind them.

Tanya watched them walk away. 'Do you think Luke is going to marry that girl, Papa?'

'Good heavens, child, what an extraordinary thing to say.'

'Because if he is, she's not nearly good enough for him. Luke is so clever.'

'Perhaps too clever for his own good.'

'What do you mean by that?'

'Luke is a man with a conscience,' went on her father, 'and it is not a comfortable thing to possess.' And if anyone knew about that, he thought wryly, then he did. Twelve years married to a woman he could not love, and as a matter of conscience too loyal to abandon her.

'Come along,' he said briskly, 'a bite of lunch and then back to work. I have patients waiting for me.'

'And I promised to join Giovanni at Christie's. There is a French cabinet coming up in which he's particularly interested.'

Luke took them to Bertorelli's in Soho, which on the strength of a loan from Colin he could just about afford. It was quiet there, the food was good, and old man Bertorelli came round with a basket of roses presenting one to each lady with all his Italian charm.

Luke's mother blushed at the extravagant compliment he paid her, but Megan only sniffed and put the flower beside her plate. Luke had not been home for some time, so there was a lot of local news to be exchanged and it was quite a while before Megan asked the burning question.

'Who are your grand friends, Luke? You never told us anything about them.'

'I've not known them long. Actually Lord Aylsham is a doctor at Guy's. I fell over and cut my head open and he stitched me up. Look!' He pushed back the hair to show the thin, newly healed scar.

His mother exclaimed over it, but Megan only frowned.

'And what about his daughter? Is she a nurse?'

'No, of course not. I was invited for a weekend,' he went on reluctantly. 'They have a country house near Ely.'

'Country house, fancy, how grand! Our Luke'll be getting too big for his boots soon, too posh to be seen talking to the likes of us.'

'Don't talk nasty like that, Megan,' said his mother reprovingly. 'I'm sure Luke would never be like that – besides, he may be a lord, but he spoke so kindly. He seemed a very nice man.'

'Oh, he is, Ma, he is, but we don't want to talk about them, do we?' said Luke quickly. 'You're only up here for a few hours. Is there anything you'd like to see before you get the train home?'

'There is just one,' said his mother shyly. 'I've always wanted to see where the King and Queen live. Is that a long way? Could we just take a peep?'

'Of course we can. We'll take a taxi.'

'Oh no, Luke.' She was shocked. 'You mustn't waste your money like that.'

'Nonsense, this is a special day.'

He took her arm in a very masterful way and stopped a cruising taxi just outside the door.

After they had gazed at Buckingham Palace and she had admired the Guards in their sentry boxes, they strolled in St James's Park and presently sat in deck chairs in the hazy sunshine. While his mother dozed a little, worn out from the early start and all the excitement, Luke took Megan's arm and they walked round the lake looking at the pelicans, the secretary birds and the other exotic species.

'Do you know, Megan, there has been a lake here with all kinds of birds since the time of Charles II,' he said, 'it was called Rosamund's Pond then, a favourite trysting place for lovers. His father James actually kept a menagerie. They say there was a wild boar and a bear and even an elephant.'

But Megan was not interested in history. She had pulled off the ugly hat, and the breeze blew little tendrils of hair from the plaits coiled round her ears.

She said, 'What does it mean, this extra prize they have given you? Is it money?'

'Not exactly. It's a kind of grant so that I can go on working at the university and take my MA.'

'And you'd have to stay on in London studying, I suppose?'

'Well, it would be a little difficult to write a thesis in Tredegar, wouldn't it?' Suddenly what had been boiling up in him ever since the morning burst out before he could stop himself. 'I never really expected it, Megan, but now I've won it I simply can't let it go. You see, with an MA under my belt I could get a much better job, a teaching post in a public school perhaps, even an assistant lectureship at a university.'

'Tredegar's not good enough for you any longer, is that it? None of us matter – not Dai or your sisters or me, not even your mother.'

He turned on her indignantly. 'You know that's not true. Of course they matter to me. You're being unfair. What's the point of it all if I don't take what is being offered to me? I've worked damned hard for it these last three years and am I to throw all that away?'

'Oh, I've no doubt you've worked in your way, but what about the rest of the family, what about Dai and your sisters and your mother? Haven't they done their bit? Your mother's nearly killed herself to earn money to send to you *and* keep the rest of them going – all that time Dai was out of work, how do you think they managed? They would have gone under if it hadn't been for her.'

'I know all that, Megan.'

'Do you? I wonder. I know what you're thinking right now. What's old Megan saying all this for? I'll tell you why. Because no one else will put it straight, and I love your mother. Ever since my father had that accident, she's been like a rock. I've been closer than your sisters because they're so much younger and don't understand as much as I do. She has been dreaming of the day when you'd come home, her grand, clever son. She was crying with pride when Mr Pritchard talked about the post at the grammar school. Do you know that one day last winter she collapsed in the mine manager's office? They brought her home in an ambulance. "Not ill," said the doctor, "just worn out and half starved." For days afterwards she crept about like a ghost. She never told you any of that, did she?'

'No, she didn't,' Luke said, shocked and distressed. 'I never wanted her to do that, never.'

'And she won't say a word now. She'll never let on how she's hurt. She'll go on working and giving and you'll go on taking and taking till she drops dead. Can't you take this post if it's offered and still accept this prize or whatever it is?'

'No, I can't. You don't understand what it means.'

'Oh, I know I'm ignorant, but there's one thing I'm pretty sure of. It's not just working for this MA, if that's what it's called, it's that girl, isn't it? That's why you want to stay in London. I could see it, sticking out plain as a pikestaff. "My wonderful, clever Luke,"' she mimicked mincingly. 'Who does she think she is, with her fancy manners and her fine clothes? A princess or something?'

'As a matter of fact, that is exactly what she is. Her mother was a Russian princess.'

'Oh my, fancy that! Russian too, then what's she doing over here? If you think she'll look twice at you, then you must be dotty – condescending little bitch!'

'Stop it, Megan, stop it!'

'Why should I stop? I thought you had more sense, Luke Jones, more pride, than to go crawling round people like that. You wait till I tell Dai what his little brother is up to. You should hear what he says about the Russians now he is thinking of joining the Reds. The way you were looking at them made me want to laugh. Lord this, Princess that, inviting you to their country house, the boy from some dirty old mining village in Wales. That must have given their friends a good laugh, or didn't you happen to notice it?'

She had hit harder than she knew. 'Shut up, Megan!' he said, then furious as much with himself as with her, he slapped her cheek hard.

She stared at him for a moment and then unexpectedly he saw the tears start to her eyes.

'I'm sorry,' he muttered, 'I'm sorry.'

'It doesn't matter.' She pulled out a handkerchief and dabbed at her eyes.

He looked at her for a moment, old childish memories forcing their way up, and suddenly he despised himself.

'Don't cry, Megan. Nothing is settled yet. I've got to have time to think.'

'Oh, you'll do exactly what you want to do, you always have,' she said bitterly. 'You'll please yourself. You won't think twice about us.' She scrubbed at her face angrily, aware that though it was all true enough, the real motive behind her attack was the plain fact that he was growing away from her, that what had existed between them as boy and girl had long since faded. She was just Megan, the girl next door he had known all his life, someone to be pitied with her sick old father, while he was the man she loved and wanted and would always want, and she guessed that however hard she fought he would never be hers.

'Come on,' he said and took hold of her arm.

She shook him off and walked quickly back to the row of chairs. His mother was awake and looking for them when they rejoined her.

'I wondered where you two had got to,' she said, stifling a yawn. 'I could do with a cup of tea.'

'So could I,' sighed Megan.

'Right. Time's getting on. We'll go and find some tea and then I'll take you to the station.'

At Paddington he saw them on to the train and kissed them goodbye. His mother clung to him weeping suddenly, hating to let him go.

'I will be home soon,' he promised and meant it, but the weeks passed and he still stayed on in London, existing somehow on a series of temporary jobs and beginning to type out the contents of the fat exercise books on an ancient typewriter bequeathed to him by Colin. James Tait's influence had secured for his son a cub reporter's job on the *Glasgow Herald*.

'I'm awa' to bonny Scotland,' he announced in an atrocious Scots accent, 'reporting on haggis suppers and Rabbie Burns Nights and Celtic kicking a football about, God help me, while you'll be communing with great minds in the groves of Academe.'

'Lucky dog. I'd give my eye teeth to do what you'll be doing.'

'No, you wouldn't, not your style at all. You're destined to be the next bestseller. In no time at all I shall be writing in the gossip column of how I once shared digs with the great man and lapped up the deathless prose dripping from his pen.'

'Oh, go to hell!'

'That's just where I *am* going just as fast as I can,' Colin went on gloomily. 'Pa says it's a stepping stone to Fleet Street if I'm lucky – a damned big "if" in my opinion.'

But he departed cheerfully, full of bounce as usual, leaving Luke to consultations with stuffy university authorities who looked him up and down disparagingly, assuming that he was properly grateful, not likely to diverge one inch from the proper pursuit of knowledge, and would behave with a decent dignity and decorum. He came out feeling battered and wondering if he was crazy. Maybe he should throw it all up now, go home to Wales, grab at the opportunity offered to him, settle for the humdrum life in Tredegar except – except that stubborn desire for freedom still burned inside him and would not be stilled.

One afternoon in early September he walked briskly up Bond Street in search of Giovanni's gallery. He had put it off time and time again. There was absolutely no basis for Megan's absurd suggestion that he was hankering after the unattainable, and now he would prove it, he told himself; but all the same, they had been so decent to him, it was only right to pay a courtesy call before he went off to Wales.

The gallery was in Maddox Street. He saw the name etched discreetly in gold and hesitated before he took a deep breath, pushed open the door, and boldly went in. Pale grey walls, thick carpet under his feet, an air of dignity and elegance, one or two choice pieces of furniture, a Buhl cabinet, a fine Queen Anne bureau, a small table in exquisite marquetry, on the wall a flower painting by one of the finest of the Dutch masters.

A young man, elegantly dressed in a morning coat with a discreet flower in his buttonhole, appeared from the back.

'May I help you, sir?'

'I was actually looking for . . . for Tanya . . . Miss Aylsham.'

'Certainly, sir.' He had a faintly supercilious smile, as if he were well accustomed to young men of all types coming in search of the lovely Miss Aylsham. He waved a slim hand in the direction of a curving antique staircase with a balustrade of wrought iron and brass. 'She will be in our Russian room.'

Luke climbed up slowly, awed and impressed.

Tanya saw him appear and stand hesitantly for a moment, looking for her. She had been piqued and disappointed that her overtures of friendship had produced no result. Most young men whom she deigned to favour fell over their feet to show their appreciation. They arrived with flowers and expensive chocolates, armed with invitations to luncheon or to the *thé dansant* at the Ritz, or with tickets for the opera or the latest musical at the Gaiety with the promise of a tête-à-tête afterwards at the Café de Paris.

Some she accepted, a great many more she turned down. She had the reputation of being what Diana called 'a choosy bitch'. The theatrical circles in which she moved were more outspoken in their comments than the usual band of well-bred debutante escorts. She had never really shown a great deal of interest in any of them, much to her Aunt Hester's annoyance. It really was most unfair that Penelope, still unmarried and likely to remain so, was left on the shelf while her cousin, half Russian and apt to come out with disconcerting remarks, turned up her nose at all kinds of enticing invitations that with a little clever manoeuvring could have ended in a very successful engagement.

But then Tanya was looking for something quite different, something that would sweep her off her feet into unimaginable happiness. She was pursuing an ideal, just as her mother had done with such unhappy results. 'You're looking for a dream lover, and believe me there are not many about these days, if there ever were,' said Diana practically. 'You're twenty-two, my pet, and not a schoolgirl. Come down to earth.' Tanya laughed at her, but nevertheless, in her secret, most innermost heart, she was still young and innocent enough to cherish the idea. Not that Luke in his rather ill-fitting navy blue suit seemed ever likely to fulfil that dream, but all the same something warm and generous in her complex temperament had responded to him with an immediate liking.

She came to greet him with outstretched hand. 'How lovely of you to come. I hoped you would one day, and it so happens that I'm all on my own this afternoon. Giovanni is at a sale, and Lucy, who shares with me, has slipped out for a couple of hours.'

She wore the green silk dress which suited her so well. Her eyes are green too, he said to himself, why didn't I notice it before, and he knew almost at once, with an uneasy certainty, that Megan had been right after all. A good part of his determination to pursue his own particular dream and remain in London was so that one day he would possess something worthwhile to lay at the feet of this delectable creature.

Of course, none of these hidden thoughts appeared on the surface. They were quiet and rather shy with one another. She led him round the gallery, pointing out some of Giovanni's finest items and displaying what to his ignorant eyes appeared an expert knowledge of antiques and particularly of the Russian articles, the icons, the fine jewellery, the eggshell china with a royal monogram, which formed a good part of the collection.

He looked and admired, was confounded by the prices asked, and whenever he could without it being too obvious watched the play of light and shadow on his companion's charming face.

Presently she stopped and smiled up at him. 'I'm afraid I've talked myself dry. Are you hopelessly bored? Would you like some tea?'

'May I take you out somewhere?' God knows where and what it would cost in Bond Street, but what the hell!

'I'm afraid I can't leave the gallery just now,' she said apologetically, 'but I can brew up a cup at the back if that will be all right.'

'Rather, it sounds terrific.'

So in what perhaps had once been a kind of outhouse she put on a kettle and they drank China tea with lemon out of Meissen cups and ate huge sticky buns laid out on a Sèvres plate that had once graced a table at Versailles, talking and talking about anything and everything until she was called away to deal with a customer.

He stood in the doorway and watched her. The woman was

obviously Russian, so slight she looked as if a puff of wind would
blow her away, and dressed in a curious collection of exquisite silks
that must once have been a blaze of colour but were now faded
and worn. Priceless black lace covered her white hair, long silk
skirts rustled as she moved, and an embroidered shawl was
wrapped with a kind of careless grace round a tiny figure upright
as a ramrod. She was obviously selling rather than buying, and
though Luke could not understand what they were saying, he was
impressed by Tanya's gentleness, her sympathy, a kind of grace
and courtesy from a young girl to one who could have been her
grandmother.

When she came back to him she said, 'Poor soul. She has come
here so often before. I think this must be about the last thing she
has to sell.'

'Who is she?'

'She is the Countess Skorsky. One of her many nephews was a
family friend. We used to call him Uncle Val when he came to stay
at Dannskoye. He was murdered when the Bolsheviki stormed the
Winter Palace.' She held out her hand. 'Do you see this?'

It was a tiny icon, no more than two inches square, on a fine
gold chain.

'It's the kind of thing mothers used to give their sons when they
went away to the university or into the army, a kind of talisman to
keep them safe. This must have been returned to her when her son
was killed in the war. How cruel to be forced to part with it.'

'Is it valuable?'

'Not terribly. I tried to sound hopeful, but I don't know how
Giovanni will feel. He is kind, but he has to run a business. He
can't afford to be too generous.'

She sighed as she put the icon carefully away.

It was a tiny incident, but he knew then with an absolute
certainty that he had not been wrong that day on the Ravensley
lake. This girl in some inexplicable way had captured him, body
and spirit, something he had never really believed in until it
happened to himself. This young woman with her beauty and her
inconsistency, with her charm and vagaries, her sweetness and
sudden cruelties, was the woman he wanted, would always want,
even though at present he had absolutely nothing at all with which
to go to her father and say, 'I want to marry your daughter.' He

could imagine Dr Aylsham's lifted eyebrows, his quizzical smile, but given time he would have something to offer, by God he would!

'We're going away soon,' she was saying, 'we usually spend a month with Uncle Niki in the South of France.' She sighed. 'There isn't all that much to do there, but it's lovely to be together again, to speak Russian with each other. We ride his horses and help to pick the olive crop, and my cousins are tremendous fun. They rush madly about in their taxis, and in between their picking up rich tourists, Paul and Nicola and I go with them.'

'What about Andy?'

'He comes when he can, but not this year. He's still working like fury at the hospital, and he wouldn't leave Diana, not while the play is still running.' She glanced at him. 'Why don't you come with us? There's heaps of room in the old farmhouse and Aunt Sonia wouldn't mind. She loves visitors.'

For one second the very thought dazzled him, then he came down to earth with a bump. What on earth would he be doing there in that kind of society?

'I wish I could, but I'm afraid it wouldn't be possible.'

Then the intimacy between them was abruptly broken by Lucy coming back. Tall, graceful, older than Tanya, her shrewd eyes summed Luke up and found him wanting, and she treated him with a chilling courtesy when they were introduced.

'Won't you stay and meet Giovanni?' urged Tanya, but he shook his head.

'I'm off to Wales tomorrow. I ought to get packed.'

'We'll meet in the autumn, won't we?'

'Yes, of course,' he said fervently and made up his mind that, come what may, he would be back in London by then.

She came to the door with him and waved him on his way. He looked back to see her standing there, a sylph in her green dress, a dream girl, but very much flesh and blood too. 'If you think she'll look twice at you, then you must be dotty,' Megan had said. Well, if he was crazy, he was in it now up to his neck, and he didn't care. One day, he vowed to himself, one day, and he let it carry him forward with a great surge of energy and hope.

* * *

He did not enjoy the week he spent in Tredegar. He was ashamed to find that, despite his painful love for his mother, his affection for his coltish sisters endlessly giggling over their boyfriends and squabbling over who would wear what out of their scanty wardrobe, his appreciation of Megan's real goodness of heart in the way she cared for her sick old father with his uncertain temper, he felt hopelessly stifled, only too aware that he had grown away from them, from the whole close-knit community, and could never again become part of it.

He had spent an evening with Dai, furiously irritated because Elspeth was such a sloppily incompetent housewife. His mother had brought up six children, two of whom had died early, and had heroically kept the whole household going during his father's long bouts of illness, so why couldn't Elspeth manage with only two? The hot, untidy little kitchen smelled of stale food, of washing and scorched ironing, of wet nappies and the sour-sweet smell of babies, with Owen, the latest addition, screaming himself purple.

Afterwards, when they strolled down to the pub, there had been Dai's sly hints – wasn't it high time he gave up his flighty ambitions and contributed something useful to the family budget? Dai, very much the elder brother, holding forth and setting his teeth on edge.

'Now you listen to me, Luke lad. From what I've been hearing you're getting yourself mixed up with the wrong kind of folk up there in London, lords and such, and they'll do you no good at all.'

'That was Megan, I suppose?'

'Aye, she did let on a bit. Not too much, mind, but I could read between the lines all right. There's a girl too, isn't there, eh?' He gave Luke a playful dig in the ribs. 'Well, that's only natural, can't be expected to live like a monk. But you want to watch out, look where you're going – sweet as honey to your face, those flashy types, and stab you in the back before you've time to draw breath.'

'You don't know her, Dai.'

'Don't you believe it! They're all the same, and I wasn't born yesterday. I had my fill of girls, nice and nasty, before Elspeth.'

Dai, growing more confidential with a pint of bitter inside him, leaned across the slopped, dirty table and whispered, because there were ears pricked everywhere only too ready to inform, and he couldn't afford to lose his precarious hold on a decent job, not with two hungry mouths to feed and another suspected.

'For God's sake, Dai, not another! Don't you ever stop to think? Aren't two enough with Elspeth the way she is.'

'There's nowt wrong with Elspeth. She's a good girl and she does the best she can,' Dai said in quick defence.

'Oh, I know, I know.'

He knew too that Dai must have been through hell the last year or two, so who was he to judge? What else could a man do when the empty days and long nights stretched ahead endlessly? The quick comfort to be found in bed cost nothing.

Dai had given a sharp look around him and pulled his chair closer.

'Never mind about that now. There's something else. I've not breathed a word to anyone yet. Ma would go up the wall, but I've joined the Reds, signed up with the Communists, went over to Maerdy specially. They've got it fixed up fine there: communal kitchens, hunger marches, delegations to confront the bosses – that's the way to do it. There was even a chap over from the Soviet Union bringing a banner, all red and gold it was, from Moscow. They keep it in the Workers' Institute, even draped it over the coffin when a member died.' His eyes were shining. 'I heard him speak myself. They've got the right ideas over there, no doubt about that. It gave you a sense of power, made you feel like a man, not some bloody slave – all those bosses stuffing their pockets with the results of our sweat. Penhale's one of the worst of them. Growing fat and rich on it, he is. And that boy of his, home from Oxford, lording it about the town with his painted women, trying it on with Beth Morgan, and she falling for him, silly little fool, till her father got wind of it and packed her off to her auntie in Nant-y-glo.'

'You're talking crazy, Dai. Don't you know what is being said about it up in London? The government's so jumpy, you'd think a Communist was hiding under every bed. They could come down on the lot of you, and then where will you be? Out of a job and on the dole again.'

'Not this time, not if I'm careful – and I am that, damned careful.' He sat back in his chair, looking Luke over with a hint of contempt. 'Haven't you grown cautious all of a sudden? Is that what all that book learning does for you? Makes you soft and flabby, no guts? Don't you remember Grandfather and what he

79

used to tell about the past? A hundred years ago it was, called themselves the Scotch Cattle and rampaged all over Merthyr Tydfil, organizing strikes, teaching the workers the importance of acting collectively. They made the ironmasters sit up, didn't they? Wasn't our great-great-grandfather hanged for it *and* buried like a martyr? You used to be proud – made us feel great just to hear about it, didn't it? Well, now it's up to us again.'

'Grandfather never believed in riot and murder.'

'Neither do we if we can get what we want peacefully. It's our rights we're asking for, that's all, our human right to live out our lives and bring up our children decently.'

'In Russia they are massacring their own people in the name of those very rights.'

'Propaganda!' said Dai scornfully. 'Is that what your smart friends are telling you? Don't believe all you hear – and I tell you something, boy, and I mean it. If we don't do something pretty quick, there'll be bloody revolution right here in Wales!'

They had gone on arguing about it, but Luke could get nowhere against Dai's blind belief: he clung to it like a new religion which had given him hope.

The last two days of Luke's stay, he tramped up into the hills, eating and sleeping rough, glad to be alone while he tried to make up his mind. The grass was beginning to turn brown at the end of summer, and in the early mornings mists blew about the hills, clearing to a gentle sunshine and sometimes to rain, and alone up there, in a great silence far from the stifling little house, the pressures, the poverty, the heroism and the hopelessness, he came to a decision.

There could be no half-measures. He could not split himself in two. He would go his own way, but he would work too in whatever way he could, and he would keep only enough to live, all the rest must come to his mother. She would know how best to use it. Only in that way could he salve his conscience and turn down the easy choice, the teaching post which would bind him in the shackles of Tredegar for ever.

It seemed ironic that, after all his grand resolutions, the only work he could find when he got back to London was packing boxes of

Christmas decorations for some ten hours a day. The economic slump in the United States had permeated throughout Europe bringing widespread unemployment everywhere. There were long queues for the most trivial work, and no matter how menial or how badly paid, it was instantly snapped up.

No one knew how the fire started that morning in the packing room of the big department store. Maybe a carelessly dropped cigarette end, maybe deliberate sabotage in protest against the long hours of work and the starvation wages.

Luke didn't notice it at first. He was working automatically, his mind occupied with other things, his only defence against the repetitive, soul-destroying labour that was better than nothing and did mean that he could eat. He awoke suddenly out of his absorption to hear someone screaming. There was a smell of burning, a sudden sheet of flame. A girl's flimsy cotton frock had caught alight and was flaring up. People were standing staring, momentarily paralysed, but Luke had been in a fire once before. He tore off his work coat and flung it round her, beating out the flames. She tripped and he fell on top of her to the floor. Someone else had the wit to run for the fire buckets. In a few minutes it was all over, nothing left but a smouldering mass smothered in sand and water.

The girl in his arms moaned a little. He unwrapped the coat carefully. Her dress, her underwear were badly burned, her hair scorched.

'Better get a doctor quickly and an ambulance,' he said hoarsely.

He was conscious now that his own hands were burned, one of them badly. He hugged them against him as the pain began. The floor manager had appeared and began asking angry questions, then sooner than they had expected the ambulance was there, and the doctor.

'Lucky someone had some common sense,' he muttered, bending over the girl, who mercifully had fainted. 'She's not so bad as I feared, no major burns as far as I can see. Gently now, take her up gently.'

The ambulance men were lifting her on to the stretcher and spreading the blanket. The doctor turned to Luke.

'Better let me look at those hands of yours, young man.'

'I'm all right.'

The doctor grunted. He spread some kind of ointment over them and wrapped them in bandages.

'Don't leave them,' he warned. 'Best go along to the hospital and get them dressed.'

The owners of the store held an immediate inquest as to how the fire had started and who was to blame. With a shock Luke discovered his own unpopularity. It was true that he'd not mixed with the other workers, had held himself aloof – not deliberately, but simply because he had nothing in common with them. He had shown a certain impatience with their constant grumbles and complaints, and now, perhaps out of spite – who does he think he is with his high and mighty airs? – the finger was being pointed at him. He carried cigarettes in his pocket, he had been seen to snatch an opportunity for a surreptitious smoke. The floor manager, glad to escape any accusations of laxity, added his opinion. Temporary staff could be dismissed out of hand. At the end of the day Luke found himself with a couple of pounds in his pocket but out of a job and in very considerable pain. His right hand was the worst, so he could not even try to forget the pain in work. He had hoped to complete the typing of his precious novel before he must settle down to his academic thesis. Now he could do nothing. He bore it for three days, then, after a sleepless night of agony and with an arm beginning to swell ominously, he realized the doctor might have been right. His only experience of hospitals had been Guy's, so he walked there late one afternoon, his arm in an improvised sling, and by a lucky chance it was Andy who was dealing with Casualty that day.

He glanced up as the nurse ushered Luke in. 'Well, look who's here. Tanya said you'd gone home to Wales. What have you been doing to yourself?'

He frowned as he unwrapped the bandages. 'Whoever treated this ought to have been shot. Why didn't you come before? Better sit down, old man. I'm afraid it's going to be hellishly painful.'

It was. Luke gritted his teeth while Andy cut and probed into the lacerated flesh before putting on fresh bandages. He patted Luke on the shoulder afterwards with a friendly grin.

'Cheer up. I think we've just about stopped you from losing your hand this time. Tell you what. I'm off duty in about half an hour.

If you like to hang about I'll buy you a drink and we'll have a chat.'

'I'd like that.'

'Good. Nurse, take Mr Jones to one of the dressing rooms and find him a cup of tea.'

He'd have hated to confess it, but he was glad to sit down and sip the hot reviving tea she brought him until, about an hour later, Andy looked in.

'Come on. It's about opening time, and there's a very decent little pub just up the road.'

It was on the riverbank, small and snug. Andy came back from the bar carrying two whiskies and two large ham sandwiches.

'Can't always stomach English beer,' he said cheerfully, 'and you need something to buck you up.'

Luke eyed the ham sandwich doubtfully. 'You shouldn't have . . .'

'Oh, go on, man, tuck in. I hate eating alone. The family are still in France. They won't be home for another week or two, so I've volunteered to take over night duty.'

Andy was rapidly developing something of his father's skill in diagnosing patients' conditions and had already guessed that Luke was on edge, a man being pulled several ways as well as being desperately hard up. Wisely he said nothing, only shook his head decisively when, their drinks finished, Luke got to his feet.

'What about another? My shot this time,' Luke said.

'Not for me. I'm due back in half an hour, and authority won't look kindly on their fledgling doctor breathing whisky fumes all over the casualties.'

'No, I suppose not.' Luke sat down again thankfully. 'How is Diana?'

'Beautiful as ever, damn her!' Andy said, and when Luke looked surprised he went on quickly, 'Oh, don't get me wrong. I'm still one of her most fervent admirers. She's just had an astounding bit of luck, as a matter of fact. Her principal fell ill suddenly and Di stepped in literally at an hour's notice, and by pure chance one of the critics was in the house that night on a second visit. Nothing much to write about in August, so he went into eulogies about this brilliant young actress in his Sunday column. The theatre was packed the following night and all the week she played, since

83

when, she tells me, most of the threatrical world has been on the telephone.'

'But that's terrific. Good for her. She's really going places, isn't she?'

'Looks like it.' Andy took out a cigarette case, offered it to Luke, and lit both cigarettes before asking almost casually, 'Tell me, what would you do if a young woman refused to marry you but offered to sleep with you whenever you wished?'

Luke stared at him, astonished and slightly shocked. 'You mean . . . Diana?' he asked incredulously.

'Yes, Diana.'

'But isn't that rather . . .?' In Tredegar it happened often enough that a girl was pregnant before she was married, and it was accepted because marriage was the ultimate aim and young people were often impatient when circumstances – no money, no place to live, difficult parents – stood in the way; but anything else . . . that was a different matter. 'Does she mean it?' he said at last.

'Oh yes, she means it all right. Diana always means what she says. And she wants it as much as I do, but she also wants to be free – to have her cake and eat it, as the boring old saying goes.'

'And you?'

'I don't know, Luke, I honestly don't know. It made me so angry that we had a violent row and I walked out on her.'

'What will you do now?'

Andy sighed. 'God knows. Go back, I suppose, when I can't endure it any longer.' He suddenly brought his fist down on the table so hard that the glasses jumped and Luke caught them just in time. 'God, what fools we are! I told her to go to hell, and the very next night was creeping into the theatre just to watch her from the back of the circle.'

'But Diana is – what would her parents say?'

'General Sir Harry Harcourt would probably like to have me publicly horsewhipped. Pa would be a good deal more tolerant. He has learned to be, in a hard school, but all the same he wouldn't exactly approve, and if he wants to he can make you feel pretty small. Oh well –' He ground out his cigarette and got up. 'Having poured out my troubles I must go back and settle a few for other people – mainly physical, thank goodness. Don't neglect those hands of yours, Luke. Come in the day after tomorrow – before if you're in pain or it swells up again. They need watching.'

'Thanks. I will.'

He looked after Andy as he strode away. He was only a year or so older than himself, and yet somehow he seemed much more mature, already grappling with deep emotional problems to which there seemed no easy answer. He wondered what he would do if one day Tanya was to make that same offer, and the quick flood of heat that raced through him, the sudden stirring of his blood, left him in very little doubt.

5

'Princes on white chargers and knights in shining armour are distinctly thin on the ground just now,' Diana had once said with a laugh. But she was wrong, thought Tanya, because here without a doubt was one of them, even to the white horse, an Arab with proudly arched neck and huge dark eyes, and a princely rider all in black – boots, breeches, high-necked pullover. No golden helmet, but hair a deep bronze burnished by the early morning sun, a face olive-skinned and too lean for classical beauty, with high cheekbones, tilted eyebrows that gave him a faintly oriental look, like the Tartars who used to ride in to the Easter fairs with their wild shaggy ponies. As for his eyes – she could never say afterwards what colour they were or what it was that made them look so strange, only that, for the few seconds on that narrow path high in the hills above Grasse, their brilliance held her riveted so that she could not move, could not speak, until with a slight inclination of his head he drew aside to let her pass and she shivered suddenly with an odd feeling of release as if he had held her prisoner and had now set her free. Then he had ridden on, straight-backed, not turning his head, until he disappeared round the curve of the mountain path.

Of course it was absurd, utterly ridiculous. She laughed at herself as she shook off the sensation that in those few seconds something had happened, something momentous. It was still very early, not yet seven, and though the September sun was warm, it was not the burning heat of midsummer; yet she felt a prickle of sweat down her back and between her breasts under the thin cotton shirt. A few seconds later she heard the others calling out to her as they came into view, her cousin Boris with his young sister Elena, and tagging behind them Paul and Nicola.

'Where did you get to?' they were asking.

'You disappeared so suddenly.'

86

'We thought you'd gone over the edge.'

'Of course I didn't, silly. I took the side path, that's all. Did you see that man?'

'What man?'

'You must have seen him, all in black on a white horse.'

'We didn't see anyone. You must have imagined it,' said Nicola flatly.

'Of course I didn't. He was here blocking the path before he moved aside to let me through.'

'It must have been the ghost,' said Elena wide-eyed, 'the ghost of Roquelaire. The peasants say he walks these mountain slopes still.'

'Not in broad daylight,' said Boris crushingly. 'More likely someone from the villa in the next valley.'

'Why? Who lives there?'

'They're Swiss, I believe, in trade and disgustingly rich. They only come here in the summer and often have guests staying with them. Come on, all of you.' He began to shepherd his flock together. 'We've come far enough. Back to breakfast. Yuri and I have to work today. We're taking a party of tourists all along the coast to Marseilles.'

'Americans?'

'No, Germans this time.'

They wound down in single file along the narrow path, the air sweet with the scent of thyme, heavy with the ripe fruits of autumn on these richly wooded slopes, and Tanya tried to dismiss the whole incident from her mind. But she could not quite escape the nagging doubt that somehow an opportunity had been missed, a chance lost.

'Who was the ghost of Roquelaire?' she asked Elena as they rode side by side along the widened track.

'Oh, it's one of those old tales. Mamma would prefer me not to talk to the peasants, but I like listening to their stories. This one is about a young man who was base-born, and his natural father hated him so much that he decided to have him murdered so that he could never inherit Roquelaire. But the servant ordered to commit the crime took pity on the baby and abandoned it where it was sure to be discovered and cared for. Years later he came back to take his revenge and the two of them fought a deadly battle high up on one of the mountain peaks. He overcame his cruel father and hurled him down to his death in the river below, but in his moment of triumph the stones crumbled under his feet and he followed his victim into the gorge.'

'Did he die?'

'No, worse than that. He lived, but only as a helpless cripple watching the castle he had fought for crumble to ruin around him.'

'What a horrible fate.'

'Wasn't it?' said Boris, coming up beside them. '"Vengeance is mine," saith the Lord, and all that. Don't listen to Elena. Her head is stuffed with gruesome tales like that. You ought not to spend so much time chattering to servants, my girl. Good thing you'll soon be going back to school.'

Paul had edged his horse up on the other side of Elena, and now he said, 'Why shouldn't she talk to them if she wants to? The country people know and understand more than you think. Don't be such a snob.'

Boris grinned. 'Hark at him! Found yourself a champion, have you, my child?'

Elena blushed angrily. 'I'm not a child. I'm nearly seventeen,' she said defiantly. She put a hand on top of Paul's, and they exchanged a secret smile.

It struck Tanya that her delicate young brother was growing a little too fond of his cousin, and Father would certainly not approve. She wondered if she ought to speak to him about it, then dismissed it from her mind. Very soon now the holidays would be over and they would be going home to England. She wondered if she would ever see the stranger again.

No one knew why the estate was called Les Coquilles when they were so far from the sea and there wasn't a shell to be seen, but it had its own quiet beauty. As they rode up the long drive, the old house with its pepperpot turrets lay baking in the mellow sunshine, half château, half farmhouse, with its outbuildings and huge barns. Terracotta pots spilling over with geraniums stood on the stone patio, bougainvillea clambered over the ancient walls, a tawny cat basked in the heat, and Elena's big white dog raised a sleepy head to greet them. There was peace and serenity to be found up here in the hills, and its pervading spirit, strangely enough, was not Tanya's Uncle Niki, hard though he worked with his flocks of sheep, his olive groves and the vineyards climbing up the terraced slopes, but her Aunt Sonia.

She never ceased to marvel at how this small slim woman, still elegant even in country cotton and linen apron, who had danced with princes at the Winter Palace, had seen her husband's father and grandfather cruelly assassinated on her wedding day, had been forced to watch while her most valued possessions were pillaged and smashed by the greedy hands of peasants, yet retained such strength and calmness of spirit. In the early days, after escaping from Russia with two growing boys and a baby daughter, she had not scorned to bake the bread, to cook meals for husband and children, and even now presided over simmering pans of soup, of jams and preserves, and tended the rows of beehives that lay gathering honey under the old apple trees. There were times when Tanya wished passionately that she could be more like her.

'How can you be so happy, so content with your life,' she would ask, 'when you have lost so much?'

Sonia only smiled, pushing back the dark hair with a small hand roughened now but still shapely. 'Why shouldn't I be content when, compared with others, I have so much – my husband, my children. We can eat, we can still watch the seasons come and go, and they are wonderfully beautiful here. Of course I worry when I see Niki near to killing himself with such hard work; I catch my breath with fear every time I remember Boris and his passion for fast cars; it hurts me not to be able to give Elena the kind of fun a young girl ought to enjoy when she is growing up; but you learn to accept, to find contentment in small things, never to ask too much from life.'

'That's easy for you, you had everything once, but I can't seem to find my way. I'm not like Di. She knew she wanted to be an actress from the very beginning and she has fought for it, but everything I try to do flies away from me.'

'Do you never stop to think about what you have instead of hankering after what is beyond your grasp? You have a lovely home, a family, the best father in the world.'

'Oh, Papa thinks more of Galina than he does of any of us. It's always been like that.'

'That's not true, Tanya. Isn't it time you grew up and forgot this old grudge against your stepmother?'

'Why should I? She stole him from my mother, and now she steals him from us.'

Sonia sighed. This stupid prejudice which soured her niece's relations with Galina, and to some extent with her father, reminded Sonia of Tanya's mother. She and Nina had grown up together, closer than sisters, both as children and as young girls. Nina had been lovely, volatile, demanding everything, expecting ecstatic happiness as her right, snatching at life with greedy hands and, when she did not find what she sought, rebelling against cruel fate, never realizing that you must earn your happiness until the very end, when she had died tragically in saving the life of the husband whose love she could never win. Something of that wild, restless spirit – too much of it – lived in her daughter, and Sonia feared for her.

A few days before they must leave for home they cast aside their country clothes and went on a jaunt down to the coast.

'My party,' Simon told Sonia. 'We've been living on your bounty all these weeks, now it's my turn.'

So Sonia stripped off her cotton gown and brought out one of the evening dresses she so seldom wore, fastening round her neck the last of the Malinsky heirlooms, which she said laughingly she was clinging to until the olive crop failed or the vines developed phylloxera or the sheep all died of scab, when it would have to go the way of the rest. Niki wore at his throat the jewelled cross awarded by the Tsar in those far off days; and Tanya, looking, as her father said, like a dryad from the green forests, fastened her mother's diamonds in her small ears.

They dined extravagantly at the Hôtel Splendide and then went on to the Casino at Monte Carlo, where rich Americans and wealthy tourists stared at the distinguished party which, astonishingly, included their very own taxi driver in impeccable evening dress, his fair hair burnished to gold under the chandeliers.

The great room, its crimson and gold glittering under the crystal lights, was crowded. Every nationality under the sun seemed to be gathered there, handsomely dressed, some of them so old that their desiccated bones appeared strung together with wire and they jerked like marionettes as they hung over the tables, faces avid with greed and hope and envy. There were impoverished aristocrats alongside war profiteers, loud-voiced and vulgar with bulging wallets. There were the sad middle-aged still clinging to fast-fading dreams, lovers and those looking for love, newlyweds full of excitement at some lucky win, and those desperate, white-faced and wild of eye. None of their party could afford to gamble beyond a few throws for luck except Boris, who much to his mother's disgust would sometimes toss all his hard-earned cash on the table, laughing when he lost and pouring it into his mother's lap when, more rarely, he won.

His father indulgently gave Tanya a handful of chips, and Boris found a place for her at one of the great tables. With beginner's luck she won again and again, and her little pile grew appreciably until, flushed with success, she recklessly put the whole lot on the same favourite number and inevitably lost it all.

'Damn!' she muttered under her breath, with a look of such comical dismay that she quite entranced the elderly gentleman sitting beside her. She was pushing back her chair to get up when a long slim hand came over her shoulder and dropped half a dozen chips in front of her.

She looked up in surprise, expecting to see Boris, and instead met the eyes of the stranger on the mountain. He was standing just behind her, no longer the black knight, but in elegant evening dress that somehow had the effect of making him look even more exotic and different from everyone else in the room.

'Try these for me,' he said.

He spoke in French, but she guessed at once that it was not his native tongue.

'Oh, I couldn't, I couldn't possibly accept . . .'

'Play them,' he commanded. 'If you win, it's yours, if you lose . . .' He gave a little shrug.

She hesitated for a moment, uncertain what to do, and then recklessly pushed them on what had been her winning number. Within a few seconds, astonishingly, the whole pile was being thrust towards her. She laughed because it was so absurd, such an extraordinary chance, and turned to hand over his winnings – and he was gone, vanished almost as if he had never been there.

'Did you see where he went? He was just behind me,' she asked, but she might have been talking to the air. No one took any notice; they were pressing up against her, eager for a place at the table.

She picked up the chips, crammed them into her evening bag, and got up, going from group to group in search of him; but he was nowhere to be found in the great room. Except for the winnings in her bag he might never have existed.

She confided in Boris, who knew nearly everyone, describing him as well as she could. Obligingly he made a few discreet enquiries and came back with the information that a man answering his description had already left. They did not know his name but understood he had come with a party from the Villa Valéry.

'The Swiss you told us about?'

'That's right. One odd thing though,' Boris went on, frowning. 'He asked particularly about us – who we were, especially your father and Galina and you.'

'Asked about us? But why?'

Boris shrugged. 'God knows. Probably some eccentric, you get all kinds of odd fish here. He didn't follow up his enquiries, did he?'

'I don't know,' Tanya said slowly, 'I don't know. Perhaps he did in a way.'

'I shouldn't worry about it. Cash the chips, put the money in your handbag, and forget about him.'

But that she found hard to do, and later that evening there was another puzzling incident.

She went back to her father and found him looking concerned.

'Galina is feeling a little upset. Yuri is going to drive us home.'

'Is she ill? Shall I come with you?'

'No, my dear, it's nothing. The heat in here, I expect. You stay and enjoy yourself. Boris will bring you back with your uncle and aunt.'

In the car Galina said, 'Am I making a complete fool of myself, Simon?'

'No, of course not, but it must be a chance resemblance. How could it be anything else?'

'I don't know. I only know that, for a moment when that young

92

man paused and looked straight at me, I could have been looking into the face of Igor Livinov.'

Simon frowned. Igor Livinov, the tough, hardened revolutionary who had long ago driven them apart, who had haunted their lives in Russia till the very last hour, whose clutches they had barely escaped all those years ago.

Galina was looking at him. 'Could he have had a son, do you think?'

'It's possible, but that young man was twenty-eight or twenty-nine at least, so that would be before . . .'

'Before Igor came into my life and into yours.'

'Yes, and in any case what harm can he do us now?'

'I wish I knew.'

He was right, of course, but she still trembled. It was as if a sleeping tiger had suddenly awakened, had opened wide his great jaws, had stretched out a cruel paw – and yet why should it reach out to touch them? Simon had never concerned himself with politics, had never allied himself with any particular party. His mission had always been to heal and save life as far as he could, never to destroy. She thought of the friends they had left behind in Russia, dear friends who had been swallowed up in that vast upheaval as if they had never existed. It had distressed her greatly during the first months in England, and Russia was still her country, she could not escape from that. Her roots were there, it was where she had grown up, where she and Simon had fallen in love, where her son had been born. She shuddered suddenly and clutched at her husband's hand as if for reassurance.

'I know it's foolish, I know you will think I'm turning neurotic, but I had a frightening certainty that in some way this chance meeting spelled danger.' She turned to look at him, her large hazel eyes filled with anxiety. 'Simon, you know I'm not given to feelings like these, but for a moment it was very, very real. You will take care of yourself, darling, won't you?'

She did not yet realize that the danger threatened not so much her and her husband, but those dear to them, and in a way neither of them could have imagined or believed possible.

* * *

A month later Tanya and Diana were sitting close together on the hearthrug in front of a cheerful little fire (for although it was only October the nights had turned decidedly chilly), indulging in what they used to call a 'good old chinwag'. Between them was a pot of coffee and a wedge of Nanny Gibbons' slab cake, stuffed with fruit and covered in a delightful goo of almonds and brown sugar, which she had been baking for nursery teas ever since she had first come to Chalfont Manor as under-nursemaid when General Sir Harry Harcourt was still in rompers.

'Madly bad for the figure, but gorgeous all the same,' sighed Diana, stuffing in the last rich crumbly mouthful. 'Remember how the girls used to make a rush for the tuck boxes when they arrived in Lausanne? Nanny supplies it non-stop. She is convinced that I'm pining away. "It's not right," she says, "to look like two boards nailed together, Miss Di. Gentlemen like to feel there's something substantial to get hold of not just skin and bone," and then she goes red as a peony in case she has said something indelicate.' Diana sat back and licked her sticky fingers like a dainty cat washing its paws. 'Now tell me all about your adventures on the Côte d'Azur,' she said.

'There weren't any, not really, only one very tiny one. You tell your news first.'

'Well, it is rather exciting. You see, the play closes in a few months, just after Christmas actually, and after that three of us are going to get together and stage a little season of our own. What do you think of that?'

'What kind of season?'

'Oh, not boring old West End successes, but real drama.' Diana's eyes shone. 'Ibsen, Chekhov, Shaw, James Joyce – plays with real meaty acting parts.'

'But how can you? I mean, won't it be wildly expensive.'

Diana turned to look at her, the fire throwing strange lights and shadows over her expressive face, the eyes under the dark red cap of her hair glowing with enthusiasm.

'Not the way we intend to do it. It won't be grand, it will be very cosy and intimate. We've found a tiny theatre up two flights of stairs in Knightsbridge. It's called the Lantern and only holds about a hundred, but it's absolutely right for what we want to do.'

'Who's we?'

'There is Barry Dean – you remember him? He plays the young lead in our show, fearfully good-looking *and* knows it, but he did marvels at Stratford and he was at the Old Vic last year. Then there is Craig and me.'

'Who is Craig?'

'Craig Vassall. He's American and absolutely marvellous. It was his idea really, and he will direct the plays. We will each put in some money – probably about three hundred pounds – and won't take any salary, of course. We shall be sticking our necks out, but lots of people are interested already, and it's going to succeed, I know it is, I feel it in my bones! They have this kind of fringe theatre in out-of-town New York, Craig says, and we've talked and talked about it and now it's going to come off, and I simply can't wait for the play to finish and get started on it.'

'This Craig,' said Tanya doubtfully, 'what's he like? Is he in love with you, by any chance?'

'Goodness, no. He's not like that at all. Theatre is all he dreams about. Girls in his world are actresses or they're nothing, mostly nothing. He happens to think I've got what it takes, if you know what I mean, and I did get a lot of publicity when I took over the lead in the summer. Craig came to see the show five times! It's going to be the most tremendous fun if it comes off – if it does – we could go simply anywhere,' she went on dreamily.

'Lucky old you,' said Tanya enviously. 'Why can't I find something thrilling to do like that?'

'But darling, you could if you tried, you're so clever. You know, the thing is that you've had it easy, you've never felt you simply had to escape from your awful family like I have. When I think of your father, so handsome, so glamorous still, and so wonderfully easy to talk to, and compare him with boring old Daddy, I could spit, and as for my brother! Darling, you won't marry Cecil, will you, not even if he's the last man left alive? I couldn't bear it if you did.'

'No fear of that,' said Tanya fervently.

'Now go on, tell about you. What has happened to that lovely son of the Welsh pits? I must say I rather took to him.'

'I haven't seen him since we got back, but Andy has. They seem to have started up a kind of pub friendship. He got his hands horribly burned in some frightful fire at the place where he was working and Andy treated them for him.' She turned to look at her friend. 'Does Andy know about this theatre venture?'

'Not yet. I haven't seen him lately. We had a row and he stalked out in high dudgeon.'

'Andy did? That's not a bit like him,' said Tanya incredulously. 'What did you quarrel about?'

'Oh, this and that. He pops into the theatre occasionally and watches from the back of the circle. The girl who sells the chocolates tells me. "Your gentleman was in again, Miss Di," she says and smirks. Makes me feel like the housemaid.'

Tanya guessed that, though Diana dismissed it so lightly, the quarrel meant a great deal more to her than she was willing to admit. She was tempted to tell her about the stranger and that odd episode at the Casino, but Di was so practical, so down-to-earth. With a few careless words its magic could be destroyed, and somehow she didn't want that to happen. She still had the money, which cashed up had amounted to more than five hundred pounds, and she had kept it intact, with a queer sort of feeling that, if she ever met him again, it would provide a link between them.

She looked up to see Diana's eyes fixed on her thoughtfully.

'I've just had an idea,' Diana said. 'Would you like to come in with us? I don't mean with money, unless you want to, but just to work as part of the team.'

'Could I – but how? I can't act, you know that. Remember how frightful I was in that Molière play at Lausanne?'

'God, yes, absolutely dire, wasn't it? No, I wasn't thinking of the acting side, but we're going to need lots of help with sets and costumes and you're absolutely wizard at things like that.'

'I'd love to, if you think I could.'

'Of course you could, especially if we put on one of the Russians. We'll be working on a shoestring, you know, so we'll have to beg, borrow or steal most of the props. I don't know what Nanny will have to say if I carry off the furniture from the flat and we're reduced to eating off the floor! We're going to need one or two strong men too, and someone with a gift for words to take on publicity. What about roping in your Welshman? Andy says he's frightfully brainy. I'm certain he could help.'

'What about the others – Barry and Craig? Will they mind?'

'Not if you're any good they won't,' Diana said frankly. 'And you will be, I'm quite certain of that. Tell you what – I'll throw a little party here one Sunday, then you can all meet up.'

'Can I tell Andy about it?'

'If you like. He came come along too if he condescends to be interested.'

'You know perfectly well he's interested in anything *you* do. What has happened between you two?'

'Oh, nothing really.' Diana got to her feet and picked up the tray. 'I'll just take this through to the kitchen, then we'd better get to bed. It's fearfully late and I've got an understudy call at ten – a bit unnecessary now, but our director is a stickler for the rules.'

When she came back Tanya asked, 'Has Andy been proposing to you again?'

'He does it regularly. It's becoming a bore,' Diana replied flippantly. 'Last time I turned him down but offered to sleep with him if that's what he wanted.'

'Diana, you didn't!' Although she knew that kind of thing did happen nowadays, even among their own set, Tanya was still shocked. It simply wasn't done when it was one's closest friend and one's own brother. 'Was it a joke?' she asked.

'Oh no, I meant it.' There was a touch of defiance in Diana's voice.

'What did he say?'

'Flew into a rage, stormed out of the house, and slammed the door, since when I've not seen him.'

'Do you mind very much?'

'Of course I mind. I mind like hell,' Diana said violently. 'Well, that's enough about that. I'm going to bed. Put the guard up in front of the fire, will you, or Nanny will have my blood in the morning for trying to burn the house down. Goodnight.'

She went quickly out of the room, but not before Tanya heard the suspicious shake in her voice and guessed that tears were not all that far away. Diana was already fighting a battle between ambition and love and, however she decided, one or other of them would suffer, probably both. Why was life so full of problems? thought Tanya as she poked angrily at the fire before putting up the guard. One dreamed of being grown up, of escaping restraint, of being free to choose, and discovered snags at every step of the way. She was going to take very good care not to fall in love rashly, and in the meantime there was this exciting suggestion from Diana. She went off to bed happier than she had been for a long time, her mind already teeming with ideas, and was suddenly aware of how much she was looking forward to meeting Luke again.

It was Andy who told Luke about the party. They had taken to meeting occasionally at the friendly little pub near the hospital and had grown to appreciate each other's company.

'What kind of party is it?' Luke asked cautiously.

'Mostly theatre folk, I imagine. Tanya tells me that a few of them are planning some sort of crazy venture putting on plays that no one in their right senses wants to see, like Ibsen and Joyce and Strindberg.'

Luke grinned. 'Don't be such a philistine. Will Tanya be there?'

'Lord, yes. They've already got her hooked good and proper. You'd better look out or they'll rope you in too.'

'I wouldn't mind. I'm interested in plays. Drama is the subject of the thesis I'm beginning to work on. "German Influence on the British Theatre after the Hanoverian Accession". Sounds impossibly pompous, doesn't it? But no one else appears to have thought of it and that's what counts. Also it's going to mean a trip to Germany to do some research.'

'Lucky dog. I wouldn't mind getting away for a while.'

'Couldn't your father wangle a course for you at some foreign hospital?'

'Perhaps. He's not all-powerful, you know. Will you go on Sunday?'

'I might,' Luke said airily, and knew he wouldn't miss it for the world. He ached to see Tanya again and had been fighting a desire to rush round to Giovanni's gallery as soon as he knew she was back. Now the opportunity was being offered to him and he could take it without seeming to push. 'How about you?'

'Oh, I don't know. I'm not mad about theatre parties – a bunch of inflated egos all showing off at the tops of their voices.'

But all the same Andy did turn up with Tanya. He received a cool nod from Diana and found that in actual fact he had been rather unfair. There were only about a dozen gathered in the old-fashioned sitting room of the Curzon Street flat, and though they talked almost exclusively of the parts they had played, were playing now, or hoped to play in the future, they were for the most part quiet, well-behaved and very friendly, accepting Luke at face value and joking with Andy, whom most of them had met before.

Barry Dean, who was quite excessively good-looking, was holding forth about some skulduggery performed by his rascally agent to an admiring group among whom was Tanya. Luke looked at her hungrily. She had not yet lost the light tan from long days spent in the sun, and she seemed to him so beautiful and so unattainable that he felt a sudden wave of depression. Then Diana, smiling dazzlingly, was beside him and taking his hand.

'I'm so glad you have come as there's someone I particularly want you to meet. Come on.'

She threaded her way through the room pulling him after her, and he found himself facing a slight man with dark smouldering eyes, a lop-sided smile and a shock of unruly black hair.

'Craig Vassall, meet Luke Llewellyn Jones. He's terribly clever, an absolute wizard with words, and is going to write us all up, aren't you, Luke?' said Diana, not giving him time to protest. 'Now you two can get to know one another while I hunt up some more food.'

'She sure is a crazy kid,' drawled his new acquaintance, giving him a hard handshake and looking him up and down critically. 'Glad to meet you, Luke. Are you all you're cracked up to be?'

'God knows, but I'm darned certain I'd like to have a try.'

It was very soon obvious that Craig Vassall, who with his white face and spiky hair looked not unlike one of the clowns in Bertram Mills' circus, was an extremely forceful young man with a number of very original and startling ideas on almost every subject. They were soon engaged in a lively argument over books and plays they either liked or disliked and Luke began to enjoy himself. The time went by almost too quickly.

Around midnight the party started to break up, with trains to catch, taxis to be hunted up and early morning film calls taking most of the guests away.

'Gorgeous party, darling.'

'Marvellous food.'

'Heavenly drinkies.'

'Jolly lucky being able to use Daddy's flat,' someone murmured enviously amid the hugs and kisses and thank-yous.

And it was just then that Cecil suddenly erupted into their midst, regrettably very drunk.

He had let himself in with his own key and stood on the threshold eyeing them owlishly. Luke noticed that Diana looked angry and apprehensive at the same time.

'What's going on?' Cecil said loudly. 'A party? And why wasn't I asked?'

'I thought you were down at Chalfont this weekend,' said his sister quickly. 'Anyway everyone's just going.'

'Oh, they are, are they, and about time too.' He moved into the centre of the room and looked about him insolently while some of the actors who had met him before edged towards the door. Tanya made a move towards Luke and Cecil's eye fell on her.

'What the devil are you doing here? Are you hoping to tread the boards like my little sister?' he demanded.

'Oh, be quiet, Cecil. Don't be an ass,' she said impatiently.

But he went on relentlessly. 'And you brought your Welsh boy with you, did you? I thought we'd taught him to go back to his stinking valleys. We'll have to try harder next time, won't we?' He smiled unpleasantly and looked around him. 'Who else do I know? What about you, Master Barry Pretty Boy Dean, the Henry Irving of the second-rates?'

'Now look here,' spluttered the actor. 'You can't get away with saying things like that.'

'Can't I? Try and stop me. This is my flat. Get out of it if you don't like my manners.'

'Shut up, Cecil,' said Diana furiously. 'You're drunk.'

'Not so drunk as you think, dear sister. Does Papa know whom you're entertaining all on your own up here? What are they after, all of them, the food or the drinks, or is it you, like old sawbones here who won't take no for an answer?' And he gave Andy a violent push that sent him sprawling backwards. Before he could retaliate Cecil's eye had fallen on Craig. His eyes narrowed. He looked him up and down with a scalding contempt. 'What the hell are you doing here, Jew boy?'

There was a terrible silence. Craig did not move, but his eyes blazed in his white face before he said, very quietly, 'What do you want us to do with this pest, Diana? Shall we throw him out?'

'He *is* my brother,' she said unhappily. 'He does live here.'

'Right. Just show me where. Luke, give me a hand.'

Between them they frogmarched the furiously protesting Cecil across the room, down the passage, and into the bedroom Diana indicated, pushing him unceremoniously through the door and locking it.

'That's that,' said Craig, dusting off his hands and ignoring the shouts and frenzied banging on the door. 'Let him sleep it off.'

Diana said tremulously, 'Craig, I'm terribly sorry. I could murder my brother. That was unforgivable.'

'Nonsense, girl,' he said calmly, putting an arm round her shoulders. 'Do you imagine it is the first time someone has used a big stick on me? My grandfather was a Polish Jew called Jacob Vassalowsky. When the pogrom drove him and others like him out of their village near Cracow, he fled to the States, and because no one could pronounce Vassalowsky let alone spell it, my father changed it to Vassall. And I'm not ashamed of any of it. I'm bloody proud, if you really want to know.'

'Bravo,' said Luke to himself, filled with fellow feeling. 'Bravo!'

If the incident left a nasty taste in the mouth, it also had the effect of drawing them closer together as if in defiance of the insult. Diana made more coffee and Craig began to outline his plans, and they talked and talked, each one of them defending his or her favourite play and arguing far into the night. It was very late indeed before Luke had a moment alone with Tanya as he helped her to wash up glasses and coffee cups in the kitchen leaving Andy tidying the room with Diana.

Gently she touched his injured hands, healed now but still showing scars from the burning.

'Andy said you were terribly brave about it.'

'Not really. It was a case of needs must.'

'It seems ages since we talked. I want to hear all about everything. Can we meet sometimes? I'm staying with Di tonight.'

'What about having a meal with me tomorrow evening?'

'Yes please, somewhere nice and quiet where we can talk.'

'Do you mean that?' he said, his mind racing.

'Of course I do.'

'Right then. I'll come and collect you when the gallery closes.'

'What a vile beast Cecil is,' she went on, plunging her hands into the hot soapy water. 'Di says he's got himself mixed up with the Mosley crowd, parading around in black shirts. What do they call themselves? Fascists or something. The General would have a fit if he knew. He calls Mussolini "that spaghetti bounder". Cecil is not going to forgive you or Craig in a hurry.'

'I don't think I'll let it worry me too much,' said Luke sturdily, far too elated to allow Cecil's enmity to trouble him.

He walked home that night feeling quite unusually happy, all the anxieties and frustrations of the summer put firmly behind him. From a meagre existence on a diet of bread and soup eked out by the occasional meal tentatively offered by Andy, who had guessed at his plight, he was now modestly affluent.

He felt vaguely guilty at profiting from another's misfortune, but thanks to a car accident that had crippled one of his fellow graduates at King's he had been offered a temporary teaching post in a small private school on the outskirts of London. Forcing the love of literature and the rudiments of English grammar into the minds of unwilling eleven-year-olds was not exactly the fulfilment of his ambitions, but it did give him a livelihood and he leaped at the opportunity. There were quite a few preliminary skirmishes, but he had not grown up in a tough mining village for nothing. The boys suddenly discovered that their new teacher was not only a lover of poetry and fine prose but, if pushed, could retaliate swiftly and very much to the purpose, particularly at any impudence at the expense of Wales and things Welsh.

As one of them remarked ruefully to his classmates, 'Better look out, chaps, L.J. can be tough!'

This last month he had sent off the first repayment he had ever been able to make to his mother, and now that the burden of gratitude had lifted a little he felt free to go his own way and indulge in his own particular dream.

6

Though he did not realize it, the next few months were to be the happiest Luke would know for a very long time. He found more pleasure in teaching scruffy small boys than he had expected. He had money – not a lot, but somehow he could make it sufficient. He had begun to work on his academic thesis. The bulky exercise books had been reduced to a neat typescript which he read straight through; he was appalled by its glaring faults and began happily to edit and revise, boldly cutting the worst of the purple passages. Above all he had his lovely girl, or at any rate a great deal of her company. The budding theatre plans brought them together, and she seemed to enjoy the simple pleasures he could offer. They constantly ate together, at Bertorelli's when he could afford it, at quiet cafés where the food was good but cheap when funds were low. Once, when his back was turned, Tanya hurriedly paid the bill, and he stalked out of the restaurant in an icy rage with her racing after him.

'I'm sorry I'm not Cecil,' he said furiously. 'If we're reduced to tea and a bun, then that's what we'll have and like it. I'm not your gigolo.'

'Oh, Luke,' she exclaimed, between laughter and tears, 'you couldn't be like that in a hundred years. And if you *were* Cecil, I wouldn't be seen dead with you.'

He stopped. 'Do you mean that?'

'You know I do.'

'Sometimes I'm not sure . . .'

Then the absurdity of it struck him. He smiled reluctantly and she slipped an arm through his.

'Forgiven?'

'All right, but never again.'

'Never!' she promised.

Under the inspired leadership of Craig Vassall, the theatre

scheme grew and matured. Their opening play was to be a new translation of Ibsen's *Hedda Gabler*.

'Don't tell me,' he said when the others looked at him aghast. 'Don't tell me that Diana is too young for Hedda. I know that, but she has the right dramatic intensity and that's what's important, all those emotions churning beneath the marble exterior. Barry Dean is an absolute natural for Løvborg, that poetic wastrel "with vine leaves in his hair" whom Hedda sends to his death through love and hate and jealousy.'

'And what about the other parts?' asked Luke.

Craig tapped his big nose slyly. 'Your English theatre is in the doldrums. I've got a number of actors up my sleeve who're dying for a chance to play in something worthwhile provided it's not for too long.'

He was right. They were young, idealistic, and so full of an engaging enthusiasm that interest began to be aroused in theatre circles. Colin came down for a few days, was included in one of their impromptu meetings and immediately fell in love with Diana. He promised to persuade his old man to get them a mention in the national press.

'It's not his scene, I'm afraid, he's up to his neck in politics. He's off to Germany soon to try and get a lead-in on this new man – what's his name? Adolf Hitler. Looks like a window cleaner but seems to be making a hell of a big noise. Pa meets with his cronies at the Press Club. I'll ask him to spread it around.' And he was as good as his word.

The press were not all that interested in their lofty ideals, but two former debutantes with notable fathers made a story in a dull week. The girls were photographed leaving Curzon Street arm in arm, and the escape from Russia was revived and retold.

The Lantern had an excellent if tiny stage and a well-equipped auditorium, but it had not been in use for some time. Luke recruited helpers, and they spent hours of their spare time cleaning, getting rid of rubbish, and splashing on paint to give it a new and brighter look. His days were crammed, and during all these weeks he fell more and more in love with Tanya and slowly began to realize that, though sometimes she seemed very close to him, she was not in the least in love with him.

They sat hand in hand in the upper circle at Noël Coward's

Bittersweet, and he lent her his handkerchief to mop up her tears when the hero met his untimely death. They laughed with sheer delight at the acid wit of *Private Lives* and sat on a hard seat in the gallery of the Old Vic to see *Hamlet* in its entirety with John Gielgud. But he never tried to make love to her, never went further than the cool kiss on meeting and parting.

He wondered afterwards how much difference it might have made if he had not been inhibited by the plain fact that her father was Lord Aylsham, by the respect he felt for him, by the gracious old house in Wimpole Street when he was invited there, by the beauty and dignity of Ravensley. He should have rushed his fences, but something held him back. The time would come, he told himself; it *must* come when he had his MA, when his novel was published. Meanwhile he clung to what he had.

He was not aware that Aunt Hester had telephoned her brother-in-law, her voice trembling with outrage.

'I suppose you know your daughter is running around with a bunch of actors. I've never liked that Diana Harcourt – fast, that's what she is, if not worse. I feel sorry for her parents. I don't know what the General would say, or poor Grace, if they knew half of what she gets up to in their flat now that she has been permitted to live there.'

'And what exactly does she get up to?' asked the doctor drily.

'You know what I mean – parties going on to all hours, drinking too much, and goodness knows what else. Cecil happened to mention it when I ran into him the other day. The poor boy is quite upset about it. It seems Diana has met some American Jew and has quite fallen under his influence.'

'And what is wrong with an American Jew?' said Simon calmly. 'They are usually well thought of in artistic circles. In any case Andy thinks Craig Vassall is quite exceptionally brilliant.'

'Does he indeed? But of course Andy is besotted with the wretched girl – always has been, more's the pity. I can't think why you don't put a stop to it.'

'Andy is not a child, Hester. I can't order his life, not now.'

'That's as may be, but he ought to take more care of his sister. She goes simply everywhere with that miner's son. Penny happened to see them lunching together in one of those common cafés in Soho, giggling together over sandwiches and coffee with a lot of workmen.'

'And what was Penny doing there, may I ask?' enquired the doctor ironically, and then went on quickly, cutting short Hester's outraged splutter. 'I'm really quite capable of looking after my daughter. I know all about the theatre venture she is concerned with, and I approve of it. I'm pleased to see her taking an intelligent interest in something so worthwhile instead of wasting her time at a lot of frivolous parties.'

'Oh, Simon, you're impossible. You're quite out of touch with what is going on and don't seem to care in the least how it reflects on me. And what is this I've been hearing about Nicola wanting to train as a vet? I never heard anything so preposterous. I hope you're not encouraging her?'

'It's her present craze and I see no harm in it. At her age I wanted to be a professional jockey. Time will show whether it is serious.'

'I've no patience with you. You don't seem to have any notion of playing a proper part in society, and Galina encourages the children to do just as they please.'

'My dear Hester,' he said, losing all patience, 'my wife and I have far more important things to attend to than cutting a dash in the social scene, and you really do not need to concern yourself. The family don't require help from you, or from anyone else come to that. Now I really can't waste any more time. I'm due at the hospital.'

He put down the telephone and swore quietly to himself. He heartily disliked his sister-in-law, but all the same he had better have a word with Andy, and perhaps Luke for that matter. Experience had taught him that to interfere too blatantly with the young nowadays only provoked rebellion, and he thought that a sharp eye and the occasional word of advice casually dropped in paid off a great deal better. There was very little that they didn't tell him, and he knew that in the main he had their trust and confidence, and that was what was important.

Luke went home for Christmas and found that his mother had saved the money he had sent and spent it on the luxuries the family had been short of for so long – the turkey and plum pudding, the mince pies and chocolates and fruit. They were all there crammed into the tiny house: Dai and the heavily pregnant Elspeth; the two-year-old Maeve and Owen the baby; his two sisters with their boyfriends; and Megan in and out, though denied a share of the Christmas feast since her grudging old father obstinately refused to join in his neighbours' merrymaking.

Luke had brought small gifts, and they made a great deal of fuss of him as donor of the good things. He hated every minute of it, acutely aware that beneath the smiles and jokes, the pulling of the crackers and the wearing of silly hats, there was an undercurrent of discontent, of envy perhaps, almost of dislike; because try as he would, he could not join in the fun wholeheartedly as he once might have done, and they knew it.

Dai was bitter because the newly elected Labour government, under its leader Ramsay MacDonald, was doing so little for the working men and women who had put them there in faith and hope. One of the members of the Communist group had been gaoled for three months and lost his job for openly speaking out against them at a political rally, and a boy, who might have been like Luke himself ten years before, lost his scholarship because his father had joined openly in a march under the red banners.

'For God's sake be careful, Dai,' urged Luke. 'Don't take any silly risks.'

'If someone doesn't make a move, then we'll get nowhere,' growled his brother. 'It's all very fine for you, swanning about up there in London with your grand friends having a fine old time. What do you care? The rest of us can go hang.'

'That's not true. I do care. I'm not doing nothing, you know. I'm working damned hard. Just because it's the kind of thing you don't understand or care about you condemn it. I've been lucky enough to break free, and I intend to remain free, and that's something you can't stick, can you? It chokes you up with envy, doesn't it? Well, is that my fault?'

Then at the sight of Dai's stricken face he stopped. 'Oh hell! I shouldn't have said that.'

'Maybe it needed to be said.' Dai slapped him on the back. 'Come on, boyo, let's have another drink and agree to differ, shall we?'

But beneath the laughter and good fellowship the bitterness remained.

He saw it strongly in Megan's father, crippled for so many years and his tiny disablement pension cut to the very bone.

He went in to see him, carrying a bottle of whisky he had given up a good deal to buy. The old man accepted it with grudging thanks.

'Bribery, is it now, Luke? No need to butter me up, you know. Better to bring something for Megan here. Looks for your letters she does, day after day, and precious few there are coming. I've told her over and over. He's got away from you, my girl, he's his own life, he has other fish to fry, pretty ones maybe. Waiting for me to die, she is, then she'll be off like a rocket to London, decking herself up lovely, out to catch a husband before it's too late.'

'You shouldn't say things like that, Dada,' said Megan.

'And why shouldn't I then? Aren't they true enough? What else have you to look forward to, girl, tied to an old cripple like me?'

It made Luke feel uncomfortable, and afterwards Megan said, 'You shouldn't take too much notice of what he says. When the pain's bad he lashes out, and if you happen to be there, then you get it right in the neck. Don't I know it? It's kind of you to bring the whisky. He's not much else to look forward to.'

He had brought her a string of glittering beads which Tanya had helped him choose. They looked hopelessly out of place on her old plaid frock, but she smiled as she fingered them.

'They're lovely. However did you know I just love that pretty colour? I'll wear them at the New Year's Eve party at the Methodist Hall – that's if he'll let me go. Sometimes when he's badly, he doesn't like to be left alone.' And sometimes when he was not badly, but just couldn't bear her to go off and enjoy herself, thought Luke. Poor Megan! She was looking up at him almost pleadingly. 'You'll be staying over for that, won't you?'

And he knew he couldn't, though he had intended to. He would have to dance with her, put on a show of affection when he felt only pity, giving her false hopes, which would only be cruel.

'I wish I could, but I can't. Exams, you know, I must work.'

'Do you still see that girl – you know – the one you called Princess?'

'Now and again,' he said and knew she didn't believe him.

He made excuses and left after three days, glad to get back to his bare little room, to his books and his work, even though Tanya and most of his new friends were out of town still celebrating the holiday.

Hedda Gabler opened at the end of March and Luke, standing at the back of the auditorium, was a great deal more keyed up and on edge than the actors. The curtain went up on a scene as authentic as Tanya could contrive, and a faint ripple of surprised appreciation ran through the house, which was crammed with family, friends and social acquaintances. There were also one or two members of the critical confraternity: the *Times* man very dignified and with a faint look of condescension as he pushed his way into his seat; someone from a literary magazine who looked like an Oxford don; one or two writers from the popular press rushing in late as they stopped to polish off the whisky offered for their entertainment in the tiny bar.

'Where did all that fine furniture spring from?' whispered Andy, who had materialized beside Luke.

'Tanya scrounged a good deal of it from Giovanni. It's worth a fortune. God help us if anything happens to it!'

'Is he here?'

'In the front row watching it like a hawk.'

Diana's first entrance caused a stir of intense interest. She looked marvellously in character in a dark green gown which she and Tanya had concocted between them. Her red hair was swept back austerely, showing the fine, clear-cut features.

Andy drew a quick breath. 'Is she going to pull it off? Is she, Luke? What do you think?'

'Craig has done wonders with her at rehearsals.'

Andy's hands gripped the brass rail that ran along behind the seats so hard that his knuckles whitened.

'If she makes a success, a real success, then I've lost her, and if she doesn't . . .'

'If she doesn't, she'll come running back to you,' said Luke tactlessly, meaning to comfort. Andy turned on him furiously.

'I don't want that. I don't want to be a refuge in trouble, a poor second best. What the hell is the good of that?' Someone in the back row turned round and glared at him. 'One thing is sure,' Andy whispered. 'Whichever way it goes, I can't win.'

Presently he disappeared, as if he couldn't bear to watch any longer, and was replaced by Tanya. She took Luke's arm.

'How's it going? I couldn't get round before.'

'Very well, I think.'

'Do look at Di's parents. I don't think the General understands one single world. *A Little Bit of Fluff* is more his mark. And her mother is shocked. They'd far rather be seeing her as some simpering ingénue.'

'Your father looks interested.'

'Oh, Papa is quite a good judge. He thinks we're taking a fearful risk, but rather approves. If we pull it off, won't Aunt Hester be sick!'

There was no doubt of the play's success on that first night, but then it was bound to be a success with so many friends in front, all taken aback at the sheer professionalism of the group when they had condescendingly expected some little amateur effort. But it was the critical reaction later that week that sent their spirits rocketing up into the skies.

'The artistic integrity and intellectual grasp of Craig Vassall's production of this great play bodes well for the future of the talented group,' wrote one. 'Flawless performances, especially from Miss Diana Harcourt,' said another. *The Times* was more restrained, but a popular daily went to town with a photograph of Diana and the caption 'Ex-debutante makes theatrical history'. The literary magazine outdid itself: 'The living art of the theatre today is in the hands of experimental groups such as this. A truly notable production, and I advise the serious intellectual theatre-going public to lose no time in visiting the unpretentious little Lantern.' They certainly did, crowding in so that the run had to be extended from three weeks to five, and on the last night even eminent late-comers were reduced to sitting on the floor or up the steps while the second production, Chekhov's *Seagull*, was already heavily booked.

Not that Craig allowed their success to go to their heads.

'We're not society playboys,' he said, 'we're serious people engaged in worthwhile work.'

So the last night of the run was not celebrated with a frivolous party. Instead those chiefly concerned went back to Curzon Street and indulged in nothing more extravagant than a bottle or two of the General's champagne and a pile of Nanny's delicious sandwiches, with Craig insisting that everyone should leave at a reasonable hour.

'Now look here, chaps,' he said, glass in one hand, sandwich in the other. 'We've a dress rehearsal on Monday and we open on Wednesday with a very tricky play indeed, and the audience is going to be damned critical. Much more is going to be expected from us, very much more. We've done it once, and to make any impact the second production has got to be ten times better. It's like a second novel. If the first achieves any kind of success, then the follow-up has got to be twice as brilliant. You'd agree with me there, wouldn't you, Luke?'

Luke nodded ruefully. Craig was so right – provided the first had got somewhere. His manuscript had started on its travels and had already been returned twice. He was beginning to hate the postman's knock and the fat parcel looking more and more tired.

'Have a nice quiet week-end, duckie,' went on Craig, kissing Diana lightly and patting her cheek. 'Hedda was damned good, but Nina has got to be startling – and you know why, don't you?'

'How could I forget? I'm grateful, Craig, I can't tell you how grateful.'

'We're going right up to the top, you and I, just you remember that.' He gave her a quick hug and went clattering down the stairs after the others.

Andy said quietly, 'See Tanya back to Wimpole Street for me, will you, Luke? I'm due back at the hospital later.'

'Right. We'd better get a taxi.'

Outside the front door Tanya said, 'Let's go down to Ravensley tomorrow. I seem to have lived for weeks and weeks on the smell of greasepaint, size, dusty clothes, frowsty costumiers, furniture polish, and endless cups of tea and buns. Oh for some of Betsy's cooking and a cold wind blowing across the Fens! Can you come, Luke?'

'I don't see why not. School doesn't open again till Tuesday.'

'Why do you suppose Andy was so eager to get rid of us?' she asked when they were in the taxi.

'I think I can guess. He probably wants to have it out with Diana once and for all.'

'You mean about Craig?'

'Well, they have become pretty close.'

The same thought was in both their minds, but they didn't put it into words: Tanya out of a kind of shyness and Luke because he would not betray Andy's confidence.

'I think Nanny has gone to bed,' said Diana, picking up glasses when the others had gone. 'I'll go and make us some more coffee.'

'No, don't.'

'But if you've got to go back to Guy's and work through the night, you ought to have something.'

'As a matter of fact I'm not going back.'

She stopped on her way to the door and frowned at him. 'Then why say so?'

'I wanted to talk to you.'

'Oh, Andy, not now, not at this time of night.'

'It's as good a time as any, and I never seem to get you alone these days.'

She came back resignedly and sat on the sofa. 'What is it you want to talk about?' she asked.

He was standing in front of the fire staring down at her, and she sensed the tenseness in him – a kind of suppressed anger, though he spoke quietly enough.

'To start with I'd like to know why Craig is so insistent that you should make a hit in this next play.'

'Isn't it obvious?'

'No, it isn't. Something is going on between you two, that's what is obvious. Is it too much to ask what it is?'

'It's nothing much, only I've kept quiet about it because he hasn't mentioned it to any of the others yet.' She got up and moved away from him, putting plates together on the table, before she went on reluctantly. 'If you must know, there are some people coming over from the States, important people. If they're impressed it could mean a great deal to him. You see, there's a play he has written. They've read it and like it, and there is a big

112

chance he could be asked to direct it and it could end up on Broadway.'

'Have you read it?'

'Yes, I have, and I think it's really something, original, quite startling.' She could not keep the enthusiasm out of her voice. 'He's had plays done before in out-of-town theatres, but this is different. This could really take him somewhere.'

'And you too?'

'And me too perhaps. There's a marvellous part – if they like me.'

'And would you go if the chance came?'

'Of course I would, like a shot. I'd be a damned fool not to, wouldn't I?'

'So as far as I'm concerned, it's kiss and farewell, is that what you mean?'

She turned to him. 'No, of course it isn't. If it does come off, and it's still a big if, it would only be for a short time, six months perhaps.'

'And after that?'

She shrugged her shoulders. 'How can I tell? In this business nothing is certain. Who knows what may turn up?'

'It's this fellow Craig, isn't it? He's the one that matters, not me, nor your parents, nor anyone else. He has you dancing on a string like some damned puppet, one jerk and you are racing after him.'

'Oh, for God's sake, don't be jealous, not you, Andy. I thought you had more sense. I'm not in love with Craig, not in the very least, but I admire him tremendously as a man of the theatre and if I had the chance to go on working with him, here or in America or anywhere, I'd fall over my feet to go – so now you know.'

'Well, that's pretty straight. I don't know what the hell I'm doing here. I'd better go.'

She was immediately repentant. 'No, Andy, no, don't go, please don't go, not like that. I can't bear to see you hurt. I'd do anything to make you feel as happy about it as I am.'

'I could not love thee, Dear, so much, loved I not honour more,' he quoted drily, 'only for "honour" substitute "theatre".' And then quite suddenly the anger burst out of him. 'Damn you, woman, don't you realize the hell I've been through all these weeks? Don't

113

you know what love is? I thought we had something real and warm and living between us.'

'So we have.'

'Then prove it.' He had gripped her by the shoulders and was shaking her. She tried to push him away.

'Andy, don't be a fool. Let me go.'

'No.' His fingers were digging fiercely into her flesh. 'You made me an offer once. Do you remember? Now I'm going to hold you to it.'

'Andy, please . . .'

But he was too strong. She tried to resist him but stumbled backwards on to the sofa, and he fell beside her, holding her in his arms, kissing her savagely. She struggled at first, and then slowly he felt her relax. Her mouth softened and opened under his, her arms went round him. After a little he drew away and looked into her face, running his finger down the lovely curve of her cheek.

'Shall I go or stay?' he murmured huskily.

In the light of the table lamp her eyes were dark pools under the long lashes, but excitement lurked there, the strong attraction she had fought for so long. Why oh why was life so unfair? She lay still, staring up into the taut, lean face, then with one hand she began to unbutton her white silk blouse, and reached up to pull him down to her.

7

On that afternoon in early May there was a smell of spring in the air at Ravensley, even in the stable yard where Tanya and Nicola had joined forces to persuade Luke on to a horse. He was resisting strongly.

'But it's so easy,' said Nicola, who had ridden since she was three years old. 'There's nothing to be afraid of.'

'I'm not afraid,' he protested, 'it's just that I don't like the look in that big brute's eyes.'

'Blackie has the sweetest temperament,' said Jake, who was standing by to give assistance. 'She wouldn't hurt a fly. Now, you put your foot here in the stirrup, sir, then I'll give you a leg up and Bob's your uncle.'

'Is it? Oh, all right.' He gritted his teeth. 'I'll have a go. You can only die once.'

'That's the ticket.'

Once settled in the saddle it didn't seem so bad, even though the ground appeared a very long way away. He went twice round the stable yard with Jake yelling instructions.

'Sit back! Grip with your knees! That's right now. Don't pull on the reins too hard. Go with the horse, sir, don't fight her!'

He glanced at the two girls who were watching him, giggling quietly, and pronounced himself ready to start off.

They rode out all three of them taking it gently so that he began to fall in with the rhythm of the mare, and after the first terrible jolt when all his bones seemed to crack at once, he even learned to ease comfortably into the rise and fall of the trot.

They rode down one of the green avenues of the park. There were still drifts of daffodils along the edges and glimpses of late primroses under the trees, and he started to enjoy himself. Presently they came to a tiny stream and followed along the grassy bank, and all might have gone off splendidly if Cecil hadn't suddenly appeared at the far end of the path.

'Oh Lord, look what's turned up!' muttered Nicola disgustedly, and Tanya frowned as he came cantering up to join them.

'Mother heard you were down this weekend and wondered if Di had come with you,' he said breathlessly. 'I offered to ride over and find out.'

'Well, she's not here. She's busy with extra rehearsals for the new play. We open on Wednesday,' replied Tanya shortly.

'Oh, is that what it is? You know what Mother is like. If she doesn't hear for a week or two she worries about her daughter amongst a lot of wild actors.' He gave his high-pitched giggle and looked around. 'Isn't Andy here?'

'No. It's his Sunday at the hospital,' said Tanya, glancing pointedly at Luke. 'I'm sorry, Cecil, but we must be getting back. Jake has to drive Nicola to school this evening.'

Cecil ignored her, looking across at Luke with a sly grin.

'Taffy was a Welshman, but Taffy can also ride a horse, I see. Who'd have thought it? Let's see what you can do, shall we? What about racing me to the bridge?'

'No!' said Tanya quickly, but Luke forestalled her, recognizing a challenge and unwilling to let it go unanswered.

'Right,' he said, 'I'm on. Shall we go?'

Before anyone could say anything he had dug his heels into Blackie and the startled mare leaped forward. It was not a great distance and he'd never felt so frightened in his life, but he stuck on somehow until they reached the narrow plank bridge over the tiny stream. He knew he couldn't pull Blackie up. Cecil, far more experienced, came up beside him, deliberately jostling against him so that the mare shied and with the bit between her teeth took the jump awkwardly, clearing the stream and unsaddling Luke so that he sailed clean over her head.

He rolled over and over on the soft turf and into the tangled reeds. The next moment Tanya had raced up and was off her horse.

'That was your fault,' she yelled furiously at Cecil. 'I saw what you did.'

'Am I to blame if the fool can't control his horse?'

'Go away!' she screamed at him. 'Go away and never, never

116

come back!' She was on her knees. 'Luke, Luke darling, are you hurt?'

He sat up, dazed, but thankful to find himself still all in one piece.

'I'm all right, I think,' he muttered. 'Only winded.'

She sat back on her heels. 'Thank goodness. I'd like to *kill* Cecil Harcourt.'

'Not on my account, please.'

He managed a shaky laugh and got to his feet a little gingerly.

'What's the right procedure? Get straight back on if I can, is that it?'

'Are you sure?' She was looking at him with an anxious frown.

By this time Nicola had come back leading the repentant Blackie, now looking rather ashamed of herself, and somehow or other he clambered back into the saddle, aware of a number of bruises in very unfamiliar parts of his body, but with a peculiar sort of satisfaction all the same. He was quite unconscious of the fact that Cecil had notched up another black mark in the score he was slowly building up against Tanya and this unwelcome intruder.

Dr Aylsham met them as they came in. He noticed Luke's muddy jacket and his obvious limp and asked what had happened.

'I fell off my horse,' Luke said lightly.

'It was Cecil's fault,' added Nicola, still burning with righteous indignation. 'He rammed him at that little bridge across the stream.'

'Did he, indeed? And why was that?'

'Out of spite, I expect. Tanya sent him off with a flea in his ear.'

'Nicola, I don't think your headmistress would approve of you using expressions like that.'

'It's very expressive though, isn't it?' she said thoughtfully. 'I wonder where it comes from? Do you know, Luke?'

'Only that it was in use in the fifteenth century, when nearly everyone had fleas and one in your ear biting hard could be very nasty.'

Nicola went off into peals of laughter. 'I think that's gorgeous. I must remember to tell our English mistress that. How clever of you to know.'

'I don't like to think what her opinion of us will be if you do,'

117

remarked her father. 'And now after all that what about Luke? Did you suffer any serious damage?'

'Nothing, sir, really – a few bruises, that's all.'

'You'd better see my wife about those. She has a whole cupboardful of liniments and embrocations.'

'Do I have to go back to school this evening?' pleaded Nicola, hanging on to her father's arm.

'Yes, my pet, you do.'

Nicola was a weekly boarder at an exclusive school near Ely. This little argument took place every Sunday evening, and though she never got her way she was always hopeful.

She heaved a sigh. 'In that case I shall have to eat the most enormous tea.'

'Why, greedy-guts?' said her sister, coming into the hall from the stables where she had gone with the horses. 'You're much too fat already.'

'I'm not, am I, Papa? She is being beastly.'

'Pleasantly plump,' he said, patting her on top of the head.

'Sunday suppers at St Bride's are *awful*, things like cold semolina or tapioca, frogspawn, ugh!'

It was when Nicola was tucking into toasted tea cakes and two hefty slices of Betsy's special angel cake that Dr Aylsham asked casually why Andy had not come down with them.

'He's at the hospital,' said Tanya.

'I didn't think it was his turn.'

She exchanged a look with Luke and went on smoothly, 'I think he mentioned he was taking over someone else's stint.'

Her father frowned but made no comment. Later, standing on the steps waiting for Jake to bring the car round, Nicola took Luke's arm.

'Is Andy having an *affair* with Di?' she asked in a stage whisper.

'Good heavens, child, what do you know about things like that?'

'Don't be such a prig,' she said scornfully. 'Of course I know. You should hear some of the girls at school. And I'm not a child. I'm fourteen. Juliet was married and bedded when she was fourteen.'

'Nicola! You shouldn't say things like that.'

'Why not? Shakespeare does.'

'You're not Shakespeare, and in any case I wouldn't dream of discussing your brother with you.'

'That means he is, and it's all so useless.' She sighed. 'Diana will never marry him. She's wedded to her art.'

She was such a quaint mixture of childish candour and schoolgirl sophistication that he burst out laughing.

She pulled away from him. 'Don't make fun of me. It's not fair.'

'I'm sorry, Nicola. I wasn't laughing *at* you, really I wasn't.'

'I know. It's just because you're grown up and I'm not, but you see I've got such a very long way to go to catch up.'

By that time the car was there. She gave him a quick hug before she climbed into the front seat beside Jake, and waved as they drove off.

She was right in a way, he thought, as he went back into the house. Her brothers and her sister were so much older than she was that she was constantly making a valiant attempt to bridge the gap, and despite the love and warmth it wasn't always easy.

They spent a quiet evening. Tanya was more subdued than usual, more ready to please, and after supper she put on the gramophone, playing some of her father's favourite Mozart rather than the jazz she preferred. The room was filled with the lovely harp and flute concerto when the telephone rang, shrilly, stridently, cutting across the delicious harmony, and presently Jake knocked and came in.

'It's the police, sir. There's been an accident on the railway. The Superintendent would like to speak to you.'

'That sounds like trouble. Very well, I'll come.'

Tanya turned off the gramophone. 'I wonder where it is?' she said, and then they were silent, waiting a little apprehensively until the doctor came back.

'It's some way north of Ely,' he said. 'It seems the London express has collided with a goods train.'

'Is it serious?' asked his wife.

'Yes, it is – very serious. Several coaches have overturned and a good number of people have been injured. I'm afraid I must go. They're going to need all the help they can get.'

'I'll come with you,' she said, getting up. 'We'd better take blankets and sheets and anything else we think may be useful.'

Luke said, 'May I go with you? I can't do much for the injured, but I'm sure I can help in some way.'

'We'll all go,' said Tanya quickly. 'Shall I ask Betsy to fill the Thermos flasks with hot tea, and what about brandy, Papa?'

'Good idea. Ask Jake to fetch it for us while I put things together.'

They were soon ready, and with Jake driving faster through the narrow lanes than Luke could have believed possible they reached the scene of the disaster within an hour.

It was dark by then, and gigantic flares lit up a horrifying scene that might have sprung from the brush of some surrealistic painter. Three carriages had crumpled into one another like a child's toy train and had toppled over the embankment into a fearful mass of mangled iron, splintered wood and smashed glass.

People were screaming, shouting, weeping or simply dumb with agony and shock. Ambulances had already arrived, and the dead and badly injured were being placed on the stretchers. Police were everywhere, and the fire brigade, who had come with their equipment and were working desperately to free those still caught in the tangled wreckage. Doctors were working against time to help the worst cases, and Simon Aylsham went at once to join them. Luke and Tanya began to unload the car. Galina took bandages and sheets to the nurses who were dealing with the innumerable injuries caused by the flying glass. Children were crying pitifully or running distractedly among the scattered and smashed luggage; teddy bears, dolls, intimate articles of clothing had tumbled out of cases and were being trodden into the mud. There were passengers trying helplessly to gather their possessions together while others, dazed and shivering with shock, were weeping uncontrollably. Luke, who had once been involved in a pit accident, began to gather them together, getting out blankets and rugs to wrap round them, urging them to sit down and wait quietly until help arrived to take them away to safety.

Tanya had lifted out the big Thermos flasks. Her face was white, and her hands were shaking so much she had difficulty in unscrewing the cap.

'Are you all right?' whispered Luke.

She nodded, making a determined effort to swallow down the nausea, to control the shivering.

'It's just the blood. I hate it, but I'm all right now. I'm *all right*. I can do this. Leave it to me.'

She began to talk gently to those still in great distress, persuading them to drink the hot sweet tea, while Luke, after one glance at her, went off to help in dragging out victims still trapped in the wreckage, trying to comfort them, supporting those who had been injured until one of the doctors could take over.

It was a good deal later, and the hectic pace had slackened a little, when a policeman approached Dr Aylsham as he straightened up from dealing with a young woman whose leg had been broken in two places.

'Could I have a word with you, sir?'

'Yes, what is it?' he asked a little brusquely.

'I wonder if you could help us?'

He saw the stretcher lifted into the ambulance before he turned round.

'In what way?'

'There's a man trapped under some very heavy wreckage. It's going to take an hour or two before he can be freed, and in the meantime he is in some danger.'

'Is he injured? In pain?'

'Very likely, but more than that. We'd like to warn him to remain very still and not struggle as it could collapse further on to him, but he doesn't seem to understand. He must be some kind of a foreigner and we can't make out what he is saying.'

'What is he? French, German?'

'I think some of us might have been able to manage that, but it's a strange lingo none of us have heard before. We wondered whether you might be able to interpret it.'

'Well, I can only try. Where is he?'

The carriage must have rolled on to him so that the unfortunate man was pinned across the thighs beneath the length of the iron steps. The rescuers had brought their lifting equipment but had not yet been able to raise it sufficiently to drag him out.

Simon knelt down, getting as close as he could. He tried French and German, a few words of Italian, with no result; then as a last chance he spoke in Russian and saw a flicker of recognition cross the bearded face. The whisper was so faint he had to move forward

121

to catch the sound. He listened intently, spoke something reassuring, and stood up.

'He is Russian,' he said briefly, 'and he says he is in great pain and bleeding badly. How long will it take before you can free him?'

'A couple of hours at least.'

'If an artery is damaged he could die in that time. Could I crawl close enough to him to give an injection and try to stop the bleeding?'

'I wouldn't advise it, sir. It could be dangerous.'

'All the same I think I'll have to try. I'll need some light. Has anyone got a torch?'

'I don't think I can allow you to take the risk, sir,' began the Police Superintendent.

'You'll have to, won't you?' said the doctor crisply. 'I'll take the responsibility. Will someone hold the torch for me?'

'I will,' said Luke.

'Good. Come on then.'

By this time a little crowd had gathered, attracted by the scent of drama as people always are in the most dangerous circumstances.

Simon prepared his hypodermic, took a swab and bandages, and began to crawl along the narrow tunnel under the fallen carriage, followed by Luke carrying the torch.

They moved very slowly inch by inch so as not to jolt anything, which might precipitate a further fall. Once there was an ominous creak and the whole tangled mass shifted a little. They stopped, holding their breath, till the tiny movement settled, then infinitely carefully they inched forward again.

Galina was watching with the others, absolutely still, afraid to move or make a sound, and only just aware that Tanya had come up beside her and in that moment of frightened tension had taken her hand.

Simon spoke slowly and clearly. 'I'm going to give you an injection that will ease the pain, and then try to stop the bleeding. In an hour or so they hope to set you free.'

He edged a little nearer and Luke switched on the torch. It lit the trapped man's lean face, with its stubble of beard, his eyes flickered open and he tried to raise his head a little.

'Who are you?' he whispered.

'I'm a doctor.' Simon had cut away the torn sleeve and shirt. 'Hold steady now.'

'I thought . . . I thought . . . Is your name Simon?' The voice was no more than a thread of sound.

'Yes, it is. Now take a deep breath.'

Simon slowly pressed the syringe, but not before Luke had heard a sigh, almost of satisfaction. He had understood nothing of what had been said, but it had an eerie quality as if there were some kind of link between the injured foreigner and the man beside him. Then Simon quickly and deftly pressed the swab into place and bandaged the thigh to stop the pumping blood. Afterwards, very slowly, they backed out.

A sigh of relief went through the little group who had been watching. Lady Aylsham said nothing, but the look on her face told Luke what agony she had been through and the infinite relief she felt at seeing her husband emerge safely. Tanya was more exuberant. She reached up impulsively to kiss her father's cheek and then threw her arms round Luke and hugged him.

'Here, here, what's all this about?' he said, smiling a little shakily.

'You were so brave. I'd never have been able to do that.'

There was still a great deal they could do to help, and an hour or so later the smashed carriage had been raised and the foreigner brought out. His eyes opened as Simon bent over him and said something in Russian that brought a ghost of a smile to the haggard face. The stretcher was carried away and the police chief turned to the doctor.

'I wonder if you'd mind accompanying us to the hospital, sir? We may have trouble in dealing with this poor fellow and we'd be grateful for your help.'

'Certainly. I intended to come in any case.'

Lady Aylsham said, 'I'd like to go with my husband, Superintendent. I am a doctor too. I promise not to be a nuisance.'

'I'm sure we shall be very thankful, my lady. They are going to be grossly overworked tonight. Every hospital in the district has been alerted.'

Simon turned to Luke. 'Jake will drive you and Tanya home. I don't know when we shall get back, but take care of her.'

'I will, sir. You can rely on me.'

'Good boy. Come along, my dear, we must go. The ambulance is waiting for us.'

There was nothing more they could do now, so Tanya put the Thermos flasks in the boot while Luke picked up the rugs and blankets that had been discarded.

It was not until they were in the car that Tanya turned to him.

'That Russian *knew* Papa, didn't he? Did you see how he looked at him?'

'Yes, I did.'

'And Galina too.'

'Possibly. Tanya, I don't think we should talk about it, not to anyone outside of ourselves, I mean.'

'Why? Do you think he might be a . . . a spy . . . or something?'

'No, of course not, that's much too melodramatic. I just don't think we should say anything about it to the servants or to anyone until your father comes back.'

He could not explain why he felt so strongly about it. It was just that lying in the semi-darkness, hearing the unfamiliar whispered words, sensing some link between the stranger and Simon Aylsham, he had felt a breath of danger, something stretching out from the past to threaten the family he had grown to know and love and whom until this moment he had believed so safe and secure in their fine rich home. Until he knew what it was, it was best to say nothing.

It was long past midnight by the time they reached Ravensley, and the servants had gone to bed, but a carefully banked fire burned in the drawing room and Mrs Alison came down in her dressing gown to ask if there was anything they needed.

'Father has gone to the hospital and Lady Aylsham with him,' explained Tanya.

'Were there many injured there?'

'A very great many, and several already dead. It was terrible.'

'Poor souls, what a tragedy. It must have been a shocking experience for you, Miss Tanya, and for you too, sir. Would you like me to make you both a hot drink?'

'It's very late and you've had a long day. You go up to bed, Mrs Alison. Luke and I will look after ourselves. We'll wait up for a while in case my father telephones.'

'If you're quite sure,' said the housekeeper, a little doubtful at leaving the two young people alone together. That Welsh boy had always seemed a decent enough lad, even if he wasn't in their league. (Like most upper-class servants she was much more of a snob than her employers.) She was persuaded to go at last, and Tanya heaved a sigh of relief.

'I just felt I didn't want to go on talking and talking about it, and I'm sure you don't.' She looked down with a grimace of disgust at the bloodstains on her skirt where she had nursed some of the injured children. 'I'm going to take this off. You go through and put the kettle on, Luke, then I'll make us some coffee. I don't think I could look another cup of tea in the face.'

When she came into the kitchen she had run a comb through her hair and put on a dark blue velvet dressing gown that buttoned from her neck to her feet. He thought she looked like a blonde angel from one of the medieval Italian paintings, and in reaction to the horrors of the night he wanted to take her in his arms, feel her warm and alive, smell the fragrance that always clung about her, hold her close against any possible harm.

She was spooning the newly ground coffee into the big brown jug and he poured on the boiling water.

'Are you hungry?' she asked. 'Shall I make you a sandwich?'

'No, I don't think so. What about you?'

She shook her head. He took up the tray and they went back into the drawing room.

'I think we'll have some of Papa's brandy,' she said suddenly. 'I don't like it usually. It makes me think of being ill and the time I had two teeth taken out and fainted when I came home, but tonight is different. I need bracing, don't you?'

She fetched the decanter from the dining room and brought it with two glasses to a small table close to the fire.

They sat close together on the rug, and she leaned back against the sofa.

'When something like this happens it makes you feel grateful that you're alive, doesn't it?' she said.

'I know what you mean. You feel guilty, too, because you're all right and they aren't. Silly, isn't it, when it is not your fault? Would you like coffee first and brandy afterwards?'

'Yes, please.'

He poured the coffee and they sipped it gratefully, relaxing in the warm circle of the firelight with only one shaded lamp. Presently he poured a little of the brandy into the two glasses and handed her one.

'Do you realize that it's just about a year since you knocked me down and I came here for the first time?'

'Is it as long as that? We ought to drink to it.'

They clinked glasses and sipped the brandy before Luke went on.

'Do you remember the afternoon we spent on the river?'

'Yes,' she said dreamily, 'and you told me about Wales and Llewellyn and your grandfather.'

The room was filled with shadows. In the golden pool of light they seemed very close, cut off from the rest of the world, and he suddenly knew it was now or never. He had a wild, crazy desire to take her in his arms and kiss and kiss and kiss, but that would have been a madness that could lead anywhere.

He said unsteadily, 'That was the moment when I fell in love with you.'

Her eyes widened. 'Just like that?'

'Just like that. It hit me like a bolt of lightning.'

She was looking up at him with a tiny smile. '"It is too rash, too unadvis'd, too sudden."'

Was she teasing him? Making fun of him? He took her up on it.

'"Too like the lightning which doth cease to be ere one can say it lightens."' Then he couldn't stand it any longer. 'To hell with Shakespeare!' he said violently and leaned forward, taking the brandy glass out of her hand and setting it on the table.

'I'm not joking. I'm serious, Tanya. I've thought of nothing else all this year. I want to marry you. I want you for my wife . . . No, don't speak, not yet . . . I know what you will say – it's absurd, it's impossible – and you're right. I know what your father would say – how can I dare to take you away from all this, ask you to live with me in one miserable room up two flights of stairs? But it's going to be different soon, in another year perhaps. Will you hate being a schoolmaster's wife, my darling? But it won't be for long, I swear it won't. I have all kinds of plans and ambitions for both of us, and together there's nothing, absolutely nothing, that we couldn't do. I've thought of it, I've dreamed of it all these months.' And carried away by his own tempestuous rush of words he drew

126

her towards him, kissing her more deeply, more passionately, more thrillingly, than any of the young men who had fumbled at her at dances or grabbed hold of her in the taxi driving home, and she made no move to stop him.

He was kissing her eyes, her cheeks, her mouth, one hand tangled in her hair and the other daring to unbutton the neck of her dressing gown, kissing her throat and the swell of her breast so that she trembled, her whole being shaken by sensations she had never felt before, wanting it to go on and yet half fearing it.

Presently he drew back a little and said hoarsely, 'Do you love me just a little, Tanya? Say you do.'

She was not sure whether this was love or not, but she was aware of a tremendous tenderness towards him. She put up a hand and stroked his cheek almost wonderingly.

'Dear Luke,' she murmured. She had thought of him like a brother, almost like Andy and Paul, a dear companion not a lover; now it was surprisingly, shockingly different.

He was kissing her again with a kind of hungry tenderness as her lips opened under his. She closed her eyes, all her senses tinglingly alive. This was a Luke she didn't know, and on this night alone together in this quiet house who knows what might have happened if Luke had not hesitated, if he had let his passion overcome his scruples, if her father had not said "Take care of her", if the telephone had not rung loudly, breaking into their intimacy, so that for a moment, dazed, they hardly knew what it was that had split them apart.

Then Tanya sat up, pushing back her tumbled hair.

'That must be Papa. I'd better answer it.'

Jake was already halfway down the stairs when she went out into the hall, but she motioned him back, saying, 'I'll take it.'

Luke was on his feet when she came back.

'That was Father. He and Galina are staying at the hospital overnight. He wants me to send Jake across to pick them up tomorrow morning.'

'Did he say why? Was it that man, the Russian?'

'Why do you say that?'

'I don't know. It was just something the Superintendent said about needing his help.'

'Father didn't mention him.'

She came to the hearth but the spell was broken. They could not go back to where they had left off.

She began to put the cups and glasses on a tray.

'I'll just put these outside and then we'd better go to bed. We have a dress rehearsal at the Lantern tomorrow.'

'Yes.'

He took the tray from her and carried it through to the kitchen. When he came back into the room she was kneeling by the fire poking it into grey ash. He knelt beside her and took the poker out of her hand.

'Tanya, I meant what I said tonight, every word.'

'I know you did.'

'You're not angry with me?'

'Angry? Oh no. Dear Luke, I'm very, very fond of you.'

She leaned forward and kissed him on the lips, but before he could take hold of her she had got quickly to her feet and slipped away from him.

He looked after her, suddenly overwhelmed with blank despair, a feeling that he had been given his chance and had missed it. Perhaps it was just his bad luck that, during the busy week that followed, the stranger from Monte Carlo reappeared and Tanya met Dirk von Richter again.

Part Two

TANYA
1931

8

He came into the gallery one morning when Tanya was on the upper floor, but she saw the tall man in the well-cut dark suit, the black hat with a buccaneering curve to the brim, and wondered who he was. Then Giovanni called to her, he turned to look up, and the face was that of the stranger. The surprise took her breath away for a moment, then she rallied as she came down the stairs.

Giovanni, all smiles, was saying, 'Tanya my dear, allow me to introduce Herr von Richter from Switzerland. His father often did business with me in the old days in St Petersburg. This young lady, my dear sir, is . . .'

'Tatiana Malinskaya, the daughter of Lord Aylsham, the celebrated surgeon,' said the stranger with the hint of a smile.

'You know one another?' exclaimed Giovanni.

'We met for a few moments in the Casino at Monte Carlo last summer.' His English was only very slightly accented. 'Dare I hope you remember me, Miss Aylsham?'

'Indeed I do.'

She held out her hand and he kissed it with a courtly foreign grace.

'Well, that's splendid,' said Giovanni, his Italian curiosity vastly intrigued. 'Herr von Richter is particularly interested in our icons, Tanya. Perhaps you would show them to him. Tanya is very knowledgeable, my dear von Richter, she will tell you all their history. Forgive me if I have to leave you in her hands, but I do have a very important appointment.'

'Of course, Signor Ricci. We shall meet again very soon, I hope. My father has spoken of you so often that I am delighted to make your acquaintance at last.'

They spoke for a few minutes longer, then Giovanni took his leave and Tanya was left alone with him.

'We keep our icons with the Russian collection in the upper gallery,' she said, 'if you care to come with me, Herr von Richter.'

'Lead on,' he said and followed her up the curving staircase.

For the next hour she showed him the range of icons, some of them extremely ancient, speaking intelligently of their age, quality, history and value, and guessed by the care and reverence with which he handled them, and by his informed comments, that he knew as much about the subject as she did, and possibly more.

'They are very fine,' he said at last, laying down the last one on its bed of velvet. 'I would be buying for my father, of course, but I am sure he would be particularly interested in the Byzantine Christos.'

'It is the best we have, and the most expensive.'

'Price is of no consequence. It is the quality that matters.'

'I think you may be quite certain of its authenticity, Herr von Richter.' She folded over the covering, returned the painting to the cabinet, and then looked up at him. 'When we met in the Casino you loaned me a stake which won quite a lot of money, but when I looked for you to return it you had gone.'

'My friends had to leave, so I was obliged to go with them.'

'What made you give it to me?'

'You looked so forlorn, like a child whose cherished bag of sweets has been stolen from her. I couldn't resist it.'

She might have seemed like a child then, but was very far from that now.

'I still have the money we won between us. I kept it to return to you.'

'Were you so sure we would meet again?'

'I think I was always sure of that.'

The lighting in the gallery was subdued for the sake of the valuable furniture and paintings on show, but as he looked down at her she was captured by those strange eyes that at moments had a queer golden brilliance like the eyes of an animal glimpsed in the dark, a tiger perhaps or a hunting leopard.

Then she shook the fancy away from her. 'Is there anything else you would like me to show you?'

'Not immediately, but would you do me the honour of dining with me this evening?'

She caught her breath in surprise. It was all happening far too quickly, and she drew back, afraid of seeming too forward, too readily available.

'I'm sorry,' she replied coolly, 'but I already have an engagement for this evening.'

'Tomorrow then, what about luncheon?' When she still hesitated, he went on with a charmingly diffident smile, 'Do I seem as if I'm – how do you say? – rushing my fences? If so, I'm sorry, but you see, Miss Aylsham, this is my first visit to London, and as I'm only here for a couple of days I should welcome advice as to how I should use my time to the best advantage.'

Two days! She hid her acute disappointment. 'I'm afraid you will not be able to see much in that short time.'

He made a little foreign gesture. 'Unluckily I am obliged to go to Paris and then on to Berlin to meet colleagues of my father, but I shall hope to return soon and next time stay longer. In the meantime won't you take pity on me? I am staying at the Savoy. We could lunch at the Grill and then you could tell me where I should go in this old and beautiful London of yours.'

He was very persuasive. 'If you put it like that I can hardly refuse, can I?'

'So you will come? Wonderful! Shall we say one o'clock at the Savoy, and please tell Signor Ricci that I will see him in the morning about the icon and arrange for it to be despatched to Switzerland.'

At the door he held her hand for a moment in both of his before raising it to his lips, and as she watched him walk away Lucy, who had been engaged with another customer, came up beside her.

'Aren't you the lucky one? He's quite something, isn't he? Where did he spring from?'

'Switzerland, so Giovanni said,' replied Tanya offhandedly. 'Apparently he needs a guide to show him tourist London.'

'And filthy rich too, from the look of him – fortunate old you! Better take care, darling. He probably swallows little girls alive.'

'He can't do much in two days,' said Tanya coolly and went back into the gallery.

Lucy was always scornful of what she called Tanya's camp followers, and more than a little envious, though she would never have admitted it. She cherished left-wing views and was fond of stating loudly – outside the gallery – that girls like Tanya from

133

rich homes ought not to be taking the bread out of the mouths of decent young women who were on the dole because they couldn't get a job.

Giovanni came back and was delighted to hear of the successful sale of one of the most valuable items in his shop.

'You did well, my dear. He could be a useful customer for the future,' he said.

'Who is he?' she asked, trying to sound casual.

'His father, or rather his stepfather, is the Baron von Richter, a German Swiss living in Zurich. He is a passionate collector and has some of the very finest examples of Byzantine art in his possession.'

'Why do you say stepfather?'

'Well, it seems that the Baron married late in life and there was a whiff of scandal about it. She was Russian, remarkably beautiful by all accounts but . . .' Giovanni made an expressive gesture.

'Do you mean she had been his mistress?'

'Perhaps, or someone else's, no one quite knows. The boy was her son. He would have been about twelve, I suppose. It was just before the war broke out, and since he had no children the Baron brought him up and educated him. I should say that Dirk von Richter has done pretty well for himself.'

'Who was his real father?'

Giovanni shrugged. 'Who knows? One of many, perhaps, but it's all old history now and he has taken very good care to adopt his stepfather's name. Nowadays no one would dream of questioning his credentials.'

So Dirk, as she had already begun to think of him, had a Russian mother, perhaps a Russian father too. If anything it added to his fascination. She meant to keep that luncheon date, and she dressed very carefully the next morning in a new suit of golden yellow silk, the pleated skirt swinging round her slim legs, with bronze shoes and handbag, and a daring Robin Hood cap with a feather that curled against the blonde hair.

'Heavens!' exclaimed Andy at breakfast when she rushed in to snatch a cup of coffee. 'Who are you trying to captivate today, the Prince of Wales?'

'It's a business lunch with one of Giovanni's clients,' she replied austerely.

'Poor fellow. He won't know what's hit him.'

'Oh, shut up, Andy,' she said crossly.

'Now, now, children, no quarrelling over your food,' said her father, glancing up from *The Times*, 'it's bad for the digestion, and for heaven's sake *eat* something, Tanya. You can't exist on half a slice of toast.'

'Can't wait. I'm late already,' she said, hurriedly gulping her coffee.

'Good hunting!' Andy called after her as she dashed out.

At the Savoy the food had been chosen with exquisite care. They drank champagne and lingered over the coffee. Afterwards, since the day was so fine, they strolled in St James's Park so that she could point out Horse Guards and Buckingham Palace. A gentle sun shining through the new leaves turned them into quivering gold, and the air seemed newly washed with the promise of summer. He talked entertainingly of a visit to Venice when the city seemed to float in an opalescent light, of the Byzantine frescoes at Rimini and the glories of Florence. He had a dry sense of humour, and a witty irreverence towards some of the artists he had met in his travels which made her laugh, so that by the time they reached the Ritz and sat drinking lemon tea they were already on intimate terms.

Everything he did had grace and perfection, she thought, swaying in his arms in a slow tango or in the floating rhythm of the waltz. The *thé dansant* which she had so often scorned seemed that afternoon to have become heaven, and it was only afterwards that she realized that though she had told him a great deal about Ravensley, about her father, about the family and Russia, he had told her nothing at all personal about himself.

With Giovanni's permission she spent the whole of the next day with him, and if anyone had told her that a walk around the Tower of London and an afternoon at the Royal Academy's Summer Exhibition would be utterly entrancing, she would have laughed at them, but so it proved.

From the first moment, perhaps even from that chance meeting in the South of France, something had happened between them, as if they met on some other planet that was different from anything

135

else. She tried to reason herself out of it and failed, feeling instead utterly desolate that the time was so short, that he would be gone and might never come back – and no one, no one at all, had any inkling that his visit and the one or two casual questions he had asked had anything at all to do with a certain Russian who was now lying in Guy's Hospital under Dr Aylsham's care, still very sick, and giving the police one or two uneasy headaches.

'Hallo, stranger,' said Diana early the following week when Tanya came into her cupboard-like dressing room at the Lantern. 'What happened to you? Craig wanted to know where you'd got to at the first reading of the new play.'

'I know. I'm sorry, but Giovanni had a very important client. I had to take him round London for a couple of days.'

'What was he like? Tall, dark and handsome, or short, fat and very, very rich?'

'Bit of both actually,' said Tanya evasively.

'You've a dreamy look about you,' said Diana, eyeing her curiously, 'rather as if you weren't quite with us. Don't let your client go to your head or else our Luke will have something to say.'

'Actually he's gone off to Paris,' said Tanya shortly, 'so there's not much chance of that. Now tell me your news. Is it good or bad?'

'Like yours, a bit of both. The Americans came on the first night, oozed charm, and said precisely nothing to the purpose. They're coming again, but in any case the whole project is shelved till next year. You need the patience of Job in this business.'

Tanya looked at her, frowning. 'But you wouldn't give it up, would you? Not even for Andy.'

Diana said slowly, 'You know what Nina says in the last act of *The Seagull*. Well, every time I speak those lines, I know it is exactly how I feel. "I am a real actress," ' she repeated softly, ' "I act with enjoyment, with enthusiasm, I am intoxicated when I'm on the stage and feel that I am splendid . . . Now I know, I understand that what matters is not fame, not glory, not what I dreamed of but knowing how to be patient, to bear one's cross and have faith and when I think of my vocation I'm not afraid of it." Oh Lord.'

She broke off suddenly. 'Listen to me carrying on. How dare I be so presumptuous? I'd better get off my soap box and shut up.'

'Let's hope Andy doesn't run off and shoot himself like poor Constantin in the play,' said Tanya drily.

'Andy's not a dreamy poet, he's a realist.'

'But he *is* half Russian.'

'Oh heavens, what are we being so idiotically gloomy about? Probably nothing will come of any of it anyway, and just look at the time. It's after seven and I'm not nearly ready. See you afterwards, darling, and then we'll let our hair down and tell each other every gory detail.'

During the next few weeks Tanya was in an uncertain, difficult mood, telling herself it was impossible to fall in love in a couple of days and yet finding everyone and everything around her flat, dull and uninteresting. Craig had decided to end the season with Shaw's *Candida* because it gave a splendid part to Barry, who was not a little jealous of Diana's great success, but even more because it gave Di an opportunity to show another side of her talent in the calm young woman who realizes that the tempestuous poet demanding her love is far more self-reliant in his artistic egoism than her big, blustering, vulnerable husband and makes her choice without hesitation. Tanya attended meetings and did what she was asked to do, but her enthusiasm had begun to wane.

There were no more cosy lunches with Luke, no more exciting expeditions in search of props, and he began to wonder unhappily whether the night after the accident, when he had confessed his love and his hopes, had driven a barrier between them which he did not know how to surmount.

The family, finding her irritable and out of humour, decided that Tanya was having one of her tantrums and left her severely alone. Andy, still poised between hope and despair, tried to tell himself that he was winning his war for Diana, and his father, usually sensitive to his children's needs, had other, more pressing preoccupations.

They had begun with the railway accident and the extraordinary coincidence that had brought him close to the Russian whose life he had helped to save, and had carried him back to those troubled years before the Revolution had split his life apart. The police, searching through the victim's pockets and finding no papers of identification and no visible means of support, questioned Dr Aylsham closely.

He answered with caution. 'Yes, it is true that I knew him once in Russia many years ago. His name is Leonid Pavlov,' he said.

A nondescript individual in plain clothes who had remained in the background during the enquiry looked up, his eyes behind his spectacles suddenly full of a sharp intelligence.

Simon knew him as Mr Brown – quiet, anonymous, unassuming, with a deceptively gentle manner. He had been interrogated by him long and patiently when he first came to England and was anxious to settle the position of his wife and half-Russian family. Whether he was from MI5 or part of Special Branch, the arm of the police that dealt with security, Simon was never quite sure.

'Pavlov?' Mr Brown repeated thoughtfully. 'I seem to have heard that name mentioned. Wasn't he quite high up in a certain section of the Party? Has this unfortunate fellow communicated with you or your family at any time, Doctor?'

'No, he has not. I'm afraid I'm as much in the dark as you are as to why he should have been on that train.'

'Forgive me,' persisted Mr Brown, 'but wasn't your wife at one time banished to Siberia by the Tsarist *Okhrana* for complicity in a political assassination?'

'She was the innocent victim of a police purge,' he said coldly. 'You must know how often that occurred.'

'And still does, I understand. Still, it could provide a link.'

'And what exactly does that mean?'

'We don't know yet, do we?'

Mr Brown's irritating calmness had the effect of making Simon feel like a fool who had allowed himself to be skilfully manipulated, and he said, 'Wouldn't it be more sensible to leave all these questions until Leonid Pavlov is well enough to answer for himself?'

'And how long is that likely to be?'

'That is something I am unable to tell you at this stage. Certainly not for some days.'

'Very well, Doctor, but we would be glad to be informed as soon as he is fit to be interviewed.'

There it had to be left. The injuries caused by the fallen railway carriage had been very severe. The thigh was shattered, and the lengthy operation necessary, coupled with his poor physical condition, brought the patient very close to death. As soon as it was practical Dr Aylsham had him removed from the small hospital in Ely to Guy's, where he could be under his own eye, and after a second operation he began very slowly to pick up a little strength.

He had been there for about a fortnight when Simon went into the private room where he was lying at police request so that he could be unobtrusively guarded.

He opened the door quietly to see Galina sitting beside the bed, the sick man's hand in hers, and a look of such tenderness on her face that just for an instant he was aware of a spasm of jealousy quickly suppressed. Not that he had any cause to doubt her love or loyalty; but there had been years when he had been trapped in his unhappy marriage and Leon had been close to her in exile in Siberia and afterwards in the same medical unit at the battlefront – years when Leon had been passionately in love with her, imploring her to marry him – years when, against all common sense, Simon had tortured himself with the question he dared not ask: had they or had they not been lovers? Once in the army hospital, when a soldier crazed with fear and hatred had tried to kill him, it was Leon who had thrown himself between them, taking in his own breast the bullets intended for him. How strange that after all these years he had in a way been able to repay that debt. Memories, memories . . . He thrust them behind him and went into the room.

'Sister tells me that you had a much better night,' he said cheerfully. 'Are you feeling stronger?'

'I'd feel a lot better without this,' Leon said wryly, passing a hand over the stubble on his chin.

'I think we could arrange that for you,' said Galina, trying to smile. It was difficult to reconcile the sick, grey-haired man in the bed with the Leon she remembered, strong as an oak, ruggedly handsome, without whose strength and companionship she could never have survived those agonizing Siberian years.

Simon drew up a chair on the other side of the bed.

'I'm being badgered by the police, and also it seems by Special Branch. They are unable to make up their minds whether you are

139

a spy or a defector with something to sell, and they badly want to ask questions.'

'I'd rather talk to you first.'

'Whenever you feel up to it. I think I can keep them at bay for a little longer.'

Leon looked from one to the other. 'Since we've been thrown together like this, I want you to know that I've not fled from my country out of cowardice and I'm not betraying my fellow Russians, it's only that . . .' He stopped, closing his eyes for a moment as if to gather strength. 'Oh God, it's so difficult to know where to start.'

Simon said gently, 'Don't exhaust yourself. Would you rather leave it till another time – tomorrow perhaps?'

'No, better get it over with. We were good friends once, even if we did both want the same woman,' he said drily. 'Galina chose wisely, Vicky was not so fortunate.'

'Where is Vicky now?'

'You don't think I'd have run and left her behind, do you?' he said harshly. 'Vicky is dead and our son with her. They died while I was in prison.'

Galina said nothing, only touched his hand, and she felt his fingers clutch hers for an instant. Vicky, the English Red Cross nurse from the London slums whose sturdy courage and sense of fun had helped to make intolerable conditions tolerable, and who had nursed Leon devotedly back to health when the bullets meant for Simon had brought him near to death.

Leon said, 'Could I have something to drink?'

Simon brought the glass of fruit juice and helped him to sit up a little, piling the pillows behind him.

'Are you sure you feel fit enough to talk? We don't want to bring back the fever.'

'I'm all right,' Leon said irritably.

It seemed then that the sick man could not be stopped, and the doctor judged it best to let him speak and relieve his mind of what troubled him. He took the glass from him and put it on the table beside the bed.

'Carry on,' he said. 'Tell us what has brought you here.'

'It's not a very edifying story.' He paused, frowning as if trying to concentrate. 'That year after you and Galina had gone, I told myself that when the war was over, when the first problems had been ironed out, then conditions *must* be better for everyone. You know well enough that I had never had any patience with the Tsar and his government and always believed the rich had had it too good for too long – present company excepted.' For an instant there was a glimpse of the old independence and dry sense of humour. 'It was a bare enough living, food was scarce and expensive, and my old parents, with whom we were living, had barely enough to keep them alive, but if you remember I did have some mining experience. Iron and coal were most desperately needed, so I was given employment in Magnitogorsk, where some American engineers had been imported. I worked along with them for a time and things seemed to go fairly well with us. Anyone with ability could work his way up if he kept his mouth shut and concentrated on the job in hand. Vicky had her baby and for a while we were even happy.'

He shut his eyes for a moment as if the memory of that lost happiness was almost unbearable.

Galina said softly, 'What happened to change it?'

He took another sip of the orange juice and braced himself to go on.

'It's strange, isn't it, how slow one is to realize what conditions are really like for others when you are living in comparative comfort. You wilfully blind yourself. It took some time before I knew how impossible it was to improve production when the workers were living in hell – hopelessly undernourished, appalling sanitary conditions, frightful living quarters, filthy and bug-ridden, no medical care of any kind. Was it any wonder that they died quicker than flies and no one cared? Why worry when there were always more slave workers brought in from the labour camps? Thousands, millions perhaps, driven from the rural districts because of this insane scheme to turn the peasant holdings into collective farms, were being herded into cattle trucks. Hundreds of them froze to death or died from starvation before they even reached their destinations. On our own sites they were fatally injured because there was never enough time to set up proper safeguards on the machinery. I saw it every day and it began to sicken me. I spoke out against it. I wrote letters of protest. I went to Moscow myself to plead with the authorities. Vicky begged me to keep my big mouth shut but now it had become impossible. You see, I had not yet fully realized that the whole system was riddled with spies reporting to the secret police. I had been too successful. There were plenty who were envious, and it was so easy. You remember, Galina, how we hated the *Okhrana*, those slimy Tsarist police, but then we didn't know about the *Cheka*, the GPU. It no longer mattered what you did, but who you were, and your father before you. Every action, every idle word, was reported. Within a few weeks I was arrested and sent to a labour camp while Vicky and our four-year-old son were forced to leave our tiny apartment and live as best they could.'

He paused and stared in front of him, not knowing how to tell them of the horror of that labour camp, so far from the clinically clean room, from the two friends who seemed to have been living in another world. How describe the all-pervading filth, the stench, the bloated rats, the camp food, thin vegetable soup, sometimes carrots, sometimes black cabbage, sometimes simply groats and when times were particularly bad shredded nettles, a bread ration strictly rationed by each man's quota of work done, bread often snatched by the strong from the weak, brutal clubbings for those too sick to crawl to their work shift, the firing squad for those who shirked or rebelled?

He bit it back, swallowed hard, and went on.

'I was there for five years, and one day the news filtered through that Vicky and our boy had died in the plague that raged through Magnitogorsk. After that I no longer cared whether I lived till the next morning or not, and ironically it was then that I was taken out of the work crew and brought before the Camp Commandant.

'"I understand you have some training as an engineer," he said, "so it has been decided that you can be of more use in that capacity than here. It could mean a job, new clothes, decent living quarters."

'By then I knew too well what such promises were worth. "What do I have to do for such rewards?" I asked cynically. "You work for the State, isn't that enough?" was the reply.

'That day I was allowed to scrub off the prison grime under the ice-cold water of the pump. I was given clothing still stained with the blood of the latest victim to be shot, but at that moment I would have done anything, made a pact with the devil himself, rather than go back to the dreary hell of the camp. I didn't know what was going to be demanded of me.'

He was silent for a moment before he forced himself to go on. 'I was taken to the Lubianka in Moscow, the offices of the GPU. I had no trust in the promises given to me, and I was right. I was told what I had to do. I would be working under the head of the section, and one of my duties, apart from the work quota, was to spy on him. Every chance remark, every word spoken even when drunk, every girl he bedded, all must be included in my weekly report. You see, that is the system. Everyone, no matter who they are, is set to spy on another so that every action, every slightest word spoken in anger or exasperation, holds danger and such old-fashioned notions as trust, loyalty, affection, love, no longer have any meaning.'

He lay back wearily against his pillows. 'You think I exaggerate, that these are the fancies of a sick man, but I swear to God it is the truth.'

Simon said gently, 'I think I know you well enough not to doubt that. What did you do?'

'Oh, they were very clever. I was not the first, and it isn't difficult to persuade those who have been through the nightmare of a labour camp. Why is it, Simon, that when there is a revolution for good, worthy reasons, when men work for it with sincere and honest idealism, that all the scum rise to the surface and the honest, the decent, are their hopeless victims?'

'I can't answer that question any more easily than you can,' said Simon slowly. 'I suppose it comes out of uncertainty. It is basically fear, fear for the future, fear of losing what they have won at such a terrible cost.'

'Perhaps you're right. All I know is that by then I cared nothing for any of the ideals I had once cherished. Vicky and our son had gone, so I had nothing more to lose. I agreed to their demands and thought to myself that I would do it in my own way. I'd lie in my reports, I'm make sure the information I passed on could do no harm to anyone; but after a few months it didn't work. They were cleverer than I was; they guessed what I was doing and set someone to spy on me. It was like being caught up in a sticky spider's web of deceit from which you can never break free – the more you struggle, the more you are entangled. The man I worked with was decent enough. He invited me to his rooms, he gave me privileges, and to deceive him, to report his every word, sickened me. Who can guard their tongue day and night, drunk or sober? The only way I could fight my way out of the tissue of lies was to escape, even though I risked death at every step. It was worth the danger to feel clean again.'

'How long ago was that?'

'It was the end of March when the ice begins to break up. There were terrible floods. I joined one of the rescue parties and after a day or so contrived to get lost. With any luck I have been reported drowned with a great many others.'

Perhaps that was true, though Simon doubted it. Too much interest was already being shown in Leon. He had obviously once held a more important position in the Party network than he had confessed to, and Stalin, who had held the country in an iron grip ever since Lenin's death, could not let one of their own escape his clutches without punishment. Leon could be in great danger, but he would have to let that pass for the time being. Surely here in the hospital he would be safe enough.

He smiled encouragingly. 'It must have been a devil of a journey across Europe.'

'It was. I walked most of the way. It's the easiest thing to do if you've no papers and little money. There are homeless people everywhere and it's extraordinary how you are accepted. I lived rough. I worked for food when I could. I starved more often than not. I was sick for two weeks lying in a peasant's barn, and the farmer's wife cared for me as tenderly as if I'd been her brother.' He smiled wryly. 'It took away some of the bitterness, restored a little of my lost faith in humanity. I got a passage in a ship by signing on as part of the crew, and the little I earned was stolen by my bunk mate. I stowed away on that train knowing only that it was bound for London, and trusting to luck to escape detection. An accident was the last thing I thought of.'

'You must have known you could always come to us,' murmured Galina reproachfully.

'It's twelve years ago, Galina. You are rich, established, well known – Lady Aylsham, eh? Like a whiff of the old days, isn't it? How did I know what you would feel? I didn't want to come to you as a beggar.'

'Don't speak like that, Leon,' she said. 'Friends are for life, for good times and for bad. It breaks my heart to hear how much you have suffered.'

'It wasn't all bad,' he said wearily. 'Perhaps I was simply unlucky, perhaps I found it too hard to conform. All those weeks when I was tramping through rain and sun, on good roads and on bad, I thought perhaps I can tell them something of it, make them understand how much our people are suffering, but would they listen, would they care?'

'Some will,' said Simon, 'but it's too vast for outsiders to comprehend. Russia must find her own solution. And now, I'm afraid, I'm going to play the physician. No more talking, no more distressing yourself over what you cannot alter.' He got to his feet. 'Rest is what you need if you're going to recover your health and your strength.'

Leon's face was grey with fatigue, but a little of the torment had gone out of his eyes. Simon eased him back against the pillows.

'I'm going to send Sister with something that will help you to sleep. Tomorrow perhaps we can talk again. We can begin to think to the future.'

Leon said nothing, but he caught at Galina's hand and kissed it as she drew the bed covers over him. She smiled and touched his cheek gently before she went out with her husband.

They had read of it in the newspapers and tales had filtered through from time to time, but to hear the story, raw and authentic, from someone who had once been so close to them made it painfully real. Simon knew it had distressed Galina greatly. It was still her country, to which she was bound by so many ties. Her mother still lived there, and there were other dear friends who had vanished. Only a few years before, when the Quakers had organized a mission to carry food and medicines to the worst hit areas around Kiev and in the Ukraine, he had had great difficulty in preventing her from going with them. Too much publicity had been given to their escape, he pointed out, and to return would be more likely to endanger the brave missionaries than help them.

For the time being he judged it wise to say little about Leon, even among the family and close friends. Only Andy, working with his father at the hospital, knew who he was, why he was there and something of what he had gone through. So it was he who

145

telephoned his father very late one night only a couple of days after Leon had told them his story.

It was about two o'clock in the morning when the telephone rang beside the bed, and Simon, long accustomed to emergency calls, was instantly awake and quietly dealing with it.

'Andy here, Father. Could you come? It's Leon.'

'What's the trouble?'

'Difficult to say. I'd rather you were here.'

'Very well. I'll be with you as soon as I can.'

He put the telephone down and slid quietly out of the bed. Galina stirred sleepily.

'What is it?'

'Emergency call from Guy's. I'll have to go. No need for you to worry, my dear. Go back to sleep.'

He dressed quickly and went out to where the car was always kept readily available. Traffic at that hour in the morning was light and he was soon at the hospital. Andy was waiting for him.

'What's wrong?' Simon asked quickly. 'Is he dead?'

'No, fortunately, but you will see.'

The room looked as if a hurricane had blown through it – tables and chairs overturned, water and smashed glass on the floor, with medical equipment thrown down and broken.

'We found him half out of the bed and in a pretty bad way, but I don't think he is seriously hurt. I've given him an injection just to make sure.'

The police guard had his own explanation to offer.

'It was about one o'clock, sir,' he said, 'and I'd settled down for the night. A man came along the corridor. I assumed he was one of the doctors on his usual nightly round. I don't know them all by sight. He nodded to me and went in. I thought nothing of it until suddenly there was a crash. I rushed in. The patient was half out of the bed and struggling violently with the fellow in the white coat. There must have been quite a battle. When he saw me the man tore himself free, muttered something, and was gone out of the room before I could stop him. I raised the alarm but no one had seen him. He had vanished as if he'd never existed.'

It was easy to understand, of course. At that hour of the night no one would have questioned the white-coated figure quietly going about the sleeping hospital. Emergencies on the wards could arise at any hour and had to be dealt with by whoever was on duty.

Andy held up the shattered remains of a hypodermic needle.

'He must have stepped on it as he escaped. Easy to guess what it contained. Leon would have been dead in a matter of seconds. God knows how he managed to fight him off.' They looked at one another. 'Did you expect something like this might happen, Pa?'

'I thought it possible, but not so soon and not here.'

The Special Branch man said, 'I've put a call through to Headquarters, Doctor. They should be here any moment now. With your permission it would be best if this is thought to be just an ordinary medical emergency in the patient's condition.'

'Yes, yes, I understand. I'll make sure the staff are kept in the dark as to what has really happened.'

The man in the spectacles and with the quietly authoritative manner arrived and unobtrusively took complete charge of the proceedings.

When Leon had recovered sufficiently to be interrogated, questions were asked and there were lengthy discussions behind closed doors. Not a word leaked out to the press, only a discreet four-line paragraph to the effect that yet another victim of the railway disaster had unfortunately died, bringing the total of dead to a distressing seventeen.

'Let them believe they have succeeded in their dirty work,' Mr Brown told Simon. 'In that way this poor fellow should be out of danger at least for the time being. But what are we to do with him in the meantime? That's the awkward question.'

'May I make a suggestion? As you no doubt know, I have a country place in a fairly remote part of the Fens. Speaking medically, what he needs is at least a couple of months of quiet convalescence. He could spend it there in any way he likes.'

Mr Brown eyed him speculatively. 'It's just possible it could be dangerous for you.'

'I've lived with danger before now.'

'It would certainly help us.'

'If your people will co-operate, it can be arranged from this end.'

'Very well. I think I can safely say we will do all we can, and we are obliged to you, Doctor.' He smiled thinly. 'Or should I say my lord?'

'I think we can dispense with those formalities.'

So 'the body' was removed, ostensibly to the mortuary, but in actual fact to Wimpole Street, under Galina's care, and then the following week to Ravensley. The staff were informed that the sick gentleman was a distant cousin of her ladyship who had fled out of that barbarous country.

'And after all who could blame him?' remarked Mrs Alison to Jake, who was helping her prepare the big sunny room on the first floor. 'You know all about that, don't you, Mr Starling?'

He nodded gravely. 'I do indeed, Mrs A. I've never ceased to feel grateful that the Master got away when he did.'

Not that Leon submitted without a very determined protest.

'Once I'm able to walk I can look after myself,' he said. 'I didn't come here to put you and Galina into any kind of danger.'

'You're not going to be able to walk except with extreme difficulty for at least another three months,' said Simon firmly. 'In fact, though I don't want to depress you, you're probably going to limp for the rest of your life.'

Raging against his helplessness, Leon's strongly independent spirit rose up in rebellion, and it took all Galina's tact and diplomacy to persuade him to listen to reason.

'Why is Father making such a fuss over this Russian?' said Tanya discontentedly to Andy a week or two later when they were both at Ravensley for the weekend. 'He even hinted that I might shift out of my bedroom because it is nearer to the kitchens and easier for Alice to carry up meals.'

'And you refused, I suppose?'

'Well, I didn't really see why I should.'

They were in the stable yard and the horses had already been brought out. Andy finished tightening the girths of Blackie's saddle before he turned to her.

'You're a selfish little beast, aren't you, Tanya? Never a thought for anyone but yourself.'

'That's not fair.'

'Yes it is. As a matter of fact Leon is a very decent chap. I saw quite a lot of him in Petersburg when I was a boy. He used to tell me about his work. If things had turned out differently he and Galina might have been married.'

'So that's why she moons over him like she does. I knew there was something,' said Tanya triumphantly. 'I wonder Pa puts up with it.'

Andy turned on her furiously. 'That's a perfectly loathsome thing to say. I don't know what's wrong with you lately, but you've been pretty unbearable to live with, and I'm not the only one to think so. What the hell do you think you're doing to Luke?'

'I'm not doing anything, so far as I know,' she retorted, 'and I'll thank you not to discuss me with him. If there is anything he doesn't like, let him say it to me, not go whining to you.'

She swung herself into the saddle without waiting for his helping hand and went clattering out of the gate and down the drive, angry with herself, knowing that she had behaved badly and that Andy was perfectly right, yet unable to stop herself hitting out at everything around her simply because the man she had fallen for, the one man she had ever passionately wanted, that charming, intriguing, fascinating Dirk von Richter, had disappeared as she had known he would without a word or sign. Surely if those hours they had spent together, the looks between them, that one long passionate kiss, had meant anything to him at all, he would have written, he would have done something, not just left days and weeks of utter blankness between them.

She rode for a couple of hours till she was weary and Rags was sweating badly, then came back in chastened mood. She unsaddled the mare, rubbed her down, and then went in to wash and change for luncheon before going in search of her father.

She found him in the library hunting for something and slipped her arm through his as she had done when she was still a little girl.

'I'm sorry I was such a pig, Papa. You can put your Russian into my room if you like. I'll ask Alice to help me move out all my things.'

He looked down at her, smiling because it was so like Tanya to blow up and then repent.

'That's very generous of you, pet, but there is no need. It's all settled, and perhaps he is better where he is, tucked away in that wing of the house. He won't be up and about for a good while yet. I know we haven't told you much about it, but the fact is that I

149

didn't want you children to be involved. He and I were very good friends once. We went through some pretty bad times together during the war and afterwards. He has lost his wife and son and a great deal more than that, faith and loyalty all betrayed while we have been lucky. Sometimes, you know, you have to pay for the good things life has given you.' He turned back to the shelves. 'I really must do something about getting things sorted out in here. I know I had some Russian books somewhere that Leon might like to have. Come and help me look for them.'

Later they went into luncheon arm in arm, and Galina saw them laughing together and was thankful. She knew how close was the bond between father and daughter and would never willingly do anything to endanger it. Andy joined them, the temporary rift between them forgotten, but Tanya's restless mood remained and led to a consequence no one could have foreseen.

9

'Di, have you had an invite to Ollie's birthday party next week?' asked Tanya a few days later, calling in to a rehearsal at the Lantern.

Diana looked up from the script she was studying. 'As a matter of fact I have, but I'm not going.'

'Why ever not? It could be fun.'

'For one thing it's on a Saturday and I couldn't get there till nearly midnight, and for another I never could stand Olivia Winter even at school. Silly little ninny, and now she dyes her hair bright pink and goes swanning around Europe as a model when Daddy is so beastly rich she doesn't need to lift her little finger.'

'Well, I think I shall go,' said Tanya and suddenly giggled. 'I know. I'll take Luke.'

'I shouldn't imagine it's his kind of thing at all,' objected Diana, 'and anyway you can't gatecrash.'

'Yes I can. Olivia will never notice and Luke will go anywhere with me if I ask him.'

'You really are a hard-hearted little bitch, aren't you?'

'Now don't you start. I had Andy on at me at the weekend. I like Luke – I like him very much – but I can't help it if I'm not in love with him,' she said defiantly.

'Maybe not, but just because you know he'd lie down and willingly let you trample all over him is no reason why you should make use of him.'

'I don't do any such thing,' said Tanya indignantly. 'And Luke is not nearly so easy-going as you seem to think.'

'I'm very glad to hear it.'

'Anyway you can't talk. What about you and Andy?'

'That's different,' said Diana austerely. 'I only hope you don't regret this party, that's all. I don't trust Ollie and her gang not to

151

go a great deal too far. Now beetle off, I'm busy.' She went back to studying her script.

It was a beautiful July evening, warm and very still, the setting sun gilding the sky and sending long slanting rays across the windscreen as they drove down through Slough and Maidenhead to Henley. At first Luke had been pleasantly surprised when Tanya asked him to go with her, and then doubts began to creep in.

'I don't know this friend of yours. She will be wondering who the devil I am,' he protested.

'No she won't, she'll probably never even notice. There'll be a fearful crowd, I expect, but it's a gorgeous spot on the river. You'll love it. Oh, do come, Luke darling. I don't seem to have been anywhere exciting for ages. Don't be a spoilsport.'

She was very appealing and persuasive and he always found her difficult to resist, so rather reluctantly he gave in.

It certainly was a charming setting, a Queen Anne house with its white walls festooned with creeper and climbing roses, long windows opening on to lawns that ran down to the water's edge, the gardens scented with flowers and bespangled with coloured lanterns, the long silvery stretches of the Thames shaded here and there by gigantic willows. To start with it was almost too perfect – long tables loaded with delicious food, white-coated waiters everywhere with trays of champagne and other, more exotic drinks, an orchestra playing dreamily, the dancers spilling out from the drawing room on to the closely shaved grass.

Tanya was effusively welcomed by a young woman looking rather like a mermaid in a tight silver sequinned dress that revealed far more than it covered.

'You don't mind me bringing Luke with me, do you, Ollie?' murmured Tanya.

'Course not, darling. Wow!' she drawled, looking up admiringly at Luke from her five foot two inches. 'How I do lurve the strong silent type!'

Then with a giggle and a heady wave of perfume she had floated off to greet the next arrivals.

It felt wonderful to be dancing with Tanya again, to hold her in his arms, her fair head close to his, whispering intimately together, laughing at their own particular jokes. She had always been unpredictable. Perhaps he had been mistaken in believing her cold and withdrawn from him. The evening promised to be far more pleasant than he had anticipated. The enchantment lasted till just after midnight when two loaded cars came thundering up the drive and a party of girls and young men spilled out of them, charging across the lawns, singing raucously at the tops of their voices, and waving huge coloured balloons.

'Cecil!' shrieked Ollie, flinging herself into the arms of the ringleader. 'I thought you were never coming.'

'Never say die, duckie, till the last minute. Didn't I promise, and here I am large as life. Came on from another party further down river. Meet my pals!' and he waved his hand expansively at the group who had gathered behind him.

The musicians had stopped playing, the dancers stood still, staring, and Cecil glanced around him.

'What the devil's going on, Ollie? Thought it was a birthday party not an Irish wake. Come on, chaps, let's put some pep into it!'

It was extraordinary what a very short time it took for the peace and tranquillity of the evening to be wrecked. The very same people who had been quietly sipping drinks and sedately dancing were suddenly turned into wild-eyed lunatics shrieking with laughter, chasing each other through the gardens, indulging in ridiculous practical jokes, grabbing at the balloons and bursting them. Presently, with Cecil acting as leader they had formed up into a long snake-like line dancing the conga through the drawing room, up the stairs, in and out of the corridors of the old house, leaving overturned chairs and smashed ornaments in their wake, glasses and dishes of food swept off the long tables as they surged heedlessly by.

They went charging down to the river, some of them piling into a couple of punts which they launched unsteadily into midstream, someone dangerously wielding the long pole, until one of the girls fell in, screaming in terror, while the others fell over one another helpless with laughter. It was left to Luke to wade into the water up to his knees to drag her out, slimy weed caught up in the long hair and twisted round the naked shoulders. She burst into

153

hysterical sobs as he took her back to the house and gave her over to the care of one of the housemaids.

When he came back they were dancing again, but he had lost sight of Tanya. She was nowhere among the couples, and he went back into the house to hunt for her, flinging open doors one after the other. In a quiet sitting room an elderly couple looked up and gave him a tentative smile. They must be Ollie's parents, and he wondered what they thought of the goings-on downstairs. He slammed another door hastily at the sight of the naked couple grappling together on the bed, his heart missing a beat as he glimpsed the fair head. Thank God it wasn't Tanya! Everything that was most puritanical in him rose up in revolt. He was not staying in this house another minute and neither was Tanya. He'd make damned sure of that.

He found her at last in the drawing room, which had become a temporary oasis of quiet. The band was playing softly, the theme song from *Bittersweet*, and she was sitting among them singing it very quietly. In his relief the small dreamy voice went immediately to his heart. He waited till it was finished, then he went across to her, putting an arm round her waist and kissing her on the cheek.

'That was lovely, darling, and now let's get out of here.'

'I can't go without saying goodbye to Ollie.'

'Yes you can. Let's go.'

He took her hand but, before they could move, Cecil had grabbed hold of him and dragged him away from her.

'Oh no you don't, Welsh boy. You're not Tanya's keeper. She belongs with us.'

'Like hell she does. Get out of my way.'

He gave Cecil a violent push that sent him reeling back against one of the bandsmen and picked Tanya up, pushing his way through the guests who stood staring, carrying her across the lawns to the drive and dumping her in the seat of her little red car.

But he wasn't quite quick enough. Before he could get round to the other side, Cecil was there and had climbed in beside her. She tried to push him out but he would not budge.

Luke seized him by the shoulders, but two young men who had followed Cecil pulled him away, giggling like maniacs.

'I'm going home,' screamed Tanya defiantly, 'so if you must come, you can jolly well walk back.'

Luke just had time to scramble into the dickey seat behind them before the car shot off, while Cecil's two pals piled into the one behind and accelerated after them.

He didn't think he would ever forget that nightmare journey. They were a mile or so outside Henley, and they roared down the country road in the pitch darkness and thundered through the little sleeping town. They careered over the old stone bridge and up the long steep hill past dark overhanging trees. Fortunately at two o'clock on a Sunday morning there was little traffic on the roads, but Tanya was driving much too fast and at the same time trying to fend off Cecil, who was drunkenly giggling, his arm round her shoulders, his face nuzzling into her neck.

It was in Maidenhead Thicket that the accident happened. The road was closely wooded on either side, which made it very dark. There was some kind of obstruction ahead. The narrow beam of the headlights picked it out. Tanya swerved to avoid it just as Cecil tried to kiss her. She took a hand from the steering wheel to thrust him off, and round the bend came another car. She saw it a second too late, and there was a deafening crash as she ripped along the side of it and bounced off. The impact threw her forward into the splintered windscreen. The car behind struck them in the back, smashing the rear lights and nearly throwing Luke out. His wrist cracked as he hung on trying to steady himself.

For a moment the shock held them all paralysed. Then the two in the car behind tumbled out and Luke leaped over the side and went at once to Tanya. She was slumped over the wheel and he realized she had been knocked unconscious. Cecil, white-faced and badly bruised, was staring stupidly at the blood running down her face and at the glass that was scattered everywhere. His two friends, quickly sobered by the realization of what had happened and what it could mean for all of them, grabbed hold of him and pulled him out.

'Come on, let's get out of here.'

'We can't, we can't leave her, supposing she's dead?' he said helplessly and began to cry.

'All the more reason to get away. Don't be a damned fool. It wasn't your fault. Let someone else deal with it and take the rap.'

'You can't go, not like that,' exclaimed Luke, appalled.

'You'll be all right,' shouted one of them callously. 'We'll stop in Maidenhead. Tell the police. Send someone back.'

They bundled Cecil into their own car, and before Luke could stop them had roared away into the dark night.

He took hold of Tanya and as gently as he could eased her into the passenger seat. She was bleeding profusely from a deep cut on her forehead, and he took out his handkerchief, folded it into a pad, and fixed it temporarily with the jewelled bandeau she had tied around her head.

There were no houses nearby, nowhere at all where he could go for help. He fought down a rising panic and went to the other car. The driver, a middle-aged man, had fallen across the wheel, his body horribly twisted, only one side of his face exposed. Luke had a dreadful conviction that he was dead, and then what would happen to Tanya when the police arrived?

He stood still for a moment, trying to decide what to do for the best. Should he walk on, look for a house and a telephone, or should he stay and hope the others had done what they said they would do? He had come back to Tanya and was taking her limp hand in his when he heard a car coming. The road was partly blocked and the driver pulled up and got out.

'Well, you've got yourself into a pretty pickle,' he said, coming towards Luke. 'What are you going to do about it?'

'What *can* I do?' He hesitated. 'There was another car. They said they would contact the police.'

'And an ambulance, I hope, you look as if you need one.' He peered at Tanya. 'Is she all right?'

'I don't know. It seems to have knocked her out.'

The man went across to the other car, raised the driver's head, and made a brief examination.

'Well, I'm no doctor, but I should say that chap is in a pretty bad way. Don't like to shift him without expert advice.' He came back to Luke. 'Look, I'll go and make damned sure someone comes back. You look pretty ragged yourself. Want some brandy? I have a flask.'

'No, better not, thanks all the same.'

'Perhaps you're right.' He clapped a hand on Luke's shoulder. 'Take it easy, son. I'll do what I can.'

There was another agonizing wait, then thankfully an ambulance, siren screaming, came rolling down the road followed closely by a police car.

It was an infinite relief to let the experts take over. The ambulance men were very efficient. The stretchers came out and Tanya was placed gently on one of them. It took longer to extricate the other driver and he groaned as they raised him. At least he was still alive.

'Where are you taking them?' asked Luke.

'Maidenhead. You all right, sir?'

He had forgotten about himself. Now suddenly he realized how badly bruised he was, and the throbbing pain of his sprained wrist.

'I'll do.'

'Right you are. We'll be off. Sooner we get this lot to the hospital the better.'

They drove away at top speed, and then the police took over, asking who they were, where they were going, and where they had come from.

'Templecombe Manor, did you say?' The two policemen exchanged glances. It seemed that Ollie's wild parties were already known to them.

'Were you driving the car, sir?'

He had to make an instant decision. Supposing the other man died? He had a vision of Tanya being interrogated, heavily fined, sent to prison perhaps. The police were hard on reckless drivers. It had happened once or twice before.

'Yes,' he said quickly, 'yes, I was,' and knew he had committed himself.

'Licence, please.'

'I – I haven't one.'

'Not with you or none at all.'

'None at all, I'm afraid.'

'I see.' The policeman shut his notebook with a snap. 'You'd better come back to the station with me. We can take all the particulars there, and we'll have to see about these cars being shifted. This way, sir.'

An hour later he was still at the police station going over the details and racked with anxiety about Tanya. He had said nothing about Cecil or his friends. He could not bring himself to describe

157

the disgusting pawing at Tanya which had played a large part in causing the accident, especially as it was not they who had informed the police. They had taken very good care not to be implicated in any way, and he felt a burning resentment at the callousness that had left him with two gravely injured people to face the consequences alone.

A policewoman brought him a cup of tea from the canteen and spoke to the officer in charge.

'We've got through to Lord Aylsham, sir. Luckily he is in London this weekend. He is coming down. He should be here within the hour. We're still trying to contact the other driver's wife.'

Luke looked from one to the other. 'Could I go to the hospital? Could I wait there? I'd like to know how seriously Miss Aylsham is hurt.'

'I don't see why not. You know her father, do you, young man? Well, you'll have to face up to him some time, I suppose.' He nodded to the young woman. 'Find a driver, will you, to run Mr Jones up to the hospital.'

The night wore on and the waiting seemed to stretch endlessly. He had made a rash statement, had accepted responsibility, and that was the end of it, but he still had to face Tanya's father. It did not make it any easier. He was sitting in the draughty hall with still another cup of tea when Simon Aylsham came down the stairs, and he went to meet him.

'How is she?' Luke asked.

'Not too bad – a great number of bruises and cuts, a suspected cracked rib and a nasty case of concussion. We can't be quite sure, but I don't think it will be too serious. She is coming round now but can't remember anything about it. However, that's quite common in cases like this. She will have to stay here for a few days, I'm afraid. How about you?'

'Only my wrist. They've bound it up for me.'

'I gather from the police that you were driving, Luke. Why was that?'

He realized suddenly that enmeshing oneself in lies had unforeseen pitfalls. Tanya's father would not be easy to deceive, but once he had started he had no option but to stick to his story.

'Tanya wasn't feeling well,' he improvised, 'so I offered to take over. I have driven occasionally, you know, for fun, when we've been down at Ravensley.'

'Have you?' Dr Aylsham was frowning at him. 'Tanya wasn't drunk, was she?'

'No,' he said indignantly. 'Neither of us had had more than a glass or two of champagne.'

'I see. What happened?'

'It was very dark. I had to overtake. He came round a bend pretty fast and I must have misjudged the distance. I'm desperately sorry.'

'It's a serious offence driving without a licence. You could be prosecuted.'

'I didn't think about that.'

'No. I don't suppose you did, nor that you were likely to be involved in an accident,' said Simon Aylsham drily. 'We must be thankful that it is no worse.'

'What about the other driver? No one here will tell me anything about him.'

'He's not so good. Badly damaged a couple of ribs when he was thrown against the wheel, a broken leg as well as severe concussion.'

'He won't die . . .'

'I should say that's very unlikely. I don't think you need have that on your conscience.' He put a hand on Luke's shoulder. 'Cheer up, lad. I'm driving back to London. You had better come with me. There's nothing more that I can do here for the time being, and I've made sure that Tanya is in good hands.'

They didn't talk much in the car. Reaction had set in and Luke felt desperately tired.

Dr Aylsham said once, 'I was not aware that you knew Olivia Winter.'

'I don't, but Tanya asked me to go with her when Diana and Andy cried off.'

'I suppose it's old-fashioned, but I can't say I care very much for the kind of crowd she goes around with. If I'd known Tanya was going I might have put my foot down and forbidden it.'

Luke gave him a quick glance. 'Forgive me, sir, but would she have listened to you?'

'Oh, she does sometimes take notice of what I say.'

Simon dropped Luke at his lodgings.

'Don't worry about it too much. We'll get through it somehow,' he said kindly enough before he drove away.

Luke climbed wearily up the two flights of stairs with a strong feeling that he had played the fool and got himself into a tight corner that was going to prove difficult to get out of. Just how very tight it was he didn't realize till a day later, when he saw the newspaper headlines and his precarious world began to collapse about him.

A local reporter who had a nose for a good story happened to be at the hospital that night on another case. The ex-debutante daughter of Lord Aylsham in a smash-up with her Welsh miner boyfriend coming from one of those riotously dashing upper-class parties that were always in the news like the Astors' at Cliveden – it was all too good to be true! It was his chance to send it through to a London daily before anyone else could snatch it from him. With no national crisis looming on the horizon it got a good spread in the popular press and even a paragraph in *The Times*, spiced by the fact that the delinquent boyfriend had been the scholar of the year at London University. Was this the way, they hinted reproachfully, that he wasted his time and the taxpayers' money, careering through the country roads in the middle of the night without any heed for the safety of decent citizens? Much was made of the unfortunate victim, father of four, seriously ill, likely to be crippled for life while the wretched cause of this unnecessary accident went scot free.

The melodramatic language might almost have been laughable if the results had not been so serious.

The first frosty reaction came from the headmaster of the small private school when Luke went back for the last week of term. It was made very clear to him that such behaviour could not be tolerated in one of their teachers. What parents would be willing to entrust their precious darlings to the care of such an irresponsible young man? The suggestion already discussed that he might continue in the autumn was quietly dropped.

The question of his bursary, which still had a year to run, hung in the balance. Some university dons held puritanical views. His case would be considered, but he would be very fortunate to escape with a severe reprimand.

He worried more about what his mother would feel, her shock and disappointment, the neighbours bringing the newspapers, gloating over the spicier details, pointing out that it was only to be expected of him, abandoning a decent upbringing and hankering after the fleshpots of high society.

Dai rang him up that very night, his voice crackling over the public telephone.

'Didn't I warn you what would happen, Luke boy? But you wouldn't listen, would you? This is what comes of mixing with people out of your own class. I knew it from the start. She's no good to you. Didn't Megan tell you the same thing? What do you think they're saying in Tredegar? All nudging one another, pleased as punch. That Luke Jones, going to the bad he is, too big for his boots, always was, thought himself so grand, a cut above the rest of us, and now likely as not to end up in prison. How do you think Ma likes it, and the girls . . .?' On and on he went until Luke, exasperated, cut him short.

'For God's sake, Dai, I wasn't drunk and I haven't murdered anyone yet, so shut up about it, will you?' And he slammed the receiver down.

It was sheeting with rain on the day he was summoned to attend the Magistrates' Court at Reading. He went down by train and trudged through the streaming streets. It was one of those grey mornings when England forgets it is supposed to have a summer. The waiting room was cold and cheerless with stained green walls. There were other people sitting there looking unhappy. His feet in his thin shoes were damp and he felt chilled and depressed. In the court he took the oath and answered the questions fired at him as briefly as he could, wondering grimly if he was committing perjury and what the punishment was likely to be if he were found out.

The Magistrate looked at him severely over his rimless glasses. 'When you say your companion was feeling unwell, do you mean that she was drunk?'

'No,' he said angrily. 'No, I don't. Neither of us was drunk.'

He was furious at the implication and afraid that in the eyes of the press and the public his denial would not be believed, though, to do them justice, the police had not implied any such thing.

'You are an educated young man, a graduate of a notable university,' went on the Magistrate. 'You should be providing an example to others not so fortunate as yourself, not flouting the law in this irresponsible fashion. You are extremely fortunate that the man you have wantonly injured is now making a recovery. You will be fined one hundred pounds for driving without a licence and to the public danger, and let it be a lesson to you for the future.'

He drew a deep breath. He hadn't known what to expect, but one hundred pounds was a stunning blow. How in the world was he ever going to pay it?

Afterwards he sought out the Clerk of the Court. He had to make it clear that it would be paid somehow even if it had to be done in instalments, but he must be given time.

The Clerk, a dried-up stick of a man, anxious to get out to his lunch, looked him up and down disparagingly.

'The fine is paid,' he said and shut up his book.

'Paid? But it can't be. Paid by whom?'

'How should I know? It was handed to me in cash, and you are very lucky, young man, to have someone generous enough to pay for your wilful folly. Now good morning to you.'

He took up his books and papers and walked away, leaving Luke breathless, not knowing whether he was grateful or angry. It could only be one person, of course; it had to be Tanya's father. All his pride rose up in rebellion. He couldn't accept it, especially not from him. This was *his* affair; he had taken it upon himself and, however difficult, he would settle it in his own way.

He had been tempted to stop at Maidenhead on his way home and ask to see Tanya. In the last weeks he had sent her flowers and written a note. He had rung the hospital every day to ask how she was, but however much he longed to see her he must talk to her father first.

Back in London he telephoned Wimpole Street and spoke to Lady Aylsham.

'The doctor is not here, Luke. He has gone down to fetch Tanya. They are allowing her to come home today. They should be back by early evening. Come and dine with us if you wish.'

'Thank you, but no. I'd like to come afterwards if I may.'

'Yes, of course. I expect we shall put Tanya to bed as soon as

162

she arrives, but my husband will be here if you want to talk to him.'

He guessed that she knew what had happened that day, for when he called about nine o'clock he was not shown into the drawing room as usual but into the room where the doctor saw his patients. It was handsomely furnished with deep red leather armchairs, a fine antique desk and a glass-fronted Sheraton bookcase against the wall. A silver tray with bottles and decanters stood on a small table by the desk.

'Ah, Luke,' said Simon Aylsham cheerfully when he came in. 'I'm glad you've called. I want to talk to you. Would you like a drink?'

'No thank you.' He stood obstinately defiant and came bluntly to the point. 'It was you, wasn't it, who paid that fine today?'

'Yes, it was. I sent Jake with what I hoped would be sufficient to cover it, and in actual fact my guess was pretty nearly right.'

'You shouldn't have done it,' Luke burst out. 'It was my affair. I can pay my own debts. I don't need to beg from anyone.'

'Very well. If you feel so strongly about it, you can pay me back. Shall we say a pound a week? Now sit down, Luke, for heaven's sake, and don't stand there glowering at me like an avenging angel.' He poured two small drinks and pushed the glass of whisky across the table. 'Drink that, and when you have calmed down, perhaps you'll tell me the truth for once. It was not you who was driving that car that night, was it?'

'Why do you ask?' he mumbled, taken aback.

'Tanya has begun to remember. Today she saw for the first time one of the newspapers describing the case and she is extremely upset. She remembers quite clearly leaving Templecombe Manor, she remembers Cecil being offensive to her in the car, but after that everything has become a blank. Now you're not going to tell me that you forced the car to stop, got rid of Cecil and his friends somehow, and then took over the wheel yourself, are you?'

It sounded ridiculous, and he knew he couldn't keep up the lie in face of the grey eyes watching him steadily.

'No, no, it wasn't like that.'

'Good. Now we've got that out of the way perhaps you'll be good enough to tell me exactly what *did* happen.'

'I suppose I must,' he muttered reluctantly.

'Certainly you must. Now come on, boy, stop spinning fairy tales.'

'All right.' Very briefly he sketched in what had happened at the party, how Cecil had pursued them, and how he and his two pals had vanished at the crucial moment. 'I couldn't tell the police all about that. It had sickened me, and they wouldn't have believed me anyway. What proof did I have? They'd taken very good care to disappear.'

'So when the police *did* arrive, you took the blame on yourself.'

'I did it on the spur of the moment, and afterwards I had to go along with it.'

'Why so chivalrous, may I ask?'

Luke got up from the chair, paced angrily about the room, and swung back to face the doctor across his desk.

'You know why. You must have guessed. I love your daughter, Lord Aylsham. I want her for my wife more than anything else in the world, and I couldn't bear the thought that she might have to suffer interrogation in court, perhaps even be sent to prison if the other driver died. It all happened so quickly I had to decide with no time to think, and I couldn't let that happen to her.'

'I see. Does Tanya know that you are in love with her?'

'Yes, she does. I told her once – that night after the railway accident.'

'And what did she say? Does she return your love?'

'No, I wish to God she did.' He came back and sat down again, feeling utterly deflated and more and more certain that he had now damned himself for ever. 'She was sweet and friendly and kind, but she is not in love with me.' Simon was looking at him thoughtfully and he went on rather desperately, 'I know I'm not what you would wish for your daughter. My father was a miner, I've no money and no immediate prospects. I've thought of that over and over again, but give me time, just a little time, and I will get somewhere. I'll make her proud of me, I swear I will, and you too.'

'I'm sure you will, Luke,' the doctor said quietly, 'I've never doubted your ability. It's not you who worries me, it's Tanya. She can be difficult to handle. She is volatile, changeable, and trying to keep her tied is like holding a wild bird in a cage. If she sets her heart on someone or something no one can hold her. You think it

164

strange that I should say this about my own daughter, but, you see, I knew her mother, and Tanya is very like her.'

For a moment Luke glimpsed a shadow of pain on the doctor's face, as though he stared back into a past he did not want to remember, then it had vanished.

'I'm afraid you must take your chance with her,' he said wryly.

'You mean I can still see her? You're not forbidding us to meet?'

'My dear boy, we're living in the twentieth century. I can't lock my child up, however much I may disapprove of the company she keeps. I can only advise and perhaps try to guide.'

'Could I see her now – tonight?'

'She is in bed and asleep, I hope. She is still not fully recovered. Tomorrow perhaps.'

Luke got up. 'I'd better go.'

'Not for a moment. There is something further. I'd not expected this declaration of yours, I must confess. It makes what I intended to say to you a little more difficult. You must understand that by taking on Tanya's guilt you have put me very greatly in your debt.'

'Oh no,' Luke said quickly. 'I thought only of Tanya, not of anything else.'

'Maybe you did, but the fact remains that I can't put it right, it's much too late. To proclaim the truth now would lay you open to a charge of perjury, to contempt of court, all kinds of problems, added to which nobody would believe it for a single minute.'

'It doesn't matter,' said Luke stubbornly. 'I can manage.'

'But it does matter. I cannot allow you to suffer financially or in any other way because of my daughter's irresponsible behaviour.' He paused for a moment, seeing the prickly look of obstinacy on Luke's face and uncertain how to word it without seeming to patronize. 'For some time,' he went on at last, 'I've had it in mind to ask if you would do something for me, and now this seems a good time to bring it up.'

Luke stared at him. 'Anything, of course, if it is within my power.'

'Do you remember some time ago we spoke about the library at Ravensley? Would you like to sort it out, catalogue it, put it in order for me, on a proper financial basis naturally?'

It could solve a lot of immediate problems, it was the kind of thing he'd love to do, it would give him time to complete his thesis

– but had the Doctor made the offer just out of pity, just because he thought he owed Luke something on account of Tanya?

He said slowly, 'I don't want any payment. I'll do it for you for nothing.'

'Now it's my turn to be difficult,' the Doctor said drily. 'You don't know what you may be called upon to do. Frank Carroll will no doubt borrow you to help him with his farm accounts, Nicola can be very demanding, and don't think I'm giving you free access to Tanya. As soon as she is fit enough to travel I'm taking her to spend the rest of the summer with her Uncle Niki at Les Coquilles. Go home for a few days, Luke, think about it, and let me know how you feel.' He rose to his feet. 'Now you'd better come and talk to my wife. She will tell you when you can have a word with Tanya.'

When he left shortly afterwards, with the promise that he could call and see Tanya the following afternoon, he wondered why he did not feel more elated. He had not been forbidden the house, had in fact been offered a closer relationship with the family who had become so important to him; but he was also aware, with a sinking of the heart, that the doctor knew his daughter a great deal better than he did and rated his chances of winning her love too low to be any kind of a threat. It was a dispiriting conclusion.

'Lord knows if I've done the right thing by that boy,' said Simon Aylsham to his wife when Luke had gone. 'But I couldn't let Tanya turn the whole action of the law upside down, especially when she doesn't really remember a damn thing about it. It would only make matters worse. Your suggestion of doing over the library was a godsend, my dear. I think he fell for it. Did you realize the boy is crazily in love with Tanya?'

'I did guess at it.'

'Did you, by God, and never said a word to me. What about Tanya?'

'She's not in love with him – not yet at any rate.' She looked across at her husband's frown. 'What would you have said if she was, if they had come asking for permission to marry – would you have refused your consent?'

'Much good that would do,' he said ruefully. 'Tanya would

probably take the bit between her teeth and run off with him. I wouldn't have said no, but I would have told them to wait for a while. All our acquaintances, most especially Hester, would think I was off my head of course, but I never took very much heed of class distinctions. It's whether people are right for each other that's important, and that's something very difficult to assess.'

Galina knew better than anyone that Simon, with his unorthodox views and the very different life he had led in Russia, had found it hard to grow accustomed to the rules of English society, still very rigid despite the war years and their aftermath. She knew only too well how many people still looked askance at her, the Russian woman whose past was so dubious. With his help she had lived it down, but it was still there.

She said slowly, 'Do you think Luke is right for Tanya?'

'Certainly not yet. He's not mature enough. He wouldn't know how to handle her. She would run rings round him in the first few weeks.' He sighed. 'Oh Lord, what's the use of speculating? She'll probably go her own way whatever we say. We'll pack her off to France for a month or two. Sonia is always a good influence.'

He did not know that by that simple decision he was to bring about the very result he would have done anything in the world to prevent.

Luke arrived on the stroke of three, bringing with him a bunch of yellow roses from the florist's – stiff, prickly and a little like Tanya's mood that afternoon.

Though her own memory was blurred she knew now what had happened that night. Her father had explained it very carefully. She knew she ought to feel grateful to Luke, who had saved her from a great deal of unpleasantness at considerable risk to himself, and instead was aware of a faint feeling of resentment. He didn't *have* to do it, did he, and it created an awkwardness between them which neither of them could bridge. They were making polite conversation like strangers rather than old friends.

She thanked him for the flowers. 'What do you think? Cecil had the cheek to send a huge bouquet. I was so angry that I told the messenger to take them straight back.'

'He won't have liked that.'

'Papa said he ran away.'

'It was those pals of his. They forced him to go.'

'Anyone with an ounce of guts would have faced it out with you.'

She wanted to say 'Why did you take the blame?' and knew he would answer 'Because I love you,' and felt she just didn't want to face up to it. She took refuge in trivialities.

'Di came to see me. *Candida* had a good write-up and she has been offered a contract with the BBC rep. Andy is cock-a-hoop about it because now she won't be waltzing off to the States with Craig.'

He moved his chair nearer to the sofa on which she was lying. She looked so pale, so lovely and fragile, that he ached to take her in his arms, but he didn't dare.

'How do you feel now? Are you still in pain?' he asked.

'Only now and again. It hurts if I move quickly, and my face feels stiff where it was bruised.'

'Your father has asked me to work for him. Did he tell you?'

'Yes. You and your books – you'll like that, won't you?' She put up a hand and touched his cheek. 'I wish you were coming with me to Les Coquilles. I shall be lonely there.'

'You will have your cousins.' He took her hand in his. 'I'm going to miss you horribly.'

For a few seconds the old feeling of companionship flowed back between them. He leaned forward to kiss her cheek, and she moved her head a little so that her lips brushed his. Then the door opened and Galina came in, followed by the servant carrying a loaded tray.

'I thought we might have tea together,' she said briskly, 'then I'm afraid you must go, Luke. Tanya still tires very quickly.'

They drank the tea and talked of ordinary everyday things until it was time for Luke to go.

As the door closed behind him, Tanya swung her legs to the floor and crossed restlessly to the window. Outside, the small London garden was bathed in the warm, buttery glow of late afternoon sun.

'I suppose you are wishing I was going to marry Luke, then you'd be rid of me,' she said without turning round.

Galina had begun to put the teacups together on the tray. 'Why should I want to be rid of you?' she said evenly.

Tanya swung round on her. 'Then you'd have Father all to yourself.'

'Don't you think that's a very silly thing to say? You're not your father's only child, you know.' Galina picked up the tray. 'Open the door for me, will you?'

'The servants will do that.'

'They have a great deal to do.'

'Oh, all right. If you must do their work for them.'

She crossed to the door, flung it open, and shut it behind her stepmother with an unnecessary slam.

She stood uncertainly for a second. She had wanted to say 'Sorry' and somehow the word had stuck in her throat. Then abruptly she made up her mind. If she was going to be banished to Les Coquilles, she might as well make the best of it. She had a sudden vision of Dirk von Richter on that day she had seen him first, riding towards her down the mountain path.

With an unexpected burst of energy she ran up the stairs and began to hunt through her wardrobe, tossing out its contents one by one. Everything looked dreary, uninteresting, out-of-date. She would ask Papa for some money and spend a day in the shops, new shirts for riding, something light and thin for lying in the sun. She would persuade Boris to take her into Monte Carlo, and for that she would need something really glamorous. Di was the one to help her choose. She would get in touch with her now, arrange to meet tomorrow. She let the wave of excitement carry her along, thrusting aside, as she had done so often before, everything that was difficult, uncomfortable, frustrating. She pushed the pile of clothes to the floor and picked up the telephone.

10

A bar of early morning sunlight slanting through the uncurtained window woke Tanya from a shallow sleep so that, dazzled, she shut her eyes against it and for a fleeting moment wondered where she was.

She had been at Les Coquilles for nearly a week and for the first time since that wretched motor accident felt new life, new energy pulsing through her. She lay for a few minutes longer revelling in the sensation of renewed health, then she was out of bed, crossing to the window, pushing out the casement, breathing in great gulps of the clean, pine-scented air.

She could hear the servants moving about their early morning tasks. A boy went by below whistling as he swung his pail, someone was singing at their work. It was only just after six, but everyone was always up and about early in the old farmhouse. For the last few days she had been allowed breakfast in bed, all the privileges of a semi-invalid, but not this morning. She had been giving in to it for too long. She plunged her face into a basin of cold water and dressed quickly, jodhpurs, boots, white silk shirt, yellow cashmere pullover. She ran a comb through her hair and then went down the stairs of the old turret and out into the garden.

There had been light rain during the night, and after the scorching heat of summer the air was sparkling and unbelievably fresh. She had no one to ride with her that morning. Her father had brought her out there but had only stayed a couple of days, the burden of his Russian charge, the threat of danger, still causing him considerable anxiety. Her cousins were away, Boris in Tunisia on holiday, Yuri taking an extra course at the Sorbonne in Paris, Elena spendng a few weeks in Florence with a schoolfriend, but she did not really mind being alone.

In the stable yard Marco grinned and touched his cap to her.

He brought out Minette, and the mare pushed her nose against her shoulder.

'Glad to see me, old girl?' she whispered as she fondled her.

Then she was in the saddle and away up the path they usually took, climbing into the hills. How good it was to feel alive once more!

She pushed on further than they had ever gone before, the path skirting a deep ravine and climbing slowly up and up. It was then as she edged round a narrow corner that she saw the solitary horseman ahead of her standing motionless on the top of the ridge, and though he had his back to her she knew immediately that it was Dirk von Richter, a year almost to the day when she had seen him first. Was it coincidence or had he heard that she was there? News travelled swiftly from one villa to another across these valleys.

Should she go on or should she turn back? She was still angry with him because he had vanished and never returned as he had promised. Then, while she hesitated, the mare shifted restlessly, a large stone went bouncing down the slope, and he swung round, looking straight at her. After that she had no choice. She went on slowly and steadily up the steep path until she could rein in beside him. He had turned back to gaze out across the wooded valley and almost perpendicular ravine. Far below there was a silver gleam of water winding through overhanging trees, and on the opposite slope, perched on what seemed an almost impregnable precipice, were the ruined walls of a castle, the grey turrets half covered with a thick mat of climbing ivies.

'I love this view,' he murmured half to himself. 'Always I must come here when I am at the Villa Valéry.'

'It's certainly wildly beautiful, but rather frightening too. What is the castle?'

'They call it Roquelaire.'

Roquelaire! The tale Elena had told them last summer – the boy who sought revenge, and found it at the expense of his own life, condemned to live a helpless cripple in a mouldering inheritance.

'It has a grim history, hasn't it?'

'You know it?'

'My cousin told me about it. The peasants say his ghost still walks these hills.'

'Do you believe that?'

'I don't know. Perhaps. There is an atmosphere, isn't there? Something brooding, something endlessly frustrated.'

'That's in your own mind. He achieved what he set out to do. That should be enough for any man.'

There was a decision, a conviction in his voice, that surprised her. The sun had disappeared behind a black cloud, and a gust of wind seemingly out of nowhere suddenly swirled around them. She shivered and he smiled down at her.

'It would seem he doesn't approve of us talking about him. I think we've had enough of ghosts and desperate deeds. Shall we go back?'

The eeriness, the dark shadow, the sense of something evil vanished as they climbed down in single file, and then as the path widened they were riding side by side, talking so easily and happily that she forgot the grudge she had held against him.

He was speaking of the new art gallery he had visited in Berlin. 'My stepfather would like me to take it over for a year and run it. I meant to return to England weeks ago but he was taken ill.'

'Not seriously, I hope?'

'Luckily, no, but bad enough. A slight stroke. He has made a good recovery, but his doctors thought a few weeks at the Villa Valéry were just the thing to set him up. I couldn't let him travel alone, so I waited till he was strong enough and then came with him. We arrived yesterday. Now tell me about yourself.'

'Not much to tell. I had a car accident, nothing very bad, but my father insisted on a few weeks here. Unfortunately my cousins are all away.'

'So here we are, both of us, stranded, I with the Baron who wants nothing more than to doze and read in the sun, and you with your uncle and aunt who no doubt have their own affairs to occupy them – so what are we going to do? It's obvious, isn't it? We must find our amusements together. What do you say?'

There was a moment of doubt. What was she committing herself to? Then the memory of the two days they had spent together in London flowed back and she smiled up at him.

'Sounds wonderful. When shall we start?'

'Meet me here tomorrow at the same time and we will make plans. Is it a bargain?'

172

'It's a bargain.'

She held out her hand and he clapped his own on it, those strange eyes of his meeting hers as he raised it to his lips and lightly kissed it.

'Signed and sealed.'

And so began those magical few weeks in which she lived solely in the present, giving little or no thought to the future, and was unbelievably happy.

They met on the following day and made a plan of campaign so that the weeks formed a kind of pattern. Always in the early morning they rode together up into the hills, silvery green with olives, more often than not ending on the high ridge overlooking Roquelaire, which seemed to hold some strange fascination for him. They would part where the road divided, Dirk going on to the Villa Valéry while Tanya raced into Les Coquilles to breakfast quickly and change out of her riding clothes before hurrying to meet him where he waited outside the huge gates in the long, low, black Lagonda. They would drive away, always exploring something new, villages, towns, places of rare beauty or historic interest, sometimes picnicking (the chef at the Villa Valéry had the knack of producing delicious snacks and rare delicacies), sometimes stopping at a country inn and lunching on crisp home-baked bread and goat's cheese with garlic and black grapes, huge and luscious, washed down by rough country wine.

There were candle-lit dinners at luxury hotels in Nice or Cannes, or at the Colombe d'Or at Cagnes-sur-Mer where Renoir had lived out his last days and the hotel walls were covered with paintings by Chagall, Bonnard, Picasso, Miró and many other artists given in exchange for delicious meals.

After a few days Sonia became worried. Tanya was constantly flying in and out of the house, stopping only to swallow a cup of coffee or to change her clothes.

'Who is this man?' she asked, coming into the bedroom one evening and watching her niece peel off her thin summer frock before hunting through her wardrobe, slim and straight in her white satin camiknickers. 'Don't you think your uncle and I should meet him?'

'Oh, don't be so old-fashioned, Auntie. His name is Dirk von Richter. He is one of Giovanni's most valued clients. That's where I met him. He's Swiss and very respectable. We just both happen to like the same kind of things, that's all.'

'Does your father know him?'

'Oh, don't *worry* about me,' she said impatiently, avoiding the question. 'It's simply that his stepfather is not very well and has to rest a good deal, so he's at a loose end just as I am, and it seems sensible to see something of each other. You can't really expect me to mope at home all day and do nothing. It is supposed to be a holiday.'

Then she was gone, wearing a delectable evening gown of some pale green gauzy material sprinkled with silver stars that shimmered as she moved. Dirk said they reminded him of fireflies under a summer moon.

But Sonia was still anxious.

'Do you think we should write to Simon about this business of Tanya?' she asked her husband that same night.

'Oh, for heaven's sake! Why disturb him for nothing? It's just a summer flirtation. Let the girl enjoy herself. Tanya's no fool, you know. I don't think she'll be led astray. I tell you what. I'll telephone the Villa Valéry. Ask him formally to dine with us one evening. He can hardly refuse. Then we can take a good look at him. Will that make you feel better about it?'

It did not happen immediately, partly because Niki was a busy man and what with the olive crop and the grape harvest had much to occupy his mind, and partly because, when he did at last telephone, he was told that the Baron von Richter was indisposed and could not be brought to the telephone, and somehow messages left for his son either did not reach him or were not at once followed up.

As the days went by and they grew closer, Tanya was finding that in many ways Dirk was totally unexpected. He combined a liking for the rich, luxurious things of life with a passion for beauty stretching from antiquity to the paintings of Matisse and Picasso. His long fingers would caress an antique bronze head or an oriental jade carving with an almost sensuous pleasure, and she had not yet realized that within her elegant, sophisticated companion there

174

still lived the boy who had grown up during his most impressionable years in hatred and bitterness and disillusionment, who had been starved of love and beauty and kindness and still nursed a dream of revenge against the forces that had placed him and his dead mother there.

Once they ate their lunch by the Fontaine de Vaucluse, where the mysterious pool welling from the deep heart of the mountain pours its silver stream through the cascades of the river – the lovely spot where the poet Petrarch first saw the sixteen-year-old Laura in her green dress with violets in her hands and loved her from afar all the years of his life.

'Could you do that, Dirk, live all your life with a dream?'

'I doubt if any man could,' he said idly, 'and certainly Petrarch didn't. He managed to father two illegitimate children by another woman.'

'Oh, now you've spoiled it all, bringing down a heavenly passion to an earthly one.'

But he only laughed and leaned forward, lightly touching her lips with his and then pulling her to her feet.

'Come, lazybones, we've other things to see.'

They spent an afternoon at a tiny fishing village where Tanya pulled off shoes and stockings, paddling like a child in the limpidly warm sea, and Dirk roared with laughter, swinging her into his arms when she shrieked as the burning hot white sand scorched her bare feet.

They drank their morning coffee at Avignon opposite the half-crumbling bridge of St Bénezet, built six hundred years before by the peasant boy to save wayfarers from death in the rushing waters of the Rhône. Tanya took a few dancing steps singing softly –

> 'Sur le pont d'Avignon
> L'on y danse,
> L'on y danse . . .'

And Dirk pulled her on to his lap and gave her a smacking kiss, to the scandalized pleasure of an elderly lady at the next table who took them for a honeymoon couple.

On a breathlessly hot afternoon they walked around the castle of Tarascon, where King René had once entertained a court of troubadours singing of beauty and heartbreak and love.

'And enjoyed it on the sly in some of these dark corridors, I'll be bound,' remarked Dirk cynically.

They went dancing at Monte Carlo and lost money in the Casino, remembering the night when he had given her the chips. It was as if in these few weeks he wanted to cram in everything that most delighted him and carried her along with him.

One evening at her particular urging they went slumming in Marseilles, walking through the tortuous, colourful, crowded streets in the old quarter where people of every nationality seemed to rub shoulders and no woman dared to walk alone. He wore his black pullover and slacks, and she her oldest dress with a red scarf knotted in the neck and a beret on the bright hair.

'We look like an apache with his woman,' she giggled.

'That's what we want to look like.'

They ate in one of the better cafés, the food roughly served but the best bouillabaisse she had ever tasted, rich with lobster and crab and what she thought was probably squid, and it was there that something odd happened. There were half a dozen men lounging at a nearby table, sailors probably, speaking a motley of languages. One of them, whose fair hair and Slav features made him outstanding, glanced at them again and again. When Dirk got up to pay the bill he sauntered over to them and said something. Tanya saw Dirk's face darken. He replied briefly and harshly, but she caught the words and knew it was Russian.

'Not here, you fool, not here,' Dirk said.

But the man persisted. He edged nearer, his eyes on Tanya, and with a swift, brutal gesture Dirk hit him across the face. He staggered back, one hand going to his bleeding lip. His friends half rose from their seats and for a moment danger hung in the air. Then Dirk threw a handful of money on the table, took Tanya by the arm, and strode out of the café, hurrying her through the narrow streets and into a broader thoroughfare until they reached the place where they had left the car.

'Who was that man?' she asked breathlessly as he flung open the door and pushed her in. 'Were they Communists?'

'God knows. Some damned insolent fellow asking for money. I didn't like the way he looked at you.'

But she did not quite believe him. She had a queer feeling that

176

the fair-haired man had known him, that there was some connection between them, but she did not question him. Close as they had become in many ways, there were still areas of Dirk's life about which she knew nothing.

She would lie in bed at night and think back over the day. If this was love, then she was knee-deep in it. She was fascinated, intrigued and physically very aware of him, though he never overstepped the mark, never tried to catch her unawares as other men had done. His kisses were part of their joyous companionship, given as a compliment to her looks or because some moment moved them deeply or lightly, gaily, amidst their laughter. Sometimes she was shocked at her own desire for more. His hand brushing down her bare arm could make every nerve tingle. Once when they were swimming and their bodies became entangled she shuddered with pleasure pressed against his breast, feeling his heart beat, her body moving rhythmically with his. But although they shared so much and talked so freely, she still felt she only knew part of him, the outer person he chose to reveal and not the inner self, the depths that two lovers should be able to reach in one another. He never spoke of his own childhood, and only once mentioned his mother. It was one day when, after driving in the hills through the blazing heat of midday, they stopped in search of a cool drink. The village was a poor place, the stone cottages half tumbled down, and the children playing in the dust of the gutter stared at them like animals through dirty tangled hair.

'There's little enough here for tourists,' said the innkeeper sourly, putting out the best he had for these well-dressed customers. 'There aren't many interested in that old fresco on the wall of the church.'

'What's the story?' asked Dirk idly, grimacing at Tanya because of the sharp acid taste of the wine.

It seemed that the lord of the local castle, which had long since crumbled to dust, defied the church and his priests by holding feasts of lust and debauchery instead of prayer and repentance during the holy season of Lent, and the wrath of God had descended on him and his guests.

'Is it true?' asked Tanya.

The landlord shrugged his shoulders. 'Take a look and make up your own minds.'

The church was tiny, with grey stone walls hung with a fungus like great leprous patches. Rank grass grew around the tombstones that nobody tended. It was pitch dark when they pushed open the door and groped their way into the porch, but perhaps for the sake of the odd tourist it boasted electric light. Dirk fell over a pew before he found the switch, then suddenly like a cinema screen the whole extraordinary thirteenth-century panorama burst upon them, colours fading here and there, paint peeling off in places, but an astonishing picture of medieval life touched with beauty, with superstition and terror.

The figures, men, women, even children and animals, danced, writhing together, coupling with obscene gestures, so vividly alive that Tanya had a queer feeling that at any moment one or another of them would come dancing off the wall to take her hand and lead her in and out of the wooden benches. Two of the figures were constant throughout the whole pageant. One was Death or maybe the devil; black, menacing, hooded, he moved from one to the other, and as he touched them their faces twisted into abject terror. The other was a woman, beautiful with long, floating red hair that fell around her naked breasts. She too seemed to move from one to the other, sometimes tempting, sometimes lying in a lover's arms, head thrown back in a frenzy of sensual delight.

They walked along the length of it and then Dirk stopped. He was gazing at the woman, whose outstretched hand now touched the head of a small boy crouched at her feet.

'My mother had hair like that,' he said. 'When I was a child she used to unbind it till it reached her waist and let me brush it for her. I can feel it now in my fingers, soft as silk and yet vibrant with life. I wonder who *she* was.'

'The Count's wife perhaps.'

'No man would allow his wife to be portrayed like that. These thirteenth-century painters lived in the midst of plague, war and death, and they certainly knew how to depict the wrath of God. Come on, let's go. It gives me the shivers.'

One afternoon when they had come back from one of their trips earlier than usual he asked her if she would like to visit his stepfather.

178

'Yes, very much, if he is well enough.'

'He's quite recovered but does not care for too much company.'

She felt a little nervous, anxious to make a good impression and feeling grubby and dishevelled from a long day in the car.

'You can freshen up if you wish, but I doubt if he will even notice. Such things never worry him.'

She did not know what she had expected, a rotund German perhaps or a solid commonplace Swiss. Johann von Richter fitted neither of these descriptions. He was tall and spare, frowning a little behind gold-rimmed eyeglasses, with a small brown beard and a gentle manner. He was carelessly dressed, a silk scarf tucked into the neck instead of the high formal collar. He treated her with an exquisite courtesy and reminded her of an absent-minded professor of literature rather than an astute financier who had made enough money to indulge his love of fabulously expensive antiques.

They drank lemon tea and he spoke of the early years before the war when he had frequently come to St Petersburg and visited Giovanni's gallery.

'I never had the pleasure of meeting your grandfather, Prince Malinsky, but I remember your grandmother well, a very formidable old lady.'

'Grandfather was assassinated before I was born, but Grandmother used to terrify me and my brothers. She never wore anything but black and was terribly strict, so that when we went to Dannskoye for the holidays we used to pray that she would be away on one of her frequent visits to relatives. She never got over the shock of being forced to leave Russia.'

With a stab of pity she remembered that frightening figure of her childhood reduced to a shrunken old lady, bewildered and lost in a strange new world.

When it was time to leave he kissed her hand, holding it for a moment in his own.

'Thank you for sparing an hour of your time to a dull old man,' he said. 'Perhaps you will come again.'

'I'd like to very much if Dirk will bring me.'

The Baron looked after them, his brown eyes thoughtful behind the thick spectacles. The girl was lovely, but she had breeding too, an instinctive courtesy and gentleness, not at all like so many of these strident, demanding young women of the post-war generation. It was the first time Dirk had brought one of his women to meet him, and he wondered. Sometimes he felt he did not really know him at all. He let his thoughts run back for a moment to Varya Andreyevna, who so many years ago now had come applying for a post as his housekeeper – a flame-haired beauty living on her wits since she had been exiled from Russia as a red-hot revolutionary. What was she doing applying for such a menial post, he had asked himself, and yet for some inexplicable reason he had picked her out from the other, sober, quietly dressed, far more suitable applicants, and with her had come her son, thirteen years old, a handsome savage who had looked at him warily, prepared to hate, ready to defend to his last breath the mother he loved. If anyone had told him then that two years later he would marry her, he would have laughed in their face; but against all advice, all prophecies of disaster, he had gone his own way, and the success of their marriage had confounded all the critics.

Those had been good years when she had made his lonely bachelorhood blossom, when he had sent that farouche boy to the best school in Switzerland and on to university in Leipzig, treating him like his own son and being rewarded by a flowering of affection between them; but in all this tranquil pleasure, mother and son had remained an enigma. He had never plumbed the depths, never really learned what they sought in their inmost hearts, and sometimes it had made him afraid for them.

In her last illness it was to her son she had turned, as if they shared between them some secret purpose from which he was excluded – or was he just imagining it because of his distress at losing her he had grown to love so deeply?

The evening was growing chill. He summoned the servant to take in the chairs and rugs before returning slowly to the house. Perhaps this girl with her charm and beauty would give the boy what he needed, an anchor to still his restlessness, a settled home, maybe children.

The evening Dirk spent with the Malinskys at Les Coquilles was not so successful. On the surface it was very pleasant. Sonia had gone to a great deal of trouble. The dining room with its white

walls and dark beams was softly lit by the three-branched candelabra, one of the few surviving relics of the old days. The food was
simple but superbly cooked and served. Boris had returned the day
before from Tunisia and talked entertainingly of his adventures in
the desert. Dirk responded with some of his own experiences and
paid charming deference to his host and hostess, and yet afterwards
Tanya knew they had not liked him and was immediately on the
defensive.

'The chap is a bounder, an adventurer,' said Boris in his
forthright way. 'You keep clear of him, my pet.'

'That's quite the stupidest thing I've ever heard you say, and
completely untrue,' said Tanya defiantly, 'and I've absolutely no
intention of doing any such thing.'

'Don't say I didn't warn you when you come a cropper.'

'Oh, don't be an ass, Boris. I'm not a child. I know what I'm
doing.'

'No more to be said then, is there?' He gave her a quick hug and
kiss.

But it still worried her a little. Boris could be shrewd in his
judgement of people.

Privately to her husband Sonia said, 'He has everything, looks,
charm, background, money, and according to report a most
respectable stepfather, so why do I dislike him?'

'Perhaps for that very reason, my dear: he has too much in his
favour. I had a different impression,' went on Niki thoughtfully.
'He seemed to me to be playing a part, and like a supremely good
actor has been playing it for so long that he almost believes in it
himself. But underneath there is the real person, and what that is
like is anyone's guess.'

They were right in one way and wrong in another, but that was
something they did not find out for a very long time, and then
something unexpected happened that made the careful letter which
Sonia was writing to Tanya's father totally unnecessary and she
tore it up.

The weeks had gone by so quickly that it was difficult to imagine
that it was the end of September. Tanya had been at Les Coquilles
for more than six weeks and it was time to think about going home.

181

Sometimes in the dark hours of the night when she woke and random uncontrollable thoughts went flitting through her mind, she wondered if she was pursuing a dream. She would go back to England, life would return to its commonplace level, and she would never see Dirk again. In all this time, and though they had shared so much, he had never once said 'I love you,' never once spoken of a future together, never yet made her feel that she had become an integral part of his life and not simply an amusing companion with whom to while away what could have been long, tedious weeks. She would be overcome with a leaden depression, a fear that the bottom could so easily fall out of her world and the next step would be into chaos – a feeling that fortunately vanished when she woke to find the sun was shining on another day of promise and she could resolutely put the night's horrors behind her.

A week after Dirk had dined at Les Coquilles he asked her if she would like a trip in his friends' cabin cruiser which was in the harbour at Cap Ferrat. It had not been possible before as the boat had been undergoing an overhaul, but now that was completed and he suggested they might try it out by taking it down the coast towards Marseilles.

'Sounds terrific,' she said.

'Better bring a coat. The wind can be cool at sea.'

They lunched early at one of the luxury hotels at St Jean Cap Ferrat, the most exclusive district of the Côte d'Azur, and then went on board the *Lorelei*. A man in seaman's jersey and boots came to meet them. He and Dirk spoke together while she looked around her, then he saluted them and leaped across the craft moored between them and the landing stage.

'Do we go alone?' she asked in surprise.

'Don't worry. I've done it often before. I won't drown you.'

It was a perfect afternoon. She pulled off the little jacket she wore over her pleated white sun dress and lay stretched on the deck watching him at the wheel. The sun had lost the scorching heat of midsummer and was tempered by a fresh salt breeze. The sea was like an enormous stretch of shot blue silk gently rippling.

They went further than they had intended, lured on and on, just far enough out to feel they were at sea and yet in sight of the hills, the clustering white houses, the huge multi-coloured sprawl of Marseilles, and beyond towards the delta of the Rhône and the

182

wide stretches of the Camargue where the little black bulls roamed the lagoons and Tanya saw flamingoes rise in a spell-binding cloud of white and sunset pink.

It was late by the time they came gliding back into the harbour of Cap Ferrat and Dirk slowly manoeuvred the cruiser into her mooring place.

'I thought we might eat on board,' he said, glancing down at Tanya. 'I'm well stocked with food. You can come to the galley and take your pick. I can cook too, if Madame would care for an *omelette aux fines herbes* or even a steak.'

She suddenly realized how very isolated they were. Dusk was already creeping into the corners, and though the hotels where dinners were still being served were well lighted, the harbour was mainly silent and deserted except for laughter from a distant yacht where a party was in progress.

She hesitated and he smiled. 'What's wrong? Are you afraid of dining tête à tête with me? Surely we've gone beyond that?'

Suddenly she felt foolish standing there like a blushing school-girl. After all she had spent hours and hours alone with him during the past weeks, so why be so prudish now? Only there *was* a difference; she sensed it and then thrust it aside.

'It's only that it is rather late and I thought they might be wondering where I was.'

'We'll go ashore and I'll drive you straight home if that's what you want.'

There was a faintly derisive note in his voice and that settled it.

'No, don't let's do that. It would be much more fun to eat together first. Let's explore and see what you've got hidden away.'

It was a merry meal and they prepared it together, Dirk mixing the salad while she cooked an omelette. There were huge, delicious prawns, slices of cold chicken, and a bottle of Chambertin, cool and fragrant, which he produced like a conjuror out of an ice bucket.

It was nearly eleven o'clock by the time he brought the coffee he had brewed himself. On deck it was dark already, but in the cabin the lamp spread a warm, mellow glow.

She glanced up at the ship's clock mounted high up on the wall and got up to put her coffee cup on the table.

'It's fearfully late. When we've drunk this we really ought to go.

183

My aunt will be thinking we're both at the bottom of the sea by now.'

'Not yet. There's plenty of time.'

He reached up an arm and pulled her down beside him on the long bunk seat. He kissed her long and deeply. It was what she had waited for, had longed for, and her whole body responded to him helplessly, joyfully. He teased her lips open and something within her seemed to melt into an ecstasy of love and desire. His mouth was still on hers as one hand crept up and slipped down the strap of her sun dress, his long fingers gently caressing her breast. She trembled as his lips moved to her throat and then to her shoulder. She closed her eyes, irresistibly drawn towards him; and then abruptly and unexpectedly, like a douche of ice-cold water, she realized what was happening to her and reacted fiercely against it. It came over her in a wave of anger and she struggled to free herself. So this was what he thought of her, this was how he saw her and the hours they had spent together, not love, not something true and lasting, but what Boris called contemptuously 'an easy lay'. But she was not like that, she was not just anyone, a girl to be picked up, made love to and discarded. She was the Princess Tanya Malinsky. She fought to get away from him, and surprisingly he let her go.

She stood up, summoning all her dignity.

'I agreed to dine with you, but I didn't bargain to spend the night with you. Can we go now, please?'

He uncoiled himself from the seat, standing in front of her looking so formidable that she shivered, but she stood her ground bravely.

'No,' he said, 'no, we're not going. We've the whole night before us. Isn't this what you've been waiting for all these weeks? Well, my darling, now it's here.'

He picked her up and carried her through into the sleeping cabin and deposited her on the bunk bed. But now she was angry, furiously angry and frightened at the same time. She scrambled across the bunk to escape, and when he pulled her back she bit the hand holding her so savagely that he exclaimed and let her go.

'That's no way to say thank you, my girl.'

She was on her knees and hitting out at him with the first weapon that came to hand, which happened to be a hairbrush.

Infuriatingly he began to laugh as he wound a handkerchief round his bleeding wrist, and if she hadn't been so terribly distressed she might have realized that he was not putting up much of a fight. If he had wanted to, he could have overcome her easily, but she was able to escape from him, run through the adjoining cabin, up the hatchway and out on to the open deck without too much trouble.

The night was velvety dark, the only points of light the lanterns burning on the boats scattered throughout the harbour. She shivered in her thin dress as the wind blew in from the open sea. She could hear him coming up the stairs behind her and jumped from the cruiser on to the boat that lay between her and the landing stage. Water splashed up and soaked her feet and legs. She jumped again, falling to her knees on the rough cobbles and ripping her thin silk stockings.

She looked back once and saw him standing on the deck, but he was making no attempt to follow her. He was smiling to himself, and if she had only known, she had passed the acid test; but all she could think of just then was to get away as quickly as possible. Limping badly she climbed up the steps and made for one of the hotels, realizing with a sinking heart that she had left her handbag behind so that she had no money to hire a taxi. She stumbled into the palatial doorway and stood still for a moment, dazzled by the brilliant lights in the pillared hall. Her leg was bleeding profusely under the ripped stocking, her dress was torn off one shoulder, and her hair was in wild disorder. A shocked waiter came towards her. This was not at all the kind of person they expected or welcomed. She summoned up all her strength and faced him boldly.

'I have met with an accident,' she said as firmly as she could, 'and – and I've lost my handbag. Could you – is it possible for you to make a telephone call for me?'

The waiter looked at her, frowning uncertainly, several guests paused to stare, then the man at the reception desk came forward.

'Whom do you wish us to telephone, madame?' he said smoothly. Some of the younger members of the aristocracy were known to indulge in wild parties. It did not pay to be too hasty.

'My uncle, Prince Nicolai Malinsky, at Les Coquilles.'

For an instant she felt her head swim and the man took her arm.

'Better come into my office, madame.'

He led her into a small room behind the reception desk, fetched her a glass of water, and asked for the telephone number. She watched anxiously as he put through the call.

'There is a young lady here asking for you, Monsieur le Prince. She appears to have met with an accident.'

He waited a moment, then handed her the telephone. With infinite relief she heard the familiar voice.

'Boris Malinsky here. Is that you, Tanya? What's wrong?'

'Boris, I'm at the hotel by the harbour at Cap Ferrat. Can you come and fetch me? I've lost my handbag and I haven't any money.' She tried hard to speak calmly, but he heard the suspicion of a sob in her voice and asked no more questions.

'Of course I'll come, pet. Are you all right? I'll be there as soon as I can, but it will take a little time. Let me have another word with the manager.'

She handed over the instrument, and whatever Boris said it had the desired effect. The man became all courtesy, conducting her to the powder room where the attendant provided her with fresh stockings and where she could wash off the blood and tidy her hair and dress. Then she was ushered to a quiet corner of the lounge, supplied with a tray of coffee, and left to pull herself together while she waited.

It was nearly an hour before Boris came through the doors. She saw the reception clerk point her out, and he came across at once, taking in her appearance with one swift glance.

'What's happened? We thought you were spending the day sailing down the Med.'

'So we were. I can't talk about it, Boris, I can't. Can we go?'

'Yes, of course. Here, you'd better put this on.' He handed her the white woollen coat he was carrying over his arm and she huddled gratefully into it. 'I borrowed one of Mamma's jackets, thought you might need it. It's cool in the car.'

'What did you tell them?'

'They're out this evening on an errand of mercy. One of Mamma's lame ducks – the old Countess Suvitsky – has been taken ill. She's poor as a church mouse, so Mamma thought she had to lend a helping hand and Father drove her down there. What have you done with von Richter?'

'He's still on the *Lorelei* for all I know – or care.'

'It's like that, is it?' With a heroic effort Boris stopped himself from saying 'What did I tell you?' as he helped her to her feet. 'Do you want me to go across there and punch him on the nose?'

She managed a wan smile. 'No, Boris, nice of you to offer, but I don't think it would help at all. I just want to go home.'

'Right. I'll settle with the hotel and off we go.'

He tucked a rug round her in the open sports car and they drove mainly in silence up the tortuous winding roads to Les Coquilles.

Once she said in a small voice, 'Don't say too much about tonight to Aunt Sonia, will you?'

'Not a word. They won't be back till some time tomorrow anyway.' He gave her a conspiratorial grin. 'Car broke down and you telephoned for help. How about that?'

'Boris, you're a brick.'

'Always ready to lend a hand, that's me.'

'I want to go home to England as soon as possible. Do you think you can arrange it for me?'

'Bit sudden, isn't it?'

'Not really. I've been thinking of it for days. It's time I went back. I've been here for long enough.'

He made no comment, only thought the more, and within a couple of days he drove her to the railway station and saw her on to the Paris express.

'Sure you don't want me to do anything?' he asked when she kissed him goodbye.

'No, it's all right.'

'Don't fret too much. These things happen.'

'Yes, of course.'

She waved to him as the train drew out of the station and then sat back on the seat, the magazines he had bought for her lying unopened in her lap. She was closing the door on what had been a marvellous few weeks, and she wanted to cry because it had ended so badly and because in her secret heart she still wondered if somehow it had all been her own fault. Should she have stayed? Should she simply have laughed at him? That's what Diana would have done, not behaved like an outraged virgin. Dirk had telephoned twice and she had refused to speak to him. Now she regretted it. She gazed at the latest fashions unseeing and read through a whole article without taking in a single word of it, seeing Dirk's face on every page, hearing his voice with its slight, endearing accent, remembering the last glimpse she had of him, standing on the deck, his face shadowy in the light of the ship's lantern – laughing at her, that was the worst of all. She did not realize that sometimes laughter runs close to relief; it can mean pleasure or affection or even love.

The train clattered through a tunnel, and when they came out of it and she had wiped the smuts from her face, she had made up her mind, not yet aware how very difficult it was going to prove, to put Dirk von Richter out of her life.

11

It was October, warm golden days which England occasionally enjoys after an indifferent summer, and even on the Fens, where winds come blowing in sabre-toothed from the North Sea, there were moments of tranquillity still filled with birdsong, with the scent of woodsmoke from the bonfires of burning leaves, and the spicy autumn tang of the dying meadowsweet and bog myrtle.

Luke had been at Ravensley for two months. It had not been an easy decision, and he had walked about London for a couple of days in a state of uncertainty. It seemed too easy. That strong puritanical streak in him demanded difficulties to be overcome and so far his life had provided plenty of them. It was in fact not clinched until the day he met Andy for a drink and a sandwich in the little pub by the Thames.

It was a warm evening and they carried their glasses outside.

'Have you told Pa yet whether you're going to take up his offer?' asked Andy, relaxing gratefully after a long hard day.

'No.' Luke shifted uncomfortably. 'I don't feel I ought to take advantage of his generosity just because of this affair of Tanya and the car.'

'What a fellow you are for making mountains out of nothing at all. As a matter of fact you'll be doing him a service. He's worried about this Russian chap. Uncle Frank is about, of course, but he's not often at the house. I think Father would like to feel there was someone reliable at Ravensley keeping an eye on him when he can't be there himself.'

'I thought he was just an old friend who'd been lucky enough to get out of Russia.'

'Well, he is and he isn't. Actually we've been obliged to keep it very dark, but the Soviet would seem to have a secret police of their own just as unpleasant as the *Okhrana* ever was. Leon was a Party member, and they hate to let anyone escape their clutches.

189

They've already had one go at him, and though to all appearances they succeeded, I wouldn't trust them not to take another shot at him.'

'You mean he is in danger, you're all in danger?'

'I wouldn't quite say that, but there's a chance, a pretty remote one but it *is* there.'

'I see. I didn't know that.'

In some queer way it made all the difference. If he could do a service in return, he felt better able to accept what was offered and tackle it with a good will.

He settled into a routine, rising very early, begging a cup of tea from the kitchen to keep him going till breakfast, and during the morning working in the library, which was so full of unexpected treasures that he sometimes found it difficult to tear himself away in order to spend the afternoon and often the evening working on his thesis, which had grown in scope and needed the closest concentration.

There were distractions, of course, mostly pleasant ones. When Jake saw he could stick on a horse and was unlikely to break his neck, he was permitted to exercise Blackie on his own, and though he would never be a horseman, he enjoyed the feel of the strong body between his knees, the mare's friendly greeting when he brought her a carrot or an apple, even the stable smell of horse sweat and ammonia. Once or twice he had ridden round the estate with Frank Carroll, and his narrow view of English country life, bounded by Tredegar and University, began to widen into a greater understanding. He got to know Paul, the boy whom all the family tried to protect, and now he knew why.

'Have you got a girl you meet when you dash up to London?' Paul asked curiously one day as he watched Luke sort books into piles and note down the names.

'I have and I haven't,' he replied, careful to avoid any mention of Tanya.

'I'd like to marry my cousin Elena. She's the loveliest thing you can possibly imagine and we like all the same kind of things, but Papa would never allow it.'

'Why?' Luke asked idly, intent on his work.

'She's my first cousin for one thing, and then I'm the tainted one of the flock.'

That startled him. 'What on earth do you mean?' he said.

'Haven't they told you? I'm a haemophiliac, and you couldn't really risk passing that on, could you?'

'How long have you known about it?'

'As long as I can remember. I was always wanting to do what Andy and Tanya were doing and it was always forbidden. I've survived so far but sometimes it's been touch and go, and you wouldn't want to inflict that on the girl you love, would you?'

He had envied Paul, who seemed blessed with everything, looks, money, success, and he was doing brilliantly at Cambridge, yet would be living on a knife-edge all the days of his life. It made his envy seem very small.

Then there was Nicola, coming home from school at weekends and providing her own bombshells.

She enjoyed helping him, and armed with a duster would climb up to the top shelves, vigorously banging books together and covering herself and Luke with clouds of black dust.

One day, sitting cross-legged on the floor and sorting huge tomes of estate history into date order, she said suddenly, 'Tell me, can you commit incest with a half-brother?'

'What!' Luke nearly fell off the top of the ladder with surprise. 'What a question, and what do you know about things like that?'

'I suppose you can,' went on Nicola thoughtfully. 'After all, there was all that fuss about Byron, wasn't there? Augusta was only his half-sister, and he didn't meet her till she was grown up and married, so she must have seemed just like anyone else. Would it be the same nowadays?'

'I expect so. Why this burning interest, and surely you don't discuss topics like this in your literature classes?'

'Lord, no! Miss Pritchett goes all pink and skates round questionable subjects. I was really thinking about myself. You see, I'm so awfully in love with Andy.'

'Oh, nonsense,' he said firmly. 'Of course you're fond of him. He's your brother, and it's very right you should be, but . . .'

'Oh, it's not like that at all. He's always seemed quite different from Paul right from the beginning. When I was little I used to say I was going to marry him when I grew up, and now I understand why.'

191

'Nicola, you're talking absolute rubbish and you know you are. Andy is going to marry Diana one of these days.'

'Is he? I don't think so.'

'I hope you don't go around saying this to other people.'

'Of course I don't, but you're different.'

'I suppose I should feel flattered,' he said, coming down the ladder and ruffling her hair. 'You're a funny child.'

She jerked away. 'I'm *not* a child,' she said.

One morning a week or so later he went down himself to collect the letters left in the post box half way down the drive. There were several for the doctor and his wife and just one for himself, a long, official-looking envelope not like the cheap thin paper that came from Wales. He had half expected to see his manuscript returned again and was relieved that there was no parcel. Up to now it had been sent back five times, and only one of the rejection slips had said kindly, 'Perhaps you would care to let us see more of your work at some time.'

He took the letter with him into the dining room. Leon was seated at the table and they exchanged a friendly nod. The Russian's scanty English, which had grown rusty during the intervening tumultuous years, was beginning to come back to him, but conversation between them was necessarily limited. Luke helped himself to poached haddock, poured some coffee, and split open the white envelope. His eye ran down the page.

'My God!' he exclaimed. 'My God, I don't believe it!'

Leon looked up. 'It is good news, yes?'

'Very good, unbelievably good.'

He took a quick gulp of coffee, burnt his mouth, and read the letter again.

It stated quite clearly that the writer had read the manuscript with considerable interest, and if the author cared to telephone and make an appointment for one day the following week, they might perhaps discuss it and come to some mutually satisfactory agreement.

Luke read the letter a dozen times before gingerly he made the phone call. A warm friendly voice assured him that Hugh Carter would be pleased to see him on Wednesday next at eleven o'clock.

He lived in a state of euphoria for the rest of the week, not saying a word to anyone, with a superstitious certainty that if he did so something terrible would happen. Hugh Carter would drop dead or the publishing house would go into bankruptcy before anything could be settled.

What should an aspiring author wear at his first interview? There wasn't really much choice. He settled at last for his one decent suit and set off for London far too early, convinced that if he didn't the train would break down and he would never arrive at all.

He was lucky in more ways than one. The Cambrian Press was small but was run by two youngish men of vision and determination. In a couple of years they had already achieved one near-bestseller and had acquired a good deal of critical approval for an unusual and interesting list. Hugh Carter, who was thirty-five and had been born in a remote village in North Wales called Clynnog Fawr, prided himself on possessing a nose for talent and for a potential winner. He had sensed something new and vigorous in this young Welshman's story, which was set in the previous century but was still vibrant with an authenticity that must have come from personal contacts. (Luke never realized how much he had absorbed from that grandfather of his.) The reading public had begun to look for books of this kind, earthy, realistic, romantic, with flashes of poetry and the fierce intolerance of youth. They could do with what Hugh's partner called 'a jolly good read', and it had not escaped Hugh's astute mind that this youngster had already got himself in the news, even if unfortunately. It meant that his name would attract attention, and publicity of any kind was always valuable. There were crudities, of course, too many passages of purple prose, a tendency to obscure the plot with too much historical detail, but these were problems easy to overcome.

The interview went well. Hugh Carter had not been back to Clynnog Fawr since he left it at the age of nine and remembered little except for the Tudor church of St Beuno, a miracle-working saint who had the reputation of raising the dead, but put two Welshmen together and they would soon strike sparks from one another.

Luke emerged into the street an hour or so later dazed with talk and filled with a sense of achievement combined with the comfort-able assurance that when the alterations were completed he could look forward to receiving a cheque for fifty pounds as an advance on royalties. It seemed like illimitable wealth on that joyous morning that a drizzly rain and a sharp wind could do nothing to spoil.

He simply had to tell someone, and who better than Tanya to share his triumph with him? He had not seen her since she had returned from France. To his disappointment she had not come down with her father at the weekend, but now if she was free he would take her out to lunch. They would go to some splendid restaurant where they could celebrate in style his marvellous stroke of good fortune. He left the Cambrian Press in Maiden Lane, skirted St Martin-in-the-Fields, crossed Trafalgar Square, walked up the Haymarket, stopping in Piccadilly Circus to buy a dozen pink roses from a flower-seller's basket, and then made his way through the back streets to Giovanni's gallery.

He pushed through the glass doors, ran up the circular stairs, opened his mouth to call her name, and then stopped dead.

He could see Tanya, but she was not alone. A tall man was with her, a man with a dark, hawk-like face, and Luke knew at once that he was no customer. They were standing intimately close. Tanya was looking up at him with a light in her face that he had never seen before. He could not hear what she said, but her companion bent his head and kissed her, her arms went round him, and they melted together into a long embrace that was oblivious of anyone around them.

Luke stood staring at them, filled with a deep and passionate anger that seemed to well up and choke him so that he could not bear to watch a moment longer. He turned and went blindly down the stairs and out on to the pavement. In Bond Street people stared in amazement at the young man who strode through them unheedingly, who paused for an instant staring down at the flowers in his hand and then tossed them into the gutter. He walked on and on, barely conscious of where he was going, filled with bitter anger and disappointment, until very gradually good sense began to return. She had never told him that she loved him, had never promised him anything. He had let it grow in his own mind until it had become almost a certainty that now had been brutally torn to shreds, and he only had himself to blame. His first bounding joy and excitement was abruptly killed. Part of it had belonged to her and now it had vanished.

Who was the man? Where had she met him? Why hadn't he

been mentioned? The family usually talked pretty freely about each other. There were few hidden secrets. His mind seethed with unanswered questions.

The thrill had gone out of the morning. Of course a great deal of the satisfaction and sense of achievement would return, but joy, so rare and transient a feeling, had gone for ever. He went back to Ravensley that afternoon in a very different mood from when he had started out.

Giovanni's gallery seemed an absurd place for a reconciliation, and perhaps that was why Dirk had chosen it. She had to listen to him there, she could not run away as she had been doing consistently ever since that evening on the *Lorelei*. He had followed her to London as soon as he had made sure the Baron was in good hands. He had telephoned Diana's flat, he had rung up Wimpole Street.

'There's that foreigner with the very sexy accent asking for you again,' said Andy lightly for the third time that week. 'Aren't you going to put the poor devil out of his misery?'

'I've no wish to speak to him.'

'That's all very well,' grumbled her brother, 'but I'm running out of plausible excuses not to bring you to the phone.'

The very next day Dirk had come to the gallery. She had been carefully unpacking a new and valuable picture when she felt him come up behind her. She recognized the long hand with the one gold ring that was put on hers, and jerked away.

'No, Dirk.'

'At least listen to me, Tanya, that's all I ask.'

'What is there to say?'

'A very great deal.'

She turned to face him then, and her treacherous heart seemed suddenly to miss a beat, because she had been thinking and thinking about him night and day ever since she had come home, and now he was there in the flesh and so much more difficult to resist.

'Let's go somewhere and talk,' he urged.

'We can talk here.'

'Very well, but it's not easy.'

195

He was not a boy, but a man with considerable experience of women, but how explain to her that she was the first one he had passionately desired, just as he desired to own a beautiful picture or an exquisite piece of sculpture, but even more than that. How could he make her understand his tortured boyhood, the violent love/hate relationship with his beautiful mother that had made him what he was? One day perhaps he could tell her, but not now. Tanya possessed all the elusive, elegant charm of her aristocratic Russian ancestors. She had a mind he could train and influence, but he had to be sure, hadn't he? Women had fallen for him far too easily, ready to betray him with other men, trying to trap him by falling into bed with him, an easy capture that bored him unutterably. Tanya had not been like that. She had faced him with flaming anger and outraged innocence, and that was what he demanded from the woman he would make his wife.

Even with his suavity and charm the explanation came out lame and disjointed and for that very reason bore the stamp of truth, but it was not well received.

'You mean you were trying me out, testing me?' she said bluntly, with a burning indignation.

'Believe me, I had no intention of keeping it up. If you had not turned on me like a wild cat defending your honour it would all have ended, a joke we could have laughed at together. You turned the tables on me. Look at what you did. I bear the scar still.'

He pushed up his cuff and she saw the small mark on his wrist. It nearly won his case for him. She wanted to laugh as she remembered now she had belaboured him with a hairbrush and how easily he had let her escape him.

She said with dignity, 'I still think you behaved outrageously.'

'I know, I admit it, but can't you find it in your heart to forgive me? I've come, Tanya, to ask you to be my wife. Must I first pour dust and ashes on my head before I go down on my knees?'

Marry him? So all those dreams of hers were true after all. It was a dazzling prospect, but she was not going to give in too easily.

'I don't know. I would have to think about it,' she said.

'Yes, of course, but in the meantime am I forgiven?'

'Perhaps – in time.'

'Not in time but now. Like this.'

He leaned forward and kissed her very gently, and all her

defences crumbled. She let him take her in his arms, forgetting her anger and her grievance, only dimly aware of the footsteps on the stairs that abruptly ceased.

When Dirk released her she said, 'Did you hear someone come in just then?'

'Does it matter if they did?'

'No, I suppose not.'

'Have dinner with me this evening, my darling. There is so much to discuss, so much I want to tell you.'

For the very first time he was speaking to her in Russian, and she didn't know then that it was the ultimate acceptance, the link with his hidden Russian birth of which he was still immensely proud. She only knew that it thrilled her as nothing else had done, taking her back to the fabulous days of her childhood.

For the next few weeks she saw Dirk almost every day, sometimes for lunch or dinner, sometimes only for a few snatched minutes, occasionally with friends since he had a number of acquaintances in artistic circles. He had hired a car, and on Saturdays they would drive out into the country which, though it was November now, was still lovely with the last tints of autumn. They would eat at some Cotswold inn close to a blazing fire, or occasionally go dancing in one of the riverside hotels, always a mecca for the bright young things of society.

But she did not yet bring him to meet the family and could not really explain why. It was as if he was still something secret to herself and she didn't want to share him with anyone. She went down to Ravensley for the occasional weekend and was so sweet and loving to everyone that they were all slightly surprised. What had happened to their wayward, difficult Tanya? Nicola said openly, 'She must be sickening for something nasty,' and her father remarked to his wife, 'Sonia must have done her good. I really believe Tanya is growing up at last.'

Only Luke wondered. His knowledge weighed upon him. Should he say something about it? To Andy perhaps? Then he drew back. If he had not run, if he had gone forward boldly and been introduced, it would have been different. As it was he felt like the most unpleasant kind of eavesdropper and so he kept silent. But it was inevitable that someone would find out.

Diana ran into them one day when they were lunching at the

Savoy Grill and waved discreetly from a distance. Afterwards, when Tanya dropped into the flat, she looked at her questioningly.

'I saw the two of you yesterday. Who is he? The Swiss?'

'Yes, he is, as a matter of fact. I met him again in France during the summer.'

'Quite a heart-throb, I must say,' commented Diana drily. 'Is he in love with you?'

'He says he is.'

'And you?'

'I'm going to marry him, Diana.'

'Just like that?'

'Just exactly like that.'

Diana raised delicately pencilled eyebrows. 'What does Papa have to say?'

'He doesn't know yet.'

'Don't you think you ought to tell him?'

'There's plenty of time.'

'Hadn't you better go easy, darling? You haven't known him all that long.'

'Quite long enough.'

'For the lightning to strike?'

'Yes, it was rather like that. Am I mad? Am I crazy to trust to it, Di? I'm so wildly happy and so frightened.'

'Of what?'

'I don't know.' She put out a hand and Diana clasped it. 'Love makes you horribly vulnerable, doesn't it, and I always thought it was all so simple.'

'You'll learn, darling,' said Diana. 'You'll learn.'

Then suddenly everything seemed to happen at once and the balloon went up.

Craig had come over from the States again and Andy had been persuaded to lunch with him and Diana at the Ivy, largely patronized by London's theatre people, and in sheer self-defence against the brilliant and voluble American he had urged Luke to join them.

Craig was holding forth about his future plans while Andy jealously watched the glow on Diana's face as she listened, and Luke, who had delivered his amended manuscript that morning, was pondering whether he should confide his own news to them.

He glanced round the crowded room where the cream of the acting profession were eating, talking and laughing, and thought how strange it was that two years ago he would never have dared to set foot in the place and now, thanks to the Aylshams, such pleasures had become quite usual.

The door opened again, half a dozen people came in, and with them was Cecil with his latest flame, a young dancer from Cochran's revue. He saw them at once and strolled across on the way to his own table.

'Well, if it isn't my dear little sister and our friend from the USA with the Welsh boyo! What has happened to Tanya? Why isn't she one of the merry throng?'

'Any reason why she should be?' said Andy coolly.

'Only that she seems to be everywhere lately with that dago boyfriend of hers.'

Andy's mouth tightened. 'And what exactly do you mean by that?'

'What I say, old boy, didn't you know? Lord knows where he springs from, but he's apparently rich as Croesus and sports a silver-grey Lagonda which I wouldn't mind myself. Tanya is quite the little gold-digger these days, isn't she?'

'You keep your dirty tongue off my sister.'

'Certainly, when you keep your grubby hands off Diana.'

Andy sprang to his feet. 'What the hell do you mean?'

'Deny it if you can.'

Cecil was shrilly triumphant and Andy picked up the half-empty glass and threw its contents into his face. The wine trickled ludicrously down his chin. In another moment they could have been at each other's throats. Luke half rose from his chair, then the girl was tugging at Cecil's arm and the waiter was beside them offering a clean napkin.

'Allow me, sir, and your table is this way,' he said smoothly.

People at nearby tables were staring at them. For an instant Cecil did not move, then he snatched the napkin from the waiter and let the girl lead him away.

Andy dropped back in his seat and Diana put her hand on his.

'Take no notice. You know what Cecil is.'

'Yes, of course. Sorry about that, Craig. Go on with what you were saying.'

Afterwards, walking down St Martin's Lane, Luke said, 'Cecil won't forgive you for that.'

'To hell with Cecil. It's Tanya I'm thinking of. Do you know anything about this?'

'I did see them together once. I thought perhaps he was one of Giovanni's clients.'

'What the devil is Tanya up to?'

Andy had always felt a responsibility for his sister, and at the first opportunity he tackled her about it. She flared up indignantly.

'I like him. Why shouldn't I go out and about with him if I wish to? What's it got to do with Cecil Harcourt?'

'Nothing at all, but quite a lot to do with us if it causes talk.'

'Oh, talk!' she said contemptuously. 'Who cares about that?'

'Don't try to get out of it, Tanya. Is it serious?'

'Yes, it is. He has asked me to marry him.'

'In that case why hasn't he spoken to Father about it?'

'Oh, for heaven's sake, don't be so old-fashioned. We're not living in the Middle Ages. He doesn't have to ask permission to speak to me. Besides, I told him to wait for a while.'

'Why? Are you ashamed of him?'

'No,' she said angrily, 'of course I'm not.'

'Then bring him to see us.'

'To be looked over and criticized and judged as if he were a prize ox?'

'Tanya, you know very well that Pa isn't like that.'

'Yes, I do know. All right,' she went on reluctantly. 'I'll ask him to come down to Ravensley next Sunday. Will that do?'

Andy put out an arm and drew her close to him, speaking gently in the Russian of their shared childhood.

'What is it, my pet? What are you worrying about?'

'I'm not sure,' she whispered. 'I love him so much and I'm so afraid of things going wrong.'

'Silly puss.' He kissed her hair. 'Why should they?'

But things did go wrong, very wrong, and for reasons neither of them would have dreamed possible.

12

'Of course I will come,' said Dirk when she suggested it. 'I would like to meet Lord Aylsham. I want to tell him how much I love his daughter.'

For this reason there was an air of anticipation at Ravensley on that Sunday morning. Nicola and Paul were eaten up with curiosity as to whom Tanya would turn up with this time. Simon Aylsham, forewarned by Andy, was not too pleased. He had not thought that Tanya would bring a stranger into their midst and expect him to be accepted as a sort of foregone conclusion.

'What am I supposed to do?' he grumbled to his wife that morning. 'Welcome him with open arms into the family circle when I know nothing at all about him?'

'You know what Tanya is,' said Galina soothingly. 'It's probably a nine days' wonder and she will have changed her mind about him by the end of the week. She has done it before. Sonia would have warned us if it had been really serious.'

Luke simply absented himself. To watch Tanya with this stranger, to realize that he had lost her so irrevocably, was more than he could endure. Perhaps in time he could accept it, but certainly not yet. He got up very early, begged some sandwiches from Betsy in the kitchen, put on his heaviest coat and strongest pair of boots, and set off for a long tramp, anywhere so long as it was far away from Ravensley.

Leon, whose health had greatly improved even though he still could not walk without a stick, had begged Simon to let him work in the gardens.

'I'm not much of a man for books, never was really,' he said, 'but the good earth, what's buried in it and what grows in it, that's what still interests me. My hands itch to be at work.'

'Speaking as a doctor, don't go too hard at it, not at first,' warned Simon, 'but as mental therapy I should say it's the best possible thing. Frank will help to suggest something you can do.'

So he went into details of drainage with the new machinery that was replacing the old windmills across the Fens, and in his spare time took upon himself the creation of a herb garden which had been one of Galina's dreams. Whenever she was there, they pored over catalogues and worked together on the design and the plantings.

He was on his hands and knees weeding the front borders when the long bonnet of the Lagonda came smoothly up the drive. He looked up as Dirk parked it carefully and got out. The two men stared at one another for an instant.

'So this is where you have found refuge, Leonid Alexandrovich, how interesting,' Dirk said pleasantly.

'Yes, I work here.'

It had been a simple exchange but it was in the familiar Russian, and a knot of anxiety tightened inside him. Here he was known by a different name, and yet this stanger had addressed him familiarly.

Then Tanya came running down the steps, putting her arms round her lover and leading him into the house, while Leon sat back on his heels. For an instant he had believed he saw again the lean bony face of the high-ranking official in the Lubianka, the man who had coldly and relentlessly given him his instructions, no choice between death and betrayal, sending him to spy on the man with whom he would work in the mines of Magnitogorsk. Only of course it couldn't be he, that man had been middle-aged already, while this Dirk von Richter could not be more than thirty. He went back to his work, but the sweat was cold on his back. It was not for himself. He had long accepted that his life could be forfeited, he was living on borrowed time, but there were his friends, Simon who had been so generous, Galina whom he still loved. Somehow he must convey a warning.

To all outside appearances the day went smoothly. Sunday luncheon had always been a family affair when Betsy excelled herself with splendid roasts and delicious sweets, a time when they were very often all together discussing each other's doings, when conversation ranged from personal matters to politics and could become boisterous so that guests were apt to feel a little neglected. If Simon and his wife had been shocked to discover that Tanya's chosen husband was the young man glimpsed a year ago in the Monte Carlo Casino, no one would have guessed it. Simon carved the beef and kept the conversation on reasonable levels. Galina was paler than usual and ate little but made sure everyone had what they wanted. Only Leon, who had joined them and who normally enjoyed the give and take in a variety of languages, was unusually silent.

It was a fine winter's day. A touch of frost silvered the bare black bones of the trees and turned the spiders' webs into nets of diamonds on the long holly hedge as they walked out that afternoon. Nicola was running ahead with the dogs, Andy and Paul were discussing some knotty problem, and Tanya was finding a new joy in showing Dirk the home she had once pretended to despise and had grown to love dearly. He, whose boyhood had known only grinding poverty and bitter, painful humiliation, caught a glimpse of happy family life and wondered if one day, when the burning mission he carried within him had at last been fulfilled, he too might find contentment in such a simple existence.

They came back to tea in front of a blazing fire, the dogs stretched on the rugs, plates of hot scones keeping warm in the hearth, wedges of Betsy's chocolate cake.

'What do you think of him?' whispered Paul to Nicola under cover of fetching her another cup of tea.

'I'm not sure,' she said judiciously. 'He's frightfully thrilling to look at, rather like one of Elinor Glyn's heroes – you know, the one that throws you across his saddlebow and rides off into the sunset – but he doesn't really fit in, does he?' She giggled suddenly. 'If he were mine, I'd keep him for Sundays and have a nice, comfortable, ordinary husband for everyday.'

'Anyone know what has happened to Luke?' enquired Tanya. 'I haven't seen him all day.'

'He had a sudden passion to explore marsh churches, Lord knows why,' said Andy teasingly. 'Luke is one of Tanya's beaux, Dirk. You will get used to finding them under your feet wherever you go.'

'Don't be such a pig,' muttered his sister, knowing quite well, with a tiny qualm of conscience, why Luke had deliberately avoided them. She got to her feet. 'Let's have some music. Have we anything new?'

Under cover of the lively strains of Henry Hall's recently formed dance orchestra, Dirk approached his host.

'I wonder if I could have a few words with you in private, Lord Aylsham?'

'Yes, of course.'

Simon saw the anxious look Tanya gave them as he led the way into the library, and wondered now the moment had come what the devil he was going to say.

Earlier that afternoon when the young people had gone out walking, Galina had come to him bringing Leon with her.

'Simon, you cannot allow Tanya to marry this man,' she said vehemently. 'Now that I've seen him again I am positive that if he is not the son of Igor Livinov, then he is closely connected with him. He may call himself Dirk von Richter but he's not Swiss or German. Did you see his face, did you hear him join in when the children were telling that Russian joke?'

'Wait a moment, my dear, we can't rush blindly into this. We don't know anything about him for certain, and until we do, we must not pass judgement.'

'It's your daughter's happiness, maybe her very life,' went on Galina urgently. 'Leon, tell Simon what you told me.'

They were speaking in Russian for his benefit and kept their voices low, though none of the servants, with the possible exception of Jake, would have understood a word.

'All I'm certain of is this,' said Leon, speaking slowly. 'His face is that of the man in the Lubianka who condemned me to a living death. He has those same eyes – eyes that can strip you naked and leave you shuddering and without defence. When you've been through hell, you don't forget the face of the devil who sent you there. This man who likes to call himself von Richter is the living image of Igor Livinov, and he *knew* who I was.'

Simon was thinking of that now as he waved his guest to a chair and seated himself at the desk, still piled with Luke's careful lists.

Was it true or wasn't it? And even if it was, can you condemn a man for what his father is or has been?

He said, 'Would you care for a drink? Brandy, whisky, vodka? I can ring for it.'

'No thank you. I would like to smoke if I may.'

'Certainly.'

Judge a man's reactions not by his eyes but by his hands. Von Richter appeared absolutely calm, but his hand shook slightly as he held up the gold lighter. He took a long pull at the black and gold Sobranie before he said, 'I guess you know why I wish to speak to you.'

'Tanya has told me that you have asked her to marry you.'

'That is so and she has accepted me, so now it is for me to – how do you say? – lay my cards on the table.'

'To be perfectly frank, Herr von Richter, my daughter has taken me by surprise. A few days ago I knew nothing at all about you, and before I permit her to marry you I should have to know a great deal more.'

'I believe Tanya is of age, is she not?'

'She is certainly over twenty-one; but all the same, we have a close and loving relationship, and I would not wish her to go into marriage rashly and break the links that hold the family together.'

'Very well. Here are the facts.' He got to his feet and began pacing up and down the room. 'My stepfather, the Baron von Richter, is a Swiss banker, retired now but wealthy and with a lifelong passion for collecting and sometimes selling antiques. My mother, Varya Andreyevna, was Russian – not as aristocratic as the Malinskys and yourself, but of decent enough family, driven out of Russia much as happened to you. I was five years old when we came to live in Geneva, and it was a bare enough living for many years until she became the Baron's housekeeper and subsequently his wife. He sent me to school and to Leipzig. I hold a degree in modern languages and fine arts and for many years now have managed some of the art galleries in which he has a financial interest.'

Simon had the strange feeling that, plausible as it was, this was a prepared statement delivered almost by rote, and though possibly near to the truth also left a very great deal out.

He said gently, 'May I ask who your father was?'

Dirk stopped his pacing and faced his host across the desk, his eyes flashing golden in the mellow light of the lamp so that, for an instant, Simon glimpsed something of what Leon had described. Then he went on very quietly.

'There I do have something to confess. I never knew my father, or even who he was. On that my mother was always silent. The fact is that I am illegitimate. Till the Baron adopted me as his son I was called Mikhail Androv, which was my mother's name. Surely you, Dr Aylsham – who are, I understand, well known for your liberal, perhaps even unorthodox, views – would not hold that against me?'

He was right. Simon was essentially fair-minded. It was not the fact of Dirk's birth that provided the stumbling block, it was something else, much more inexplicable. He had stated his case frankly and openly, yet like Sonia, like Niki, Simon could not quite believe it.

He sat back in the desk chair watching the lean, handsome face with its undeniable charm and its arrogance, trying to probe beneath it to what was essential.

'Does Tanya know about this?' he asked.

'Some of it. I took her to meet my stepfather in France, and he was greatly impressed. I told him of my intention before I left for England, and he was delighted. His health is precarious, otherwise he would have come with me and taken the opportunity of meeting you and your wife. I may say that when I marry he is willing to give me a larger personal allowance apart from what I earn as his representative abroad.'

In many respects this Dirk von Richter could be considered highly eligible and yet . . . Simon wanted to pick holes in the facts presented to him and found it difficult.

'When do you propose to marry?' he asked.

'Almost immediately, certainly before the end of the year.'

'Oh no, that is quite out of the question. It is barely four weeks away.'

'I know, but it so happens that in the spring I have a commitment to work in our Paris gallery, and from there, possibly at the end of the year, I shall go on to Berlin. The gallery there has been going through some sort of a crisis, and my stepfather relies on me to put it together and set it on the right path once more. I have told Tanya this. She is very anxious to be with me and to work alongside me.'

It sounded eminently reasonable, but Simon still had a strong feeling that to allow Tanya to marry this stranger would be like throwing her to the wolves. He must have time to find out more, to be satisfied that this was something real and not mere infatuation on her part.

He leaned forward. 'I realize your problem, but I don't think you entirely understand what this means. Tanya may be twenty-three, but in many ways she is very young for her age, and you have known one another for such a very short time. I know that your work in the art world will deeply interest and excite her, but if you marry so quickly she will be leaving everything she has ever known. Except for you she will be alone and, I may say, friendless in foreign countries, living out of necessity an unsettled life with no permanent home. I would like to suggest you wait a while, six months perhaps, until you have fulfilled your Paris commitment, and then if you both feel the same about each other we can think again.'

'Lord Aylsham,' Dirk said with a touch of irony, 'do you imagine that Tanya will be happy with a decision of this kind?'

'Possibly not. Tanya is impulsive and sometimes acts thoughtlessly, but she usually listens to me.'

'Do I take it that you are withholding your consent to our marriage?'

'For the time being, yes, I am. I hope you understand.'

'Oh yes, I understand, but I doubt very much if Tanya will.' He glanced at his watch. 'It is growing late. Perhaps it would be best if I go now.'

'You do not need to leave. We can offer you a bed for the night if you wish. At least stay and sup with us.'

'No. I will say goodbye to your wife and Tanya and then go. In any case I must be in London tomorrow morning.'

He did not offer to shake hands, simply gave a correct little bow and went out of the room, leaving Simon uneasily sure that he might have won for the moment but Dirk von Richter was definitely not defeated.

In the hall Tanya was saying, 'Why must you go?'

'It's better if I do. I don't think your Papa likes me very much.'

'What do you mean? What did he say to you?'

'He will tell you himself.'

'I'll see you tomorrow, won't I?'

'Of course. I'll telephone. We'll lunch together.'

She clung to him as he kissed her, watched him go down the steps to his car, then went back to the library, brushing past Luke, who had just come in and was taking off his coat and boots in the hall.

In the dining room Andy, Paul and Nicola were already at the table helping themselves to the cold supper laid out for them as usual on Sunday evenings.

'What's up?' Luke asked. 'Tanya went by me looking black as thunder.'

'We gather Pa has put his foot down,' said Andy through a mouthful of cold beef.

'Forbidden her to marry him, do you mean?' Despite common sense Luke felt his heart give a sudden leap of hope.

'Not exactly. He's said they must wait, and that doesn't please her ladyship at all.'

In the library Galina had joined her husband, and Tanya faced them both, taut and strung up, ready to do battle for her love.

'What have you been saying to Dirk?' she demanded. 'Why have you told him to go?'

'I didn't tell him to go,' her father replied. 'It was his own decision. All I suggested was that you and he should wait a little, six months at least, and then see how you both feel.'

'Why, why? I shall never change. Didn't he tell you how important it is that we marry now? Then we can work together in Paris and Berlin. It's wonderful. It's what I've always wanted to do, and now you've spoiled it all. Why should we wait?'

'What are you afraid of?' asked Galina quietly. 'That if he goes away, he will not come back?'

'No, of course not. It's hateful of you to suggest that. But he won't be here. I shan't see him for months and months. Can't you understand? Anything may happen.'

'Listen to me, my pet, listen quietly, and try to be sensible,' said her father patiently, taking her hand and pulling her close to him. 'You've only known Dirk for a couple of months, if that. Your mother and I, with your brothers, met him for the first time today. How can I allow you to marry a man of whom we know so very little? How can I let him take you away, leading a helter-skelter sort of life in France and Germany, no settled home, far from all of us? To my mind, marriage is a partnership for life, it is not lightly undertaken; and if you have let your feelings, your infatuation, carry you away, then it is I who must think for you.'

'It is not infatuation, Papa, I truly love him.'

'I know you think you do, and if it is so, if it proves real and lasting, what will a few months matter? They will be gone in a flash.' He put his arm round her. She leaned against his shoulder and he stroked her hair. 'You must learn to be patient.'

'Your father is right,' said Galina gently. 'This is serious, not something to be entered into so rashly, without careful thought.'

She meant well, but it was a mistake. Tanya turned on her instantly.

'Oh, you would say that. You've always opposed everything I've ever wanted to do. You don't want me to be happy, you never have.'

'That's not true.'

'Oh yes it is. You're jealous because Papa loves me more than you, because he sees my mother in me, and you can't bear that, can you? You've hated me for that ever since she died.'

'Be quiet, Tanya. You're talking nonsense,' said her father wearily.

And Galina, out of her very real anxiety for the girl, lost all patience.

'Your father has not told you everything. When we saw this man first for a few minutes in the Monte Carlo Casino I was struck, and, I may say, horrified, to see his likeness to a man we knew in Russia, a man who did your father and me the greatest possible harm.'

Tanya stared at her. 'I don't believe you. You're making it up.'

'Indeed I'm not. Until today we had no reason to think that it was the same man, but were appalled when he came into the room. I couldn't believe that fate had played such a cruel trick as to bring Igor Livinov into our lives after so many years.'

'But what has this man to do with Dirk?' said Tanya slowly.

'We don't know yet. That is what we *must* have time to find out. It is true, Tanya, you must believe me. I know his stepfather is Swiss, but Dirk is Russian, he has admitted as much to your father. But he has not told him everything. Igor Livinov is a great man in the Soviet of today. He is part of the secret police, the GPU, and he holds great power. It could be he who organized this murderous attack on Leon in the hospital.'

'And you believe that Dirk has something to do with things like that? You must be crazy. You should have heard the things he said when we were together in France. He hates the Bolsheviki as much as we do.'

'How can you be sure of that? Listen to me, Tanya. I have never spoken of this to any of you, it was too painful, but it was this man, this Livinov, who drove your father and me apart . . .'

'No,' said Simon quickly. 'No, Galina, leave it . . .'

But she ignored him and went on with an effort. 'A short time before we were to have been married, when your father was in England with your grandfather, who was dying, this man . . . raped me brutally, heartlessly. When I knew I was pregnant, I ran away, I hid myself, and it was not till months later, till I knew with certainty that the child I bore was not his but your father's son, that I felt I could go back to your father. But by then it was too late. Believing me to have gone out of his life, he was married to your mother. Through his savage attack Livinov condemned us to years of misery. You will say that this has nothing to do with Dirk, but how do we know? How can we be sure? When Leon saw him arrive today, he was as shocked and distressed as I was.'

'Oh yes, Leon – everything *he* says is right, isn't it?' Tanya shook it away from her, refusing to believe. 'How do you know he's not a Communist, a spy, and that assault in the hospital was not just a pretence to deceive you and Father? But of course, he's part of your past, isn't he? He was in love with you then and he still is now. Do you imagine I haven't seen the way he looks at you? Do you think I haven't noticed how much time you spend with him? The herb garden is a lovely excuse, isn't it? Haven't you noticed it, Papa? Doesn't it ever worry you?'

The bitter words spilled out, the pent-up jealousy that had built up over the years.

'Stop it, Tanya,' said her father sharply. 'Don't you dare say such things.'

'Why?' Can't you face up to them? She can say what she likes about me, but if I say anything about her, then it's all wrong. Perhaps this Igor Livinov didn't rape her, perhaps he was her lover all along, and afterwards you swallowed her sad story whole.'

'Tanya, for God's sake!'

Moved by a gust of uncontrollable anger, Simon slapped his daughter's face hard.

She gasped, her hand flying to her cheek. 'You've never hit me before.'

'Perhaps I should have done it more often. I'm sorry but I will not stand here listening to such outrageous accusations against Galina.'

'Galina, Galina, it's always Galina, isn't it? You think more of her than any of us. I'll never forgive you for this, never, never!' And she ran out of the library, up the stairs and into her own room, flinging herself on the bed in a passion of tears and self-pity.

'Damnation!' exclaimed Simon. 'Why did I have to lose my temper?'

'She deserved it.'

'And why did you have to say all that to her? It only made things worse.'

'Someone had to. She has to realize why we feel as we do. She has to be stopped. You are too soft with her, Simon. You always have been.'

'She's my daughter, for God's sake. I love the child.'

'She's not a child. She's a self-willed, obstinate young woman. You must realize that.'

'Oh hell!' He turned away. 'She will set us quarrelling if we're not careful.'

'You don't believe that Leon and I are . . .'

'No, of course I don't.'

She gave him a long look. Random accusations can sometimes contain barbs that pierce and fester.

'If you wish we can give up this garden project.'

'No, no, leave it. I don't think she even realized what she was saying.'

'I don't hate her, Simon. I would love her if she would let me. I want her to be happy. Should I go to her? She loves you so much. She will be very wretched about this quarrel.'

'No, better let things cool down. She'll get over it.' He sighed. 'Pray God that I can make her see reason.'

For once he was wrong in his judgement. Tanya was up very early, and had packed a suitcase and written a hasty note. Jake brought it to Simon when he was pouring coffee for breakfast.

'Miss Tanya asked me to give you this, sir.'

'Where is she?'

211

'Gone, sir. She came down when I was getting the car out to drive Miss Nicola to school. She asked me to drop her at the railway station.'

'I see. Thank you, Jake.'

He slit open the envelope and stared at the few scrawled sentences. Then he went out and up the stairs, leaving the coffee cooling.

Galina, half-dressed, turned to him as he burst in.

'What has happened?' she asked.

'She's bolted. Packed a bag and gone to this man. Here – read what she says. "I shall be at the Savoy with Dirk and I'm never coming back."'

'You'll have to go there, Simon. You will have to bring her away.'

'Yes, but what then? What can I do if she is determined? One of our ancestors tied his daughter to a bedpost and did his best to beat her into submission, and even he failed,' he said wryly, 'and I can hardly improve on that. But I won't have my daughter running abroad with her lover and marrying in some hole-and-corner registry office as if she were a pregnant housemaid, and that's what she will do if I turn my back on her. If it has to be, if I can't prevent it, then she shall be married properly.'

'Oh, Simon, I'm desperately sorry. Was it my fault? Did I say too much?'

'No, it's not your fault, nor is it mine. Somewhere, if there is a somewhere, Nina must be laughing her head off at me. I'll be lucky if I don't have an outraged Hester on the telephone. She has a nose for scandal, and how she'll love something like this. Oh, why couldn't Tanya have picked on Luke? A horde of Welsh miners as in-laws would have been preferable to this. I'd better go now before anything worse happens. Will you telephone the hospital and tell them that I'll be late?'

'Yes, of course.'

'Wish me luck.'

She reached up to kiss him, and he stopped only to swallow a cup of cold coffee before driving to London as fast as the early morning traffic permitted.

* * *

Tanya had reached town before eight o'clock, took a taxi to the Savoy, and asked for Dirk. She was told that Herr von Richter was in the breakfast room, so she left her suitcase at the reception desk and went in search of him.

He was not alone. A small thin man was with him, grey hair, grey suit, grey pointed face reminding her vaguely of the river rats she and Andy used to prod out of their holes on the Fens. They both rose as she approached the table, and she saw the surprise on Dirk's face. He nodded to his companion, who gave her a sly knowing glance before he left.

'Who was that?' she asked, frowning.

'No one of importance – a fellow who runs messages for me, that's all. Darling, what has brought you here?'

'I know what my father said to you last night, about waiting months and months to be married. We – we quarrelled over it, so I left early this morning. I came straight to you, Dirk. I'm over twenty-one, I can do as I like. He can't stop me. We can be married just as we said we would before you go to Paris.' She saw him frown and felt a momentary panic. 'We can, can't we?'

'Of course we can. It can be arranged through the Swiss Embassy. But, dearest, I don't want it to be like that. You are fond of your father. It will make you very unhappy, won't it, and I would not wish that.'

If she had expected him, in true romantic style, to crush her to his heart, tell her what a brave, wonderful girl she was, fling her into his car, and drive off to paradise, it didn't work out like that. Instead he was eminently reasonable and very anxious for her good name.

'I will take a room for you in the hotel where you can leave your bag for the time being, and then perhaps we can think quietly what to do next.'

He summoned the waiter, gave his order, and then turned back to her.

'What about breakfast? We'll have some fresh coffee and toast.'

Running away in a dramatic bid for freedom had fallen rather flat, and Tanya suddenly woke up to the plain fact that it was definitely not done to be breakfasting with a young man, not a husband or a brother, in the public room of a large hotel where she could be seen by any of their many acquaintances. Dirk calmly went on eating, poured the fresh coffee when it came, and urged her to take some grapefruit and fresh toast.

It was all so different from what she had imagined, and it was disconcerting to find that, even in moments of crisis, one did get hungry. Reluctantly she began to butter the toast.

When they had eaten, she said tentatively, 'I must look perfectly dreadful. I'll go up to the room and tidy up.'

He took her arm, and as they came out of the breakfast room an enterprising press photographer, who had been tracking a film star who was staying at the hotel, took a couple of quick shots on the off-chance. You never knew what you could sell.

Dirk fetched her key, saw her into the lift, and was coming back to pick up a newspaper when he saw Simon come through the doors. He went to meet him.

'Good morning, Lord Aylsham. I have been expecting you ever since Tanya turned up about an hour ago. She has gone to the room I booked for her. Shall we wait for her in the lounge?'

Simon, whose anger with the arrogant young man who had stolen his daughter had been steadily growing with every mile, was taken aback by this calm, reasonable attitude.

'I've come to take Tanya home with me,' he said stiffly.

'Of course. I was quite sure you would. I did warn you, didn't I, that Tanya would not see the situation quite as you do?'

The implication that this foreigner understood his daughter better than he did was so infuriating that Simon found it difficult to speak civilly.

'I suppose you believe you have won?' he said.

'I'm quite sure I have. You know perfectly well that I have only to say the word and Tanya will come with me in the boat train to Calais and we shall have to be married in Paris.'

'I could not possibly allow her to do that.'

'No, of course you couldn't, neither would I want it. I'm not proposing an elopement. I don't think there will be any necessity, do you?'

Simon had a strong desire to wipe the smile off the handsome face, but he knew that violence would serve no purpose.

He said, 'Suppose we wait until we hear what Tanya has to say.'

'Certainly.' Dirk summoned a page and sent him on his errand

and then glanced at his unwilling guest. 'May I order you something? Coffee perhaps? It's a little early for anything stronger.'

'Thank you, no.'

At the moment, he thought it would probably choke him. The damnable fellow had him at a disadvantage and was obviously enjoying it. They waited in an uneasy silence. Dirk took out his cigarette case, offered it politely, was refused, and lit up himself.

Presently they saw Tanya come hurrying through the door and rose to their feet. She stopped when she saw her father. She had combed her hair and freshened her make-up, but she looked very young and vulnerable standing there masking nerves with a show of defiance, and Simon's heart went out to her.

'Tanya, my dear, I'm here to take you home with me.'

'I'm not going with you. I don't want to talk to you.'

'Yes, you do, my darling.' Dirk put an arm round her shoulders. 'Now, come and sit down. There are one or two matters to discuss before he takes you away.'

'I'm not going away. I'm staying here with you.'

'No, my dearest, it would not be suitable. Besides, in a few days I shall be going to Zurich. My stepfather will want to meet Lord Aylsham, and would be very distressed if he were not present at our wedding.'

'Wedding?' Tanya looked from Dirk to her father.

'Yes. Perhaps before we part this morning we could fix a date.'

'I think you underrate my powers of persuasion,' said Simon drily. 'I'm not giving you my blessing yet.'

'Oh, but you will. If I judge you rightly, you would not want any shadow of scandal to fall on your daughter and it would, you know, if we were to run off together and wait until we got to Paris before we married.'

Smooth silky manner, and beneath it a will of steel. For a moment Simon was back in the cold dirty room in the Bolsheviki Headquarters at Sevastopol, fighting with Igor Livinov for the freedom, the very life, of Galina and his son. Was that resemblance fancied, or was it real? Who *was* this man? Again and again he felt as Niki had done before him, that Dirk von Richter was a superb actor playing a part he had planned for himself. And this was the man who had ensnared his daughter, and she would go with him, he knew that now, whether he gave his consent or not.

He stood up. 'It's time to leave,' he said brusquely. 'I've been here long enough. I'm not simply Tanya's father. I'm a doctor with patients who depend on me. I will let you know my decision.'

'Dirk,' said Tanya pitifully. 'Dirk, please . . .'

'Go with your father,' he said. 'He won't shut you up in his castle on bread and water, believe me.' He tilted up her chin to look at him. 'I'll see you tomorrow.'

'You promise?'

'Of course – and before you go I have something for you. I meant to give it to you when we lunched together today.' He brought a small box from an inner pocket and opened it. Inside was a ring, not unduly large or flashy, but of exquisite workmanship, a ruby surrounded by tiny diamonds, the stone flashing rosy beneath the overhead lights. 'I'm not going to say it was my mother's or belonged to ancestors about whom I know nothing. I saw it in a shop in Florence and knew it was what I wanted for my future bride, if ever I had one.'

'Isn't this a little premature?' said Simon drily.

'No, I don't think so.' Dirk took Tanya's hand and slipped the ring on to the third finger, and then kissed her gently. 'Till tomorrow,' he said.

The next morning in the gossip column of one of the popular daily newspapers there appeared a photograph with a caption – *'The Honourable Tanya Aylsham breakfasting at the Savoy with wealthy art lover Dirk von Richter. Do we scent romance?'*

It was not a paper that Simon would ordinarily see, but Galina found the servants poring over it in the kitchen and borrowed it.

'That'll set the tongues wagging,' he said disgustedly. 'If Hester telephones, tell her I'm locked in the operating theatre and can talk to no one.'

Down in Tredegar Megan had seen it too. Elspeth, nursing her third baby, stared down at it spread out on the kitchen table.

'She's pretty enough,' she said grudgingly. 'Is that the girl Luke has set his heart on?'

'I saw her once that time we went up to London. Dressed to kill she was, all airs and graces, trying to make me look a booby and treating Luke as if she owned him!'

'Doesn't look much like it now, does it? Dai always said as how Luke never had no chance and was doing himself no good up there. I must say that Dirk whatever-his-name-is looks a fair treat, doesn't he?' Elspeth went on enviously. 'Bit like Clark Gable in that film down at the Roxy.'

What the devil did you do when your daughter set her heart on a man whom you instinctively disliked and distrusted but against whom you could prove absolutely nothing? Simon went to see his old friend Nigel Drew, with whom he had shared some eventful years in Russia. Nigel was in the diplomatic service and was taking a holiday in England while awaiting posting to Berlin. In his quiet way he knew almost everyone, and had his finger on a number of useful sources of information.

They sat over drinks in the smoking room of the Garrick Club, haunt of actors, writers, journalists and politicians, to which they both belonged.

'I've seen the fellow about,' he said thoughtfully. 'Met him at a couple of parties – quiet, good manners, doesn't give much away. My dear Simon, his stepfather, Baron von Richter, is of the utmost respectability, even if he did marry his housekeeper, who possibly had been his mistress. After all, it is not a crime, and if his adopted son has a murky past it's been long forgotten. Aren't you just a little prejudiced simply because he's taking Tanya out of this country for a year or two and you hate parting with her?'

'I admit that's part of it – but it's more, much more. Galina is convinced that he is linked with Igor Livinov, so you don't need me to tell you how strongly she feels about it; and there is certainly a kind of resemblance that comes and goes.'

Nigel smiled. 'What do you suspect? A rabid Communist masquerading beneath the skin of a wealthy capitalist? I doubt it, but I do happen to be acquainted with someone in MI5. I could have a quiet word with him if you like.'

'I'd be grateful if you would, though in her present mood I think Tanya would run off with him if he turned out to be the blackest criminal on record.'

'As bad as that, is it? Look here, old chap, don't you think you and Galina are worrying yourselves over something that may never

217

materialize; and even if it does, Tanya is grown up now. If she has made a mistake, she will have to live with it.'

'And all we can do is stand by to pick up the pieces. Is that what you mean?'

'Something like that. Children have a habit of going their own way, good advice or not. You can't protect them all their lives.' Nigel glanced across at his friend's frowning face. 'I seem to remember you doing much the same yourself years ago, but you survived disaster and so will Tanya.'

Simon sighed. 'You're probably right, but poke about a little for me, will you?'

'If he's taking her to Berlin in a year or so, I shall be able to keep an eye on them.'

'Are you looking forward to this posting?'

'Not particularly. I don't much fancy this fellow Adolf Hitler. Germany went through a bad time after the war. They're ripe for change, but what will it be? For better or for worse? I'm getting too old for this game, Simon, and I'm afraid I smell trouble.'

They went on talking with the ease of old friends till Simon had to leave.

'You won't forget?' he asked as they parted.

So Nigel discreetly asked his questions and came up with nothing useful. MI5 expressed no interest whatsoever in Dirk von Richter.

The old happy confidence between father and daughter had vanished for the time being. He couldn't get through to her – no one could, not even Andy. She was deaf to all persuasion. She slipped out to meet Dirk as often as she could, and when he was away in Switzerland flowers or some charming trifle arrived at the house for her every day. She was edgy and difficult over everything, and it was a trying time for the whole family, especially Galina, on whom fell the burden of all the preparations.

'I don't *want* one of those ghastly fashionable weddings,' said Tanya irritably. 'I hate them. I just want it to be Dirk and me and the family, and at the Russian Church.'

So the date was fixed for December 21st, an announcement appeared in *The Times*, invitations were sent out, and arrangements were made.

There were moments during those few fraught weeks when it seemed grossly unfair to Simon that, after the trauma of having to escape from Russia, with the tragic death of his wife, the pressures of making a new life and settling the family in England, Tanya should choose someone totally unsuitable and Andy, closest to him of all his children, should fall in love with a girl who stubbornly refused to marry him. He gravely suspected the boy of indulging in a red-hot affair with Diana, and one of these days there would be the devil to pay when Sir Harry Harcourt found out, as he inevitably would sooner or later.

Those weeks were hell for Luke too. He realized that he had been living in a dream of his own making, but that didn't make it any less painful, and he couldn't back out of it. He couldn't just go away. He had a commitment to fulfil towards his benefactor, and was not going to let him down. The fact that the family guessed his feelings and were particularly kind and thoughtful towards him only made it worse.

One day Simon came into the library when he was sitting at the desk, pen in hand, staring bleakly into a dismal future. He put a hand on the boy's shoulder.

'It's the very devil, isn't it? I went through it once, and do you know what saved me – a cholera epidemic. Work's the thing, work day and night. It's the only anodyne.'

He was right. Luke set to work on a new novel, working at it doggedly, pouring into it all the joys, agonies and frustrations of the past year, aware that it was probably grossly overwritten and probably self-pitying, but finding a grim satisfaction in turning it into a world of his own creation.

It was only a week or so before the wedding when Tanya said to Diana, 'It's not going to be a grand affair and I'm not having bridesmaids, not even Nicola, but I would like you to be there with me. Would you mind?'

For perhaps the last time the girls were sitting on the rug in front of the fire, drinking tea and exchanging confidences as they had done so many times before.

'Of course I will. I hoped you'd ask me. What do I have to do? Is is any different from our church?'

'Not essentially, but more beautiful, more impressive. When I was about nine my mother took me to the wedding of a friend of hers. I remember thinking then that's what I would like when I grow up.'

'And now it's here. Are you happy about it?'

'Yes, of course I am, wildly happy.'

Diana, who knew about the family disapproval, gave her a quick glance but made no further comment. She leaned forward, the firelight playing on the lovely curve of her cheek, then she said suddenly, 'Craig has asked me to marry him.'

'What!' Startled, Tanya sat up. 'But you couldn't, not now, not after . . .'

'I said no, but he'll ask me again, I know he will.' She grimaced. 'He can be very persistent when he wants something.'

'But you always said he was not the marrying kind.'

'I didn't think he was. I believe he contemplates a kind of working partnership.'

'But you can't be in love with him?'

'No, I'm not, but I like him. We think alike. I respect his mind.'

'That's not enough, not nearly enough.'

'Isn't it? How do you know? It might be safer.'

'Who wants to be safe?' Tanya looked concerned. 'This will kill Andy.'

'No, it won't. Andy is tougher than any of us.'

'But why, Diana, why? I thought you and he were so very close.'

'We are, and that's why. If we marry we'll kill what is between us. Can't you understand that? I've thought and thought about it. Next year there is going to be a chance for me in America, and if I take it, it could go further, perhaps even Hollywood. I'm determined to get there, Tanya, right to the top, but how can I drag Andy along with me? He's a dedicated doctor. I know that. I admire him for it. And if I give it all up and marry him, what will happen? In a year or so I shall be turning his life into hell. I know myself only too well. To part now is the best way to preserve what we've had together, not destroy it.'

'I couldn't do that. I couldn't bear the thought of losing Dirk,' said Tanya fervently.

'You might have to.'

'Why do you say that?'

'I don't know. Perhaps because we know so little about him.'

'When, Diana? When are you going to make the break?'

'I don't know yet. It's not easy. Next spring perhaps, before Craig goes back to the States.'

They sat close together, staring into the fire as if seeing their future in the flames, so different from childish dreams, so many hard decisions to make, a little afraid of what was to come, but vividly, thrillingly alive.

For a society wedding the gathering of guests was small, only the family and close friends. Dirk's stepfather had arrived, and charmed everyone with his gentle manner, but apart from a few acquaintances in the art world, the bridegroom stood almost alone.

It snowed that morning, a thick mantle over rooftops and pavements, hanging like snowy clusters of blossom on bushes and the skeleton boughs of trees. In the car that took them to the church Simon looked out on a white world and was beset by memories: the wedding of Niki and Sonia, with the horror of the bomb that killed their father and grandfather, spreading blood and carnage among the guests; his own wedding in St Isaac's Cathedral, a grand affair with over two hundred guests. When Tanya had come down the stairs in her white satin wedding gown and long filmy veil, her mother's diamonds glittering in her ears, she was so poignantly like Nina, so radiantly beautiful, that he had felt choked. Such a confident dream of happiness could be so easily betrayed.

At the church, when she put her gloved hand on his arm, she looked up at him and smiled, her eyes brilliant with unshed tears, and he knew that the constraint, the anger, that had been between them all these weeks had melted away.

Aunt Hester, in a handsome dress and coat trimmed with sable, stood beside her large, complacent husband frowning at Penelope, the plain, unmarried daughter who was sniffing into her lace handkerchief. She looked around her with strong disapproval. It was all so theatrical, so un-English, from the bridegroom with his flashy film-star looks to the church with its dark, rich Byzantine paintings gleaming with gold, the priest in his magnificent jewelled

221

cope and mitre, the sonorous Russian choir, the crowns held above the heads of the bride and groom, the white silk scarf bound round their hands as they were led three times round the altar. It wasn't decent, it wasn't proper, more like some play at Drury Lane than a real marriage. Whatever was her brother-in-law thinking of to allow it? And Diana too, in pale green silk, the full skirt billowing out from her slim waist, a wisp of tulle and one white rose on her gleaming copper hair – fast, that was what she was, carrying on with Andy and at the same time being seen everywhere with that American Jew who was standing discreetly at the back far too flamboyantly dressed. She glanced at General Sir Harry Harcourt and his wife, innocents both, with Cecil beside them fidgeting through the long ceremony. Someone ought to warn them about their daughter before it was too late.

It was lucky perhaps that she didn't see Luke. He had not intended to be there at all, and then at the last moment couldn't keep away. The misery of seeing Tanya married to that foreign bounder was rather like the masochistic pleasure of pressing on a half-healed wound or an aching tooth.

He was staying in London for a day or two. Colin, who had come down on a flying visit, had given him the key of his father's flat in Bayswater.

'The old man's abroad,' he had said, 'so there's nobody to do anything for you, but if you want a bed for a night you're very welcome to use it.'

He could have stayed at Wimpole Street, but it helped to be alone. The reception was at the Ritz, but he couldn't endure the thought of having to smile pleasantly, to chat, to drink their health in champagne. After the service he would go back to Bayswater.

They were to spend the first night of their honeymoon at Dover, then cross over to Paris for a week or two, and afterwards there was the long drive down into Spain.

'If you've never seen the gardens of the Alhambra and enjoyed an Andalusian spring, then it's high time you did,' Dirk had said when they had talked about it.

They would leave the snow and freezing fogs behind them and make love among the lemon groves, climb the Sierra alive with the purple pink flowers of the cystus, go to the Holy Week ceremonies of Seville. There had been talk of trouble; the Communists – Republicans, as they called themselves – had been rioting against the government and had been put down harshly and bloodily by the Fascist General Franco, but that was only in the cities, in Barcelona and Madrid. It would not come anywhere near them.

In a flush of happiness Tanya hugged everyone when it was time to leave that afternoon – her father, her brothers and sister, even her stepmother. Simon thought she looked more like sixteen than twenty-three in her slim travelling dress under the mink coat and fur hat which had been his gift to her. Nicola and the boys were pelting them with confetti as they got into the car. Dirk was driving them down to Dover, where the new Lagonda would be shipped to travel with them to France.

The best suite the hotel could offer them still looked a trifle shabby, even though at Dirk's command there were flowers everywhere. When the porter had brought up their luggage, had been tipped and had closed the door behind him, Tanya looked around her with a little nervous laugh.

'I feel like the heroine of a Victorian novel about to embark on an illicit love affair,' she said. 'I can't believe that we are really married at last.'

'I assure you that we are. When I want something, nothing is allowed to stand in my way. Haven't you found that out yet?' With a sudden brusque movement he swung her into his arms, holding her so tightly that she gasped. 'Are you properly frightened of me?'

'Terrified,' she exclaimed breathlessly.

Then he laughed and released her. 'We'll soon remedy that.'

A bottle of champagne stood in the ice bucket on the table. He opened it, filled two glasses, and handed one to her.

'To us,' he said.

'Don't you think we've had enough?'

'It's good to be a little drunk on one's wedding night.'

Out of the many memories of that day there were two which stood out, simply because of what happened later.

After they had dined and danced a little in the hotel's ballroom, where a small orchestra plodded through a languid foxtrot, they went up to bed.

A gas fire glowed, but the room was still cold, and Tanya

shivered a little in her thin silk nightgown which Diana had helped her to choose. Dirk came in from the bathroom and slipped off his dressing gown. He was wearing black pyjama trousers but no jacket, and as he turned to throw the gown over a chair she saw clearly the scars on his back. They were faint but unmistakable. Once as a child she had seen one of her grandmother's serfs flogged, a shuddering memory she had tried to forget. She knelt upright on the bed and touched his back caressingly.

'How did you get them?' she whispered, and was taken aback by the fierceness of his reaction.

'Don't! Don't touch them!' he said and caught her hand in an iron grip. Then he saw the surprise, the consternation on her face, and relaxed. 'I'm sorry, my love. It was a very long time ago when I was a boy, but I suppose one still remains sensitive.'

'Oh, darling, I'm sorry, I'm so sorry.' She put her arms round him, burying her head in his neck.

He tilted up her face and kissed her lingeringly, then with deliberate slowness slipped the nightgown from her shoulders and kissed her throat and her breasts as his hands slid down her body.

He made love to her that night slowly and expertly, treating her like a rare and valuable object, wooing her with skill and expertise, bringing her to a physical delight that she had never experienced or dreamed of, and she was not to realize till long afterwards that that was to be one of the things that went wrong. He was always in some strange way remote from her. They were never two people wildly in love, groping clumsily towards one another with joy and laughter to find utter and complete fulfilment not just of body but of mind and spirit.

She fell asleep in his arms, and for some reason had a terrifying dream in which she found herself alone in some vast and terrible place that smelled dank like an underground cavern or the vault of a tomb, a place where she wandered hopelessly, crying his name and receiving no answer. When she woke in the early morning and groped for him, he was not at her side. She sat up in sudden panic, the dream still with her. The winter morning was dark. She felt for the switch of the lamp beside the bed and then she saw him. He was standing at the window, the curtains drawn back, staring out at what must at that hour have been a sombre, wintry sea. In profile his face looked remote, unapproachable, the face of a stranger.

She whispered, 'Dirk, what is it? What's wrong?'

He turned and smiled so that the stranger vanished into the familiar.

'Nothing wrong. I couldn't sleep, that's all, and sometimes I feel a need to get up and walk about. It's early yet. Go back to sleep again.'

'Not unless you come too.'

He hesitated, then crossed to the bed, taking off his dressing gown and slipping between the sheets beside her.

She shivered at the touch of his hands.

'You'll take cold if you do things like that. What were you thinking about? You looked so – so different.'

'Nothing very much. How best to plan the weeks ahead.'

But although she laughed and nestled happily against him, for the first time she didn't altogether believe him.

13

It was dark by the time Luke got back to the flat. He had spent most of the afternoon tramping through Green Park, Hyde Park and Kensington Gardens. In the streets the pavements were already trodden into black mud, but in the parks the snow still lay thick and untouched except for the footprints of a solitary walker like himself, the pawmarks of dogs and the intricate tracery of birds' feet.

The flat was the ground floor of a tall house in a quiet square, built for some prosperous merchant in Victorian times and now converted into three spacious and expensive apartments. He did not really feel cold until he opened the door and the chill, the dark, the emptiness seemed to engulf him. He was a fool, he thought, he could have gone back to Wimpole Street. There would have been warmth and food and companionship, only he did not want to share the day's event with anyone. He could have dropped in to one of the neighbouring pubs where the locals gathered in friendly fashion and there drunk himself into a stupor, but he didn't want that either. Then what the hell did he want? Work, Dr Aylsham had said, work – well, that was something he could do.

'How's the new book coming along?' Hugh Carter had asked only a day or so before, telephoning him to say he would be getting proofs pretty soon and there was a chance, a fairly good chance, of an American sale. And it was all too damned late! If this had only happened a few months ago ... But would it have made any difference? Probably not. Oh hell!

He knelt down to light the gas fire, turned it on high, and then went into the kitchen. He looked at the few items of food he had brought in – some eggs, one or two tins – and decided he didn't want any of it. He put on a kettle, brewed a pot of tea, cut a hunk of bread and cheese and carried it through into the sitting room. He drew up a chair to the fire and, while he ate and drank, read through what he had written during the past week, slashing at it mercilessly. Presently he began to write, and gradually as the ideas flowed he wrote on and on, while the tea grew cold and most of the bread and cheese remained uneaten.

He was roused out of his absorption by a ringing of the front door bell. It could be Colin, of course, coming down unexpectedly from Glasgow, or James Tait returning earlier than expected from abroad, but they would have had their own keys, so who else knew he was there except the Aylshams? He glanced at the clock and saw it was eight already. He must have been sitting cramped over his writing for nearly three hours. The bell rang again, longer this time. He scrambled to his feet, went to open the door, and then stood staring in blank astonishment.

Outside on the doorstep in a long tweed coat, a thick woollen scarf knotted around her neck, snow on her shoulders and on the brown beret, stood Megan.

'Good God!' he exclaimed. 'It's you!'

'Aye, it's me all right, not me ghost.'

'But why? What are you doing here?' Then in sudden alarm, 'Has something happened?'

'Can I come in? I lost me way and my feet are that freezing.'

'Of course, come in, come in. How did you know I was here?'

'I went to Wimpole Street. The servant told me.'

'You went to . . . Oh, never mind. Tell me later.'

He took her into the sitting room, taking her coat and shaking off the snow, urging her to sit near the fire.

'Take your shoes off and warm your feet.'

'D'you mind if I take off my stockings too? They're soaked through.'

'No, go ahead. Could you do with some tea?'

'Couldn't I just!'

'Right. I'll make it.'

He carried the tray out into the kitchen and put the kettle on again. When he came back with the tea, two clean cups and some biscuits, she was sitting on the hearthrug with her bare feet tucked under her, and in her hands the sheets of paper he had hastily bundled together when he had gone to open the door.

'What's all this then?' she asked curiously. 'Some of your school work?'

'No.' And then suddenly, because he had kept it to himself for so long and simply had to tell someone, he added, 'It's a book I'm writing.'

'A book? What kind of a book? A story, do you mean, a novel like – like – ' she groped for what had been drummed into her at the council school – 'like Dickens – or that chap Evelyn something?'

'Well, a bit like that, I suppose. I've written one already last year. They're going to publish it.'

'A book – with *your* name on it – you!' She stared at him as if it did not seem possible that the boy she'd played with on the dirty pavement outside the little black houses in Tredegar could have produced a book that someone was willing to print and actually sell. 'What's it called?'

'*The Lost Leader*. It's about Wales.'

'Is it a love story?'

'Part of it. They've paid me for it already, Megan, fifty pounds now and another fifty on the day it is published.'

'A hundred pounds! Just for a bit of your old writing!'

'And that's not all. If it sells I shall get more.'

'Fancy! Why didn't you say?'

'I wanted to be sure first.'

'Did you tell *her*?'

'Who?'

'You know – the princess, the one who got herself wed today to that dishy fellow.'

His face closed up instantly. 'No, I didn't. You're the first person to be told. Now, come on, have some tea, and then tell me what's brought you to London. What about your father?'

She took the cup and sipped the tea before she answered.

'He died just over a month ago. Don't you read your letters, Luke?'

He remembered now. There had been something his mother had written. He had intended to get in touch with Megan, and then in this last, wretched month had neglected to do so.

'I'm sory,' he said quickly. 'I'm truly sorry.'

'You needn't be. He'd had a tough time. He was glad to go. It was very quick – in his sleep one night.' She nibbled at a biscuit before she went on. 'You know how we had to live. Down to the cardboard more often than not, never a penny to bless ourselves with most of the time. Well, after he'd gone, I was clearing out his things – I had to, see, there wasn't much but there was his good suit and his new boots that he'd hardly ever worn – and it was then that I found it, tucked away in the bottom of that old chest of his, nigh on thirty pounds all in bits and pieces in a box with a piece of paper – 'Have a good time, Meg,' written on it when he couldn't hardly hold a pen.' Her voice trembled a little. 'He always used to say that, d'you remember? "She'll have a good old time when I'm gone" – and I used to think he meant it sarcastic like . . .'

She paused and dabbed at her eyes with a handkerchief.

'He saved it for you, Megan.'

'He must have done, and me going for him sometimes when he made me mad. It made me feel awful because I couldn't say sorry – I had a good cry over it.'

'What are you going to do now?'

'Get a job, I suppose, a proper one. Your ma says why not go into service? I could, you know, I know all about housework – I've done it all my life – but I thought I'd have a little holiday first, come up to London, look at the shops, buy myself a new coat. I've been staying with me Auntie Mabel. She married a chap who runs a little boarding house over in Fulham, and in the winter they nearly always have a room empty.'

It was a long time since he had been in Tredegar, and she went on talking, telling him about Dai, about the boys he used to know, those who'd got away and bettered themselves like he had, others who worked down the pit or were on half-time or on the dole. What she didn't tell him was that she had seen the notice in the newspaper, noted the date of the wedding, made sure she was here at the same time, knowing that it was the end of all Luke's hopes, it had to be, it had just been a dream and now it was over. She had crept into the back of that weird church that seemed to her so extraordinary as to be almost heathen. She had seen Tanya come down the aisle and thought, this is the girl he's wanted all this time, and had hated her bitterly because of it. Then she had seen the look on Luke's face and lacked the courage to speak to him. She had intended to go home that day, had indeed gone to the station, and then on impulse put her suitcase into the left luggage office and found her way to Wimpole Street. Jake, who had come

229

up for Miss Tanya's wedding, opened the door to her. He gave her Mr Jones' address and here she was, still wondering what had made her do it, still uncertain, still hopeful – of what, she didn't choose to think.

He suddenly looked at the clock. 'Goodness,' he exclaimed, 'it's past ten. I'd better see you back to your auntie's place.'

'I've left,' she said in a small voice. 'She has a new lodger coming in this afternoon. I was going home.'

'Then why . . .?'

She bit her lip. 'I wanted to see you, Luke. I couldn't go home without seeing you.'

'That's why you went to Wimpole Street.'

'Yes. I thought you would be there and – and perhaps that Lord Aylsham wouldn't mind . . .' She looked up at him. 'Couldn't I stay here – just for the night? Nobody need know, and I can leave in the morning.'

He looked dubious. 'I've just been using the one bedroom. The bed in the other one is not even made up.'

'It doesn't matter. I could sleep in here on the sofa.'

After all, why not? Megan was almost like a sister, and he doubted if Colin or his father would raise any objection if they ever found out.

'No,' he said decidedly, 'you can have the bedroom. 'I'll stay in here.'

Now it was settled it turned into a kind of picnic. Without his realizing it the weight of his depression had begun to lift a little. It had been a relief to be with someone from the past, someone outside the fevered atmosphere he'd been living in for the past month.

He said suddenly, 'I've just realized I haven't really eaten anything all day. Are you hungry?'

'Yes, I am, but it doesn't matter. I don't mind.'

'I do. I haven't much here, but there are some tins.'

They settled for baked beans, a tin of corned beef and some scrambled eggs.

'I don't think I'd better raid Mr Tait's wine cellar, but I have some whisky,' he said.

She giggled. 'Only a very tiny one for me.'

They ate the food with relish, and toasted the new book. Then he fetched blankets, a rug and a pillow for himself and showed her the bedroom and the bathroom. Presently, undressed and in his pyjamas, he sat by the fire with another whisky and a cigarette waiting for her to finish.

'Luke . . .'

He turned and saw her standing in the doorway in her plain white petticoat. Her hair hung loosely round her shoulders. It curled a little at the edges and shone a glossy brown in the light. It struck him that he had never seen it unpinned since the days of childhood. She looked more like a schoolgirl than a woman a year older than himself.

'I haven't a nightdress. All my things are in my suitcase.'

He smiled. 'I can't help you, I'm afraid. You'll have to share my pyjamas. I'll keep the trousers, you can have the jacket.'

He slipped it off and tossed it to her. She giggled and vanished with it.

It was not until he had finished the whisky and stubbed out his cigarette that he remembered he'd left the packet and his lighter in the jacket pocket.

'Damnation!'

He hesitated, then crossed and knocked, putting his head round the door.

'May I fetch my cigarettes?'

'Of course. They're on the dressing table.'

He went in and picked them up. 'Are you warm enough?' he asked.

'Yes, I think so.'

He turned, expecting to see her in bed already, but she was not. She was standing only a few paces away from him. The jacket was much too big for her. The sleeves fell over her hands, though the hem only reached her thighs. It looked funny and yet somehow endearing, and suddenly the whole long and stressful day came to a boil. He had been vaguely aware of why she had come, and now she was standing there, trembling a little, his for the asking. He knew that the wisest thing he could do was to walk straight out of the room and shut the door, but he couldn't move. Now, probably at this very moment, the girl he loved, had worshipped for so long, was lying in the arms of another man, lost to him for ever. Did that mean that he had to live like a monk for the rest of his days?

A wave of physical hunger swept through him. He thought savagely, why not – why should he not take what she was offering to him?

He took a step forward. She was unbuttoning the jacket and it fell open, then she moved into his arms, reaching up to his mouth, her lips opening under his as he kissed her, her breasts pressing against his chest, and he let the reckless impulse sweep him away. He picked her up and carried her to the bed.

She had dreamed of it for so long that she gave herself up to him without reservation, without thought of anything but a feeling of pure triumph that it was she and not that other one, that lovely princess of his, who lay in his arms, letting herself believe, if only for this one night, that she had won his love.

Luke was awakened out of a heavy sleep by the strident sound of the telephone, and struggled out of bed to answer it, already conscious of an acute self-disgust that he had used Megan simply to alleviate his own bitter disappointment.

He pulled on his pyjama trousers and stumbled into the sitting room, shivering in the biting cold of early morning. Someone was shouting down the telephone, and it was a few minutes before he realized that it was his mother. She used the instrument so rarely that she was convinced that no one could possibly hear all those miles away unless she shouted. Gradually he began to grasp what had happened. There had been an accident at the pit, a cave-in, and Dai was trapped.

'He's not dead?'

'No, they think not yet.'

He knew only too well what it could mean, the foul air, the choking dust, the suffocation.

'When was it?'

'The evening shift, about eight o'clock. A collapse of rock, Luke boy. They're trying to get through to them. Elspeth is near off her head with worry, and the baby sick too. The girls are working away from home. I tried to speak to Megan at her auntie's house, but she says Meg has left already.'

He saw his mother, so alone, with no one to help and comfort

232

her, trying to care for three young grandchildren with Elspeth worse than useless.

He said, 'Try not to worry too much, Ma. I'll come down. Just as soon as I can get a train.'

'Oh, Luke boy, if you could!' He heard the sob of relief in her voice and how she strove to be calm. 'If you're quite sure it will be all right. I spoke to your – your doctor. He was so kind, told me where I could find you.'

Oh God, she must have telephoned Wimpole Street in the middle of the night!

'Listen, Ma, I'll be there, I promise. It will be all right, I'm sure it will.' He tried to convey a confidence he did not feel.

When he went back into the other room Megan was sitting up in the bed, the sheet clutched round her naked shoulders.

'What has happened?'

He told her briefly. 'There's been a fall in the mine workings. Dai is trapped with five others. I don't know what I can do, but I'm going down.'

'I'll go with you.'

Megan, a miner's daughter, took it surprisingly calmly. He rang the Great Western terminus and found out the time of the train. They dressed quickly, swallowed the hot tea she had made, and then went out into the freezing morning, the snow crunching under their feet. At five o'clock it was still dark, but in the Bayswater Road he managed to hail a cruising taxi.

They did not talk much on the way down, only about the chances of the men being rescued alive and what could be done for Elspeth if the worst happened. They did not speak of themselves or of what had happened between them the night before. There was a restaurant car on the train and he offered her breakfast, but she shook her head, so he went along the corridor, fetched two cups of coffee, and brought them back to the compartment.

It was after nine by the time they reached Tredegar, and they went straight to the house. The kitchen seemed more stifling and crowded than ever and smelled of cats, food and wet nappies. The three-year-old Maeve sat at the table, porridge on her face and dripping on the floor as she waved her spoon at them, his mother was patiently trying to feed the reluctant Owen in his high chair,

233

while the baby wailed incessantly in the basket cradle close beside the kitchen range.

Megan took over at once, slipping off her coat and taking the bowl and spoon from his mother.

'I'll do that,' she said, 'while you see to the baby.'

'Where's Elspeth?' asked Luke.

'At the pithead, can't get her to leave.' His mother didn't say much, but he saw the relief on her face because he was there.

'I'll go up there now. Megan can stay here with you.'

God knew what he could do, but he would at least be there with them all.

They had never been demonstrative, but his mother held tightly on to his arm for an instant.

'You do that, Luke. There ought to be some news soon.'

Despite the cold and a biting wind quite a crowd had gathered, stamping their feet as they waited. He saw Elspeth, a thick woollen shawl wrapped round her head and shoulders over her coat. She clung to him convulsively, her pretty baby face smudged with tears.

'Do something, Luke, please, please. There must be something more you can do, there must be,' she pleaded.

He hugged her and then pushed his way to the front. The cage had come up with the crew who had been trying to battle a way through, their faces in the raw light grey with fatigue and sweat.

'Can't hear a sound,' said one of them wearily. 'Seems to me they're gonners, all six o' them.'

'No, I'll not believe that, I won't believe it, not yet,' exclaimed Luke. 'I'm going down with you.'

The second crew, who were piling into the cage, stared at him blankly. One of them said roughly, 'It's no place for the likes of you, Luke lad. You'd spoil your fine clothes and your fancy shoes.'

'We've enough on our plate as 'tis, we don't want no bloody amateur shoving his nose in.'

He felt the resentment, the contempt for the one who'd got away, the outsider.

'Here you are, mate. Put these on.'

One of the miners who had already come up was thrusting the workman's overalls at him.

He took off his good coat and pulled on the rough working

clothes stiff with dirt and sweat and coal dust. Unwillingly the men made room for him in the cage.

As a boy he'd been down the pit with his father. Then it had been a thrilling adventure, but now the thick dark, the claustrophobic feeling of being trapped under the weight of tons of earth, seemed to choke him. The miners moved confidently in this strange nightmare world where he could only grope and stumble. Surprisingly, despite the cold and snow outside, it was warm down there, the air thick and heavy so that it was difficult to breathe. They were working at the far end, and for a time he laboured with them, heaving with the pick, trying to smash a way through till his shoulders ached intolerably and his hands were badly blistered. If only they could hear something, if only there was some indication that the men still lived.

He was resting for a few minutes, leaning against the shored-up wall wiping the sweat from his face, when he saw the tunnel leading off to one side.

'Wouldn't that be nearer if we worked through there?' he asked.

The foreman of the gang shook his head. 'No good, mate. It narrows to barely wide enough for a man to slide through. Dangerous too, could cause another fall.'

'We might be able to speak to them. Has anyone tried?'

'He'd be a damn fool if he did.'

'I'm willing to have a go.'

'It's a sight too risky. Like as not we'll be having to pull you out too.'

'That'll be my bad luck, won't it? Anyone got a torch?'

The foreman shrugged his shoulders but found him the light.

'Listen,' he said, 'listen all the time. A creak could mean it's beginning to move in on you.'

Luke very soon found that the miner was right. He was slithering along a passage that grew ever narrower, and the air was so foul that it was painful and sickening to breathe, but he went on doggedly. Once he felt the earth around him shiver and lay still, his heart in his mouth, cold sweat trickling down his back. If it fell in behind him he would be closed in, entombed for ever, suffocating in this black hole. Then it seemed to steady and he forced himself to crawl on, his mind flying back to the night of the railway accident. If he could do it then, he could do it now. He came at

235

last to a blank wall and knew that now if he had been right he should be that much nearer to the trapped men.

He took a deep breath and raised his voice. 'Dai, are you there?'

There was no answer, and his voice seemed to lose itself in the all-pervading blackness lit only by the tiny gleam of the torch.

Then he had an idea. Years ago when they were boys he and Dai had worked out a signalling code inspired by the wartime stories of prisoners in dungeons, adventures like *The Count of Monte Cristo* which had once enthralled him. He wondered if he could still remember it.

He groped with difficulty in an inner pocket and found the heavy penknife he carried to sharpen pencils. Slowly he tapped out a message, so many long, so many short, spelling it out.

'Dai, are you there?'

Still no response, but after a minute he tried again, louder this time and more distinct, feeling sure that the sharp sound would carry more easily than a muffled voice. After another agonizing wait he heard the answer, faint but unmistakable. He listened intently and hoped he'd got it right.

'We're all here, one very bad,' and then something he could not interpret. But they were there, they were alive. It was the incentive the rescuers needed.

He crawled back with the news. It gave the weary men fresh heart. They sent up the message and more miners came down, the sweat pouring off them in black rivulets as they worked, and by the afternoon, nearly twenty hours after the accident happened, they finally broke through. One of the six had died, but the others, starving, near to collapse, were still alive. Luke did not think he would ever forget the first sight of Dai, pinned to the ground by the heavy part of the roof that had fallen across him but the eyes in the coal-black face alive and recognizing him.

When he came up to the surface he found he was something of a hero. Men thumped him on the back, Elspeth kissed him, and another of the wives threw her arms round him and hugged him, the tears running down her face. But what had he done, for God's sake? Dai was his brother, wasn't he, the boy he'd grown up with; Dai, who'd dragged him to the council school, cuffed him in private and fought his battles for him in the playground; Dai with three babies under the age of three and a blind, unreasoning belief that Communism was the only answer for the future.

They brought the injured men up tenderly and with care. The ambulance was waiting. They all needed treatment, but Dai was the only one to cause real anxiety.

At the hospital Luke scrubbed the coal dust from his face and hands and waited. Elspeth sat trembling beside him. Presently a nurse came to speak to them.

'We don't know yet how bad it is. The doctors are busy with him now. He could have multiple injuries from the roof falling on him. It's going to take time. Why don't you both go home? Phone in to us later.'

He persuaded Elspeth to go with the plea that the children must be needing her, but he remained himself. It was the infirmary where his father had died, still running on a shoestring, grossly understaffed, the overworked doctors and nurses fighting against lack of drugs, lack of the latest techniques. Where he sat the green paint was flaking off the walls, and there was that grim hospital smell of disinfectant and drugs, of disease and sickness and death. It turned his stomach but he was determined to wait and presently the surgeon came himself, an elderly man, weary but kind, delivering an uncertain verdict.

'We'll have to operate, but not until tomorrow. He is in too poor a condition, dehydration, loss of blood,' and he went into a long explanation of which Luke grasped only part, a broken pelvis, damage to the kidneys, a fractured thighbone.

'Will he recover?' he asked bluntly.

'We hope so. Your father, if I remember rightly, died from tuberculosis, but your brother has no record of sickness, has he?'

'None that I know of.'

'Good, good.' He put a hand on Luke's arm. 'Don't wory, lad, we will be doing our best.'

But was their best good enough? He thought of that short stay of his at Guy's, the care, the attention, and he knew that even if he scraped together every penny he had it still wouldn't be enough to pay for such treatment.

Later that evening he realized he must telephone Wimpole Street. He was, after all, an employee, working for a generous

237

wage. He must at least leave a message to say he would be away for a few days. It was going to be a desolate Christmas at Tredegar.

He put through a call from a public telephone box with a pocketful of small change. It seemed to take an age while he studied the graffiti on the dirty walls, and he jumped when he heard the familiar voice.

'Aylsham here. Can I help you?'

He had not expected to speak to Simon himself, and he fell into a disjointed explanation and apology for his mother ringing them in the middle of the night.

'It was an emergency, I gather. I hope not serious?'

'Bad enough. There was a collapse in the pit. The roof fell in on my brother.'

'I'm sorry. Is he badly injured? What do the doctors say?'

And because it lay heavy upon him, the responsibility for Elspeth, for his mother, for the children, he poured out what the surgeon had told him as well as he could remember without realizing how much he conveyed of doubt and tension and anxiety.

There was a pause at the other end, then Simon said, 'I have a couple of days free. Would you like me to take a look at him?'

It took his breath away. He said, 'But I couldn't . . . I couldn't ask such a thing from you.'

'You're not asking, I'm making the offer if you think it would help.'

'Help! Oh God, it would be marvellous, but what will the doctors at the hospital say?'

'Oh, it's quite usual to call in a second opinion.'

Maybe it was, but not a man of his eminence and rank.

'Are you quite sure?' Luke asked dazedly.

'Quite sure. I'll get an early train. You might warn them at the hospital that I will be there some time in the morning and would welcome a consultation with the surgeon in charge of your brother's case.'

'I will, of course I will . . . I don't know how to thank you.'

'Don't thank me yet. There may be nothing I can do. Keep your spirits up and your brother's too. It's half the battle.'

He came away still feeling dazed, and at the house they gazed at him doubtfully, only half believing what he told them about it.

Megan said suspiciously, 'What's he doing it for – working people like us? 'Tisn't natural.'

It made Luke furious. 'He doesn't think like that,' he said.

'He must be a lot different from most, then.'

It was his mother who said quietly, 'I always thought he was a good kind man, and now I know I was right.'

Since Elspeth and the children were staying at the house with his mother, he backed out of sleeping there and took a room at the Welsh Harp. They ate a sketchy supper, and Megan came with him when he left later that evening.

'You don't want to stay at that old pub, Luke,' she said, taking his arm. 'I've still got the house, you know; the lease has a few months to run and they can't turn me out. There's plenty of room.'

He knew what that could mean. He disengaged himself gently.

'Nice of you, Meg, but I'd rather be on my own for a while. There are things I've got to work out.'

'What things?'

'Elspeth for one. How's she going to manage if Dai is sick for months, and he could be.'

'She'll get compensation.'

'That won't be much, even if they don't try to prove that it was their own negligence that caused the accident,' he said cynically.

'I'd better say goodnight then.'

'Goodnight, Meg, and thank you for all you've done to help.'

'It hasn't been much.'

He kissed her cheek hurriedly and walked quickly away, aware of her disappointment but telling himself it was for the best.

The rumour had run round, and the hospital staff, out of a feeling of outraged pride, were making a frenzied attempt to appear at their best. They didn't exactly relish a visit from some fashionable London doctor, with a handle to his name if you please, looking down his long nose at their methods and techniques. Perhaps it wouldn't have worked out so well if Dr Isaac Williams had not discovered in the first five minutes that he and Simon had both spent gruelling years as army surgeons in the war. Ikey, as he was affectionately known, would have happily passed an hour in swapping stories if his distinguished colleague hadn't firmly reminded him that he had come a very long way to see his patient.

Dai had been resentful when Luke was allowed to see him for a few minutes earlier that morning.

'What's his lordship want with me, I'd like to know? What's in it for him?' he demanded.

'Damn it! Kindness, generosity, are not found solely amongst the working classes,' Luke snapped.

'Oh God,' Dai moved his head restlessly on the pillow. 'If I'm going to go on as a cripple, I'd rather have died down that bloody pit.'

'Don't say that, don't even think it!'

Then the nurses came and Luke had to go.

There were X-rays to be studied and a lengthy examination. Time dragged while Luke waited to hear the verdict. It was late in the afternoon when, walking restlessly up and down the corridor, he saw the two doctors come out of the ward where Dai lay in his curtained bed.

Simon paused for a moment to put a hand on his shoulder.

'With Dr Williams' consent I'm going to operate early this evening. Don't hang about, boy, get out into the air. You'll feel the better for it.'

'Will he recover?'

'God willing.'

'Why did you come?'

Galina had asked him that same question before he left that morning, and he'd hardly known how to answer. It was partly because he was sorry for the boy, weighed down with responsibility at an age when he should have been enjoying the pleasures of carefree youth, but more important something in himself, a feeling that he had failed Tanya. He should have somehow saved her from a marriage he still knew in his bones to be ill-judged. This somewhat quixotic act lifted the burden a little.

'Don't put too much trust in me,' he said drily. 'I'm not infallible, no one is. Go now, Luke. Have some food. Try to keep cheerful. I'll see you later.'

The snow lay in dirty churned-up heaps along the pavements and in the gutters when Luke came out of the hospital, but a frail wintry sun was still shining fitfully, and out on the hills the air would be fresh and bitingly clean. He felt a sudden revulsion against the tightly packed little house, against his mother's stifling kitchen, Elspeth's constant tears, Megan's look of reproach, the children getting under everyone's feet. It would be dark soon, but he wound the woollen muffler more closely round his throat and strode through Tredegar up into a wide-ranging landscape that had been familiar since boyhood. It was icily cold, but it was an escape from the reek and squalor of the streets, the gloom of poverty and unemployment, of sickness and tragedy. He began slowly to fight his way out of the depression that had held him in its grip ever since he had first known that Tanya was lost to him. He walked on and on till he was exhausted and darkness crept up from the valleys with a rising mist. He came back starving, but aware of a lifting of the spirit that carried him through the next few exhausting, difficult days.

The doctors were cautiously optimistic. Simon stayed overnight so that he could monitor his patient's progress after the first, critical hours. The hospital glowed with pride and a sense of achievement. They would follow the great man's instructions to the letter. There might be need for a second repairing operation, he told them, but in the meantime he would be available in case of crisis.

The reaction of the close-knit community in that small mining town was mixed. A certain envious streak, a certain resentment, was mingled with relief. No one wanted Dai Jones to die, but why should he be picked out above the rest for special attention just because of that young brother of his with his toplofty notions, thinking himself a cut above the rest with that BA after his name, soon to be MA too, God help us, if his mother was to be believed. And what about Megan, a good girl if ever there was one, eating her heart for him and he not caring a rap? Off after some city floozie, no doubt. The resentment smouldered, and Luke was aware of it though nothing was actually said.

He drew out of the bank his precious fifty pounds and spent it lavishly on Christmas – a turkey, a few luxuries, presents for the babies. What was left he put into his mother's hands.

'They're going to need it, Ma. It'll be a long time before Dai is earning again. There'll be more, I'll see to that. Don't you worry now.'

He was buoyed up with hopes for the future, filled with a new certainty of success. The grinding necessity to repay some of what had been given to him was slowly being lifted. The worst thing was parting from Megan. In Tredegar you didn't sleep with a girl, a good girl, unless you had what they called 'intentions', and he guessed it was in Megan's mind. He had no wish to marry her, no wish whatsoever. He avoided any mention of it until the very last moment, when she came with him to the station on the morning he was to go back to London.

Some of the snow had melted by then, and the wind was raw with damp cold as they waited shivering on the platform.

She said, 'When will you be coming down again?'

'Not for some time if Dai goes on all right. I'm going to be very busy.'

'You will write, won't you?'

'Of course I will, and you too, Megan. I shall want to hear how you are and whether you find the job you want.'

'Luke,' she went on tentatively. 'Luke . . . about that night . . .'

'I think we should forget about it, don't you? It should never have happened. I should never have taken advantage of you. Don't think I don't realize that.'

'It wasn't exactly like that, was it? Luke, you don't think I'm the sort of girl who . . .'

'No, of course, I don't. How could I?'

'It's just that – that I love you, Luke . . .'

He wasn't looking at her, but he heard the tremor in her voice, and then thankfully he could see the train in the distance.

'And I'm fond of you, Megan, very fond, but we can't talk about it now, there's no time.'

He gave her a quick hug and picked up his bag. The train had come clanking into the station and pulled up.

'I must go. Goodbye, Meg, and don't forget. Let me know what happens to Dai, to everyone.'

Then he had climbed in. The door slammed. The guard waved the green flag. The train jolted forward, and he waved from the window, a little ashamed, but deeply relieved and thankful to be going back to the people he liked, the work he loved, to the new book he was writing, to hope for the future.

14

The small grey man whose face had reminded Tanya of the Fen water rats was driving slowly down the narrow country lane that led to Ravensley. The car, like himself, was small, battered and nondescript; no one would have spared it a second glance. He stopped some yards from the large wrought iron gates that were partly open, turned the car so that it was facing the way he had come, and drew discreetly into a convenient gap in the sparse woodland that bordered the lane. It was early, not much after seven, and not yet fully light. He settled down to wait. The snow had mostly gone by now, though it still lay in patches under the trees, but the wind that blew across the marshes was bitingly raw. He shivered, huddling into his thin overcoat, even though the windows were tightly shut. The service he worked for were stingy in their allowances, and certainly didn't run to a coat of good woollen cloth, fleece-lined and fur-collared, like the one sported by his immediate controller. If he didn't succeed this time he might as well turn the gun on himself, he thought morosely. He could still hear the icy, contemptuous voice when he had tried to explain the reason for his failure. A patient in hospital should have been safely drugged into sleep by midnight, not lying wakeful in the light of the shaded lamp by the bed. When he had moved softfooted towards him, hypodermic in hand, his wrist had been seized in a grip of steel. He had fought to free himself and all hell had broken loose. He had been lucky to escape. He had lain low, and was thankful to learn from the newspaper report that his victim had overestimated his strength and had died after all, so that no one need know of that desperate battle. But the report had lied. He was still very much alive, the man knew that now.

'I want him eliminated by the New Year,' went on that chilling voice, admitting of no argument. 'Take care you don't fail this time, or else . . .'

243

He didn't need to be told any more. It would be back to Moscow, back to his miserable attic, to the lowest, the most menial of jobs, with none of the luxuries to which he had grown accustomed in this cursed capitalistic country, the good food, the freedom, with no spying eyes watching every movement, no ears taking note of every idle word. Those at the top of the ladder knew how to live, he thought resentfully, staying at the Savoy Hotel, elegant clothes, lovely women at a snap of their fingers, no soiling of their hands, only the power to send poor devils like himself to do their dirty work for them. Once long ago, when he was about fifteen, he had cherished ideals, believing in the glorious Revolution that would give a fat living to everyone, but not any more. The bosses were still there; they were just different, that's all.

He awoke from his reverie to see the postman come speeding down the lane on his bicycle. He watched him go up the drive to the box fastened to a wooden post, take out the bundle of mail from his carrier, drop it in, and return, a young man whistling merrily as he came whizzing down the drive and along the lane.

It was not so easy to eliminate a man who never stirred out of the park that surrounded the great house. He had thought first of hiding somewhere in the grounds, but a cautious reconnaissance had shown him there were altogether too many people about even when the family were absent, servants, a gardener, stableboys. He'd been watching this particular routine for ten days now, and had observed that his victim came limping down the drive to collect the mail at approximately eight each morning as if it was a task he had set himself to do. It always took him a few minutes to unlock the box, take out the mail, put it in the leather pouch over his shoulder, and relock the box, during which time he was a living target. He always came alone, and it was far enough from the house to deaden the sound and give him ample time to make his escape. He looked at his watch. It was seven-forty-five, time to make a move. He got out of the car. The lane led only to Ravensley, so there was little likelihood of any traffic. He looked cautiously around him, then went through the gates and made his way silently along the edge of the scanty woodland until he was near enough to be within easy range but conveniently hidden by a huge laurel, remnant of a hedge that had once bordered the drive. Presently he saw Leonid Alexandrovich come towards him, noting dispassionately that he looked a great deal better than he had done in the hospital and was swinging along with a certain ease, though he still used a stick. He paused by the box, put down the cane, and fumbled for the key, while his assassin settled himself into position and raised the gun. He was an excellent marksman and he took careful aim for the forehead. In a couple of seconds it would all be over and he could be on his way. Unluckily he had not calculated on the unexpected.

A fresh young voice shouted, 'Is there anything for me this morning?'

A girl came running down the drive at the same time as two huge dogs broke through the woodland, one of them jumping up at him, barking furiously.

His arm jerked, a stream of Russian oaths were startled out of him, and the gun went off.

He saw his victim stagger but knew he had not killed him. He turned and ran, pursued by the dog that was still barking madly. The girl came tearing after them.

'Stop!' she screamed. 'Stop! Jason, get him!' He turned and fired. The dog yelped but still came on.

'Stop, murderer!' yelled the girl.

But he didn't stop. He kicked out viciously at the dog, flung himself into the car, and was away, roaring down the lane.

Nicola bent over the dog breathlessly. The bullet had dug a deep furrow across his shoulder and blood matted the creamy fur. He whined as she touched him. She took him by the collar and led him back up the drive.

Leon was leaning against the post. The shot had whipped through his upper arm, and blood was running down inside his sleeve and dripping through his fingers.

'Is it very bad?' she asked anxiously. 'Can you walk or shall I fetch Luke or Jake?'

'I'm all right. You pick up the letters.'

'Yes.' She watched him with a worried frown as she put the mail into the leather pouch and relocked the box. 'Did you hear what that man shouted when Jason flew at him? It was Russian.'

'Yes, I heard,' he said sombrely.

Then she had taken his undamaged arm and they went slowly back up the drive, Jason limping beside them.

At the house a concerned group gathered round the wounded man.

'Oughtn't we to call the police?' said Mrs Alison, shocked and distressed. 'A man shooting like that – who would do such a wicked thing?'

Luke exchanged a glance with Jake. 'I think we should wait till we've spoken to Lord Aylsham.'

'Papa has gone to Wales to see your brother. He went yesterday,' objected Nicola. 'He won't be back till this evening.'

'I'll put a call through to him, but what about Leon? Shall I phone the doctor?'

'There's no need. I'm all right. He only winged me,' protested Leon.

Jake was already helping him out of his coat and shirt. It seemed that the bullet had gone clean through the fleshy part of the upper arm and buried itself in his thick leather coat.

Mrs Alison fetched a bowl of warm water, towels and bandages while Jake, who had had some medical training during the war in Russia, cleansed the wound and bandaged it efficiently.

By now the first numbness had worn off. Pain and shock were beginning to take their toll, and Leon leaned back in the chair with closed eyes.

'Better take it easy, sir.'

They persuaded him to lie down with a cup of hot sweet tea and aspirins while Nicola was trying to deal with Jason. She sat on the floor with the big dog's head on her lap, speaking gently to him while Jake cut back the thick fur, dealt with the raw furrow, and put on lint with a healing ointment, winding a bandage round the dog's body to keep it in place.

'Will he be all right?' she asked anxiously.

'If he's not, then we'll take him tomorrow to the vet your uncle uses for the farm dogs and the cattle,' he said reassuringly.

'He was so brave. He went on even when that beast shot at him.'

The big dog licked her cheek when she bent down to kiss his silky head.

Luke on the telephone had been fortunate enough to contact Simon himself and told him briefly what had happened.

'We are not sure what to do. Shall we contact the police?'

'Did Leon recognize the man who shot at him?'

'We didn't question him too closely but I think he did, and Nicola is sure he spoke in Russian.'

'In that case leave it to me. I will get in touch with the right people. Your brother is doing well, Luke. It's going to take time, but there is nothing to worry about. I'll be back as soon as I can get a train.'

By early evening they were all there with Leon, holding a council of war – Simon, who had brought Galina with him from London, and Mr Brown with a man from Special Branch.

'We thought we had covered your tracks effectively,' he said to Leon. 'But somewhere there must have been a leak.'

'Not the family,' said Simon. 'I'm certain of that, and the servants have never known his real identity.'

Leon said nothing, but the memory of that Sunday morning when he had seen Dirk von Richter was vivid in his mind.

'We could give you new papers, a new identity, and send you somewhere comparatively safe. We have such places,' said Mr Brown and came up against an unexpected obstinacy.

'I'm grateful, but I'm not going anywhere,' said Leon firmly. 'I'm not running away. I've done nothing wrong. I've not betrayed my country and I have a right to live where I choose. If it's dangerous for my friends, then I will go away and find somewhere else. I've two hands, I possess certain skills, I'm not asking for anything from anybody, I can earn sufficient for my own needs. I can look after myself.'

Mr Brown sighed. He pointed out the flaws and dangers in his reasoning but Leon was adamant, and at length it was decided that he should stay at Ravensley at least until his wound was healed. After that they would have to think again.

Mr Brown wearily accepted a small whisky, refused a bed for the night, and departed as he had come, unobtrusively in his anonymous-looking car.

Having satisfied himself that Leon's arm had received the right treatment, and after being dragged by Nicola to inspect Jason in his basket, Simon was at last alone with his wife. Both of them had the same thought in their minds.

'My God, what have I done?' he said. 'I have allowed my

daughter to marry a monster. Who else but Dirk von Richter could have known and sent that assassin to complete the work he failed to accomplish at the hospital?'

'And would have succeeded but for Nicola. Do you realize, Simon, that she could have been killed? He could have shot at her as he did at the dog.'

'I know, I know. It doesn't bear thinking about. Should I have told them, Galina, of our suspicions? Should have I begged Mr Brown to investigate Dirk von Richter, to find out what lies behind that charming mask, to discover who he is and what part he is playing? He is my daughter's husband, for God's sake! How could I say it when she is writing ecstatically happy postcards from Paris, from Spain? What will she do when she finds out that she's married to a murderer masquerading as her lover?'

'Do you remember how Igor Livinov was always linked with outrages and at the crucial moment conveniently vanished? An *agent provocateur* who lets others suffer the penalty of what he has plotted. Is that what Dirk von Richter is doing?'

'I don't know, Galina, I just don't know. Does he play the role of lover to suit some purpose of his own, or is that part of him genuine? Shall we ever know?'

It was a tormenting question to which there was no answer, and Simon could share it with no one but Galina. He was tempted to write to Tanya, to explain the doubts they had of the man she had chosen for her husband, but he knew she would not believe him. It would do nothing but alienate her from him, and that was the last thing he wanted to happen. He would have liked to discuss it with Nigel, but his friend had already left to take up his post in the Berlin embassy and he did not want to trust it to letters. So he did nothing, only insisting that Leon should never move far from the house unless accompanied by Jake or Frank Carroll.

Luke had his own troubles during the weeks that followed. Why is it, he asked himself angrily, that one woman entrances you and another, perhaps far more suitable in every way, leaves you stone cold? Is it the colour of the eyes, is it the beauty of face or voice or manner, is it the flesh or the spirit, or is it just that some inexplicable spark sets another spark alight, they fuse, and one is trapped for ever?

Once he had believed that vital spark might have taken fire between him and Tanya, but he had been hopelessly wrong. Von Richter had stolen her from him, but was it real or was it infatuation? Would she wake up one day and realize the truth? He tormented himself with useless conjectures. She had sent him a postcard with a brief message – 'The gardens of the Alhambra are like paradise. How you would love the romance and the history.' Was she wilfully cruel, or just heedless in her happiness? He tossed it into the wastepaper basket, then retrieved it later like some lovesick schoolboy.

He went on working. The library was almost entirely put in order now, each book noted and listed. He was typing out the final draft of his thesis and finding time to work sporadically on the new book, but in between sentences, or when he stopped to take a breather or drink a cup of coffee, he was haunted by visions of Tanya laughing with Dirk, riding with him up into the Sierras, eating with him, lying in his arms spent with the passion of love. He would thrust them aside angrily but they kept recurring and he had to concentrate twice as hard to keep them at bay.

Towards the end of February the proofs of his novel arrived, and by the same post a fat letter from Megan. He put it aside for the moment while he opened the parcel with trembling hands. The sight of his own work, all those sentences laboured over with such care, all those chapters thought out and revised, now in print for the first time – it was a magical moment. Suddenly it was not his any longer, his own secret torment and private delight. It seemed almost inconceivable that the great wide world would soon be reading what he had written and agonized over, would be passing judgement on him. Except for Megan he still had not told anyone, hugging the secret to himself. He spread out the long galley proofs on the library table and began to read, almost as if it belonged to someone else. Tentatively he began to make corrections.

He did not open Megan's letter until the evening after he and Leon had supped together. Nicola was back at school, Paul at Cambridge, the doctor and Galina in London, so they had the whole vast house to themselves. He went back into the library for another hour at the proofs before bed and saw the letter where he had dropped it. He slit it open and began to read.

She had written about his mother, about Dai, who was now home from the hospital, not able to walk much yet but getting stronger every day. 'He'll not be going down the pit any longer. They've promised him a surface job. You'd think he'd be glad of it, but that's not old Dai. Carrying on about it, he is, pushed aside like a lame old dog, he grumbles, 'tisn't decent, 'tisn't right, but Elspeth's thankful and so is your Ma.'

The letter rambled on for another page and then came to the vital point. She'd obviously found difficulty in putting it down. She did not state it in so many words, but her meaning slowly became clear to him and it appalled him. She was pregnant. That one wretched night in Colin's flat, his own crass folly, had had its consequences.

'Please write, Luke,' she wrote, the pen trailing with a blot and something crossed out as if she were pleading with him. 'Please come if you can.'

He knew what it meant only too well. In Tredegar you didn't get a girl with child and then abandon her, not unless you were the lowest kind of selfish bastard. He had grown up in that belief. He knew what it would mean to his mother, to Dai, to the whole tightly-knit community if he did nothing about it, even if he offered to provide for the child – his child – oh God, it couldn't be true! He read the letter through twice again and knew there was no mistake. That it should happen now of all times, just when things were beginning to blossom for him.

'Let us have the proofs back in a couple of weeks or less, if you can,' Hugh Carter had written. 'We look for publication some time in June. What are your plans? Are you going for an academic career? There is a new literary magazine starting up in the autumn, there could be a chance for you there.' And an afterthought handwritten at the end: 'America has come up trumps.'

It couldn't have come at a worse moment. It would tie him down, cripple him, and he would never be able to break free. The thought of abortion crossed his mind, and he thrust it away from him. It was vile as well as dangerous, and Megan would be horrified at the very idea.

All the evening, all night he lay wakeful, wrestling with himself.

To marry her would be a disaster for her as well as for himself. They had nothing in common except a few childish memories. He had grown away from Tredegar, he'd known that for a long time, he could not go back there; and yet if they were married that was what he would have to do. He would be forced to take the first job that offered. He had hoped for a lectureship in an adult training college or even at a university – how would Megan fit into that? Or there was this even more tempting suggestion of work on a literary magazine that would probably pay little but would be full of opportunity for a young man who had only himself to think about.

He tossed and turned, unable to make up his mind, and after a time got up and paced about the cold bedroom. At last he decided to compromise, to give himself a brief time in which to think. The next morning he wrote to Megan that he understood the situation but could not come immediately. He had important work to do on the new book. He was sure she would understand how vital this was for the future, but as soon as he possibly could he would come. Was she absolutely sure? he asked. Had she seen a doctor? He added that this was something between the two of them and must be settled by themselves alone. She did not reply, and the next couple of weeks were fraught with anxiety. Please God she had not confided in his mother or anyone else in Tredegar. He dreaded the thought of them all waiting to see which way the cat would jump, laughing at him caught in the trap in spite of all his grand ideas.

He couldn't sleep, could scarcely eat with worrying over it. Dr Aylsham noticed when he came down at the weekend.

'You're looking fagged out, boy, you've been working too hard. Take it easy for a week or two,' he said.

'As a matter of fact I was going to ask if you'd mind my going down to Wales for a few days.'

'Go by all means. Stay for a week. I'd be glad to know how your brother is progressing now he is at home.'

So at the beginning of March, when the first daffodils were coming into bud down the drive at Ravensley and the wind blew in across the marshes, bringing with it flights of birds and the first faint promise of spring, he took the train to Tredegar with dread in his heart.

There was no hint of spring in Wales, no flowers blooming yet in the sooty earth. It was early afternoon when he got out of the train, a cold grey day, the streets thick with the black mud of recent sleet when he trudged through them.

He went first to his mother and she welcomed him with pleased surprise.

'Why didn't you let us know, Luke boy?' she exclaimed when he kissed her. 'I'd have got the girls over, arranged a bit of a party. Sit down now. I've got the kettle on. There'll be a cup of tea in a jiffy and one of Megan's rock buns.'

'Just a cup, Ma, that's all. I had a day or two free, so I thought I'd run down, see how Dai is coming along, and the children.'

'They're fine, just fine, thanks to your good doctor. Dai's home now, but he's not working yet. Did Megan tell you about the job? I can't help feeling glad he won't be going down that old pit again, even though the money's not so good, but to listen to Dai you'd think it was like being thrown on the scrap heap. Your da was just the same whenever he was took bad. He never wanted to desert his pals.'

'And how is Megan?' he asked casually, sipping the deep brown tea.

'Not so good these last few days. A bit feverish she is, there's a lot of this flu about. She's been doing a temporary job up at the depot, getting up at six each morning with a bitter wind down there enough to cut you in half.'

Thank God his mother didn't seem to suspect anything.

'I'll look in to see her. I've brought a few chocs, some for you and some for her.'

'You shouldn't go spending your money on us, Luke. You've got enough to do with it,' she said, but she looked pleased all the same when he gave her the pretty coloured box. 'Megan'll like those. She was always one for the sweeties, was Meg.'

He drank another cup of tea just to satisfy her and then went in next door by the back way, which was usually left open. Megan was in the tiny front room huddled close to the fire, and she glanced up as he came in. She looked pale and there were dark shadows under her eyes.

'Hallo, stranger,' she said. 'So you condescended to turn up at last.'

'I told you I'd come just as soon as I could.'

'Can't drag yourself away from your fine friends, is that it? Did you tell them why?'

'Why should I? This is something between us and no one else. I brought you these.'

'He put the box of chocolates on the table beside her, and she glanced at it indifferently.

'You'd have done better to give them to Elspeth. The kids at least would enjoy them.'

'What's the matter with you, Megan?' He pulled up a chair and sat down. 'I'm here, aren't I? I want to do anything I can to help.'

'And what does that mean? Ten bob a week to help keep the baby, or a tidy bit more to send me to Mrs Pentewan in Nant-y-glo who'll get rid of it for you?'

'Megan, how can you speak like that? I've never even thought of such a thing.'

But he had, if only fleetingly, and it made him feel guilty.

'I'm sorry,' she went on. 'You don't know what hell it's been ever since the New Year.'

'Are you quite sure?' She didn't answer, so he went on with an effort. 'Because if you are, then there's only one thing to be done. We must be married.'

'Married?' She raised her head quickly. 'D'you really mean that?'

He got up, feeling stifled by the heat in this small parlour cluttered with furniture and cheap knickknacks collected over a lifetime.

'It's not going to be easy. I haven't a job yet, and if we marry now, God knows where we can live.'

'There's this house . . .'

'And what would I be doing in Tredegar, tell me that? Go down the pit, is that what you want, or get a clerking job at the depot?'

'If it had been that other girl, the princess,' she said bitterly, 'you've have married her like a shot, wouldn't you, with a palace to live in, I suppose, job or no job?'

He stopped his pacing and looked down at her.

'Listen, Megan, Tanya is married, she's out of my life for good. What I felt for her is in the past and has nothing whatsoever to do with you, and if you think the Aylshams lead idle, good-for-nothing lives then you're quite wrong. They work as hard as anyone.'

'That's what you say. You still love her, don't you? She's the one that matters, the one you dream about. I'm only the soft fool you take to your bed.'

'All right, all right,' he said with angry impatience. 'It's done now. Don't let's argue about it. I'm here to put it right.'

She stood up then, facing him with a certain dignity, a certain pride.

'You don't want to marry me, do you? Don't think I don't know. You hate the very idea. I know what you've been thinking these last couple of weeks. How can I get out of it with decency? Where will she fit in with my clever friends – famous author, university professor with his common Welsh wife who can't even speak proper? But she is bearing my brat, so I've got to do the respectable thing by her. Well, I don't want it like that. I don't want to have to feel grateful all the days of my life. I don't want to be just someone whom you tolerate and go to bed with when you feel the need . . .'

'Megan, please . . .'

'You shut up and listen to me for a change. I'm not so stupid that I don't realize where it would all end. Tearing one another to pieces, more than likely, and I'm not having any of it. And you don't need to worry, because there is no brat – you don't owe me a thing, nothing at all, d'you hear?'

He stared at her. 'Do you mean you lied in that letter?'

'No,' she said wearily, 'it was no lie. I never wrote to you till I was sure, but in this last week I've been ill and – and – it happens sometimes – I lost it.'

'Megan, you didn't – you didn't do anything to . . .'

'I'm not that much of a fool. Oh God, I'm so miserable. I wanted it and I didn't want it. I was so afraid, and yet it would have been your child . . .'

She was crying now, shaken with great sobs, and he put his arms round her, holding her, speaking gently, soothing her as if she were one of his young sisters.

She groped for a handkerchief and he gave her his.

'Do you know what I meant to do?' she went on huskily. 'I was going to keep it up, I was going to let you believe I was pregnant till after we were married, and then . . . then there would have been no going back, would there?'

'And why didn't you?'

'Because I'm a fool. Because I love you, Luke, and I know only too well what you feel about me.'

'Megan I'm sorry, I wish there was something I could do.'

'Go away, Luke, go right away. I don't want to see you ever again. It's time, isn't it, that I picked myself up off the floor? I'm twenty-six, God help me, on the shelf already, that's what they would be saying in Tredegar.'

'There are other men, Megan,' he said helplessly.

'Of course there are, some of 'em a good deal better than you, just as there are other girls, but they are not Russian, they are not princesses, are they?'

For a second there was a link between them, both unhappy, both looking hopelessly for the unattainable.

Then Megan said fiercely, 'Go, Luke, please please go.'

He still hesitated, then bent his head, kissed her averted cheek, and went quickly.

He looked in on his mother and picked up the bag he had brought with him.

'I'll call on Dai,' he said, 'and then take the train back.'

'I hoped you'd be staying for a day or two.'

'Not this time. There's something coming up, Ma. I should be there.'

'Take care of yourself, boy.' She reached up to touch his face. 'You're not looking too spry.'

'I will.'

He gave her a quick hug and went out into the street.

It was dark by now, a bitterly cold night with a rawness in the air that promised more sleet. He paused for a moment. Dai would take it badly if he didn't call, but after the scene with Megan he felt he couldn't face the hot kitchen, the babies, Elspeth's whining, Dai suspecting something of what had happened and going on and on about it. God knows, he didn't feel particularly proud about it himself. He looked at his watch. There was a train shortly after nine o'clock. He could catch that and spend the night in London. He still had the key to Colin's flat. He set off for the station. He still felt shaken. He had not meant any of this to happen, and he blamed himself severely. Occupied with his own wretched thoughts, he did not notice the three youths hanging about on the

255

corner of the street who glanced at one another and then followed after him.

In Tredegar it was not easy to keep anything secret. Gossip, true or untrue, ran from one to the other, was chewed over and commented upon. Megan had confided her condition to nobody, but there were those who had noted her return from London with that prinked up, conceited smartie Luke Jones. They'd seen him go in and out of the house and drew their own hasty conclusions. And here he was again, lording it in his good thick coat, leaving that poor girl to manage as best she could. Wasn't it about time he was taught a bit of a lesson?

Luke was walking quickly down a long dark alley, a short cut to the station. Few people were about on this miserable evening. The youths met him head on, barring his way.

'Been having a bit of a go with Megan, have you, me boyo?' said one of them.

'What's that to do with you?' said Luke curtly.

'When are you putting up the banns, then?' asked another, edging round so that Luke could not run for it even if he had wanted to.

'What the devil are you talking about?'

'Oh doesn't he speak pretty?' said the third mockingly. 'We don't like outsiders having their fun with our girls and leaving them high and dry.'

'I'm no more of an outsider than you are. Now, get out of my way, all of you. I have a train to catch.'

'Fancy! Back to London, is it? Then take this to remember us by!' and the first speaker delivered a punch that sent him reeling backwards against the iron railing. Then they were all at him. The battle was sharp and furious. One or two people coming off the train saw what was going on and left them severely alone. Luke fought back gamely, but it was an unequal struggle, one against three, in the narrow confines of that dark alley. He was bounced from one to the other, his hat was trampled into the mud, his collar torn, and his mouth was bruised and bleeding. He tripped and fell. They kicked out at him viciously, one after the other, then all three turned and fled.

He dragged himself to his feet and hung on to the railing for a moment, trying to recover his breath. He found a handkerchief to dab at his mouth as a policeman bore down on him.

'You've some nasty bruises there, sir. Been having a bit of an accident, have you? Want to come up to police for a clean-up?'

'No, officer, I'm all right. I fell and came up against these iron spikes. I'll go into the toilet on the railway station.'

The policeman gravely picked up his battered hat and handed it to him. If some of the lads had roughed up one of these toffs – well, that kind of thing had been happening lately, and he was not saying too much about it. Native feeling in Tredegar was strong and clannish.

In the station lavatory Luke dipped his face in the cold water and tried to wipe some of the mud off his coat. The punch in the ribs, the vicious kicks, had left him stiff and bruised. It took him back to that other episode on the bank of the lake at Chalfont Manor with Cecil Harcourt and his bully boys. Not accepted in one class, and now booted out of the other. He was neither fish, flesh, nor good red herring, he thought wryly. Well, he would stand on his own feet in future. He had a queer feeling that he had broken all bonds, he was no longer tied down, he was independent; from now on he would stand alone. There was a certain lonely satisfaction in it.

It carried him through till the summer. His work on the library was finished, but he seemed to have become a fixture at Ravensley.

'You're welcome to stay till you have decided on your future,' said Simon, and it did give Luke breathing space. He satisfied that hard-working conscience of his by offering to revise the files in Frank Carroll's untidy estate office, and by spending a little time each day talking English to Leon and incidentally picking up a smattering of Russian. The new literary magazine was to start in the autumn. It would give him a salary of five pounds a week, though its future was likely to be uncertain. On the other hand his thesis had received the accolade. He had his MA degree, with a suggestion that he might turn it into an academic booklet which would give him prestige, if no financial gain, and would necessitate a trip to Germany for further research.

Life had suddenly become full of tempting possibilities, when one Saturday morning in late June the first copy of *The Lost Leader* dropped into the mailbox. It was a thrill that perhaps comes only once in a lifetime. He touched it almost with awe, the coloured jacket depicting a miner against a background with a hint of the ancient past, his name on the cover, and inside the dedication to his loved grandfather.

He took it down with him, put it casually on the breakfast table, and sat down.

'What's that?' asked Andy, peering at it across his eggs and bacon.

'Just a book I've written,' Luke said offhandedly.

'A book you've *what?*' exclaimed Nicola with her mouth full.

'Don't shout, child,' said Galina. 'What kind of a book, Luke? A textbook?'

'No, a novel.'

'You sly dog,' went on Andy, 'keeping it to yourself all this time and never letting on.'

The doctor looked up from *The Times* and enquired testily, 'What is all this? What's going on?'

Luke picked up the book and handed it to him.

'Good God!' He turned it over in his hands. 'My dear boy, this is absolutely splendid. Why didn't you tell us about it?' He riffled through the pages. 'How have you managed to write all this along with your other work?'

'I don't know. It's taken ages.'

Food was forgotten as the book was passed from one to the other, critically examined, and admired.

'Will you give me a copy, signed with your name,' said Nicola, 'so that I can show it at school and boast that I know a real author?'

'I'll give you all a copy,' said Luke expansively.

'Indeed you won't,' said Simon. 'I'll place an order with my bookseller. If a book is worth reading, then it's worth paying for.'

It became something of a talking point for the whole weekend. Diana rode over from Chalfont Manor on Sunday morning and was persuaded to stay for lunch.

'I heard a hint about you on the grapevine,' she said to Luke. 'You know, friend of a friend in the publishing world. You're going

258

to be famous, my boy. We'll have a party at the flat to celebrate. You can tell Craig all about it. He's got a finger in Hollywood.'

'I thought he'd gone back to the States,' said Andy quickly.

'No, not yet. There are one or two decisions to be made before he goes.'

'Such as?'

'Oh, just things,' she said airily. 'I must go. Mother will be having kittens if I'm late back. She is convinced I'll fall off and break my neck one of these days. Why don't you ride back with me, Andy?'

They went off together and Simon looked after them. He had never played the heavy father. He had left his children free to choose their own friends, and only now, after what had happened with Tanya, did he wonder if he had been wise. He had an uneasy feeling that Diana had come to a decision and, whatever it was, it was not going to give Andy his heart's desire. He wished he could help but knew there was nothing he could do.

Diana was in fact biding her time till she could break it gently to Andy, and it was Cecil who forced her to act brutally. Her brother had always been jealous of her, and had nursed a grievance against Andy ever since that unfortunate luncheon at the Ivy. He found an opportunity to tell his father that his beloved daughter, of whom he was so proud, was carrying on a clandestine affair with Andy Aylsham and was quite brazen about it.

The General stared at his son incredulously.

'You're mad, boy. Diana would never do such a thing.'

'I didn't want to believe it,' said Cecil virtuously. 'But now theatrical London is talking about it, and I thought you ought to know.'

Privately the General thought his son might have been better employed in defending his sister's honour rather than sneaking to him about it, but all the same, if it *were* true, then something would have to be done. The young man would have to be brought to book and obliged to marry the girl or he'd know the reason why. He had no particular wish to welcome Andy as his son-in-law, but after all his father was Lord Aylsham, good sound English stock, even if the boy was half Russian.

To tell the truth, General Sir Harry Harcourt, once well known as something of a martinet in the regiment, was a little afraid of his strong-minded daughter. She had the habit of making him feel in the wrong in the sweetest possible manner, but this time he would have to brace himself. She would have to be made to understand that this disgraceful affair could not be allowed to go on. It all sprang from allowing her to go on the stage and to use the flat when she was working in London. He should have forbidden it right from the start.

He deliberated as to whether he should approach the father first – except that he found Simon Aylsham a cool customer and could imagine his frosty reply – or should he go to the flat and catch them *in flagrante delicto*, as the saying goes? He shuddered at the thought. He didn't mention it to his wife – no point in upsetting Grace unnecessarily. He went up to London, ostensibly on business, spent a couple of nights at his club, then after dinner and a stiff brandy braced himself to face the unpleasantness and took a taxi to Curzon Street.

The party had been a great success. Some dozen young people – actors, writers, would-be critics – looked at Luke with envy and drank to his success in champagne supplied by Andy. Craig, interested in everything, promised to read the book.

'The film people are always looking for good dramatic stuff with starring parts. When does it come out in the States? Get your editor to send some copies round. You never know which one will strike lucky.'

Luke was not at all sure he wanted his novel mutilated into a film script, but there was no doubt that the money would be welcome.

They had mostly all gone by eleven o'clock. When Nanny put her head round the door there was only Luke and Craig and Andy drinking coffee with Di and talking quietly.

'Sir Harry is here,' she said in a stage whisper. 'I saw him getting out of the taxi through the basement window, Miss Diana.'

He was already coming in, big and formidable, white moustache bristling, and was clearly taken aback by what he saw. It was all so respectable, no orgy, no couple writhing together on the sofa half naked.

Diana leapt to her feet. 'Hello, Daddy, whatever are you doing up here, and so late too? Has something happened? It's not Mother, is it?'

'Your mother is down at Chalfont and perfectly well,' he said stiffly. 'I happened to be in town, so I thought I'd call on you.'

'How sweet of you. Come and sit down. Would you like some coffee, or would you prefer a drink? Andy, get Daddy a brandy.'

She had taken his hand, pulling him into the room.

'You know Luke, don't you, and this is Craig Vassall. You remember him from when we were at the Lantern.'

He allowed himself to be pushed into an armchair, then Andy was by his side putting a brandy glass in his hand. But he was not to be fobbed off. He had come here for a purpose, and he was going to get it over and done with, the sooner the better. He summoned up all his dignity.

'Now look here, young Aylsham. I understand that you've been in the habit of coming here two or three times a week all this past year. It won't do, you know, it's not done, it will have to stop.'

Before Andy could answer, Diana had completely taken charge of the situation by going off into a peal of laughter.

'What *have* they been telling you, Daddy darling? I bet it was Cecil. What did he say, for heaven's sake? That Andy and I were sleeping together?'

'Diana, please!' The General was shocked at her boldness.

But she swept on. 'All kinds of scandalous lies, I expect, knowing my brother. Really, Daddy, I'm surprised at you. You didn't believe him, did you? You know how Cecil loves to make mischief.'

'I've been begging Diana to marry me, Sir Harry,' said Andy steadily, 'but you know that already, don't you?'

'Regularly once a month for the past year,' went on Diana brightly, 'and I've always refused him. I like him very much, but marriage, that's something else.' She shrugged her pretty shoulders. Then suddenly she turned to Craig and took his hand. 'If you must know, this is the man I'm going to marry, Daddy. In a week or two we would have been coming to tell you and Mother all about it.'

'Marry!' Her father stared at her, quite speechless for a moment. 'But you can't marry Craig Vassall, he's an American.'

'And what's wrong with that?' She knelt down in front of her father, taking his hands. 'Don't be so old-fashioned. We've been waiting for a while because we wanted to be sure. You see, I'm going to play in a very important production in New York. Craig and I will be working on it together, and it was just a question of whether we would marry here, or in America after the play has opened.'

'Diana, I don't know what to say. It's not right to spring it upon me like this.'

'I wouldn't have done if you hadn't come in here breathing fire and fury. You did, you know. Listen, Daddy, Craig and I will come to Chalfont next weekend, and we'll talk it over quietly with you and with Mother. What do you say about that?'

He lumbered to his feet, blustering a little, confounded by his daughter's self-assurance.

'I'm not giving my consent immediately,' he said with dignity. 'You're my only daughter, Diana. It's not right, it's not decent. We don't do things like that in this country. I won't be rushed. Your Mr Vassall must understand that.'

'Oh, I do, Sir Harry, believe me, I do,' said Craig quickly, with the faintest hint of a smile. 'But Diana has taken me by surprise as well as you. You see, she has been saying no to me for quite a while, so I guess she's taken my breath away as well as yours, but I hope it won't be too long before you give us your blessing.'

Diana said quickly, 'Do you want to stay here tonight, Daddy? Shall I ask Nanny Gibbons to prepare a room?'

'No, my dear,' he said heavily, 'I'm better at the Club.' He looked from his daughter to Craig. 'You'd better both have lunch with me tomorrow and we'll discuss this question of marriage. I won't pretend I'm happy about it or that I approve.'

Diana slipped an arm through his. 'Don't be angry with us, Daddy. We never meant to hurt you, really we didn't.'

'I don't understand you young people nowadays, always in such a rush. It wasn't like that for your mother and me.'

'But Daddy, you must understand . . .'

'No, Diana, not now, nothing more now. I think I'd better go. Will someone be kind enough to get me a taxi.'

'I will,' said Luke and bolted from the room only too glad to escape.

The General pecked at his daughter's cheek and went unhappily after him.

A moment later when Luke came back the other three were still standing where he had left them. He sensed the explosive atmosphere and remained in the doorway, wishing profoundly that he wasn't there.

Andy was saying caustically, 'What a brilliant performance. I congratulate you, Diana, you're an even better actress than I thought you were.'

'It wasn't acting, Andy, it was for real.'

'Was it now? I suppose you know, Craig,' went on Andy in the same brittle voice, 'that Di and I have been lovers ever since *Hedda Gabler* at the Lantern?'

'I guess I did. It's not Diana's past that interests me, it's her future.'

'And her future belongs to you?'

'I believe so.'

At that Andy suddenly exploded. 'God damn it, Diana, you might have had the decency to warn me.'

'I tried to tell you, over and over again.' She was very close to tears. 'You know what I've been saying all along. How many times have we argued about it? It's better like this, really it is.'

'Better for whom? For you and Craig, I suppose, and sheer hell for me.'

'I told you if the opportunity came I would take it. You should have believed me. I can't afford to turn it down, and I don't want to.'

'Oh yes, of course, your great chance, a new star is to be born, off with the old and on with the new, and marrying Craig is part of the bargain. I don't know what I'm doing here. It's obvious I'm not wanted. I'm like yesterday's parcel, opened and enjoyed and then chucked into the dustbin. Come on, Luke, let's get out of here.'

'Andy, don't go, not like this.'

'What do you want us to do, fight for you, kill each other for you?' he said with a savage contempt. 'To hell with that. The field is yours, Craig. Go ahead. I wish you joy of it.'

He pushed her aside and stormed through the door.

'Go after him, Luke. Please, please go after him.'

He heard the appeal in Diana's voice and went quickly, deeply distressed for both of them.

Craig said quietly, 'I'm sorry he had to take it like that.'

She turned on him fiercely. 'And you go too. Don't come near me, don't touch me. Go. Go now.'

'Are you having second thoughts already?'

'I don't know what I'm thinking or feeling, only that I want to be left alone. Perhaps tomorrow it will be different.'

'All right, tomorrow it shall be. But remember this, Diana. I'm a stubborn man, and what I have won I hold on to. Life has taught me the importance of that. You gave me a promise tonight and I'm holding you to it. No going back. General Sir Harry Harcourt is not scaring me off. I'm a good deal tougher than he is.'

He stooped, kissed the top of her head, and then was gone, while Diana fought the last of many weary battles and knew that this time her boats were burned behind her and there was nothing for her to do but go forward.

Luke caught up with Andy where Curzon Street turned into Park Lane. It was past midnight, but taxis and late buses still cruised up and down.

'I'm all right,' he said drily when Luke touched his arm. 'I'm not going to throw myself under a train or shoot myself like some Russian neurotic.' He gave a short, sharp laugh. 'I don't even possess a gun. Pa put a veto on them when we were kids.'

'Do you feel like a walk? I often tramp home from a theatre or the flicks. You see completely different people at night. It's as if London were a foreign city, a hidden furtive place, filled with mystery and glamour.'

'That's your novelist's eye. I tend to see only the poor, the sick, the homeless, the derelict.'

They walked on, talking at random about everything but the events of the evening, up Park Lane, past Marble Arch and into Bayswater. Outside Colin's flat they stopped.

Luke said, 'Want to come in for a drink? Old man Tait may be there, but he won't mind.'

'No, thanks all the same. I'd better get back to Wimpole Street.' He paused and then said suddenly, 'I'm thinking of taking a spot of time off later on. What about a trip to Paris? We could look Tanya up.'

'When I was about ten I used to think of Paris as the ultimate, one of those dreams you only achieve when you are rich and famous. Well, I'm neither of those things yet, but I think I could manage about a week.'

Andy smiled. 'Not the Georges Cinq but the Rue Caumartin. I know a decent little place. Is it on?'

'It's on.'

'Good man.' He stood for a moment and then said awkwardly, 'I don't know quite what I might have done, but anyway – thanks Luke. Goodnight.'

'Goodnight, old man.'

He looked after Andy as he fumbled for his key. They were in the same boat now. They had both irretrievably lost the girl they loved, and it had drawn them closer together. He put the key in the lock and thought of Paris – the stuff of dreams that, to someone privileged like Andy, probably meant nothing at all. And Tanya – did he want to see her? He wasn't sure. When the pain sleeps, isn't it madness to rouse it again? But he would go, oh yes, he would go. There was a kind of painful pleasure in the very idea; the pull was irresistible. He was humming to himself when he closed the door quietly in case anyone else was at home and asleep, and then went thoughtfully to bed.

Part Three

DIRK
1932

15

The telephone bell rang shrilly and Tanya fell out of bed to answer it, cursing because it was still in the sitting room and her French maid didn't usually come in till nine-thirty.

'Dirk, is that you?' she said breathlessly, and then gave a squeal of mingled surprise and delight. '*Andy!* But how marvellous. Is it really you? What are you doing in Paris, and why didn't you let me know? When am I going to see you? Lunchtime today? Gorgeous. Meet me here and then we'll go out somewhere. Dirk's away for a few days. About twelve? Wonderful. I can't wait.'

She put the telephone down on its hook and stood for a moment, pleasure at the thought of seeing her brother driving out the lurking anxiety. Dirk had been away for a week with no word from him, and though there was no real need to worry, his silence for various reasons gnawed at her.

Louise, coming in half an hour later with a string bag bulging with food and a long crusty loaf under her arm, found her young mistress already brewing coffee in the kitchen and bubbling over with joy.

'What do you think? My brother is over from England and I've not seen him since the wedding. We'll be lunching out somewhere so why not take the afternoon off, Louise? My husband is still away, so we're quite free and can please ourselves.'

And a good thing too, thought Louise a little sourly. A middle-aged French widow whose husband had been killed in the last year of the war, and with a marked antipathy towards all foreigners, she had surprisingly taken Tanya to her heart and strongly disapproved of that husband of hers, Swiss, German, or whatever he liked to call himself.

'Handsome enough and with money to burn, but that's not everything as we very well know. He'd like to keep her locked up like a bird in a cage,' she said darkly to her sister, who lived up

269

near Sacré Coeur and ran a little bistro much frequented by students, artists and the like.

'Jealous, is he?'

'Jealous! Mon Dieu, he doesn't like her even to smile at another man. There's been some dust-ups over it, I can tell you. She's not one to lie down and let a man trample over her. Crazy he is about her – unhealthy, I call it. Pity he's not one of those Turks with a harem, I say. He's properly got her dancing at the end of a string. One of these days she's going to break free, then there will be ructions, you mark my words.'

'It's a good place though, isn't it?' remarked her sister, eyeing appreciatively the butter, eggs and half a Camembert cheese that Louise had brought with her.

'It'll do. She's a real lady, that one, doesn't count every sou like some I've worked for.'

The apartment overlooking the Parc Monceau was in one of the most fashionable parts of Paris. From the front windows you could see the stretches of velvet grass, the nursemaids with their elegant prams, the children of the rich running in and out of the flowerbeds with their pampered little dogs.

The rooms were already furnished but Tanya had added touches of her own, giving them grace and charm. There were one or two fine modern prints and a huge Chinese jar always filled with fresh flowers. Dirk laughed at her because she would get up early and go down to Les Halles, wandering among the flower stalls and coming back with her arms filled with whatever was in season, dripping with dew and smelling of the country.

During those first, marvellous weeks in Spain, when everything seemed drowned in bliss, she had never realized how much she was going to miss her home, the huge old rambling house, the rough and tumble of family life, arguing with Andy, teasing Luke, quarrelling with Nicola, the dogs, the horses, especially Rags – and above all her father, whose powerful personality seemed to irradiate every part of their lives.

She had wanted to go back to Ravensley for a few days just to see them all again, just to ease the bruising effect of the difficult weeks before her marriage, but Dirk refused absolutely to let her go.

'I'm not having you running home to England whenever we

have a trifling disagreement. They don't like me there, any of them, and I know exactly what will happen,' he said.

'That's ridiculous. As if I'd listen to anything they might say. I married you, didn't I, in spite of all the opposition?'

'Yes, my darling, you did, and that's the very reason. They'll be expecting to hear how badly it has turned out.'

'You don't understand, Dirk. My father is not like that.'

'You think of your father too much. It's time you grew up, Tanya.'

That argument had come after their very first quarrel. In Paris, the gallery on the Champs-Elysées was large and very elegant. She had been thrilled when Dirk took her there. Maurice Romain, the suave middle-aged Frenchman in charge, greeted her graciously, showing her round with all his considerable charm, gratifyingly impressed by her informed interest in the Russian room. Paris was filled with émigrés from Tsarist Russia, and the gallery had a notable collection ranging from fabulous items of jewellery to exquisite Fabergé works of art in gold and silver and precious stones.

She said enthusiastically, 'I would love to come and work here sometimes, meet some of your customers, talk to them.'

'I would be honoured, Madame, if you would. Someone like yourself, Russian born and a princess from the old days, would indeed be a great asset, if your husband would permit it.'

'Oh, I'm sure he will,' she said airily. 'Dirk used to admire what I did in Giovanni's gallery in London.'

But she was wrong.

Dirk said 'No' very forcefully indeed and would not be moved by any pleading or persuasion. 'No, definitely not,' he said bluntly. 'My wife does not work in a shop, and that's the end of it.'

'But it's not like that at all, and I love it. I've got all kinds of ideas, and Maurice said he would allow me to try them out. We could work on them together.'

'Oh, he did, did he? And what were you and Maurice plotting to do together behind my back?'

'Oh, for goodness' sake, Dirk, it was nothing secret. It's just that I'm interested, and I do know a great deal about it. Besides, I'm very lonely and bored when you go away. I want something to do. You did say that you would let me work with you.'

'With me perhaps, but not by showing yourself off in a public gallery.'

'That's a hateful thing to say.'

'I know what will happen. It will be you, the attractive and available Madame von Richter, who will be the attraction, and not Maurice's antiques.' He captured her hand and drew her towards him. 'I cannot endure to share you with anyone. Can't you understand that yet?'

The argument ended, as so often, in passionate reconciliation. She could never resist him when he caressed her. It aroused feelings that sometimes frightened her, and there were moments when she resented his power over her. It was as if he were afraid to let her go, as if he had to possess her wholly, living, breathing, admiring, loving, solely for his pleasure.

She gave in to his decision, but it left her dissatisfied. She had grown up with people who had a serious mission in life, her father with his dedication to medicine, Andy who was closely following in his footsteps; even her Uncle Niki was not the feckless Russian aristocrat of the gossip columns. She and Diana had always despised girls like Ollie Winter, idle, pleasure-loving, sensation-seeking. If they liked to play hard, they worked hard too. So in sheer defiance she signed up for a course of lectures at the Sorbonne and brought on one of those quarrels that Louise discreetly ignored when voices rose and doors slammed.

Tanya was thinking about it that morning when she dressed. Andy was not easily fooled. She would have to be very careful what she said to him. He must not think she regretted in any way that too hasty marriage – and she didn't, she told herself loyally, not for a single minute. Dirk was still the most wonderful person in the world; only so often he puzzled her, so often she felt that he was two people, and that beneath the handsome, charming, sophisticated exterior there lurked another, dark, shadowy person that she glimpsed only occasionally but who still remained an enigma, and there were times when it frightened her.

He would disappear for a day or a night without any really adequate explanation. In the summer something had happened that still made her shiver. They had spent a delightful morning sailing down the Seine to Passy, and were drinking coffee outside one of the open-air cafés when Dirk excused himself for a moment.

She thought nothing of it till, looking up, she saw through the windows of the restaurant that he was in close conversation with a man whose pale, bony face by a trick of the light was absolutely clear to her. Dirk came back and she thought no more about it till a few days later when, to everyone's horror, President Paul Doumer was assassinated as he stepped into his car.

Prime Minister Tardieu exploited the fact that the assassin was Russian-born. A wave of anti-Bolshevik propaganda swept through the capital, a number of people were arrested and closely questioned; but what struck a chill in Tanya was the picture of Pavel Gorgulov in the morning newspaper. The face was unmistakably that of the stranger in the café.

Dirk dismissed it at once. 'How can you possibly tell anything from a muzzy newspaper photograph? It's just one of those chance likenesses. The man I spoke to was a foreign visitor asking about the riverboat excursions.'

It could be true, of course, and yet it had made her wonder.

She paused for a moment, examining her face critically in the mirror, while that knot of anxiety inside her gave another little twist. It was a week now since the morning when Dirk had left Paris for the south.

'My stepfather has asked me to run down and see him at the villa before he returns to Zurich,' he said at breakfast.

'He's not ill again, is he? Shall I come with you?'

She liked the Baron and would have been happy to do anything that might please him.

'No, no, it's purely business. One or two financial problems have come up and it's difficult to discuss them on the telephone. You'd be bored. Besides,' – he smiled, running his finger playfully down her nose, 'you'd miss one of your precious lectures, and you'd hate that, wouldn't you? I shan't be away for more than two or three days.'

But he was. Four days went by, then five, then six, and there was still no word. Suddenly she panicked. Suppose she had been right, suppose Dirk had inadvertently been mixed up in something dangerous and had been called in for questioning? She knew it was foolish, but she put a call through to the Villa Valéry.

'Herr von Richter is not here, madame,' said the housekeeper, sounding surprised. 'Didn't you know? The Baron returned to Switzerland over a week ago.'

'I see. I must have been mistaken. I understood he was calling there.'

She put the telephone down with a cold feeling in her heart. Why had he lied? And if he wasn't at the villa, then where was he? Strangely enough, she never once thought that it might be another woman, someone from his past life about which she knew so very little. She was absolutely certain that, whatever might have happened before, it was now she whom he loved and no other. There must be some simple explanation, there had to be, but it still nagged at her.

The doorbell rang.

'That will be my brother,' she called out to Louise and rushed to open it, all her doubts and misgivings disappearing as she flung her arms round Andy's neck and hugged him.

'Hey,' he said laughing, 'what's all this? I never thought I was so popular.'

She drew back a little confused, a little shamefaced.

'It's just that I'm so very pleased to see you. It seems ages. I want to hear all your news. Letters never tell you the really interesting things. Wait till I put on my hat, then we'll go out. I thought we'd lunch in the Bois. It's quiet there and we can talk. Is that all right?'

'Fine by me.'

He thought she looked very beautiful, very chic in her navy suit and white ruffled blouse. She was thinner though, and there was something fine-drawn about her eyes, something tense and highly strung about her manner, which made him wonder if she was truly happy.

In the cab taking them to the restaurant he said casually, 'Luke came over with me. I tried to persuade him to lunch with us but he refused, said he thought he might not be welcome.'

'How silly, of course he would. I was always very fond of Luke.'

'Were you?' Andy glanced at her. 'I was never quite sure. He was crazy about you – still is, I suspect.'

'Oh, nonsense! He got over all that years ago.'

'I wouldn't like to bet on it. You know he's just had a book published, a novel which is on the way to becoming a bestseller.'

She stared at him. 'A novel? Luke? He never told me.'

'Kept it dark from all of us till the very last minute. Pa read it and was very impressed, and he's not easy to please. He's going places, is our Luke.'

She thought of the shy boy she had befriended – how long ago now, two years, three? – of how he had taken the blame for her in the motor accident, of how he had grown in stature and in responsibility, and she felt a pang of compunction and a lingering regret, as if she had carelessly thrown away something precious. It made her feel uncomfortable and she quickly pushed it aside. There was so much to talk about that they almost forgot to eat, and it was not until the coffee came that she dared to mention Diana.

'Hasn't she written to you? The last thing she and Craig wanted was a big society wedding, so they went off one morning and got themselves spliced by special licence at Caxton Hall,' said Andy with a forced brightness that didn't deceive her in the least. 'I thought the General would have a stroke he was so furious.'

She put her hand on his. 'Andy, I'm so very sorry.'

He pulled his hand away, unwilling to show how deep had been the hurt.

'Why be sorry? That's life, isn't it? Every now and then it slaps you down, and there's nothing to be done but pick yourself up again. I knew it couldn't last. Di said it often enough, but I wouldn't admit it. It was too damned painful.'

'What will you do now?'

'Work, I suppose. There's plenty of it, God knows. People still get sick. If you must know, Pa gave me hell over it. He said even if I did feel like death warmed up, it was damnably unfair to take it out on the patients, and after I'd stopped feeling like knocking him down I saw his point.'

'Poor old Andy. I could be furious with Diana.'

'Don't be. She has a right to live as she must. Anyway a chance has come up to spend a few months in Berlin. The Germans have developed some marvellous new techniques in surgery. Pa is wangling an appointment for me. You know, change of scene and all that. He'd like to go himself, but it's not so easy for him as it is for me. He can't be spared and I can.'

275

'Dirk is planning to go to Berlin. We could be there about the same time.'

'That's grand. I'd enjoy that.' He took the coffee cup she handed to him. 'When are you going to settle down, have a home of your own?'

'Not yet. Dirk is not the settling-down type. He likes to be free to be up and away whenever the fancy takes him.'

'And you? Is that what you want?'

'Of course, if he does. It's a lot less trouble.'

'And suppose a baby comes along?'

'God forbid. Dirk is not at all keen, and I couldn't cope with it, not yet awhile.'

Andy paid the bill, and they strolled arm in arm along the shady avenues of the Bois lit by a mellow September sun.

'How's Nicola?' she asked. 'Does she still want to become a vet?'

'She plagues Pa about it every so often, especially as she has become something of a heroine. Didn't she write to you about it?'

'She doesn't say much in her letters.'

He had been in two minds whether to tell her, but now he plunged in.

'If it hadn't been for her and good old Jason, Leon would have been knocked off by now.'

'Knocked off? Do you mean – killed?'

'That's it, murdered, assassinated, whatever fancy word you like to use.'

'Whatever are you talking about?'

'I'm not joking, Tanya, it's true. It was pretty grim at the time. It seems the Red Brigade decided to have another go at him. They lay in wait with a gun at Ravensley in the early morning when he walked down the drive every day to collect the post. Only, luckily for him, that day Nicola was expecting a letter from one of her new boyfriends, so she went careering down the drive with the dogs and upset our assassin's plans. It ended up with Leon being shot through the arm and Jason with a bullet digging a deep furrow across the poor old boy's back.'

'And Nicola?'

'She got off scot free fortunately, despite tearing after the fellow screaming "Stop, murderer!" but he could have taken a pot shot at her instead of the dog before he got away.'

She stared at him aghast. 'What happened?'

'She got the walking wounded back to the house. Luke got hold of Pa, and he phoned our invaluable Mr Brown. He turned up, interrogated everyone in sight to discover who had leaked the information about Leon being at Ravensley, and unfortunately came up with nothing useful. The only outsider we seemed to have entertained was your Dirk.'

'You can't believe that he had anything to do with it?'

'Well, I hope not, darling, for your sake.'

'It's ridiculous even to think of such a thing.'

'Of course it is, but it has all been pretty dire for Pa and Galina.'

It couldn't possibly be true, she thought, it couldn't, and yet certain things did begin to hang together in a very frightening way. But she couldn't talk about it, not even to Andy. They spoke of other, more cheerful things, and presently she asked when he was going back.

'In a couple of days actually, can't be spared any longer it seems, but Luke is staying on for a while. It's his first time in Paris and he's still in a state of ecstasy over it.'

'Tell him to come and see me.'

'I will. When is Dirk coming back?'

'I don't know. He didn't say.'

'Everything is all right between you, isn't it?'

'Of course it is, more than all right.'

'Good. Young marrieds, you know. It can happen.' He grinned at her, putting his arm through hers.

When they parted she clung to him for a moment. 'Give my love to Pa. Tell him I think of him often.'

He held her tightly for an instant, his voice serious. 'Tanya, if you're in any trouble at any time, you would come to us, wouldn't you?'

'Why should I be in trouble?'

'No reason. I just want you to know that whatever happens we're behind you.'

Then he was smiling again. 'I won't forget to tell old Luke to be sure and look you up.'

* * *

Ever since Andy and he had stepped out of the train at the Gare du Nord on that first evening and he was hit by the smell of Paris, that indescribable, unforgettable reek compounded of tar and garlic and Gauloise cigarettes with a dozen other, unknown ingredients, Luke had been in a state of enchantment. The great boulevards blazing with rainbow-coloured lights, the little dark streets of the Quartier Latin where the gaslight glimmered on black wet pools, the fascinating names – the Rue de la Huchette, the Rue du Chat Qui Pêche – the river winding its way through the city, filled with mystery under its ancient bridges, everything spelled magic to him.

His mind was a jumble of the books he had read, poetry, history, romance – Villon's medieval Paris of thieves and murderers illuminated by his biting, ironic wit, Abelard and his doomed love for Heloise, the Paris of Balzac, of *la belle époque*, of Dumas, of Victor Hugo, of the Lady of the Camellias and *la vie de bohème*, of Proust and Gide, of Cocteau and Paul Claude . . . Andy laughed at him because he insisted on doing the 'sights' like any glassy-eyed tourist. It was Luke's first time out of England. He had money in his pocket, behind him the rare taste of success, in front of him a new and challenging career; the only thing he shied away from was a meeting with Tanya. He had a feeling that to see her, talk with her, and know her so far out of his reach, would end in shattering his dream, and it was only after Andy had left that they did meet at last, and then purely by accident.

He had spent the morning wandering around Notre Dame in a sort of sanctified gloom heavy with the fragrance of incense and lit by hundreds of wax candles glinting on gilded statues, a vivid contrast to the bare, whitewashed Methodist chapels of his childhood, the icy cold creeping up his bare legs as he sat fidgeting through the hour-long sermon and shivering at the dramatic picture of hellfire conjured up by the fiery Welsh preacher.

He came out into a Paris veiled in the gauzy mist of September and made his way down the quays where the bookstalls spread along the riverbank.

He was hunting through some volumes of poetry all in musty brown leather bindings, Verlaine, Ronsard, Lamartine, and his hand closed on a copy of Baudelaire at the same time as another hand, on whose finger flashed a particularly fine ruby surrounded by diamonds. He looked up and found himself confronting a vision – Tanya in a black beret, a scarlet scarf knotted negligently around her throat – and for the space of a second he was taken back to that long-ago day when she had knocked him down and he saw her for the first time.

'So you *are* still here,' she was saying reproachfully. 'I've been waiting for you to call on me. Didn't Andy tell you?'

'Yes, he did, but . . .'

It was happening just as he had known it would. She was even more enchanting than he remembered. It was absurd to be so disturbed when he had thrust it firmly behind him as nothing more than a youthful folly to be put down to inexperience, like the humiliating affair with Megan. It all came flooding back, the painful rejection, the hopeless frustration, the anger and disillusion ten times worse because time had only dimmed but not destroyed. Hell, he thought rebelliously, why do I have to feel like this? Why?

> 'A rag and a bone and a hank of hair . . .
> But the fool he called her his lady fair . . .

Damn old Kipling, but he was right!

'Paris is obviously a more enticing mistress,' she said provocatively. 'Well, now I've captured you I'm not letting you go so easily. Let's have some coffee and talk. I want to hear all about this wonderful new book that's rocketing you to fame, so Andy tells me.'

'Not quite that, I'm afraid.' He found his voice at last and steadied himself.

She slipped her arm through his in her old friendly fashion.

'Come on, Luke, don't stare as if I were a ghost. Tell me all about yourself.'

The Quartier abounded in cafés where students, writers and artists still gathered to talk and argue, to laugh and sometimes noisily quarrel. They found a table that was a little apart under a striped awning, and he ordered coffee, and then sat down saying nothing for the moment, simply drinking in the subtle changes, the air of sophistication, the elegant dress, the restless movement of her hands, the faint scent of some very expensive perfume.

'What's wrong with me? Have I a large smut on my nose?' she said, laughing at him, and he realized how he had been staring.

279

'Forgive me. It's been a long time, and I was thinking how very beautiful you are. Is it marriage or is it Paris?'

She looked away. 'A little of both perhaps.'

Then the coffee came and the ice was broken. They began to talk, forgetting the first embarrassment, the words tumbling over one another as they had done in those early days on the river at Ravensley.

He told her about his brother and her father's generous gesture of help, about Andy and Diana, and the publication party Hugh Carter had given for him where he found his hand being shaken by people who had only been names to him before.

'I can't believe it even now,' he said. 'At any moment I expect to come down to earth with a bump.'

'When am I going to have a copy?' she asked.

And he thought of the book he had put in his suitcase and done nothing about.

They talked on and on till she suddenly remembered she had a lunch date.

'When are you going home, Luke?' she said.

'Very soon now. Cash is running out, but I must see Fontainebleau first.'

She hesitated and then said quickly, 'May I come? To my shame I've never yet been there.'

'Do you mean that? What about your husband?'

'Oh, bother Dirk,' she said lightly. 'He's away and hasn't seen fit to tell me when he will be back. We'll go tomorrow. I'm afraid he has the car, so we must travel by train like English trippers.' She had a faint air of defiance and he fell in with her mood.

'Sounds wonderful. Shall I pick you up at about eleven?'

'Lovely.'

He knew it was madness, but he no longer cared. He would have a day with her, and no one could take that away from him.

The next morning when they boarded the train she had a queer feeling of escape coupled with a faint sense of guilt, but she shook herself free from it. Why shouldn't she please herself, and Luke was like her brother. What harm was there in it?

The compartment was full of holidaymakers, Parisians as well as foreigners, but despite the tourists and a droning guide who made her giggle Fontainebleau was not a disappointment.

280

Long ago it had been a hunting lodge, and king after king had enlarged and beautified it. After the Revolution it fell into decay, but Napoleon had restored it to its former glory. His emblem of the bee was everywhere, painted on ceilings, embroidered on bedcoverings and curtains, woven into carpets.

Luke said, 'Versailles left me cold. All that icy splendour. I couldn't get anywhere near Louis XIV and those courtiers of his in their wigs and stuffed breeches, but this is different, isn't it? Here ghosts are all around you, here one feels *la gloire* as something very real – Napoleon probably made love in that bed, he signed his abdication at that very desk, and when he came back from Elba he reviewed his loyal Guard here before leading them to Paris and to Waterloo.'

She looked at him curiously. 'Will you put him in your next book?'

'Oh Lord no, no more history. This time I'm writing about today – and tomorrow.'

Outside in the Jardin de Diane children played, and a small boy to the admiration of his sisters stood on his head. Laughing, Luke took Tanya's arm.

'I used to be able to do that once – getting too long in the tooth now. I'm hungry. What about luncheon?'

So they ate crusty bread, creamy Brie and black grapes at one of the outdoor cafés, and afterwards strolled into the village, in and out of the market stalls. One of them was hung with tiny cages filled with birds, not only canaries but linnets and finches singing plaintively.

Tanya stared at them and then said abruptly, 'I hate to see them. Birds should be free. Let's buy one and then release it.'

He put down the few francs and they carried it into a glade of the forest. He saw her take the trembling bird into her two hands and then fling it up into the air, watching it soar up into the branches of the tree.

'It will probably die,' he said, 'if it has been bred in captivity.'

'Never mind. It will have had an hour of glorious freedom instead of months of prison in which to break its heart. Don't you agree?'

She turned to him impulsively, tripped over one of the moss-covered roots, and the next moment was in his arms.

He could not help it. He held her, slim and vibrant, close against him and then kissed her, feeling her lips soften a little. For a moment she was all his, then she had thrust him away.

'No, Luke, please . . .'

'I'm sorry. I didn't mean . . . Have I made you angry?'

'No, not angry, but I think perhaps it's time we went back.'

In the train she was quiet, but walking back to the apartment she seemed to recover her spirits.

'I have an idea,' she said suddenly, 'let's finish the day in style. Let's go somewhere to eat and dance.'

'Where do you suggest?'

'Nowhere grand and stuffy. What about Montparnasse? Everybody used to go there once – still do, most of them. We'll go to la Closerie des Lilas. It closed during the war but reopened last year. It's supposed to be marvellously exotic.'

'If you're sure that's what you want to do.'

'I'll just run into the apartment and tell Louise she may go as I'm dining out.'

He stood looking around the sitting room while she went out to the kitchen. Here she lived with Dirk von Richter. Up to now he had only seen him from a distance, only knew that the family still regarded him with dislike and suspicion. To Luke he was was still a shadowy presence. It was curious, he thought, how the room seemed filled with Tanya, books and magazines scattered everywhere, flowers crammed into a jar, a plant on the windowsill, a pair of fine kid gloves carelessly dropped on a side table, a silk scarf trailing from an armchair, but there was absolutely nothing that belonged to the man in her life. Why, he wondered, what had he to hide?

Then she came back, freshly made up and looking radiant.

'Shall we go?'

And he took her arm, feeling quite unaccountably happy, throwing caution to the winds.

Dirk came back shortly after ten o'clock, exhausted after a day-long drive along roads still infested with tourist traffic, and was unreasonably annoyed to find an empty apartment, no meal in preparation, no Louise, no wife to greet him. Where the devil was

Tanya? And why had she not left a message to say where she had gone? It was too bad of her, he thought angrily, forgetting that he had neither written nor telephoned and she had no reason to expect him back at any particular time.

He put down his suitcase, tossed aside his hat, and went to the drinks table. He poured himself a stiff brandy and paced up and down the room, his mind still battling with the events of the last few days and the problems that had occupied his thoughts for most of the three hundred miles of hard driving.

Four years ago when his mother lay dying he had made her a promise, one that he had first made years before when he was still a boy; and afterwards he had set himself a target, a mission he had confided to no one, and to fulfil it he had deliberately insinuated himself into an organization that he had believed, in his arrogance, he could use simply for his own purposes and then discard. Now he knew that all he had done was to put himself inexorably, inescapably, into a trap. He had broken the rules. He had let himself fall in love; worse still he had married, and so had let himself wide open to influences, to temptations, to human weaknesses which were not permitted. He had fought against it.

'I entered into this of my own free will,' he had said in furious pride to the stone-faced man who was implacably in charge, 'and I can leave it whenever I choose,' and had been made to realize that he was wrong, hopelessly wrong. Once you had become part of it, you could never again be free. They would never allow you out of their clutches.

He put down the glass and dropped wearily into the armchair. The silk scarf fell to the floor and he picked it up, the faint elusive perfume bringing Tanya vividly close. Very soon now he was going to have to tell her. It had been folly to believe he could keep it hidden for ever, that she would not guess, would not start questioning. He stirred restlessly. Where was she? Why wasn't she here? He had a strong need to hold her in his arms, make violent love to her, possess her wholly, lose all these tormenting thoughts and doubts in the blind fulfilment of passion.

He knew he ought to eat something. He had touched nothing since early morning, but he felt too tired to make the effort. He poured more brandy and sat on, a slow, resentful anger building up inside him; so that when at last he heard a cab draw up outside and the key in the lock, heard Tanya's voice and another with her, laughing and happy, he was ready to burst out into bitter reproaches.

He flung open the door and confronted them in the narrow hall, saw his wife, her face flushed, her hair tousled, and the young man with her whose arm still lay familiarly round her shoulders, and his anger exploded.

'Where the hell have you been?'

The laughter died out of her face. 'Dining and dancing at La Closerie de Lilas, if you must know.' She brushed past him into the sitting room. 'Why on earth didn't you let me know that you were coming home?'

'I didn't know for sure.' He glared aggressively at Luke. 'Who the devil is this?'

'His name is Luke Llewellyn Jones,' she said icily, 'and he's a friend of mine, a very dear friend. Come in, Luke, and meet my husband, Dirk von Richter.'

Luke held out his hand awkwardly. 'Delighted to meet you, Herr von Richter. I've been hearing a great deal about you from Tanya.'

'Have you indeed?' Pointedly he ignored the outstretched hand. 'Well, Mr Jones, I've just arrived home after a long and tiring journey, and I'm not in the mood for a party.'

Luke was no fool. He sensed the tense situation.

'Yes, of course, I understand. I'll say goodnight, Tanya. It's been a marvellous evening.'

She shot a defiant glance at her husband. 'Don't go, Luke. At least stay for a nightcap.'

He met Dirk's eyes and read in them an unmistakable hostility, almost as if they were rivals, which was ridiculous.

'No, better not,' he said. 'I've got a lot to do if I'm to go off home tomorrow.'

She went with him to the door.

'It's been a wonderful two days. I've enjoyed being with you so much. You will write, won't you? I'll look forward to hearing about the new book and the new job.'

She kissed his cheek before she let him go, and then came back into the sitting room, shutting the door behind her and leaning back against it.

'Did you have to be so insulting to a friend of mine?'

'Who is he?'

'A young man I've known longer than I've known you.'

'And have you been amusing yourself with him all the time I've been away?'

'And what if I have?' she said coolly. 'Do you expect me to sit here in this apartment for twenty-four hours a day waiting for you to come back?'

He was suddenly seized by a gust of anger. He took her roughly by the shoulders.

'What does this young man mean to you?'

'I've told you. He's a friend of mine.'

'And are all your friends on such intimate terms? What has he been – your lover?'

He was shaking her, his fingers digging into her flesh through the thin silk of her dress.

'How dare you say that? Let me go. You're hurting me. Is there any reason why I shouldn't spend a couple of days with him when you did not even condescend to tell me where you were?'

He dropped his hands and knew she was right. He was allowing his angry frustration to carry him away.

'You don't understand . . .'

'Oh yes I do. I understand very well. You went away for three days and stayed away for ten. I was worried sick. You could have been dead for all I knew. Wouldn't she let you go?' she went on tauntingly. 'Couldn't you bear to tear yourself away from her?'

'What the devil are you talking about?'

'The woman you went to see – the mistress you spend so much of your spare time with,' she went on wildly, not really believing her own accusations.

He took a step towards her. 'Be quiet, Tanya, you don't know what you're talking about. There is no woman, there never has been, you know that perfectly well.'

'No, I don't know, how should I? And don't tell me that you were with your stepfather, because I rang the villa and was told the Baron went back to Zurich over a week ago.'

'You rang the villa?'

'Yes, I did, was that so very wrong of me? Why did you lie to me, Dirk? Why, why?'

'There were reasons.'

'What reasons? For God's sake, I'm your wife, not your servant, not your housekeeper. I've a right to know where you go and what you are doing. Isn't that what marriage is meant to be, a sharing of each other's lives?'

'There are some things it's better that you should not know.'

'What things?' She stared at him, frowning, then said slowly, 'What does all this mean? Are you mixed up in something dangerous? Is it because of that man who killed the President?'

'Oh God, don't start on that again.'

'Andy was here while you were away. He told me about Leon, that Russian my father took to Ravensley – there has been another attack on his life.'

'So your brother has been over here, has he, poisoning your mind against me?' he said savagely. 'And you'd rather listen to him than to me. Don't you trust me, Tanya? Isn't trust also part of marriage?'

'I always believed so, now I'm not so sure.'

'Listen to me, my darling.' His voice softened. He switched to Russian, the language that had become part of their love, of their most intimate moments, his voice low and compelling. 'All the time I've been away I've thought only of coming home to you, and when I do I see you laughing and happy with another man, a stranger. Aren't I entitled to feel a little jealous, a little hurt?'

She knew what would happen if he took her in his arms; she knew only too well how difficult he was to resist. But she was not going to be won over so easily, not this time.

'No, Dirk,' she said. 'I don't want to hear any more excuses. It's very late and I'm tired. Are you hungry? Shall I get you something to eat?'

She was very cool, very distant, and he reacted against it.

'No, don't trouble yourself, I'm all right.'

'Very well. I shall go to bed.' He was standing by the table and she saw the brandy decanter and the half-filled glass. 'I shouldn't drink any more of that if I were you, not on an empty stomach. Perhaps tomorrow you will tell me where you went and why. After that we can start again. Goodnight.'

She walked away from him. He heard her go into the bedroom, and the door slammed shut with a finality that shocked him. She had never rejected him so utterly before. He knew a moment of anger and despair. It would be easy for him to stride in and take her by force, but even if he succeeded it would be useless. Tanya had too much fight in her, too much pride, and she would not forgive easily. And yet he dared not confide in her, not yet. He could not risk losing her. He must find some other way.

He picked up the glass, swallowed the last mouthful of brandy, and then, in sudden rage with her and with himself, he hurled it across the room. It hit the wall and splintered into fragments.

In their bedroom Tanya heard the crash and stood still, uncertain of what he might do. She had never defied him before. What would happen if he came bursting through the door? Would she still be brave enough to stand out against him? For the first time in her life she felt a faint tremor of fear, but of what? Of his anger? Surely not. Rather it was a fear of the unknown, of some danger that threatened them both.

But the door remained closed and she slowly relaxed, feeling limp now and somehow defeated, the anger that had buoyed her up draining away into wretchedness.

There was no sound from the other room, and after a while she began to undress, wiped the make-up from her face, and put on her nightgown. For a moment she stood irresolute. Should she go out to him? Then pride came to her rescue. Surely it was for him to come to her, for him to apologize and explain.

An hour or so later, lying sleepless, she saw the door open and knew that Dirk was standing there. He had taken off his jacket and loosened his tie. He paused for a moment and then came and sat on the edge of the bed. In the light of the bedside lamp his face looked tired and drawn, his hair ruffled as if he had been running his fingers through it. For the first time since she had known him he looked curiously vulnerable.

He said huskily, 'I'm sorry, Tanya, I'm sorry,' and though she made no move, her treacherous heart went out to him.

After a second he went on. 'I can't explain everything now, you must forgive me and take me on trust, but don't ever walk out on me again, because if you do – his voice shook a little – 'if you do, I don't know what might happen to both of us.'

He had never pleaded with her before. Always he had seemed master of himself as he was master of her, confident, self-assured, arrogant, and it moved her greatly.

She sat up and put her hand on his. 'You look exhausted. Don't talk any more now. Come to bed,' she said.

'In a moment. There is something else. In a few weeks we will be going to Berlin. There are certain affairs I have to deal with there.'

'In the gallery?'

'Partly there and elsewhere, but soon after that we will be free to look for a permanent home. Would you like that? Shall it be Switzerland near to the Baron or the South of France close to your cousins, or must I learn to live in cold foggy Britain?'

It would be something to dream about, something to discuss. How foolish she had been to doubt him.

When later he slid into the bed beside her he did not immediately pull her into his arms, caress her, make tempestuous love as he had done so often before, but instead simply drew her gently against him as if he needed more than anything the warmth and comfort of her body curving into his. That night she felt closer to the heart of this difficult and complex husband of hers than she had ever done before, but still she did not know the inmost secret that he guarded from her as he did from everyone else.

16

The first few months in Berlin proved very pleasant. It was only later that the nightmare caught her in its terrifying grip. It was not a beautiful city like Paris. It had neither the glamour nor the age-old sophistication, but to Tanya, who had never been in Germany before, it was vividly, almost stridently alive. Art and music, plays and films, seemed to be marching forward, with exciting innovations endlessly discussed and put into practice. The cruel aftermath of the war, the weariness of defeat, seemed to be over at last, and on the surface the city glittered with wealth, with enthusiasm and a kind of wild determination to taste every kind of experience no matter how bizarre.

In December the snow came. Tanya watched it from the windows of their apartment just off Unter den Linden. Thick, soft and heavy, it reminded her of winters in Petersburg still filled with the glow of childish memories. The dark political currents that were already splitting Germany apart, the violent anti-Semitism, the meetings in narrow back streets where Communists and Nazis fought out their differences savagely, crippling and murdering each other, were rarely reported in the newspapers.

She and Dirk had reached a new stage in their relationship. He was more relaxed, more ready to give as well as take. They had become friends as well as passionate lovers, and in her present contented mood she did not look ahead.

On previous visits he had made several friends, wealthy businessmen who were also art connoisseurs, men and women who frequented the gallery and knew his stepfather. They were invited to dine, eating enormously rich meals with many courses in opulent houses filled with magnificent furniture and valuable *objets d'art* – houses that Tanya, accustomed to the spacious if faded beauty of Ravensley, found little to her taste. She much preferred their acquaintances among the artistic fraternity.

Wilhelm Meister played the violin and his wife Hilde the oboe in the Berlin Philharmonic Orchestra. They lived in a pleasant suburb, and she and Dirk spent evenings with them eating sausage and liver dumplings and apfelstrudel listening to Mozart and Bach and Schubert. They would lunch lazily on the shores of the lake or walk on Sundays through the Brandenburg woods, picnic meals in their rucksacks, the skeleton trees beautiful against the snow-covered fields.

Once they met a party of Hitler Jugend, thirty or more young boys in their brown uniforms marching past in very correct formation and throwing up their arms in the Nazi salute, which had the effect of sending Tanya into a fit of the giggles.

'You should not laugh,' said Willi reproachfully, 'it is not right.'

'But it is so stupid,' she said. 'At least the old greeting of "Grüss Gott" meant something, but this "Heil Hitler" – it is simply glorifying a jumped-up politician.'

'You do not understand, you are a foreigner,' he replied austerely. 'We were less than the dust, we had nothing, nothing at all, crushed in defeat, but now we can lift up our heads again, that is what Adolf Hitler is doing for us. Soon now we shall once again mean something in Europe.'

She stared at him, finding it difficult to believe that someone like Willi, a gentle dedicated Musician, should be so easily blinded by the wild ravings of an individual like this Hitler, whom no one at home in England took really seriously.

Of course one saw the young men in their brown shirts marching about the streets, the swastikas on their shirt sleeves, collecting for party funds, pushing their boxes rudely under the noses of everyone even on Unter den Linden and the Kurfürstendamm, but Tanya thought little of it. Her father, who had once spent some months in a German hospital as a student doctor, had said, 'The Germans are a remarkable people. They will work harder than anyone, worrying a problem to a conclusion that has baffled everyone else, but they do love dressing up in uniform and marching in step,' and it seemed they still did.

That January in 1933, she was far too happy to let it worry her. Andy had arrived to take up his appointment at the hospital, and with him had come Luke and Nicola.

'Shouldn't you be at school?' she exclaimed when Luke deposited her young sister on her doorstep for luncheon.

'I thought you'd be surprised,' said Nicola cheerfully, 'but here I am and isn't it gorgeous fun? I begged, implored, and went down on my knees to Pa, but he wouldn't agree till darling Luke said he wanted to explore the library of the Friedrich Wilhelm University for some dull old book he's working on and promised to look after me when Andy was busy; so here I am. Aren't you glad to see me?'

And, astonishingly, she was. Nicola had grown in the last year. At nearly sixteen she was as tall as herself and had acquired a kind of leggy grace. No longer the cheeky, irritating schoolchild, but a young girl verging on womanhood and with a surprising maturity. After lunch, when Luke had gone off to his library, they settled down to a long cosy chat.

'Do you *like* being married?' Nicola asked at one point. 'Dirk always frightens me. He never seems quite human. You know, like Manfred, a dark stranger with a guilty secret. You remember –

'"My spirit walk'd not with the souls of men
   Nor look'd upon the earth with human eyes."'

quoted Nicola, who had been doing Byron last term.

Tanya laughed aloud. 'Don't be absurd. Dirk is very human. He gets furious if there isn't a clean shirt or he can't find his cuff links, he grumbles if I'm late for something or the dinner is not to his taste, just like everyone else.'

'Does he? How disappointing. I suppose you can't always live on a mountain top. You have to come down to earth sometimes. Are you going to have a baby soon?'

'Oh Lord, not you too! Andy was asking me that.'

'I thought married people always started having babies when they settled down.'

'Well, we've not settled down yet. Now what about you? I thought you wanted to be a vet.'

'I still do, but Pa says I've got to get Matric first then he'll think about it, and that won't be till next year,' said Nicola gloomily.

They discovered that afternoon that they could talk together with more ease than they had ever done before, and once Nicola came out with something that took Tanya's breath away. They had been speaking about Andy.

'Di walking out on him like she did hit him terribly hard,' said Nicola earnestly. 'None of us like to say much, but we all knew. I don't know how she could, do you? Andy is such a terrific person.'

'They both wanted completely different things out of life and neither would give in to the other. It was as simple as that.'

'I suppose so,' went on Nicola doubtfully, 'but I would give up anything for someone I loved.' She gave an impish grin. 'Anyway, it leaves the field clear for me.'

'Whatever do you mean? Andy is your brother.'

'No, he's not actually.' Nicola was obviously bursting to impart some tremendous secret. 'Pa told me. He said now I was fifteen I ought to know. He's not my real father.'

'What! Oh, don't be silly, Nicola, of course he is. I remember when you were born. It was that dreadful summer when the Bolsheviki broke into the house and Father was arrested at the hospital.'

'Yes, I know.' Nicola thought of Simon's grave voice and how gentle he had been with her. 'All that winter and spring he had been away at the Front with the army, and Mamma was left alone, very unhappy and worried, and it was then that it happened.'

'You mean she had an affair with another man.' Tanya was frankly incredulous. 'I can't believe it.'

'It's true. Papa told me about him. He was a soldier, and terribly brave. He'd been badly wounded and Mamma had nursed him when he was on sick leave. He had always been in love with her, only she had chosen to marry Papa, but that winter they sort of came together. He never knew about me. He was killed when the Red Army stormed the Winter Palace.'

'Valentin Skorsky,' breathed Tanya, 'that's who it was. We used to call him Uncle Val. He was very rich and we'd known him all our lives. Andy and I didn't like him much, though he was always terribly kind to us.'

She was beginning to remember the things that had happened during her father's long absence – Uncle Val turning up in his Rolls and taking her mother to balls and the opera, and he had been with them for that last Christmas at Dannskoye when it must have happened. Her cherished memories of her beautiful mother had received a sharp shock.

She said, 'Is it really true?'

'Father would never tell us anything that wasn't true, would he? I hated it at first. It made me feel sort of abandoned and lost, as if I didn't belong anywhere or to anyone. But then he explained how it all happened and how unhappy Mamma was, and somehow it made me feel better, and he made me feel that I still had him as my father even though he wasn't my real one.'

'Does Andy know?'

'Yes. Father thought he and Paul ought to be told as well as me. But it hasn't made any real difference. It's queer,' she went on thoughtfully, 'I still love Andy better than almost anyone except Pa, but I'm not "in love" with him any more. Do you understand?'

'Yes, I think I do. You're growing up, that's all. Real life is not like a Byron romance, even if sometimes it feels like one.'

The child Nicola had been enthralled by the idea of forbidden love, but she was learning to see it now in a more sensible light.

'You know,' she went on seriously, 'when I'm a vet I think I'll live with Andy, and I can do the animals while he looks after the humans. Do you think it would work?'

Tanya laughed. Nicola's imagination always tended to race ahead.

'Perhaps, perhaps not. He might find someone else he wants to marry,' she said.

'I never thought of that.'

'Well, never mind. It's a long way off, isn't it? Heavens, look at the time. We'll have some tea and then I must change. Dirk will be home soon and we're going out to dinner tonight.'

'May I come and choose what you're going to wear?'

Tanya smiled. 'You can come and look all through my wardrobe if you like.'

'Oh, gorgeous! I'd like that.'

It was not until later, after Luke had picked Nicola up and Tanya was changing for the evening, that she allowed herself to think about what her sister had told her. It was almost as if the scales had fallen from her eyes. She had hated Galina as an intruder into their cherished family life, but now she began to see her more clearly, remembering how she had stood by them during that frightful summer when Nicola was born and her father was in daily danger, how much they had all relied on her. She had seen it with the prejudiced eyes of a child, but now it was different. It was not only Nicola who was growing up.

Dirk was still inclined to be stiff with Andy and Luke, which made Tanya smile a little. They reminded her of dogs bristling and eyeing one another guardedly, but he was exceptionally generous to Nicola, with visits to the theatre and the opera, to new and startling Expressionist films which Andy frowned upon, and at Nicola's special pleading to one of the very few nightclubs where women were admitted. It was a tiny insight into that other side of Berlin life, the world of the homosexual, the transvestite, the drug taker. Nicola's eyes widened in amazement when she realized that the singer with the blonde hair and satin evening gown split to the thigh was a man singing bitter, scathing songs in a husky, disturbing voice; and she gasped openly at the young man with hair like a golden cap, with a single pearl earring and eyes darkened with mascara, who sauntered up to their table, putting an arm negligently round Dirk's shoulders and smiling slyly across the table at Luke, who looked disgusted.

'That child should not be here,' growled Andy under his breath, 'she is far too young.'

'One is never too young to discover the hard facts of life,' said Dirk drily.

There was only one disturbing moment, when they were invited to an evening party at the British Embassy and Nigel Drew, bringing Tanya a glass of champagne, drew her to one side.

'How are you and Dirk getting along in Berlin? Settling down well?' he enquired.

'I think so. Dirk has had to sack the manager of the gallery, who'd been cheating the company right and left, so he has been very busy pulling it into shape.'

'So I understand.' He glanced around and then put a hand on her arm. 'A word of warning, Tanya. Tell him to be careful about the company he keeps and the meetings he attends.'

She stared at him. He had been Uncle Nigel ever since she could remember, her father's friend, a man she trusted.

'I don't understand. What company?'

'My dear, Berlin is a melting-pot of different warring elements, Communists, Nazis, Social Democrats, and with the election coming up at the end of the month, the whole pot could boil over and people might be scalded.'

'And one of them could be Dirk?'

'Could be. Remember it.'

But when she told him, Dirk only laughed.

'Your Uncle Nigel is an old fuddy-duddy fussing over nothing important. Don't worry about it, my darling. Things are going very well for us just now.'

She went with Nicola and Luke to the railway station when they returned home. Although they had been constantly in one another's company, she had never been alone with Luke during the whole fortnight, and it was only now with Nicola safely in the compartment, a pile of magazines on her lap, with doors being slammed and the guard already walking along the platform with his green flag, that he suddenly turned to her almost desperately, cupping her face between his two hands.

'I love you,' he whispered, 'I love you very much. You do know that, don't you?'

'You shouldn't say such things, Luke, it's all over.'

There was a long whistle, the train jolted, and Nicola was anxiously looking for him out of the window.

'It will never be over, and if ever you need me I'll come,' he went on hurriedly. 'Don't forget.'

He kissed her with a firm, hard pressure and then made a leap for the slowly moving train.

She stood and watched as it moved out. He was standing behind Nicola, both of them waving, and in some curious way she felt comforted.

Nigel Drew had been right. The election on January 30th made the Nazis the biggest single party in the Reichstag, and under pressure from his ministers President Hindenburg appointed Adolf Hitler the new Chancellor of Germany. Now, the government believed, they had this troublemaker, this rabble-rouser, safely under their thumb. They couldn't have been more wrong. Bands of Brownshirts swarmed out of the back streets and began to swagger around the city feeling their power. It was a trifling incident that first showed Tanya the wind of change that was

295

blowing through Germany, and she remembered it vividly because it was the day on which she visited Dr Goldmann and he confirmed her own suspicion that she was pregnant.

Walking back to the apartment she remembered that it was Hilde Meister's birthday soon and she went into a shop to buy some small gift. In front of her a tall man in a brown uniform was arguing angrily with the attendant. Suddenly he shouted, '*Judengeschäft!*' and with a brutal gesture swept the bottle of perfume to the floor, then, pushing Tanya roughly aside, he strode out into the street.

The shop reeked of the spilled scent. The girl was crying as she knelt on the floor picking up the broken glass, and Tanya bent down to help her.

'Take care. You'll cut yourself,' she said gently. 'What happened?'

'You heard him,' said the girl bitterly through her tears. 'Jew shop! He wanted the perfume at half the price, and when I refused he smashed it. Now I shall have to pay for it out of my earnings.'

There was nothing Tanya could do except express sympathy. She made her small purchase and went home feeling shaken, not yet realizing that her own personal nightmare had only just begun.

Once, a few months after their marraige, they had talked about children, and Dirk had been very firm about it.

'Not yet, my darling. In a year or two, when we are settled in a home of our own, then we can think of a family.'

She had agreed with him quite happily, enjoying her life and not yet passionately longing for a child of her own. But the best-laid plans can go wrong and now she hesitated to tell him, keeping her pregnancy to herself for a week or so until she had a few days of unpleasant nausea and was so unwell that Dirk suggested sending for the doctor.

'There's no need,' she said, sitting up in the bed, pale but quite composed. 'I know what it is. I'm going to have a baby.'

'Oh my God, no!' He stared at her aghast. 'You can't, not now of all times. Are you sure?'

'Yes, I am, quite sure. I went to see Dr Goldmann. He says it will be born in September.'

He walked away from her. 'It's impossible, quite impossible. If it is true, then you must do something about it. You must get rid of it.'

His reaction, his anger, shocked her because she could not understand it, could see no real reason for it.

'I could never do that, never,' she said. 'It's out of the question.'

'I can't believe it,' he went on, 'I made so very sure . . .' He swung round on her. 'It's not that old flame of yours, that damned Welshman, is it? Don't think I didn't notice how close you were, how he looked at you.'

The angry colour flooded up into her face. 'You know that's not true. It's an unforgivable thing to say.'

'All right, all right, I know. I shouldn't have said it. I'm sorry. 'But you don't understand.'

'What don't I understand?'

'Never mind. We'll have to get round it somehow, I suppose, but God knows how. You couldn't have chosen a worse moment.'

'Why, Dirk, why?'

'There are reasons, important reasons.'

'What reasons?'

'You'll know – you'll know all too damned soon.'

He stared across at her for a long moment and then went abruptly out of the room, slamming the door. In reaction she felt so weak and sick and frightened, that it took all her self-control not to burst into tears.

The afternoon brought Andy. He had the habit of dropping in on her once or twice a week when he had an hour to spare, and she looked so pale, so listless, and unlike herself that he felt concerned.

They talked at random for a while before Frau Bilde, who came in to clean and sometimes cook, brought in a tray of English tea which Tanya had painstakingly taught her how to make.

When she had gone and Andy had been handed his cup, Tanya said suddenly, with a catch in her breath, 'Andy, could you give me an abortion?'

'What?' He put down the tea and stared at her. 'Is this meant to be a joke?'

'No, no, it's not, far from it.' She got up, walking agitatedly around the room before turning to face him. 'Dirk hates the very idea of a child. He was so angry about it, so – so violent.'

'He can't be allowed to hurt you like that.' All Andy's latent dislike rose to the surface. 'Let me speak to him.'

'No, no, that wouldn't do any good. He doesn't trust you or any of the family. He believes that you are all against him.' She dropped back into her chair, twisting a handkerchief between nervous fingers. 'It was so – so upsetting, so horrible, I didn't know what to do. I thought perhaps you could tell me how I could stop it.'

'There is no way. Now listen to me.' He leaned over and took both her hands in his. 'To start with, I couldn't give you an abortion, nor could any decent doctor. It's against the law, for one thing, and for another,' he managed a smile, 'Pa would kill me if I did. You are perfectly healthy, perfectly normal, it's against everything I hold good and important to destroy life deliberately.'

'You don't know what he said. He made me feel as if he hated me, as if I had deliberately done something to harm him.'

She shivered, and he tightened his grip on her hands as if giving her strength.

'Never mind what he said. Some men take it like that at first. They don't want to give up any part of the woman they love to some other – alien – being, if you can see it like that. He won't keep it up, I'm sure he won't. He loves you all right in his own peculiar way. Now, you must do nothing, nothing at all, to try and prevent it. It can be very dangerous, and if you're worried or upset about anything and you don't want to go to old Dr Goldmann, then come to me. Promise, Tanya, you must promise.'

'All right. I suppose I'll get through it somehow.' She rubbed a hand over her face. 'If only I didn't keep feeling so dreadful.'

'That won't last long. I'll prescribe something that will help you through that, and in a week or two you'll be feeling fine. Don't be afraid. I'm here. I'm with you and I'll look after you.'

Very soon after that, events both in public and in private seemed to move very fast. One very cold night towards the end of February, when the snow in the streets had hardened into dangerous, slippery ice, Tanya and Dirk were having dinner when Frau Bilde rushed in, her round plump face alight with excitement and horror. A neighbour had brought the news. The Reichstag was on fire.

'That such a dreadful thing should happen, Herr von Richter. What kind of world are we living in!'

Dirk had risen. 'It's not possible, not now, not tonight,' he said in a stifled voice, almost as if he had expected it. He threw down his napkin. 'I'll go out, take a look, find out if it is true.'

Tanya, alarmed by the look on his face, tried to stop him, but he was already out in the hall putting on his thick coat and pulling on his boots.

When he came back some hours later, his clothes, even his hair, smelled of the thick black smoke and his boots were soaked and filthy from the firemen's hoses.

All kinds of rumours tore through the city, but one thing was certain. It was no accident. It had been started deliberately. A young Dutchman, Marinus van der Lubbe, was found inside the building, seeming half dazed, matches and firelighters in his pockets. He confessed to being a Communist but swore that he had acted alone, setting fire to the historic building as a protest against the Nazis. Arguments raged back and forth, even a suggestion that the Nazis had themselves been involved in order to denounce it as a Communist crime, and the very next day Hindenburg signed an emergency decree that took away most of a citizen's basic rights. From now on newspapers would be censored, political meetings banned, private letters and telephone calls checked, and the persecution of Jews and Communists, and indeed of anyone who dared to rebel openly against Hitler and the Nazi party, emerged into the open from the dark alleys and the back streets.

All during those weeks Tanya and Dirk had lived side by side in a kind of truce and never mentioned the baby. Andy's prescription had worked. She was feeling a great deal better, sometimes so well that she almost forgot she was pregnant, and Dirk was out a great deal of the time. He explained that some of the staff at the gallery had been found to have Jewish connections, and with the new laws coming into practice difficulties had arisen.

'You are surely not dismissing them just because their grandmother happens to be Jewish?' Tanya said indignantly.

'We may be forced to do so, though, God knows, they are the best and most knowledgeable members of the staff.'

Then early in April, just as the cold began to relent and at last a few spring flowers had come into the market, the fact was brought violently and frighteningly home to her.

299

She had never thought of old Dr Goldmann as being Jewish, only that he was a wise and kind old man who used his extensive private practice to finance a long list of panel patients in one of the poorest quarters of the city. One afternoon she was walking down the narrow lane that led past his surgery when she saw him coming towards her. He was carrying a bag in one hand and a huge bunch of flowers in the other. She waved and he smiled back at her. She was wondering whether it was his wife's birthday when it happened.

The two Brownshirts came striding along the narrow pavement. The old man, hindered by his bag and the flowers, did not move out of their way quickly enough and one of them shouted 'Jewish swine!' and pushed him so roughly that he stumbled and fell to his knees, the bag going one way and the flowers another. The second man laughed and gave the old man a vicious kick that sent him sprawling forward into the mud of the road, and was then faced with an enraged Tanya, furious at the brutality and belabouring him with her umbrella.

Taken by surprise he staggered back, and then was suddenly angry. 'Jew lover!' he snarled, and slapped her face so hard that she tripped on the kerb and fell over the old man. The two men, hands on hips, roared with laughter. One of them picked up her umbrella, snapped it in half, and threw it at her, while the other kicked her hard in the stomach, throwing her across the gutter. Then, arm in arm, they swaggered on down the street.

One or two people passing on the opposite side saw what had happened but hurried on quickly, averting their eyes. It did not do to let oneself get involved in things of this kind.

She struggled to her feet, her stockings ripped, her coat covered in mud. Dr Goldmann had by now got to his knees, and she helped him up.

'You should not have done that, dear lady,' he said breathlessly. 'Those brutes are no respecters of persons, not even of women.'

'Let me help you,' she said. She picked up his bag and tried to gather the scattered flowers together.

'Leave them,' he said. 'They were for my Anna, but she will understand.' He looked at Tanya anxiously. 'Are you hurt? You had better come into the surgery. Let me take a look at you.'

'No. I'm all right. A little bruised, that's all. It's nothing. I'm not far from home.'

But she had overestimated her strength. She was not quite sure how she managed the last few yards. She felt so faint and was in such pain that she could only crawl up the front steps and let herself into the apartment before collapsing on the sofa.

Frau Bilde, coming in a little later to ask if she should bring tea, was horrified to see the state she was in. She insisted on helping her into the bedroom and undressing her. Tanya was being shaken by long shudders of pain that she had never felt before, and they frightened her.

Frau Bilde filled a hot water bottle and put it beside her.

'I'm going to telephone for the doctor,' she said gently.

'No, no, don't.' The poor man was in as bad a state as she was. 'Get in touch with the hospital. Ask for my brother,' she whispered. 'He will come.'

When Andy arrived half an hour later, he was met by an agitated Frau Bilde.

'Thank God you are here, Herr Doktor. I have been worried out of my mind.' She lowered her voice. 'She has begun to bleed.'

'What happened?'

'She was attacked,' she whispered nervously. 'Those Nazis – great brutes!'

Andy took only one look at her and said, 'Hospital for you, my girl. I'll phone for an ambulance.'

'I'm all right,' she protested feebly. 'It's only bruises. What will Dirk think when he comes home and I'm not here?'

'He can think what he pleases,' Andy said curtly. 'I want you where you can receive proper treatment.'

In ten minutes the ambulance was there, and in another ten she was being installed in a private room, Andy was there with another doctor and a nurse, and she could relax a little, let slip the tight band of anxiety and fear.

Dirk arrived at the hospital late that night and was referred to Andy.

'Frau Bilde told me. What happened? How is she?'

'As well as can be expected,' said Andy coldly, 'after being kicked in the stomach by a Nazi thug. She has lost the baby. I suppose that pleases you.'

Dirk frowned. 'What the hell do you mean by that? What did she tell you?'

'Enough. She is my sister. I don't need to be told very much.'

'How long will she have to stay here?'

'A few days. Nurse, take Herr von Richter to his wife's room.' As Dirk moved to follow, Andy stopped him. 'Be gentle with her,' he said.

'What the devil do you take me for? I love my wife.'

'Do you? I sometimes wonder.'

Tanya was drowsy from the drug she had been given, but she held out her hand to him, and he came quickly, kissing it and then her cheek.

'Did Andy tell you? I suppose it was silly of me,' she whispered, 'to do what I did, but they were such savages, and Dr Goldmann is such a kind old man.'

'Don't talk about it. Just think of getting well.'

'I suppose you're glad about the baby.'

'How could I be glad about anything that makes you unhappy?'

He sat with her until she drifted into sleep, and then went back to the empty flat. Time was growing very short. Soon he would have to tell her, he would have to give her a choice. Circumstances had changed. It had never occurred to him that they might have to part, but he loved her too much to let her be exposed to the dangers that could lie ahead. He knew now he should never have married. He should have waited till he had achieved what he had set out to do, but he had wanted her too much to run the risk of losing her, and now . . . The decision tore him in two. He might be forced to send her back to England, to that family who disliked him so much, and go on alone.

'Take it easy,' was Andy's advice when she left the hospital. 'Don't fret about it and don't do too much.' To Dirk he said quietly, 'No starting another baby yet awhile. You know what I mean.'

'I know.'

For a brief moment he thought of confiding his problem to Andy, but the dislike between them was too strong and his pride would not allow him to plead.

* * *

Beneath the apparently calm surface there was a good deal of unrest in the city. Hitler had begun to feel his power. New decrees seemed to be put into force every month controlling every aspect of life, government, trade unions, education, books, even theatres and cinemas. Every day, it seemed, there were tales whispered of men, and women too, who had defied the new rules and had been badly beaten up or had disappeared into labour camps. You never knew whether to believe them or not, but the doubt, the uneasy fear, remained.

It had been a day of sunshine and showers and Tanya had spent the afternoon in the park, where tulips already bloomed, stiff and upright like marching soldiers, and the trees were showing a haze of budding green branches. She had been home for about a fortnight and was feeling much better. The loss of the baby had distressed her, but it had been with her for so short a time, and it had been fraught with so much anxiety that it was a certain relief. Time to think about it, as Dirk said, when they were settled. After an early dinner he had gone out, explaining that he had to see a man about the changes at the gallery, and feeling tired she had gone to bed earlier than usual.

She was awakened by the slamming of a door, and lay for a second wondering what it was before she realized it must be Dirk coming back. She switched on the bedside lamp and saw with surprise that it was two o'clock. He never came home as late as that. There was a sudden heavy crash as if he had fallen over something, and she sat up in alarm. Could he be drunk? But never, never, in all the time they had been together had she known him to drink too much. She lay listening but there was no other sound, and suddenly the silence frightened her. She got up, pulled on her dressing gown, and went across the passage and into the sitting room. One light was on. A small table had been overturned, the vase on it lay smashed in a pool of water, the flowers scattered across the floor. Dirk was lying just beyond it face downward on the carpet. What could have happened? She ran to kneel beside him and saw with horror the blood that had matted the thick hair and the dark bruises on his face as he turned, trying to raise himself.

'Help me,' he mumbled thickly, and somehow she managed to haul him to his feet and into one of the armchairs. It was then that she saw the mud and dirt on his coat, his ripped shirt, the blood on his face from a split lip.

'My God, what have they done to you?' she breathed. 'Was it the Nazis? Why, Dirk, why?'

'Hitler's bully boys have two pet hates,' he muttered grimly, 'Jews and Communists.'

'But you're not a Jew . . .'

'No . . .'

For a moment she stared at him while the question hung in the air. It couldn't be true, it wasn't possible, it was too unbelievable.

She whispered, 'A Communist – you?'

'Yes.'

To her the word 'Communist' meant Bolsheviki – horror, savagery, death, the Red soldiers who had murdered her mother, put her father into deadly danger, destroyed the happiness of childhood. It was too enormous, too terrifying, to be taken in so suddenly.

She swallowed before she said, 'Your head . . . it's bleeding badly. I'll fetch water and bandages.'

He gripped her wrist. 'Did you understand what I said?'

'Yes, yes – tell me later.'

She would not let herself think about it as she collected what she needed – a bowl of water with cotton wool, a towel, liniment, bandages, plasters. When she came back she saw that he had managed to struggle out of his jacket and was sitting in his shirt sleeves, his head buried in his hands. He looked up as she came in, and the bruised mouth smiled faintly.

'Could you bring me some brandy? I'm afraid my hand is not too steady.'

'Should you have it with that head injury?'

'Be damned to that.'

She poured a small measure into a glass and gave it to him. He swallowed it at a gulp, gasped, and gave her the glass.

'That's better. Now do your worst and be quick about it. We've not much time.'

'What do you mean?'

'Never mind. Just patch me up and then we'll talk.'

She nerved herself to do what she had to. Clumsily but effectively she sponged away the blood, clipped some of the thick hair, and found the injury was less serious than she had feared. The blow had been a glancing one, otherwise it could have killed him. He winced as she dabbed at it, putting on a stinging antiseptic that Andy had once given her and fixing a plaster over it. She dealt gently with his face and with the bleeding knuckles of his right hand, but now he was growing impatient.

'That's enough,' he said, 'I'll live. Sit down, Tanya, I want to talk to you.'

She put aside the bowl and the other things she had been using, pulling up a footstool, and sat opposite him, hands clasped, her eyes fixed on his face.

'I want to know why, Dirk, why you have deceived me all this time. Why you let me believe that . . .' Her voice choked a little.

'There are reasons,' he said, 'but I can't go into those now. It would take too long, and we could be in danger, serious danger, both of us.'

'Danger? Why?'

'You know as well as I do that ever since the Reichstag fire Hitler has clamped down on all Communists. Their meetings are proscribed, many have been arrested, several have fled, a great number have gone into hiding.'

'Do they know about you?' she asked in a stifled voice.

'Not yet, but it may not be long before they do after tonight. Listen, Tanya, I was at a meeting, just a dozen of us, there were important decisions to be made. Someone must have given us away. The Nazis broke in – some of Hitler's picked bodyguard. There was a fight, several were arrested, a few of us escaped.'

'You among them?'

'Yes. The blow on the head knocked me out. They must have thought me dead already. When I came round I was lying in the gutter. I managed to crawl home somehow, but this is the point: one or other of those who've been arrested could talk. You have heard of their methods. Tortured, beaten up, anyone could squeal. So I must get out of the country as quickly and as unobtrusively as possible while I am still Dirk von Richter, wealthy partner in an elegant antique gallery and not a proscribed Communist from a back street. But first I must think about you.'

The shock had been extreme, but now she was beginning to recover from it. She felt she knew him so well, there must be reasons, weighty reasons, why he had acted as he had done. This was that dark side of his life which she had sensed and sometimes feared.

She said, 'We will go together. We are known in some quarters, and it will look the most natural thing in the world.'

But he shook his head. 'No, Tanya.' He stretched out a hand and touched her hair. 'It is best you forget about me. Go to your Embassy, to your kind Uncle Nigel, he will see that you are safe.'

She frowned at him. 'And where will you go?'

'I still have something I must do. After that . . .'

'You will come back to me?'

'Who knows?' He leaned forward and took her hand. 'Believe me, my darling, when I married you I did not know this was going to happen. I thought I saw my way quite clearly before me. A year or two and then we would be free to shape our own life. Now there could be danger, and I must not involve you in it.'

But Tanya had been reared in an atmosphere of loyalty, of love and faith in one another. Despite her doubts, despite feeling lost in a web of dark intrigue which she did not understand, she knew that you did not desert a friend or a lover in trouble. Whatever it was that bound him, whatever he had to do, she was sure of his need of her.

She said, 'No, Dirk, I'm already involved. I'm your wife and I'm going with you. You can't stop me. When do we leave?'

'No, Tanya . . .'

'You said we've not much time. Don't let's waste it arguing. Where are we going?'

'To Warsaw first and then – to Leningrad.'

'Russia!' she breathed. A long tremor of fear raced through her before she could conquer it and smile. 'It will be like going home.'

He stared at her, those strange eyes of his glowing in the dimly lit room, then he bent forward and kissed her. She could taste the blood from his wounded mouth.

After that it was Tanya who showed herself the most practical.

'You can't go out looking like that,' she said. 'People will ask questions. This morning as soon as I'm dressed I'll go to Willi and Hilde. They will help us.'

306

'No, no, you can't do that.'

'Why not? They are our friends. They are not Nazis.'

'Not yet, but they will not want to be involved. They will be afraid of trouble.'

She stared at him, feeling as if she had been precipitated into a frightening world where values had changed and nothing was normal or safe any longer.

'In that case I will go to Uncle Nigel.'

'He will want to know why,' objected Dirk.

'Perhaps, but he will do it for me.'

Nigel was indeed disturbed when she arrived early in his office at the Embassy and was engagingly frank with him.

'You were right,' she told him. 'Dirk got into some kind of a brawl with the Nazis. It was foolish, but you know what they are like. They could be after his blood. We were intending to leave Germany soon in any case. It just means going a little earlier than we meant to, that's all.'

Nigel frowned. 'And where are you going?'

She hesitated and then said airily, 'Dirk's stepfather, the Baron von Richter, intends to open an art gallery in Leningrad and wants him to assess the position there, and since we both speak Russian it seems a very good idea.'

'I don't like it, Tanya, I don't like it at all. Are you sure about it? Have you spoken to your father?'

'Oh, I shall write to Papa as soon as I get there.'

'You won't find living in the Soviet Union very comfortable just now.'

'We shan't be going to the famine areas but only to Leningrad and Moscow.'

'What do you want me to do?'

'It's just possible there may be people watching us. Could you see to everything for us, make the bookings, get our tickets?'

'If I must,' he said reluctantly. 'I'll make all the necessary arrangements for you and send tickets round to the flat.'

'Bless you. We're very grateful, both of us.'

She got up to go and he went with her to the door.

'I shall worry about you, Tanya, so take care,' he said.

'I will, Uncle, I will, I promise.'

Impulsively she kissed his cheek and then hurried away.

Nigel went back to his desk and picked up the telephone. It was obvious that her husband was in far more serious trouble than she had admitted. Maybe his old friend had been right and there was more to Dirk von Richter than had appeared on the surface. He would do what she asked, but he would also write to her father in England to let him know what his daughter was planning.

Back at the apartment Tanya forced Dirk to rest while she did most of the packing for both of them, starting at every sound and nervously waiting for the hammering on the door. But the hours passed, a special messenger came with their railway tickets and necessary visas, and somehow or other she managed to choke down a meal. Frau Bilde was given a substantial present and burst into floods of tears over it, and an Embassy car fetched them shortly before midnight.

Herr von Richter, Swiss citizen, and his Russian-born wife left Berlin with the blessing of the British on board the Continental Express bound for Warsaw and ultimately for Leningrad.

17

They did not speak much for the first hour of their journey. They were waiting for the stop at the border, after which, if they were lucky, they would begin to breathe more freely. They tensed as the train ground to a halt and the Nazi guards came clattering down the corridors examining passports and luggage, but though they were officious, though they took a long time over it, asking questions about where they were going and why, which Dirk answered with the bored arrogance of the rich, it was clear that up to now no one could have given him away. As the train jolted forward again and began to gather speed, Tanya heaved a huge sigh of relief.

The long night lay before them. Nigel had booked a first-class compartment in the wagon-lit, but neither of them had any desire to sleep. The train was very warm. She loosened her coat and took off her hat. Dirk was leaning back with his eyes closed. The marks on his face had darkened and the side of his jaw had begun to swell a little.

She said, 'Is your head very painful?'

'No more than a confounded headache.'

'I have some aspirin.' She filled a glass with water at the washbasin in the corner and brought it to him. 'Take these. They may help.'

'Why are you being so nice to me?' he asked wryly.

He swallowed the pills, replaced the glass, and sat down opposite her.

'I owe you an explanation,' he said.

'Would you rather lie down and rest first?'

'I couldn't sleep.' He moved restlessly. 'It's a long story and I don't know where to begin.'

'Why not at the beginning? We have the whole night before us.'

He looked across at her. This was not the Tanya he knew so

well, volatile, quick-tempered, apt to fly off at tangents. Somehow she had discovered an inner strength.

'You're so calm,' he said. 'Why are you so calm?'

If he only knew! Inside she was a jumble of conflicting emotions. That first, uncritical love that had put him on a pedestal, the most wonderful man in the world, and now what was he? She scarcely knew. A realization that he was vulnerable, sympathy, pity, anger at his deception mingled with a torturing anxiety, but she had chosen to go with him and she would not judge, not yet.

He began slowly, and as the train rushed through the night, eating up the miles, carrying her further and further into the unknown, the picture grew in her mind of that background of which he had so rarely spoken. The beautiful flame-haired mother, daughter of a provincial landowner, who had fallen hopelessly in love with the schoolmaster's son, a young man those elder brother had been hanged as a revolutionary by the Tsarist police and who lived only to avenge him. When he had been arrested she had gone willingly into exile with him, suffering the hardships of the labour camp in Siberia, and it was there when he knew she was pregnant that he had callously deserted her, wanting nothing that would hinder his driving purpose and leaving her, sick and unhappy, to bear the child alone.

'Did he go before you were born?'

'Yes. I was five when at last she was released. All I remember of that time is the bitter, agonizing cold and the perpetual hunger. How she kept us both alive I shall never know, but somehow we survived. By then, I believe, she had only two aims in her life, an intense burning hatred for the man who had abandoned her and a determination that I should have everything that had been denied to her. She had found a protector among the small bunch of exiles who made their way to Geneva. It was not until she sent me to school that I began to realize what my mother was and what I was. "Whore's bastard" became as familiar to me as the words in my lesson books.'

Outside in the darkness there was a long shrieking whistle as the express rounded a curve and roared on through the night. He was staring in front of him as if those harsh memories had bitten deep and he still felt the lash of them.

'Go on,' she whispered.

'Do you want to hear all this?'

'Yes, every word.'

She felt she was only now beginning to understand him, and knew a terrible regret because it could be too late.

'There were many revolutionaries in Geneva at that time,' he went on, 'plotting and quarrelling among themselves, and there was always plenty of work to be done for a pittance. My mother undertook some of it, and one day, when I was about ten, I went with her to one of their meetings and he was there.'

'Your father?'

'Yes. He had achieved the reputation by then of a ruthless worker for the cause. He went to and from Russia, and violence and death seemed to follow wherever he went. He acted while others only talked, and though some might be arrested and hanged he always seemed to escape without a scratch. He was a powerful speaker, and that day he whipped up the members to a wild enthusiasm. I admired him for it. When he came down from the platform my mother stepped out in front of him and thrust me forward.

'"Stay a moment," she said. "I'd like you to meet your son."

'I stared at him. He had a strange bony face and remarkable eyes. They turned from my mother to me, and something about that look and the icy voice, bleak as the east wind, made me shiver.

'"Are you joking, woman," he said. "There must be a dozen among us here today who could claim that privilege."

'There was a ripple of laughter. They all knew us, and I saw her eyes flame into anger at the insult as he pushed her aside and walked on. She clutched my arm so painfully that I bore the marks for days afterwards. "Look at him, look at him well," she whispered, "he is your father. One day you will force him to acknowledge you, and then you will destroy him as he has destroyed me." The passion in her voice terrified me, but at the same time it lit a fire that still burns.'

She had a sudden vision of him standing beside her on that high crag, looking across at the crumbling ruins of Roquelaire, and the brooding expression on his face when he had said, 'He achieved what he set out to do, and that should be enough for any man.' Had he meant it? Was that what was in his mind now?

'My mother was very sick that winter,' he went on, 'and I

311

realized that she was killing herself for my sake. I wanted to leave school, find some kind of work, but she would not hear of it, so I picked up odd jobs where I could. I even stole from time to time.' He smiled faintly. 'That's how I got those scars on my back. I delivered bread for a baker till he discovered that I was helping myself. For the sake of half a dozen loaves he flogged me mercilessly so that I slept on my face for weeks. Maybe it was that which made her apply for the post of housekeeper to the Baron, and wonder of wonders he engaged her. I hated him at first, as I'd hated the others who threw me a few coins and ravaged her body. I thought him rich, greedy, wanting only one thing from her, but I was wrong. He is a good man, one of the very few.'

'When did you become a Communist?'

'That's the crux of it, isn't it, Tanya? That's what you find so hard to forgive. That's why I couldn't tell you before. It was not for any political ideal. Though my mother and I spoke Russian together, though I always felt it was *my* country, the Revolution meant little to me and that winter, thanks to the Baron, I had everything I wanted.'

He got up and paced up and down the narrow carriage as if somehow he felt imprisoned. He went to the window, letting it down a few inches so that the cold night air poured in, and he took great gulps of it before closing the window again. He stood there with his back to her, leaning his head against his hands, his voice curiously muffled.

'It was the year my mother died. She had always been frail. Those early years of hunger and cold in Siberia had attacked her lungs. It was her spirit that kept her alive, that and her determination to achieve what she desired, but gradually the sickness sapped her strength. The Baron's care of her had come too late. I sat beside her bed watching her die by inches, and I made her a promise.'

In the dimly lit compartment, while the train rushed on, his voice seemed to conjure up before her eyes the macabre wall painting in that remote Provençal village, the flame-haired temptress, skeleton hands clutching at him, huge eyes in dark hollows imploring him, commanding him.

'A promise to do what?' she asked.

'Incriminate him, destroy him utterly, and to do that I had to

312

get close to him, I had to become a Communist. I had to know how they thought, how they acted, how they worked, their hates and loves and jealousies.'

At first, he told her, the older revolutionaries still living in Geneva distrusted him, but he had much to offer. He could speak several languages, he moved in a society few of them could penetrate, among men with money, position, influence. In Switzerland, where so many nationalities gathered, he could be of great service. Slowly he made himself invaluable, and learned that they were like the rest of the world, greedy, jealously fighting for power among themselves, and a few, just a very few, looking for an ideal state that does not exist.

'And what of your father?'

'He had been one of the old guard, close to Lenin before he died, and he has managed to survive under Stalin. He holds a high position in the secret police, the GPU. He is admired, hated and feared. A great many of his comrades would be only too happy to see Igor Livinov destroyed.'

'Livinov? Igor Livinov?'

In a way she had already suspected it, but certainty was still a shock. Galina, her father, they had been right. Dirk was the son of the man who had haunted their lives, had very nearly destroyed them both. They had warned her and she had refused to believe them.

She was staring at him, horror creeping into her eyes and thickening her voice.

'It was you who planned the murder of Leon, it was you who sent the assassin to the hospital, to Ravensley where he could have killed my sister, my father, my brother . . .'

'No, Tanya, no, you're wrong,' he said passionately. 'I'm not their executioner. I have never been that. All I have done is to pass on information.'

'Knowing they would act on it. That man I saw with you at the Savoy, is he their murderer?'

'I don't give the orders,' he said desperately. 'You must believe me.'

'Oh God!' She buried her head in her hands. 'I don't know what to believe. It can't be true.'

He looked down at the bowed head with a hopeless certainty

that if he had lost her, he had lost everything. He had believed himself strong enough to manipulate them to his will, and that when he had achieved his aim and found himself face to face with Igor Livinov he would be free. But now he knew that it had been as crazy a dream as that which had possessed his mother. By marrying Tanya he had given them a hold over him. That stone-faced man in Marseilles had been right. A good Communist makes no lasting attachments, he does not love nor does he hate, he never allows any such weakness to make him vulnerable.

He leaned towards her and she shrank away from him.

'Don't come near me, don't touch me.'

'Very well, but at least listen to me. When we reach Warsaw, which should be about midday, you must leave me. You must return to Europe, to England. You must go back to your father.'

It was tempting. She sat huddled into a corner staring out of the window into thick black night, facing it squarely, and knew she could not do it. She could not desert him any more than she could have deserted a hurt child or a sick dog. She turned to him with sudden hope.

'Why can't we go together, Dirk? Give up this obsession of yours. You have let it possess you beyond all reason, and what use is it? What satisfaction will there be for you even if you succeed?'

'No, I can't, not now. It's impossible.'

'Why, Dirk, why?'

But he couldn't tell her. Those others who hated, who plotted so patiently to pull down the man who had ridden so high above them, had entrapped him into their purposes. He was only the instrument. It was better for Tanya to know nothing. If, God forbid, something happened to him, she would be innocent of any involvement. They could not harm her.

'Did you love your mother so much?' she asked quietly.

'For a very long time it was she and I pitted against a hostile world. As a boy I used to dream of the day when I would face him, gun in hand, and shoot him straight between the eyes. Only then, I thought, would her spirit be avenged.'

'But that is crazy. You're not a boy now.'

'No, and nothing is simple any longer.' He got up, stretching himself wearily. 'I'm going to look for the attendant to find out if he'll make us some coffee.'

After he had gone she glanced at her watch. It was four o'clock, a dead hour of the night before the first streak of dawn brought new life, new hope. The compartment was stuffily warm, but out in the corridor someone had opened a window and the spring night was fresh and cool. She leaned her forehead against the cold glass as the train raced over the flat fields of Poland, the occasional prick of light betokening a lone farmhouse where someone lay sleepless or watched by the bed of a sick child. She knew she could not fight his obsession, but she could not let him play it out alone. Pride played a part in her stubbornness. She had chosen him in spite of opposition and would not go back on her choice. Pride and love – not the first, unquestioning passion but something deeper, because understanding was in it, and sympathy and pity, and a powerful belief that once in Russia, faced with the many problems, he would realize the folly of his promise. He would be freed from his impossible dream, and afterwards they could find a new and more real relationship.

What she did not realize, any more than he did, was that the organization of the secret police had inherited all the most terrifying aspects of the Tsarist *Okhrana* and through the *Cheka* and the GPU had long grown out of its crude beginnings. Now its tentacles were spreading far and wide. Its members spied one upon the other so that no one knew himself safe. Dirk was enmeshed in a web of intrigue of which he was aware of only part, and the only thing which Igor Livinov in his office in the Lubianka did not yet know was that the man he suspected of trying to trap him was his own son.

Dirk came back followed by the sleeping car attendant with a tray of coffee. In those first-class coaches money could buy almost any service.

They drank it hot and strong, and the trauma of the night receded a little.

'When do we reach Warsaw?' she asked the man when presently he came to fetch the tray.

'We should be in about midday, madame. Breakfast will be served from seven. Would you care to come to the restaurant car?'

'No,' said Dirk decisively. 'Bring it here. Coffee, toast, and a little fruit if you have any.'

'Certainly, sir.'

'And thank you for bringing us this.'

'No trouble, sir, none at all.' Appreciatively he eyed the large tip left on the tray. 'Anything to oblige the lady.'

When he had left, Tanya leaned back, her eyes closed.

Dirk said, 'Would you like to rest? Shall I make up the bed for you?'

'I'm all right.'

They were being polite to one another almost as if they were strangers.

He picked up the travelling rug, tucked it gently round her, and then opened the door of the compartment.

'Where are you going?'

She had a horrible vision of him hurling himself off the train.

'Only into the corridor to smoke. Try to sleep.'

'You know, I can't think of it as Leningrad,' she remarked dreamily, 'but only as the old St Petersburg.'

He turned his head. 'Does that mean . . . ?'

'I'm not running home to Papa, Dirk. I'm coming with you.'

'No, Tanya . . .'

'Don't argue. It's settled.'

He paused, then bent down and kissed her lightly before going out.

The die was cast, the decision taken. Now there was no going back, and in some queer way she welcomed it.

After the drama and stress of those first few hours on the train, the long journey from Poland through to Leningrad and the first week in the city seemed flat, dull and curiously drab. She did not know what to expect, but they had been received like all foreigners, with a grudging suspicion, and their hotel, catering almost exclusively for visitors and high Party officials, was under constant supervision, every exit and entrance closely watched. Food was severely limited and indifferently cooked, hot water was a rarity, there was no stopper in the hand basin, and the plumbing left much to be desired.

'Why?' she asked Dirk. 'Why, for God's sake? Is it because Jack is as good as his master and no one is willing to do the ordinary, necessary jobs any longer, or are they all so busy building Utopia that they forget the basic comforts of everyday living?'

It was strange, she thought, walking down the Morskaya and looking for the house which had once been home to all of them, how seeing the city after all these years was rather like one of the transformation scenes in the theatre, where by the device of lighting or shifting curtains the stage changes from brilliance into a grey, crumbling ruin.

Her childhood memories were not of the last, dark days of the war but all of dazzling light and colour – the night she was taken to a gala performance at the Maryinsky, with the Tsar and Tsarina in their box blazing with diamonds and the stalls filled with women in silks and satins and men in splendid uniforms, white, scarlet and gold. She remembered watching with Andy the gay pleasure boats filled with elegant people sailing across the Neva to the gypsy restaurants on the islands, the streets in winter bustling with sleighs and troikas with high-stepping horses and the merry sound of the bells on their scarlet harness.

Now everywhere there was an air of neglect, of poverty and a quiet despair. She gazed up at the house, the handsome door under the pillared portico battered out of all recognition, the brass fittings long since wrenched off, the steps littered with rubbish blown across them by the chill May wind. She shivered and walked quickly on.

Very few shops were open, and those that were had little to sell to the long, patient queues of women waiting for extra food or for some longed-for item of clothing rare as a snowball in summer. Any notion of setting up an art gallery with luxury *objects d'art* seemed utterly ridiculous, but of course she knew now that that was merely a cover story and that Dirk was here for some other purpose he still refused to tell her. Today he had gone to visit a high official in the Ministry of Education who had ostensibly asked him to give expert advice on some fine furniture he had recently acquired – looted more likely, thought Tanya cynically. She wondered whether one day she would see the magnificent silver candelabra with the Malinsky monogram which had stood in their drawing room adorning someone else's sideboard, find herself eating off her mother's prized Meissen dinner service, or recognize

317

on the library shelves her father's collection of rare and valuable books.

Despite the cold wind the sun was shining, and she made a sudden decision to indulge her nostalgia for the past and take the train to Dannskoye. In the old days they had travelled by carriage until Papa bought the Mercedes. She remembered the thrill of the great black car with its handsome brass fittings purring up the drive, and the children's wild excitement as they piled into it.

The little local train still ran, though the carriages looked as if they had not seen a lick of paint in twenty years. Leather had been cut from the seats to sole somebody's worn-out boots, and the floor was awash with debris that it was nobody's job to sweep out.

Dannskoye was five miles from the station and she was wondering if she would have to walk, when she saw the decrepit cab and the driver who matched it with his thick grey beard and foul-smelling pipe that he didn't even bother to remove when he spoke to her. The horse was so old and so thin that she thought it might drop dead before they got there.

She gave him a handful of money when they arrived and asked him to wait. He nodded, climbed down, hung a nosebag over the horse's head, and settled down with the enormous patience of the Russian peasant.

She walked resolutely up the drive, now thick with grass and weeds, the long trailers from the overgrown shrubs threatening to trip her up at every step, and knew suddenly that it had been a mistake to come. The old white house, once so gracious and welcoming, was a dismal ruin, robbed of everything that could be carried away, windows smashed, doors hanging on broken hinges. She stood in the hall where Aunt Sonia used to fill huge bowls with flowers, and the ghosts rushed out to meet her, long summer days when they all seemed to live out of doors, winter with the snow mountain built for them by the servants, shrieking with laughter as they slid down it with the help of Papa and Uncle Niki and Uncle Val, the dogs joining in and barking madly. She closed her eyes for a second, hearing the voices filled with joy that were completely unaware of what was to come. Then something rustled among the blown papers and rubbish, and a huge rat stared at her with eyes bright as diamonds before it scurried across the floor. Abruptly she did not want to remember any longer; it was all vanished, all gone, and would never haunt her again. She turned and ran, out of the house and headlong down the steps, to collide with a man who gripped her arm firmly and swung her round to face him.

'Who are you? What are you doing here?' he demanded.

Taken by surprise she said breathlessly, 'Nothing, nothing at all. It's only that I lived here once when I was a child.'

'The Malinskys were here then, enemies of the State, long since run off, every stinking one of them.'

She turned away and would have gone, but he stopped her, looking her up and down and frowning, noting the elegant suit, the white blouse, the fine silk stockings, the handmade shoes. There was a dawning recognition in the eyes under the bushy grey eyebrows.

'My God, you're one of them.'

She stared at him, a childish memory floating up from the past. He was Yakov, overseer of Uncle Niki's factory, and always a troublemaker. She longed to say proudly, 'Yes, I'm one of them, and it was men like you who murdered my mother,' but fortunately she realized the folly in time.

'My husband, Dirk von Richter, is Swiss,' she said haughtily.

'Papers, please.'

'By what right are you questioning me?'

'I'm in charge of this district. You are trespassing on land that belongs to the people.'

'Who've already robbed it of anything of value.'

'We do not steal. We take only what belongs to us by right.'

He examined closely the papers she took from her handbag, and then raised his head.

'Go back to where you belong, Princess Malinsky. Your kind are not wanted here.'

She took the papers from him and forced herself to walk with dignity, aware that he followed her every step of the way. It was an uncomfortable experience, and she was thankful to see her cab driver waiting. The old man opened the door for her, glared at the overseer, then spat with a slow deliberation before he climbed on to the box. Yakov stood by the wrecked gatepost and watched them drive off before moving away.

* * *

319

'You shouldn't have gone there,' said Dirk when she told him about it.

'But why? I was doing no harm.'

'Of course you weren't, but many of these minor Party officials are so uncertain of themselves they suspect everyone. The past must be eliminated, destroyed utterly, before they can go ahead with confidence.'

'Dirk, how long do we have to stay here?'

'Tomorrow you can start packing. We're going to Moscow.'

'And then?'

'There are certain things I have to do there and then we can go.'

She voiced the fear that she found hard to banish, that was always there at the back of her mind.

'You're not going to try and kill him?'

'Do I seem like a murderer?'

'I don't know, Dirk. Sometimes I feel I don't know you at all.'

'Trust me, Tanya, just trust me, that's all I ask.'

'Are you sure of that?'

'Of course I'm sure.'

But she didn't altogether believe him. She knew he had by no means told her everything, and she was afraid of what he might do and even more of what might be done to him.

That evening she wrote a long letter to her father, saying something of what she had seen that day, but a little guarded since, in this atmosphere of distrust, it seemed possible that even private letters might be censored. She said nothing at all of what Dirk had confessed to her on that last night in Berlin. Perhaps in the future, when it was all over and done with, she would be able to tell him and Galina how right they had been in one way and how wrong in another. When the letter was finished and sealed, she took it out to post herself. The woman she thought of as the spy on their corridor asked her where she was going and offered to post it for her, but she refused, suspecting uneasily that it might never reach its destination.

Two days later they boarded the train for Moscow. It was a long journey, and they took the precaution of taking a little food with them since any kind of service seemed doubtful. As usual the train was packed, but as a rich foreigner Dirk had a certain pull, and they had seats in what used to be a first-class compartment.

Bookshops had offered a very limited choice of something to read and she hesitated between Tolstoy's *Anna Karenina* and Dostoevsky's *Crime and Punishment*, finally settling for Anna.

'I read it years and years ago when I was at school, and I remember my stepmother saying once that it was the only book she had with her during all the time she was in a Siberian prison camp. Perhaps it will come in useful for me in the same way.'

She was smiling at him and he was conscious of a stab of pain. Please God, don't let anything bad happen to her.

He knew only too well that he should have insisted on her leaving him before ever they reached Russia, but when Tanya was determined she was very difficult to persuade.

He watched the golden head bent over the book. Ever since he had fallen in love with her, things had begun to change. At first, in Geneva, when he had learned about the plot that was slowly taking shape against Igor Livinov and his apparently unassailable position in the GPU, he had thrown himself into it heart and soul. Stalin disliked Livinov, fearing him and his strong influence as he had feared Trotsky and other men of the old guard who had been close to Lenin. At first it had seemed exactly what Dirk wanted, what his mother would have longed for, to see the man who had fathered him disgraced, robbed of power, exiled for life, destroyed. But in the last two years Dirk's view had altered. Livinov might be a man without human feelings towards his fellow men, but he had one undeniable quality – a loyalty to his country and to the Revolution he had himself helped to create. It might be inhuman but it was unshakeable. But now Dirk had come too far; he had in his possession every last, damning detail that would utterly destroy him, and felt suddenly sick at what he was expected to do. He had tried to withdraw a year ago at Marseilles, and refused to go any further, and had been made to realize very forcibly that there was no drawing back. He had a wife, they reminded him. No more than that, but the threat was sufficient.

He had a half-formed plan that might work and might not. So much depended on chance, and chance was a very uncertain ally.

Tanya looked up, caught his eye, and smiled.

'How is it?' he asked.

'Good.'

He had a strong desire to pull her into his arms, to hold her tight against him while he still could, but there were other people in the compartment, so all he could do was to put his hand on hers, gripping it hard for a moment.

'Not long now,' he said.

Not long before they reached Moscow, before they could leave Russia, or before the inevitable end? She was not sure, only that they were facing it together.

18

The Hotel Metropol, built at the turn of the century, still retained a faint flavour of its Victorian magnificence, though the splendour of the high gilded ceiling, the glory of the great golden candelabra, twelve feet tall, were dimmed and the alcoves and plush upholstered love seats were badly worn in places. Sadly the fountain that had once risen from the flower-fringed pool in arcs of rainbow-coloured spray had long since ceased to play.

The journey had been an exhausting one and they had neither of them had much sleep, but their rooms were booked and a note was handed to Dirk at the reception desk. He glanced at it as they were shown up to the second floor and then pushed it into his pocket with an impatient exclamation.

'What is it?' she asked apprehensively.

'Nothing very important, but it does mean I'll have to go out again almost immediately. Why don't you rest for an hour? I'll order some tea for you. I shouldn't be long.'

It was while she was unpacking the small suitcases that held their immediate necessities that she saw the pistol. It was buried beneath shirts and handkerchiefs. She was holding it in her hand, small and deadly, when she heard the knock on the door. She put it back quickly and shut the case before she called, 'Come in.'

It was the *deshurneya*, the resident spy on their floor, who came in with the tea, looking suspiciously around her and asking where her husband was.

'He has had to go out on business,' she snapped, finding this constant supervision irritating in the extreme.

She drank the tea gladly but was far too restless to lie down, and went out again, nodding airily to their frowning custodian as she went down the stairs.

She had no childish memories of Moscow to haunt her, and walked up the street and across Red Square looking about her with

323

interest despite the ever-present anxiety about what might be happening to Dirk.

Before her stretched the massive walls of the Kremlin, the very heart of Russia ever since an enterprising boyar had built the first tiny fortress on the Moscow River in the eleventh century, and which had now grown into a formidable forbidden kingdom where Stalin lived, closely guarded, every door tightly shut, like some squat gigantic spider, gathering to himself threads that spread out all over the vast empire and beyond. Directly in front of her lay the dark red basalt mausoleum where the embalmed body of Lenin lay under glass, the door guarded by soldiers with fixed bayonets while a long procession of slow-moving, patient visitors wound about the building shepherded by security guards.

Quite suddenly it frightened her. The Kremlin, the tomb, seemed to embody the menace of the last few days, the terror that had steadily grown since that night in Berlin when she first knew the truth about Dirk. Now, here at last in Moscow, he would meet his fate to win or lose. She had an irrational feeling that everyone was looking at her with hostility, the men and women in the queue, the soldiers, the passers-by, all staring at her in her elegant clothes, the alien, the outsider, the enemy. She turned and almost ran back to the hotel, taking refuge in their bedroom, standing in the middle of the floor shaking and telling herself what a fool she was to run away from shadows.

Dirk came back about an hour later and said casually, 'We must make sure we dine early this evening. I've been given tickets for the ballet,' and it was so completely ordinary, so different from what she had expected, that she didn't know whether to laugh or cry.

'Why should we be given tickets?'

'Just a courtesy to a visiting foreigner. It's *Swan Lake*. I thought you might enjoy it,' he replied lightly; but it was a great deal more than that, as had already been pointed out to him. The man who would be sharing their box was the man who would give him the final instructions, and what more innocent occasion to meet than during a pleasurable evening at the theatre?

'What do I wear?' she asked before they went down to dinner.

'Nothing too grand. It's not the Paris Opera, and evening dress is not high fashion in Soviet Russia.'

324

So she chose a dress in dark green silk with an accordion-pleated skirt springing out from a slim waist, long tight sleeves and a low-cut, heart-shaped neck. Her one jewel was an antique emerald pendant on a fine gold chain that had been Dirk's wedding present. It flashed a green fire on the creamy neck.

Despite war, tragedy and revolution, Russians still loved the ballet, and the theatre was crowded, high-ranking officials bursting out of poorly tailored dark suits, their wives in their best even if it was not the latest fashion. There were a number of curious and envious glances at Tanya as, head held high, she came through the foyer on Dirk's arm.

A couple rose to greet them when they entered the box reserved for them. A man with thick grey hair brushed straight back, a strong face, handsome in a way, but quite unremarkable except for heavy-lidded eyes that probed and missed nothing. There was an aura of immense and ruthless power about him. It was like being close to a sleeping tiger that at any moment might stretch out a paw and strike to kill. Tanya mentally shook herself. She must not give way to fancy.

'Let me introduce myself,' he said. 'Sergei Ivanovich Shukilov.' He shook Dirk's hand. 'Delighted to meet you at last, Herr von Richter, and this of course is your lovely wife.'

He bowed as he took Tanya's hand, holding it just a little too long while his eyes raked over her with a look she had long learned to recognize, a look that undressed her and summed her up. She pulled her hand abruptly away and knew by his slight smile that he had realized why. Then he had turned to the woman beside him.

'Permit me to present my wife, Anna Petrovna. Madame von Richter was born and brought up in Russia, my dear. I am sure you and she will have a great deal in common.'

She was small and delicately made, younger than her husband, about thirty-five perhaps, with a kind of fragile beauty, dressed simply but with a distinction missing from most of the other women Tanya had glimpsed as she came into the theatre; and she felt an instant attraction, as if in her she might perhaps find a friend.

The dancing of the principals was excellent, even if the general presentation was a little ragged, but Tanya found it difficult to relax and enjoy it as she might have done. She was too strung up, too aware of the oppressive presence of the man who sat just behind her. It was quite obvious that this was no accidental meeting. She stole a glance at Dirk and saw that he was looking not at the stage but at the box directly opposite, which had been empty until the curtain rose and where a man now sat alone.

At the interval Dirk and Shukilov excused themselves and went out together. The two young women, left alone, were silent for a moment, then Anna looked across at her and smiled a little shyly.

'Do forgive me. I know it's terribly rude to comment on what someone is wearing, but I do so admire your dress. Did you buy it in Paris?'

'Yes, I did, over a year ago. Dirk and I spent several months there after we were married.'

'I thought so. It is so simple and yet so very stylish.' Anna sighed. 'I always longed to go to Europe, and my father promised he would take me on a trip when I was twenty-one. Then the war came and the Revolution, so it never happened.'

'Have you always lived in Moscow?'

'I grew up here. My father was Professor of History at the University, but after he died' – she shrugged her slim shoulders – 'times were difficult, and I had to live where I could find work. My husband's government post brought him from the Ukraine to Moscow two years ago.'

The man in the opposite box, though partly hidden by the red velvet curtain, seemed to be looking directly across at them.

Tanya said casually, 'Do you happen to know the gentleman over there? I think he is trying to attract your attention.'

'I doubt it,' said Anna drily. 'I know him, of course, but not personally. He holds a very important position in the State Political Directorate – that is the GPU. He's a kind of *éminence grise* behind the Chief, if you know what I mean, but Igor Livinov very rarely attends any social function.'

Tanya's heart gave a sudden lurch. So this was the man himself, the father whom Dirk had come so far to meet . . . and destroy.

'Really? How interesting,' she said, trying to sound indifferent and putting a hand on the opera glasses lying on the ledge. 'May I?'

'Of course, but take care. He is a strange man. He may not care for being watched.'

She focused the glasses, and although she knew it was impossible, it was as if her husband's eyes were looking directly into her own. Despite the shaven head the likeness was remarkable, the moulding of the face, the high cheekbones, the mobile mouth. She might have been seeing Dirk as he would look in thirty years' time.

'A fascinating face,' she said at last, putting down the glasses.

'The face of a devil or of a saint, I've always thought,' said Anna with a wry smile. 'But if pressed, I think I'd choose the devil.'

Then the conductor returned, the orchestra began to play, and the curtain rose again.

The men had not come back, and it was during the *pas de deux* when Odile, the enchantress, uses her wiles on Prince Siegfried that Tanya was aware of a hand on her arm and a voice close to her ear.

'Leave Moscow,' whispered Anna. 'Go away as quickly as you can, tomorrow if possible. You're in great danger, both you and your husband.'

Tanya stared into the large eyes fixed on her. 'Why do you tell me this? What do you know? Is it your husband?'

But Anna only shook her head. 'Sergei tells me nothing, but I hear things. Believe me, it is true.'

Then she sat back in her chair and concentrated on the dancing, leaving Tanya shaken, only half believing, and yet finding it just one more thing to add to her fear.

At the second intermission the men came back, apologizing for being away so long and carrying a box of chocolates which Sergei Shukilov handed to Tanya with a flourish.

'I hope they don't come too late for your enjoyment,' he said.

She thanked him prettily and opened them, handing them around while the conversation became general, about how she had seen Karsavina dance in *Giselle* when she was a child, how rare it was to see a full-length ballet like this in London, and how a few years ago she had seen Diaghilev's Ballet Russe in Paris. She was also very aware that only Dirk sat silent, paler than usual. He took out a cigarette and then, realizing that smoking was forbidden, shredded it between nervous fingers, his eyes on the box opposite.

After the show was over they parted outside the theatre. Anna, with a glance at her husband, asked if they would care to go back with them for a nightcap, but Dirk refused, pleading fatigue after the tiring journey on the previous night.

Shukilov's own car waited for them, a black limousine with a uniformed driver at the wheel. Before she stepped into it Anna put a hand on Tanya's arm.

'If you're not busy, come and see me tomorrow,' she said. 'I'll be at home all day.'

Puzzled, Tanya said, 'Thank you, I'd like to, but it does depend on Dirk.'

'Yes, of course, but don't forget, will you?'

There was an urgency in her voice and in the fingers that gripped her arm, and suddenly Tanya understood what she was trying to say.

Then Anna had stepped into the car, her husband followed, and it purred away.

Alone with Dirk in their bedroom that night Tanya asked, 'Who is this Shukilov? Why did we have to meet him? What has he to do with us?'

Dirk stopped in the act of pulling off his shirt. 'He is second to Igor Livinov, what might be called his right-hand man. Any access to Livinov himself has to go through him.'

'I can't imagine *him* wishing to be second to anyone. I didn't like him. He made me shiver.'

She was sitting at the dressing table fumbling with the clasp of her gold chain, and he came to unfasten it for her. She saw his face in the mirror, saw the look of strain, the dark shadows under his eyes.

'There,' he said, 'that's done,' and dropped the necklace in front of her.

She twisted round to clasp his hand in both of hers.

'Dirk, I'm frightened,' she said urgently. 'Let's run away. Let's pack our bags and go, now, this very minute. Let's get as far away as we can.'

'It's not possible, not now. We'd get no further than the railway station.'

'You mean – we are being watched?'

328

'Almost certainly. Every step we take.'

'Why, Dirk, why?'

'Every foreigner is suspect in Russia today.'

'That's not the real reason, is it? Tonight during the ballet when we were alone together Anna whispered something to me. She said that we should go now, that we were in great danger, both of us. What did she mean? Why should she say that?'

Dirk said thoughtfully, 'I'm not sure, but rumour has it that she is not happy with her husband. Her father was a liberal thinker of the old school, and too outspoken in his views. He was arrested and sent to a labour camp, where he died miserably. She was left alone and penniless.'

Poor Anna – was that what had driven her to marry Shukilov?

'She meant what she said, Dirk, I'm certain of it, and it frightened me. When can we go?'

'Just as soon as I've done what they want me to do' was what was in his mind, but he didn't say it aloud. Instead he pressed her hands reassuringly.

'Soon, very soon now.'

They had not made love since that night in Germany. She had not rejected him, but too much had happened between them and the old intimacy seemed to have vanished. That night it was different.

Tired from the train journey and from the long, stressful day, she fell asleep quickly and into a nightmare, a repetition of the haunting dream on her wedding night when she wandered alone in some vast and empty space that smelled foul and dank, hopelessly crying out his name. She seemed to stumble over something heavy, stooped to see what it was, and saw his face distorted, the eyes staring and lifeless. She woke up in terror to find Dirk's arms around her, holding her close against him while she clung to him sobbing wildly. Later, when she had grown calmer, when they had both drowsed a little, the hunger arose, sharpened by all that had happened and by fear for the future. It flamed between them into a passion that left them both exhausted but utterly content. She fell asleep cradled in his arms, while Dirk lay wakeful through the slow hours to dawn and at last withdrew his arm very carefully and got up.

He dressed quickly and came back to look down at her. She was sleeping as peacefully as a child, the golden hair in a tangle on the pillow. He kissed her gently so as not to wake her, pulled the blankets over her, picked up the discarded nightdress from the floor, and crept silently out of the room.

When she woke some time later she found a note on the dressing table.

'You can start to pack. Have everything ready to leave as soon as I return.'

She did as he asked. She closed the travelling trunk which she had scarcely touched except to take out the green silk dress. She repacked the two suitcases, and found with a shock that the pistol was missing. He must have taken it with him. She stood staring in front of her, hearing again the roar of the express from Berlin and the quiet voice saying, 'As a boy I used to dream of the day when I would face him, gun in hand, and shoot him straight between the eyes.'

Surely that was not in his mind now? It couldn't be. It was impossible. Whatever Dirk was, he was no killer. Deep inside her she was certain of that. But why had he taken the gun, and what did he intend? The unanswered questions hammered at her mind all morning while she did everything she could to hasten their departure when the time came. The luggage packed, she went down to Reception to pay their bill. It fretted her that she did not know when he would return and so could not order a taxi.

She had dressed sensibly for travelling, a plain coat and skirt and a silk blouse, a loose fawn coat lying on the bed ready. Then there was nothing more to do but wait. She dared not leave the hotel in case he should come back and not know where she had gone, and the rest of the morning passed very slowly. She ordered some coffee and then found it tasted like mud and she could not swallow it, her throat seemed to have closed up. She looked for something to read and picked up Luke's book, which she had gone through quickly when he had given it to her in Paris and had always intended to read again, but the words of *The Lost Leader* danced on the page and made no sense. She put it in her suitcase and stationed herself by one of the windows that looked toward Dzershinski Square. That was where the Lubianka was. Dirk had pointed it out to her on their way to the theatre. There Igor

Livinov had his office, and it was from there that Dirk would surely come.

For hours he walked the streets of Moscow, through Red Square, through the Alexandrovski Gardens, down to the river, round the Kremlin, past St Basil's Cathedral, while he tried to make up his mind about what he was going to do. Lying beside the sleeping Tanya it had been impossible. He had to be out in the air, free from all personal attachments. He knew now that in the blindness of his obsession he had been manipulated; they had trumped up a case of treason against Igor Livinov, but that wasn't enough. He could be too clever for them. They wanted more, they wanted him dead, and that was why he was here, in Moscow, the loaded pistol ready to his hand.

Last night Shukilov had explained it very clearly. He would be admitted to the private sanctum, Livinov's holy of holies, where no one entered without express permission. Then, when the deed was done, he would leave quietly. It would be several hours before Shukilov would discover what had happened, and by that time he could be very far away from Moscow, travelling as he had always done as an art-loving Swiss citizen, and there would be no pursuit. He could be sure of that. Only Dirk did not trust him, he didn't trust any of them. He would cheat them, leave Livinov still alive to fight his own battles against treachery and false accusations. The fire of anger that had possessed him for so long had burned itself out. He would meet his father once face to face and then it would be over.

The appointment was for one o'clock. It was a bright sunny morning when he walked into Dzershinsky Square and paused outside the large, rather ornate nineteenth-century building which had once housed a famous insurance company and was now the headquarters of the GPU, with a fearful reputation of imprisonment, of forced confession, of torture and unexplained death.

In his office on the second floor in the very heart of the spacious building Igor Livinov sat at his plain wooden desk. The room was austere; not for him the luxuries some of his colleagues indulged in, the fine antique furniture, the Persian carpets, the looted china with the Tsarist monogram, the silver samovar with the engraved

331

coat of arms of some princely family. He despised all such frivolities. He had arrived as usual at seven o'clock, had already disposed of a heavy workload, and was conscious for almost the first time in his life of feeling tired.

He was fifty-seven. For forty years he had worked unceasingly in the cause of creating a Marxist Communist state, and he knew, with an increasing weary frustration, how very far Soviet Russia was from achieving that ideal.

He was aware from his own network of spies that a plot was being hatched against him. He guessed that Shukilov, brought from a position of supreme power in the Ukraine, now yearned to exercise that same power in Moscow, but he was not yet sure how they planned to dispose of him. Would it be by false accusation of treason and a staged trial, as had happened to Trotsky, or by the simpler, more direct method of assassination? All he was sure of was that the young man he was shortly to meet, the rich young capitalist turned Communist, was to be the instrument. He could have had him arrested, but held his hand deliberately, wanting to know how far they would go. It was a trial of strength between him and Shukilov, and what happened to Dirk von Richter was unimportant.

A young woman in a shapeless uniform blouse and skirt brought him China tea with lemon.

'I'm expecting a visitor shortly,' he said. 'Make sure that I'm not interrupted.'

'Of course, Comrade Commissar,' she said respectfully.

How plain she was, he thought idly, as he sipped his tea. Why couldn't they choose a few pretty ones?

He was not a man who ever looked back. What was done, mistake or not, was in the past, and he looked only to the future. But this morning, perhaps because of this unusual weariness, he let his mind wander over the last twenty years or so. There had been only one woman he had seriously wanted in all those austere years when he had allowed himself no personal attachments, not love or hate or any weakness that could make him vulnerable. He had possessed her once, but Galina had escaped him, had run away to her English lover. It had been his one defeat, his one regret, his one moment of savage jealousy, long put behind him.

* * *

Dirk showed his pass, proved his identity, and an armed guard led him through the hall to a small, old-fashioned lift that held the two of them with difficulty. It creaked slowly up to the second floor. He followed his escort through the iron gate and along a corridor, and was delivered over to another guard, who checked his papers once again, then opened the door, ushered him through, and shut it firmly behind him.

The man at the desk rose slowly to his feet. Father and son faced one another at last. For an instant Dirk was again that small ten-year-old boy in Geneva, trembling with excited anticipation, alight with hope, and felt once again the sharp pain of rejection and was aware of his mother's bitter shame.

Igor Livinov held out his hand.

'Welcome,' he said. 'I always like to meet personally all our executives working both in this country and abroad. Come in, bring up a chair, sit down.'

Dirk came into the centre of the room, but he did not take the proffered hand.

'Thank you, I prefer to stand.'

'As you wish.'

Livinov sat down again in the leather desk chair and subjected the young man standing before him to that penetrating look that had so often unnerved some unfortunate victim brought before him.

'I understand from our people that since you joined the Party in Geneva you have proved yourself invaluable in London, Paris and Berlin.'

'That is not the only reason why I am here.'

'Indeed?' He let his eyes run up from the handmade shoes, the well-cut suit and silk tie, till he met the eyes so curiously like his own. 'Then what is it that has brought you here?'

'Do you remember a woman called Varya Andreyevna, a beautiful woman with hair the colour of flame?.'

'Should I?'

'His face was expressionless, but the hand that had been beating a light tattoo on the desk was suddenly still.

'She was my mother.'

'And how does that concern me?'

'She named me for my father – Mikhail Igorovich.'

333

'Igor is a common name in Russia.'

Dirk ignored him and went steadily on. 'A great many years ago we met in Geneva. I was a boy then, longing for a father, eager to hero-worship, yearning to be called your son. Absurd, wasn't it, fit only for ridicule, for laughter – and you made quite sure of that, didn't you?'

'You are that boy.'

'Yes, I am that boy.'

'Is she with you?'

'She died four years ago, and I swore to her then that I would seek you out and make you pay for the years of suffering you inflicted upon her. That's why I joined the Party, that's why I have sought you, that's why I am here today.'

'For what purpose? To claim your paternity, to demand that I acknowledge you as my son?' The voice was filled with a scalding contempt.

'No, not for any of that. I want nothing that you can give me. Since I was that boy in Geneva I've longed only for one thing.'

'And what is that?'

'To kill you.'

It was said with such calm and yet with such intensity that for an instant Livinov's hand hovered over the button that would bring half a dozen guards running into the room, armed and ready. Then slowly he sat back in his chair, a curious weariness of spirit, a strange fatalism, creeping over him. He had no doubt that this was the son he had fathered so heedlessly and rejected so deliberately. They were staring at one another. He was seeing himself in this young man. He was the very embodiment of all those human emotions, all the hopes and dreams he might have enjoyed and had rigorously denied himself, and for the first time in his life he wondered if it had been worth it.

For Dirk it was different. He was seeing not the monster he had imagined, but an austere face that might have belonged to some medieval monk, to a missionary working for an impossible ideal. The obsession that had dominated his life for so long was slowly crumbling. At other times and in other circumstances it was possible that these two might have found much in common, maybe even love, but now it was too late, thirty years too late.

334

In the silence a captive fly buzzed noisily against the windowpane.

Livinov got to his feet, a strange look on his face, a look almost of resignation, of acceptance. Their eyes locked together in a battle which neither of them could win.

'Very well, Mikhail Igorovich, I am waiting,' he said at last, with a twist of the thin lips that could have been a smile.

In their absorption with one another neither of them had noticed that an inner door had opened, a door through which many a victim had passed to the interrogation rooms, the torture cells, even to death.

The shot took them both by surprise. Dirk had dreamed of it happening, and there it was. The bullet had taken Igor Livinov between the eyes. For a moment he still stood slightly swaying, then he slowly crumpled into the chair and fell forward, his head on the desk, papers scattering to the floor.

Paralysed with shock Dirk could not move, but Shukilov was beside him, thrusting the revolver into his hand, pushing him towards the inner door.

'Go, go quickly,' he breathed. 'Down the stairs, across the courtyard, through the further door. There will be a car. Leave at once. Now, don't wait.'

Still dazed, he followed the directions. The black limousine was waiting. As soon as he stumbled into the back seat it started forward, making for the hotel. He did not notice the grey military car that followed closely behind them.

19

Tanya saw the black car stop at the hotel entrance, saw Dirk leap out and race up the steps. She was at the door of their room to meet him.

'We must go now, quickly,' he said breathlessly. 'Is everything packed?'

He still held the pistol Shukilov had thrust into his hand. He flung it from him in disgust.

She looked at him aghast. The fear that had haunted her all morning had suddenly become reality.

'What has happened? Did you kill him?'

'No. He's dead, but I didn't kill him. Hurry, Tanya, hurry. Never mind the trunk. Take only the suitcases.'

But it was too late. It had always been too late. The guards were already on the stairs, thrusting aside a protesting hotel manager, terrified guests scattering in front of them. They flung open the door.

'Run,' shouted Dirk. 'Run, Tanya, through the other door, down the back staircase.'

They shot him as he was pushing her into the adjoining room. He staggered and gripped the door post. Two more shots spun him round to fall forwards through the doorway.

Tanya dropped the suitcase and came back. She fell on her knees beside him, a terrible fear flooding through her. She drew him towards her as he tried to speak.

'I didn't kill him, I swear I didn't ... I love you ...' The whispered words choked in the blood that filled his mouth. It was on her hands and staining her coat.

It had happened so quickly she couldn't believe it. She stroked his face.

'Dirk,' she said pitifully, 'Dirk,' and tried to raise him.

Then one of the guards took her by the shoulders and jerked her to her feet.

'Leave him. You must come with us.'

'No,' she said wildly. 'No. I can't leave him here alone, not like that.'

'There's nothing you can do. He's dead.'

'How can you be sure?'

She tried to fight free, but one of the other guards had now gripped an arm. She was carried along between them. She looked back from the doorway at the still figure on the floor. How could he be dead who had been so vitally alive only a few minutes before? What had happened? How had they tricked him?

'Let me go,' she screamed, 'I cannot leave him, I cannot!'

She wrenched herself away from them and would have run back to him, but they grabbed hold of her so roughly that she stumbled. Then they were forcing her forward. She was bruised and shaken, sobs gathered in her throat, but she choked them back. Pride came to her aid, pride and a certain courage she had not known she possessed until these last few weeks.

'Why are you arresting me?' she asked desperately. 'What have I done?'

'You'll soon find out,' said the one who seemed to be in command.

The third man, who was younger than the other two, had taken hold of her suitcase and the gun that Dirk had flung away from him.

They took her down in the lift. Then they were crossing the hall. The manager shrugged his shoulders helplessly as they passed the reception desk. Guests coming out of the dining room drew back, hurriedly averting their eyes. No one was protesting, no one was prepared to help.

They hustled her into the waiting car, one guard beside her while the other took his seat beside the driver. The journey was so short she guessed she was being taken to the Lubianka, but not through the grand entrance in the Square. The car drew up at a narrow door. It opened immediately, she was pushed through, marched across a wide courtyard, through another door, down a flight of steps, and then she was in a large hall with a glass dome supported by four pillars. All round were locked doors with small

337

square observation windows, rising up in several tiers. A warder unlocked one of them, urged her through, and slammed it shut after her. She heard the key turn in the massive lock.

She sank down on the narrow bed, still too numb with shock and grief to take in fully what had happened to her, but after a few minutes she tried to pull herself together and look around her. The room was small and windowless, clean enough and smelling of some powerful disinfectant. There was a table and a stool and the room was lit by a powerful electric bulb in the ceiling. Although outside it had been a warm spring day, the atmosphere here was dank, like a stone cellar which has been long shut up.

She began to realize with a very real fear that she must be in the inner prison of the Lubianka. Behind these closed doors unhappy people could be shut up for days, for weeks, interrogated, bullied, until, their spirits broken, they were ready to confess to crimes they would never dream of committing. Was that what was going to be done to her?

She shivered and rushed to the door, hammering on it in a frenzy, bruising her hands, screaming, 'Let me out! I'm innocent. I've done nothing!' until she realized the utter futility and was suddenly ashamed of her hysteria. A grating sound told her that the slide over the peephole had been moved back. Someone was peering in at her. She backed away from it, an angry pride rising up in her. She was not going to let the unknown watcher see her break down in tears and despair.

She still had blood on her hands and on her light fawn coat. There was a jug of water on the table with a tin mug, and she tried to wash it off with her handkerchief. She was not very successful, but it steadied her, helped her to shut away from her mind the terrible, agonizing moment of Dirk's death. There would be time to weep for him later; now she must try to think clearly.

It was obvious that they had never intended to let Dirk go free. At the last moment, face to face with his father, he must have found himself unable to kill him, and so someone else had done it for him and the guilt had been placed squarely on his shoulders. Was Shukilov responsible? The more she thought of it, the more certain she became. He was an ambitious man and he wanted power. She had sensed that even in the short meeting at the theatre, and he was Igor Livinov's natural successor. To achieve it he must have a scapegoat who could be silenced. He had deliberately had Dirk murdered. Why hadn't he had her killed too? Why had he brought her here? What did he intend to demand from her?

Shock, anguish, lack of food, all conspired to sap her strength. Her head ached viciously. She felt so sick and so utterly wretched that she fell face downwards on the thin brown blankets and let the surge of black despair wash over her.

It was early evening before she roused herself. She could hear voices outside, footsteps, the clatter of doors being opened and shut. She stood up to face whatever was coming, with as much calm and dignity as she could. Her turn came. The door was unlocked. Three men stood outside, an armed guard and two who looked like prison warders. One of them carried her suitcase, the other a tray of food which he placed on the table.

'I want to know why I have been brought here. I want to speak to someone in authority,' she demanded.

'All in good time, comrade, all in good time,' said the older of the two men sourly. 'Eat your supper. It's the last you'll get today.'

The man carrying her case was younger than the others. He put it down beside the bed and looked back at her lingeringly as he followed his companions out.

She was burning with angry frustration but it was still good to have her case back. It had obviously been opened and searched, then untidily repacked. Amazingly the emerald pendant was still there in its satin-lined case, but a bottle of her expensive perfume and all her silk stockings had vanished. Some female wardress must have yielded to temptation, or perhaps one of the guards had taken them for his sweetheart. It seemed a few human weaknesses still existed even in Soviet Russia.

Supper was a bowl of thin vegetable soup, a piece of black bread, and a mug of hot tea which she drank thirstily. She ate a little of the bread, but the soup with its greasy scum nauseated her and she pushed it away.

The evening and night stretched before her fretting her nerves to breaking point, hours of anguished regret that she had not somehow persuaded Dirk to give up his madness and come away with her, that somehow at the end she had failed him. Again and again she saw him fall, saw him die, the pain like a knife turning inside her. The glaring light bulb in the ceiling burned all night. It was impossible to escape it, impossible to rest or sleep. Several times during the long weary hours she heard the shutter being pushed back and knew that someone watched. The dank cold from the stone walls penetrated through the thin blankets and she lay shivering with nervous exhaustion. Once there was a scream, a long, prolonged wail of agony or frustration. She sat up, tensely waiting till all was silent again.

It was a relief when at six o'clock in the morning the door was unlocked and she was ordered to come out and bring with her the rough brown towel supplied. She was marched along the corridor to a long, cold room, a kind of wash house with a row of lavatories. There were other women there already stripped to the waist. In some ghastly way it was like a travesty of the boarding school she had once hated so much, and she felt the same loathing of having to perform all these private functions in the company of strangers. She felt their eyes upon her as she was brought in, the newcomer, the foreigner in her fine Western clothes.

She was allowed ten minutes to wash in the icy water, to use the doorless lavatory, and then was taken back to her cell.

Breakfast was brought at seven o'clock, more tea and a slice of black bread. Dinner at twelve-thirty was a bowl of tasteless stew with more black bread; supper was soup like the night before and arrived at six-thirty. After that there was nothing but the long, long hours of the night under the staring eye of the ceiling light. She tried draping the towel across her face and the watcher outside burst in, snatching it away, telling her it was forbidden. The face must always be seen. Why, she thought, did they think she would strangle herself?

For a week this same dreary routine was followed without change despite her constant demands to see someone who could tell her why she was there, why she was not being allowed to apply to the Swiss Embassy, to the British Consul. To all these questions the warders maintained a stubborn silence. She was not allowed to speak to any other prisoners in the wash house, she had no knowledge of what was happening in the outside world, and she began to wonder if their purpose was to drive her out of her mind so that she would agree to anything in order to be free. Surely some enquiry must have been made for her. After all as Dirk's wife she was a Swiss citizen. She might have been born in Russia, but her father was Lord Aylsham and he had many influential friends. All these thoughts hammered at her till she wanted to scream, and she would pace up and down the narrow cell until she was exhausted. Afterwards she never knew how she survived that first week.

Then one evening after supper the summons came. She was lying on the bed when the door was unlocked and she was ordered out. She was thankful that in an endeavour to keep up morale she had taken pains to keep her hair combed, her blouse and skirt as tidy as possible, for they gave her no time, not even to pick up her jacket.

She was led through a maze of corridors, taken up in a lift, and finally shown into an austere office furnished with little more than a desk and a row of filing cabinets. She wondered whether this room was where Dirk had met his father and received his death sentence.

Shukilov rose from behind the desk and came to meet her, all smiles and charm.

'At last, Madam von Richter. I must apologize for not having you brought here before, but you must understand that I am not entirely my own master and Comrade Livinov's assassination had caused great distress as well as many problems of administration. Come in, dear lady, sit down. It's time you and I had a little talk.'

He nodded to the guard who had brought her there, and the man went out, closing the door.

She sat down on the chair he indicated, trembling but very wary. She must be careful what she said for she guessed how cleverly he could twist her own words against her.

'Cigarette?' he asked, holding out the gold case, but she shook her head. 'Coffee then. I took the precaution of ordering a pot – real coffee too, not the rubbish they sell in the shops.'

He poured it, strong and black, and exhausted and half starved as she was the rich fragrance was almost unbearably tempting; but she felt that to yield even so little to this false kindness would be fatal.

'No thank you.'

'Well, if you will permit, I think I will.' He sipped it with obvious pleasure, and she turned away her head so as not to watch.

'Well now – to business.' He put down his cup and moved round to sit behind the desk. 'I'm afraid I must ask you a few questions.'

The charm had abruptly vanished. He was tough, formidable, the inquisitor.

'Tell me,' he began, 'which of the two Western powers was your husband working for? Was it Germany or was it Britain?'

'I don't know what you mean. Dirk was not working for any specific country. He had been a member of the party, your Party, ever since he joined them in Geneva over four years ago.'

'That, I admit, was a clever move on his part. He was very convincing, and it gave him a wonderful opportunity to serve two masters and ultimately to destroy one of the most respected members of our government.'

'Dirk did not shoot Igor Livinov. I know he didn't. He told me so himself.'

'And you believed him?'

'Dirk does not lie.'

'Isn't that a little naïve? All men lie on occasions, my dear young lady, and it was I who found him here, pistol in hand, and when unfortunately he got away from me it was I who had him followed.'

'And had him gunned down in cold blood.' She could not prevent her voice shaking.

'He was shot while attempting to escape,' he said austerely. 'There is a difference.'

'Is there? Whatever slant you care to put on it, he is dead.' She stood up suddenly, letting her anger at their devious excuses rip through her. 'Why have you brought me here to listen to this tissue of lies?'

'For a very good reason. I have here a written statement, quite simple, quite straightforward, which I must ask you to sign. That done we can begin to take steps to set you free.'

'What is it that I am accused of?'

'Read it and you will understand.'

He handed her a typewritten sheet. She ran her eyes over it with growing anger and alarm. It sounded so horribly plausible. It described in some detail a cleverly concocted plot between Dirk, Britain's secret service and Lord Aylsham, and it bore absolutely no relation to the truth.

She looked up to see him watching her.

'You know that I cannot sign this,' she said with contempt. 'It is lies, all of it lies. My father has nothing to do with any of it. He is a doctor not a politician.'

'Oh, come now, are you telling me that Lord Aylsham, who was obliged to flee from Russia some years ago, who had suffered as he believed at the hands of Igor Livinov, and who is at present harbouring a wretched defector from this country, would have allowed his beloved daughter to marry an acknowledged Communist unless it was with some hidden ulterior motive?'

'But my father didn't know about Dirk then, and neither did I, not until a month ago.' Was it really so short a time as that? It seemed as if she must have known for ever. 'You are all wrong,' she went on desperately. 'Dirk was brought here by a personal motive, one that had haunted him for years. You, who know so much, must surely also know that Igor Livinov was his natural father, a man who had callously abandoned and shamed his mother.'

'And so he came to avenge his mother's honour.' Shukilov was leaning back in his chair and smiling. 'What a remarkable fairy tale. I did not credit you with such powers of imagination. But you don't really expect me to believe it, do you?'

'It's the truth, the real truth, not idiotic lies like these.' And she tore the sheet in half and threw the pieces to the floor.

'Aren't you being a little foolish?' Shukilov got up and walked round the desk, his voice smooth as cream, eminently reasonable. 'Just sign this, it will take only a few minutes, and then I will arrange for you to be released. Oh, you may have to stay in Russia for a few months longer, but that need not be a penance.' He came close to her. She was very aware of his strong, powerful body, that of a man who found women easy game. One hand gently caressed her cheek. 'In fact it could be very agreeable. I have a dacha only a few miles from here. It can be delightful there in the summer.'

She jerked away from him.

'Don't touch me, don't come near me. Do you think I will allow Dirk's name to be blackened, my father suspected of subterfuge and spying, and all on the strength of my published confession? Never, never! Do you imagine I don't know what happened? You shot Livinov yourself, didn't you, so that you might sit here in his place, and now you think to put the blame on Dirk. Well, I'm not going to help you to place it there.'

'You fool, you damned little fool!' he said furiously. 'You don't know what you're saying. You could be condemned to a labour camp for months, for years, and I'll be the one to send you there. You've been brought up in luxury, Princess Tanya – believe me, you won't enjoy it. There's no easy living there.'

'I'd still prefer it to accepting favours from a liar and a murderer.'

Her bold defiance caught him on the raw. He struck her viciously across the face. She staggered back, catching hold of the chair to save herself from falling. She could taste the blood from her split lip. He stared at her for a moment, then moved to the desk and pressed a button.

'You can have two days,' he said harshly. 'I would advise you to think it over very seriously.'

When the guard came in, he beckoned to him. 'Take this prisoner back to the cells. She is to be kept in close confinement.'

She would far rather the decision had been made there and then while the mood of angry defiance still possessed her. Two days to think it over made it ten times worse. She had never longed so much for Ravensley, for her father's wise judgement, even for her stepmother's advice. Galina had been through something like this back in the days of the Tsar. She raged against the hypocrisy. They could not commit their murders and brazen them out, they had to paper them over with lying justifications. She had heard of labour camps, knew something of their horrors. Leon had once given her and Andy what she had guessed to be an edited version.

What should she do? All the next day she was tossed from one tormenting decision to another.

Late that night she had an unexpected visitor. It must have been after midnight and everything was very quiet. The warder on duty was the young man who had brought her suitcase. Once or twice he had given her a shy smile, and even found her a scrap of soap when her own expensive tablet was stolen in the wash house.

She heard the door being unlocked and hoped wearily she was not going to be interrogated again in the middle of the night. But it was not a guard who came in but a woman slipping through the door in a long dark coat with a scarf tied over her head. She whispered to the boy, the door was softly closed, and she pushed back the scarf.

'Anna!' exclaimed Tanya.

'Ssh, I shouldn't be here, but I happen to know that boy. He was one of Father's students in the old days.'

'Why have you come?'

'I had to. I know what Sergei is trying to do to you. Oh, why didn't you leave, both of you, while you still could?'

'If only we had. What are they saying about us in the city?'

'Very little, only that Livinov was shot by a foreign agent who has been dealt with, nothing more. No details, nothing about you.'

'What have they done with him?' she whispered.

Anna drew closer, her voice hardly more than a breath in the silence. 'I'm not sure, but there is a rumour that the Swiss Embassy may have claimed the body, but there may be no truth in it. Sergei will say nothing. It is only what I pick up here and there.'

The Baron, that kind old man – had he guessed that Dirk's love for his mother had led him to his death? If only they could have grieved for him together.

Anna was watching her with a worried frown. 'What will you do? Sergei is quite sure you will agree to what he asks. He has a poor opinion of women.'

If she had wavered before, that made up her mind for her.

'Then I shall prove him wrong,' she said quietly.

But there was something she could do. She took a deep breath, staring at Anna. It was clutching at a straw but she had to try.

'Can I trust you?' she asked.

'Would I be here otherwise?'

'Would you do something for me?'

'If I can, but sometimes I'm afraid that Sergei has me watched.'

'Could you send a message to my father in England?'

'I don't know, but I could try. Only hurry. I mustn't stay too long. They watch and listen all the time.'

Tanya found a scrap of paper in her suitcase and wrote rapidly that Dirk was dead, that she was in prison and was soon to be sent away, though where she didn't know.

There was noise outside – voices, tramping feet – they were changing the guard. An urgent knock at the door alerted them.

Anna took the folded paper. 'Where do I send it?'

Where was best in case it should be intercepted? 'To Dr Aylsham, Guy's Hospital, London. That will reach him.'

'I must go,' said Anna. 'They mustn't find me here.'

Impulsively she put her arms round Tanya and kissed her cheek.

'God go with you,' she whispered, then she slipped through the door and was gone.

The sound of marching feet died away and the heavy silence of the night flowed back, but now in the darkness ahead there was a ray of hope, faint enough, but she clung to it. It gave her strength to defy Shukilov when she stood before him once again in that bleak room. He was not smiling this time, and she knew he was angry because she had rejected him, because in some way that riled him unbearably she had conquered.

She watched him write out an order, sign and stamp it, then hold it out to the guard.

'Where am I being sent?' she asked and her voice trembled, hard as she tried to control it.

He looked across at her. His father had been a miner in the Urals. He had fought his way up through poverty and a bitter, corroding envy of the rich with their lavish clothes, their blood horses, their fine carriages and magnificent motor cars. It would have given him pleasure to take this fastidious, high-bred creature to his bed, break her spirit, bring her to her knees, as once he had taken Anna before he had tired of her.

'Far enough away to be forgotten,' he said curtly and dismissed her with a gesture of contempt.

Her feeling of triumph was short-lived. She had had the temerity to throw Shukilov's forced confession back in his face and now had to suffer the consequences. She was a convicted prisoner, sentenced to five years in a labour camp, and the treatment was a good deal rougher than any she had so far endured in the Lubianka.

It began the following morning when whe was given a brush and a pail of water and ordered to scrub out her cell. Then there was the humiliating body search. In company with about thirty other women, of all ages, all types, from respectable shopkeeper's wives to some wretched drab from the back streets, she was ordered to strip, her shrinking body examined and prodded by a middle-aged female wardress who seemed to take pleasure in inflicting as much pain and embarrassment as possible. When she

346

was dressed again her suitcase was gone through painstakingly by two of the guards, her most intimate garments pulled out and handled, her satin, lace-edged knickers held up with ribald comments and gales of laughter. One of them held the emerald pendant in his hand for a long time and she saw the greed written on his face, then he looked up, met her eyes, and threw it back. She guessed there were harsh penalties for stealing even from prisoners.

This is what she had to expect, what she would have to steel herself to endure in the weeks to come. How was she going to bear it? How long would it be before help came, as it must, surely it must!

They were packed into army trucks, so close together, so crammed one against the other, that she thought she would stifle. She must not faint, she told herself, she must not! And she managed by a heroic effort to stay on her feet till they reached the railway station. It was a relief to be out of it and marched on to the platform. It was a warm, humid day with drizzling rain, and there they waited, herded together, for four hours until a long goods train shunted slowly into the station.

Some of the vans were already packed with men on their way to hard labour in Siberia. They shouted to the bunched women, calling out coarse jokes. An empty wagon was opened and one by one the women climbed in. It was pitch dark inside and Tanya stumbled across it to a far corner, sitting on her suitcase while the other women squabbled and fought over who should have the best position. They had each been given a tin mug. A sack of black bread was lifted up with some smelly dried fish and pails of water. One of the women was appointed captain and took it upon herself to distribute the food as the train began to jolt forward.

Tanya withdrew more and more into herself as the others fought one another over the meagre portion of bread and fish. Gradually as the train roared on they began to settle down for the night. Huddled in her corner Tanya closed her eyes, trying to shut out the horror of her surroundings till she felt someone touch her arm.

The woman who had acted as captain was standing close beside her and holding out a cup of water.

'Better drink it,' she whispered. 'It's the last till our next stop and that could be twelve hours away.'

Tanya's lips were cracked and dry, still sore from the blow

Shukilov had given her. She drank the warm, stale-tasting water gratefully and handed back the cup.

'Thank you. That was kind of you.'

'It's a rotten world if we can't help one another,' said the woman. 'You're a cut above this lot, anyone can see that. My name is Maria, what's yours?'

'Tanya.'

'Right then, Tanya, a word of advice. I've been through this kind of thing before. You sit tight and don't let that rabble there steal whatever you've got in that case of yours. It's a battle, you know, from now on, and you must look out for yourself if you want to survive. Goodnight.'

It was advice that Tanya was to remember in the months that lay ahead, but just then she felt her eyes fill with foolish tears at the unexpected kindness.

All around her bodies groaned or grunted, stirring uncomfortably, some snoring already, but sleep was very far away from her. It was barely a month since that night in Berlin and yet it seemed like a year. It was still unbelievable that Dirk was dead, that she would never see him again, that the eighteen months of their marriage had vanished as if they had never been. For the first time since that terrible day the tears rolled helplessly down her face and she could not stop them. Her father had begged her not to marry him, and she had refused to listen. Dirk had implored her to leave him, and she would not go, and she had been right. If he had died alone without her she would never have forgiven herself, even though it had come to this. Somehow she had to force herself to go through with it. She had to conquer the terrible feeling of injustice. The train raced on and she dug her nails into the palms of her hands. Whatever happened she must not give up. She owed it to Dirk, she owed it to herself. She must still hold on to hope. That's what Galina had once done. Would she show herself less than the stepmother she had despised and was at last beginning to understand? What a queer way life had of hitting back at you when you least expected it.

Part Four

THE FIRE STILL BURNS
1933

20

Nicola was having a party. It wasn't really her birthday – that was in August, when she would be sixteen and grown up, thank goodness – but examinations were over, she thought she might have done pretty well in them, and if they waited till school broke up her friends would all have scattered to their various homes.

'I can't have a party of old fogies, now can I?' she asked her father plaintively.

'Meaning me, I suppose?' said Simon drily.

'Oh no, not you, Papa. I never think of you as being old.'

'After which piece of gross flattery I suppose I must say yes. Have your party, puss, and we old fogies will keep in the background. Don't wreck the house, that's all I ask.'

'May I ask Luke?'

'By all means, if he'll come. Our Luke's a busy man these days.'

So Betsy outdid herself in providing a lavish buffet table guaranteed to appeal to young people of both sexes, and Paul came down from Cambridge for the weekend bringing a couple of friends, dandies of the first water, elegance personified, who instantly became the envy and admiration of the youngsters.

By the time Andy arrived from London by the late train the party was in full swing, the drawing room doors open to the warm summer night, the gramophone screaming away at the top of its voice, and a dozen couples circulating in and out of the garden in a series of peculiar contortions which were called dancing nowadays. Somehow it made him feel rather old.

His father and Galina had retired discreetly to the library and he went to find them.

'A very odd letter was delivered to the hospital for you, Pa. I brought it down with me.'

Simon took the battered envelope but didn't open it immediately.

He received a number of peculiar letters, sometimes expressing gratitude, sometimes frantic appeals for help, occasionally abusive.

'Look who's here,' he said, 'straight from her triumph in New York.'

'Diana,' breathed Andy, and for a moment could not speak.

My God, what success and marriage could do in a year! She was no longer the girl who had laughed and wept in his arms, with whom he had argued and made love, and whom he had quarrelled with and parted from in bitterness. She was poised, cool, sophisticated, exquisitely dressed.

She came to greet him, kissing his cheek. 'Hallo, Andy, what an age it's been. Lovely to see you again.'

He stiffened against her touch, against the faint, provocative perfume that was particularly hers, against the stir in his body she instantly aroused.

'How do you happen to be here?' he asked woodenly.

'Craig has gone to Hollywood. There is a good chance of his play being turned into a film. I took the opportunity to come over for a few days, chiefly to see Mother, and Daddy too of course.'

'I see.' He had to escape until he had mastered himself. 'I must go and kiss the birthday queen. Bit of a cheat this, isn't it? Does Nicola think she'll get a double set of presents this way?'

'I wouldn't be surprised,' said Galina, smiling. 'That child has a very practical turn of mind.'

'See you all later,' he said and went out.

Nicola gave a shriek when she saw him, and detached herself from her partner to throw her arms round him and give him a hug.

'Darling Andy, I thought you weren't coming.'

'Sorry I'm late. Last-minute pressures.'

'Come and see what Pa has given me.'

She was dragging him after her through the doors and into the garden.

'Hang on,' he protested. 'What about your guests?'

'They're having a whale of a time. They don't need me.'

'Is Luke here?'

'Working the gramophone for us. He brought me some of the very latest records of Ambrose and his band. They're super.'

'Good for him.'

They reached the stable yard and Andy saw an unfamiliar head poking over the half-door, ears pricked enquiringly, nut brown with a white star, quite beautiful.

'Isn't she absolutely gorgeous?' Nicola rubbed her face against the mare's soft nose. 'Pa said I'd grown out of the old pony, and do you know what Di brought me? A real Indian outfit, buckskin tunic and leggings, all fringed, just like in the American movies. Wasn't it sweet of her?'

'After all that I'm afraid my present is going to fall very flat.'

'What is it?'

'A manual of veterinary surgery – everything you need to know about doctoring your pets from a white mouse to an elephant.'

'Oh, that's the very best of all. I've wanted one for ages, but they're so hideously expensive. How *did* you know?'

He grinned. 'A little bird whispered it to me.'

She giggled. 'That's what you used to say when I was still a baby.'

A little shyly she put her arms round his neck and kissed him on the lips. His arms tightened around her. She was so young and sweet and innocent. The knowledge that she was not actually his sister, which had seemed to matter so little when Simon had told them, had in some subtle way made a difference. Some day she was going to make some man or other very happy, lucky devil!

He rubbed his face against the soft hair. 'Come on. Time we returned and relieved old Luke. He can't be expected to work that damned thing all night.'

Back in the drawing room he offered to take over the gramophone.

'I'm all right for a bit. Diana was looking for you. She wants to say goodbye,' Luke said.

'Where is she?'

'She went into the garden, I think. She borrowed Cecil's car to drive over.'

It would be wisest not to go looking for her – but then he didn't feel wise or sensible, only wild and reckless.

She was standing beside Cecil's Aston Martin. A light breeze blew her thin silk dress against her so that it moulded the lovely shape of her breasts, the flat stomach, the long slim legs.

He said, 'You look like one of those fashion models who drape themselves over cars at the motor show.'

She laughed. 'Heaven forbid. We miss Tanya today, don't we? She would have loved all this. Any news of her?'

'Not since Dirk carted her off to Russia. Pa had one letter from Leningrad but nothing else. He doesn't say much, but I'm pretty sure he's worried.' He moved nearer to her. 'How does it feel being the talk of the town?'

'Oh, I'm not quite that, not yet, but it has felt good.'

'And you're happy?'

'Wonderfully happy.'

'And Craig?'

'Craig too. After all, he's got everything he wanted. But don't let's go on about me. I want to know about you. You never wrote.'

'Nothing to write about. I go plodding on, getting nowhere fast.'

'Don't talk like that. You have it in you to be as good a surgeon as your father, better perhaps.'

'Not a chance, not now. I've learned my limitations.'

'Are you trying to make me feel guilty?'

'Not a bit. I'm trying to stop myself making love to you here and now, this very minute, in Cecil's car.'

She gave a nervous laugh. 'That's crazy.'

'I know. I feel crazy.'

He grabbed hold of her suddenly, pulling her into his arms, kissing her savagely. She struggled and then weakened. A wave of hunger swept them together. It was almost as if their bodies knew one another in spite of their minds. Then Diana fought free.

'No, Andy, no,' she gasped shakily. 'I can't – I mustn't – Oh, God help me!'

He reached for her again, but she avoided him, opening the door of the car, scrambling in, half crying.

'Di, don't go, please stay, please . . .'

'No, no . . .'

She pressed the self-starter, let out the clutch, and the car shot forward. He fell back and watched it scorch down the drive, too shaken to move, despising himself for losing control when he had sworn to remain aloof, uncaring, master of himself.

Presently he walked slowly back to the house to find the party beginning to break up. Parents were arriving to pick up their sons and daughters. Simon was shaking hands and dispensing drinks. The girls were gathering shawls and wraps and clustering around

354

Galina to say their thank-yous. Nicola was flitting from one to the other, still happy and excited.

It was quite a time before the last goodbye was said and the last car disappeared down the drive.

It was dark now. Jake was closing the drawing room windows. Alice was picking up glasses and putting them on a tray. Nicola flopped down on one of the sofas.

'Lovely, lovely party. Why can't it go on for ever?'

'You'd be bored stiff with it if it did,' said Luke and was rewarded by Nicola sticking her tongue out at him.

'Spoilsport!'

'Off to bed with you, my girl,' said Simon. 'Alice will bring you up a hot drink later.'

'I'm not a baby.'

'You still are to us, pet,' said Galina. 'Go on, be off with you,' and she kissed her goodnight.

'Thank you for my gorgeous mare and for a super party,' said Nicola, hugging her father and then departing with a grand gesture like a queen bidding farewell to her faithful retainers.

'There's no doubt about it,' remarked Andy, 'our Nicola would have made a splendid Grand Duchess.'

'She might have been one if life had taken a different turn,' said Simon drily. 'Don't go, Andy, I want to talk to you. You too, Luke. Come into the library and shut the door.'

The two young men glanced at one another.

'What's up?' asked Andy.

'Read that.'

Simon held out the letter, the few lines on the torn sheet of paper which Tanya had written in the Lubianka nearly two months before.

'My God, this is terrible if it is true.' Andy handed the note to Luke. 'Look at that. It's not a hoax, not some kind of horrible joke, is it?'

'I wish it were,' said his father.

'But what can have happened? It sounds impossible.'

'I don't know, but I've not been happy about them ever since Nigel told us they both had to leave Berlin in a hurry because of Dirk's involvement with the Communists. Then we had Tanya's letter from Leningrad a month ago and she sounded happy enough.

355

She didn't give any hint of trouble between them or say why Dirk had taken her there, only that they intended going on to Moscow before they returned to Europe.'

Luke was staring down at the scrawled note with its pitiful message. Tanya in prison, in danger of being sent to one of their filthy labour camps, and that was weeks and weeks ago – where would she be by now? What were they doing to her, his lovely princess? The thought was unbearable. 'If ever you need me, I'll come,' he had said to her. Now that moment had arrived.

He said urgently, 'We must go to Moscow. We've got to get her out.'

'We may have to,' said Simon sombrely. 'But remember, we're dealing with a government that when it wishes can be silent as the tomb. Prising information out of the GPU can be the devil of a job. I'll start enquiries for her at once.'

Galina said thoughtfully, 'We've not yet asked ourselves *why* Dirk should go to Moscow in the first place. I know you think I was prejudiced because I saw in him a resemblance to Igor Livinov, but supposing I was right, supposing he went there for that very reason – to confront a father who had brutally rejected him and his mother?'

'Isn't that being a little fanciful, Mama?' objected Andy. 'Couldn't it be the other way round? Couldn't he be working with his father?'

Galina shook her head. 'You forget. I knew Igor Livinov. He had no human weaknesses. His only passion was the Revolution.'

'Galina could be right.' Simon was staring down at the envelope in his hand. 'There are a couple of things worth noticing about this. To start with it was not sent from Moscow but from Berlin, which explains the delay and must surely mean that somehow Tanya was able to give this to a friend, who passed it on so that there was no risk of it being intercepted. Secondly, whoever the messenger was, we've been given a clue.'

He pointed to the inside of the open flap, on which a spidery hand had written, 'This comes by way of Anna Petrovna Shukilov.'

'Now,' he went on, 'Shukilov, if I'm not mistaken, held a position of importance in the Ukraine closely connected with the GPU. To have a name could help us if we move carefully. The GPU are very like the old *Okhrana*. They take pains to preserve their anonymity,

356

but we know from Leon that Igor Livinov was a person of standing in the Lubianka. It may give us a starting point.'

They talked over every aspect of the situation, but it was hopeless to try and make plans until they had further information.

'I blame myself,' said Simon to Galina later that night, pacing up and down the bedroom. 'I should never have allowed Tanya to marry Dirk von Richter. I knew it would lead to trouble. I felt it within me and yet, God forgive me, I let her go.'

'If you had forbidden it, she would have defied you and still gone with him. It was I she was fighting, Simon, not you. If I had not come out so strongly against him, she might have listened to reason. And yet what could I have done? It's so desperately easy to be wise afterwards.'

'When I think of that child being handled by those brutes, shut up in some prison, suffering heaven knows what physical and mental torments . . .'

'I know how you feel, but Tanya was always more than just a spoiled child. I suspect she had more strength of character than either of us believed. She is not all Nina, she has a good deal of you in her, and even in the worst of prison camps you find a level on which you can exist. I did, and so will Tanya. But that doesn't mean that we mustn't do all we can to get her out. I may be guessing, but it seems to me that whatever Dirk has done, she has had the courage to stand by him, and is now being cruelly victimized for it.'

'I thought us so safe, so secure, and now this damned Livinov stretches out a hand and snatches my daughter.'

'If it *is* Livinov. Maybe he is a victim too.'

He looked at her in surprise. 'What makes you say that?'

'I don't know. Just that everything linked with Igor Livinov has always frightened me. It's as if we can never escape.'

After all these years Galina still possessed something of the fatalism of the Russian peasant, who accepts and does not question what God sends, be it good or evil.

She shivered, and Simon put an arm round her. For an instant she clung to him, finding strength in him as she had done years before when facing the man who had threatened not only their love but their very life.

* * *

357

Simon contacted that same anonymous Mr Brown from Security who had dealt with Leon's case. He listened quietly, examining the envelope and its contents with keen interest.

'Your family, my dear Aylsham, would seem to be accident-prone,' he remarked mildly. 'Or perhaps I should say Communist-prone. But we do have people in Moscow who may be able to cast some light on the situation. I'll put out some feelers and find out what information I can.'

It was a nerve-racking two weeks before he telephoned and called round to see Simon one evening at Wimpole Street, looking round the consulting room with his wintry smile.

'Quite cosy, very pleasant in fact. Is this where you tell your patients that their days are numbered?'

'I think that in most cases I can hold out hope and not deliver a death sentence,' he said drily. 'Do sit down. May I offer you a drink?'

'Thank you, no.'

'Have you any news?'

'A little – not too hopeful I'm afraid.'

'Tanya is not dead, is she?' asked Simon with a sudden stab of fear.

Mr Brown looked startled. 'No, no, certainly not. There is no indication of anything so drastic.' He sat down in one of the red leather armchairs. 'To begin with, your daughter and her husband certainly booked into the Hotel Metropol in Moscow one morning at the end of May. They left the following afternoon for an unknown destination – left in fact in some haste, the hotel manager explained, their trunk and heavy luggage being collected later.'

'Is that true?'

'It could be. On the other hand it could be what he has been instructed to say.'

'What else do you know?'

'It would appear that Igor Livinov, a high-ranking official in the Lubianka, was assassinated by the agent of some unknown political group who has been duly dealt with.'

'Does that mean murdered?'

'Almost certainly. Probably shot while trying to escape – a very useful method of disposing of an awkward situation which avoids any kind of trial. Shukilov, who is hand in glove with Stalin, would seem to have taken Livinov's place in the heirarchy of the GPU. My informant also tells me that the whole affair has been shrouded in mystery, only the bare facts appearing in *Pravda*, and there has been a good deal of speculation among the ordinary people as to what really happened.'

'And this Anna Petrovna?'

'She is Shukilov's second wife and a cut above him socially. She is minor gentry and intelligentsia, while he came up from the bottom, not that anything of that nature means much in today's Moscow. There is another interesting fact. Our man says that Shukilov and his wife with your daughter and her husband were in a box together, apparently on the best of terms, at the ballet on the evening before they disappeared.'

'So Tanya could have met her there?'

'Indeed she could. Now, my dear Aylsham, those are the facts. Beneath them I could perhaps hazard a guess. Your son-in-law was almost certainly involved in some plot against Livinov. Whether he actually did the killing is open to question, but he obviously had to be eliminated and your daughter arrested for her part in the conspiracy.'

'What in God's name induced Dirk to involve Tanya in this wretched affair?'

'I am not well acquainted with your daughter,' said Mr Brown drily, 'but if she is in love with him, is it not possible that she went along with him willingly?'

'Yes, you may be right.'

He could see Tanya so clearly, wilfully wrong-headed in her love and her loyalty.

'I've not been dealing with the Russians for so long,' went on Mr Brown, 'without learning something of their methods. They try hard to force confessions from their victims, a signed statement of guilt that they can flourish in triumph, thus whitewashing over their own dark deeds. It may sound melodramatic but it happens over and over again till someone has the courage – or perhaps I should say the folly – to hold out against them.'

'Meaning that is what Tanya may have done?'

'It is just possible. You know her better than I do.'

'And if she has, what will they have done with her?'

'That's anyone's guess, but I should say almost certainly she will have been sent to one of their labour camps.'

'But it is so grossly unjust. Can't Britain demand her release?'

'We could, but we're in a difficult position. Although she held a British passport from when you returned to this country with your family, she was born in Russia, her mother was the Princess Malinskaya, and by marriage she is a Swiss citizen. I have made a few tentative enquiries at the Swiss Embassy. Your son-in-law did not contact them, so that officially they have no direct knowledge of either his arrival or his departure, and very unfortunately his stepfather, the Baron von Richter, has suffered a second stroke and is seriously ill, far too sick even to be informed of his son's disappearance.'

'Can't we even find out where in Russia she has been sent?'

'We can try, but you don't need me to remind you how vast the country is, and obtaining lists of prisoners consigned to camps thousands of miles apart is extremely difficult, if not downright impossible.'

'Oh my God, she is a mere child still. How is she going to feel, alone and deserted in appalling conditions? Somehow we've got to get her out.'

Mr Brown frowned. 'Believe me, you have my deepest sympathy, but one thing I feel bound to impress on you. Don't go to Moscow yourself and think they will hand her over to you just like that. I know you are acquainted with the country and speak excellent Russian, but you were once a person of note in the old St Petersburg, you fled out of Russia at the Revolution and tricked one of their chief men into releasing your present wife. All that will be well known and held against you. They have long memories. I don't want to have to winkle you out of their clutches as well as your daughter. We've enough problems on our hands without that. Leave it to me. I promise we will do everything that is humanly possible to find her and work for her release.

'And that's not going to be nearly enough,' said Andy when his father discussed the situation with him. 'I know what will happen. They'll talk and talk and negotiate and achieve absolutely nothing. Tanya is not important in their scheme of things. They're not going to suggest any kind of exchange for her, that's certain. It could hang on for months, years even, and in the meantime the poor girl wil be going through hell.'

'I realized that at once, despite all the soft talk. It's going to be up to us. We must find her and we must get her away, but how, that's the problem.'

'That chap Brown is right about one thing,' said Andy thoughtfully. 'You can't go, Pa, it would be crazy. You're far too well known. If anyone is going to find out anything it must be me. I've been giving it quite a bit of thought already. When I was in Berlin I happened to meet a fellow who had taken an American medical mission there under the Red Cross. He told me some horrific stories of the famine area in the Ukraine that hardly bear thinking about. He was intending to go again some time in August. I took some details because I had half a mind to go with him.'

Simon gave him a sharp look. 'You didn't mention it.'

'There's hardly been time, has there? Now this has come up and it seems a very good idea.'

'Who is this man?'

'Dr Bartholomew Malone. He's an Irish-American and was working in New York when this scheme came up. Bart is a good chap. I'm pretty certain he'd be willing to play along if it's possible. If I can get myself out there as part of their mission, it will give me an excuse to move about. For some reason doctors are nearly always acceptable, chiefly because there are never enough of them, especially where the sick and the dying are piling up, and I have the advantage of speaking Russian, which very few of them do. Thank God we've always kept it up amongst ourselves.'

Simon would have liked to have gone himself, but was forced to see the sense of Andy's reasoning. He had already guessed the boy had a double motive for getting away. Andy had a deep and genuine affection for his sister, but there was also the plain fact that Diana was intending to spend the next two months in England. To know she was so near and yet so far out of his reach was torture, and he was not at all sure how long he was going to be able to keep himself away from her. He had come back from his six months' stint in Berlin restless and unsatisfied with his work and with his life. To return to the Russia of his boyhood to face the dangers, the problems, was something he badly needed. He began at once to follow up the contacts Bart Malone had given him, and he told Luke about it when they met for a drink in the little pub in Southwark that had become one of their favourite haunts.

'The trouble is I've got to move carefully or I'll have our Mr Brown down on me like a ton of bricks. They don't care for outsiders butting in on their preserves.'

'Have they come up with anything useful?'

'Not really. So far they have met with blank denials. As far as Moscow is concerned, Dirk von Richter and his wife left the city at the end of May and that is the last that is known about them. Obviously some kind of cover-up. So now it's up to us.'

'When do you think of going?'

'It depends on Bart Malone. It's July now. Say by the end of August at the latest.'

'I'll come with you.'

Andy stared at him. 'Don't be daft, man. How can you? You're up to the neck in all kinds of literary commitments.'

'Nothing binding, nothing that can't be broken.'

'But you can't even speak the language,' Andy objected.

'I have a smattering. I can make myself understood. I picked up quite a bit from Leon when I was at Ravensley. I've been thinking about it ever since your father showed us that letter. I've not been able to get the picture of Tanya out of my mind. How must she be feeling with Dirk gone and her life in ruins?' Andy frowned but Luke went on urgently. 'I've spoken to Colin's father, and James Tait was sympathetic. He thinks I'm dotty, of course, but he did suggest he might be able to get me a press card – you know, correspondent for one of the newspapers – though of course if I land myself in a mess they'll disown me. Still, there have been journalists going out and reporting back. It might help us in a tight corner.'

Andy was looking at him curiously. 'Do you care about Tanya so much?'

'It so happens that I do. How would you feel if it were Diana abandoned out there?'

Andy laughed suddenly. 'Oh Lord, what a couple of romantic idiots we are! We're out of place in this modern world. All right, you persuade old man Tait to give you as much cover as he can

362

and I'll get the medical side of it sewn up, then it will be heigh-ho for Moscow.'

Andy's lighthearted manner did not extend to the preparations he was making. He had, after all, left Russia when he was still a boy of twelve. He spent hours with his father and Galina drawing on their experience, studying maps, gathering as much information as he could, while Luke was coming up against some stiff opposition.

'You're off your head,' said Hugh Carter of the Cambrian Press with justifiable annoyance. 'We've invested a good deal in you. It's true that *The Lost Leader* is doing well, but it's not a runaway bestseller. We've been intending to publish the second book in August, and a nice fool I'm going to look with my prize author gallivanting off to Russia looking for a girl who is neither your wife, your fiancée nor even your mistress!'

'I'm sorry if I'm upsetting your plans,' said Luke stubbornly, 'but some things are more important than money or success.'

'Are they indeed? Sentimental tosh! My God, capture a hard-headed Welshman and he turns out to be a soft-hearted idiot running after a dream! You'll end up in some confounded prison camp in darkest Siberia and then where will I be?'

Luke grinned. 'Making capital out of it, I expect. Perhaps it will inspire me to write a masterpiece like Dostoevsky's *House of the Dead*.'

'And what kind of a bestseller do you think that's going to become in these days?' said his editor wrathfully. 'Oh, go if you must, I can't stop you, but for heaven's sake don't do anything rash. Spare a thought for those you're leaving behind you, and good luck, for by God you're going to need it!'

He received very few good wishes down at Tredegar. His brother not only accused him of being wrong-headed but of being damned ungrateful too.

'I never heard of anything so ridiculous,' stormed Dai. 'Just when things are going right for you, you must go chasing after this damn fool of a girl who has got herself into an unholy mess and no doubt richly deserves what is coming to her. She is not your responsibility.'

Luke knew better than to argue with Dai, who still clung

363

obstinately to the view that anything the new Soviet chose to do must be for the best.

'She may not be my responsibility,' he said quietly, 'but her father has been good to me, and incidentally to you too. You'd be a helpless cripple but for him. Don't we owe him something?'

'And what about Ma?' Don't you owe her something too? Just when she is beginning to take things more easily, she will be worrying herself into the grave over this.'

'If it's money that's troubling you I've still got quite a few royalties to come, and I've arranged for you to draw on my publishers.'

'It's not the bloody money, you know that,' said Dai violently. 'It's just that we don't want to think of you sticking your head into the lion's mouth for a girl who doesn't care tuppence for you.'

'Don't you mean into the bear's clutches?' said Luke humorously.

'Oh hell! You know what I mean. Why must you do these things?'

'I don't know myself sometimes. Come on, Dai, stop nagging at me and I'll buy you a drink down at the Welsh Harp.'

Strangely enough it was Megan who understood better than anyone – Megan who to everyone's surprise had been married for over a year and already had a baby son.

'Don't worry, he isn't yours,' she said when Luke bent over the cradle.

'I didn't think . . .'

'Don't tell me it didn't cross your mind when I married Alun so quick after you walked out on me. But it wasn't that. When he asked me, it seemed like a case of do-or-die, my last chance, and I still had the house and Pa's bit of money. I believe it was that he had his eye on.'

'Are you happy, Megan?'

'What's happiness? I'm all right. I've got a man with a job and we've made a child between us. Isn't that enough?'

'I don't know. Is it?'

'Poor old Luke, still hankering after the impossible, still yearning for your princess.'

'Oh, shut up, Megan, it's not that.'

'Isn't it? Poor little rich girl, isn't that what she is? Maybe she'll have learnt something by now.'

There was only one thing he found hard to give up. His MA thesis, published by the Oxford Press, had given him academic prestige, and he had been invited by Aberystwyth University to give a lecture course on drama. He had been looking forward to it, and the Head of English Studies was not at all pleased to be told that his tutor might not be back in time for the autumn term. He felt he had obtained a prize, a budding author with an excellent academic record and a Welshman into the bargain, who was now off on some wild goose chase to Russia of all places. Really, young people nowadays were totally irresponsible.

'We may be able to postpone to the New Year,' he said frostily, 'but I can't promise anything.'

So now at last they were ready to set out. Simon himself drove them down to Dover with Nicola, who had begged at the last minute to be allowed to see them off. The two young men boarded the Channel ferry ostensibly en route for a long continental trip, with a minimum of luggage and a feeling of release, even of adventure, in spite of the problems and maybe perils that lay ahead.

Nicola, standing close to Simon, said in a small voice, 'They *will* bring her back, won't they?'

'Let us hope so.'

'You miss her terribly, don't you, because she is your *real* daughter, not a make-believe one like me.'

He looked down at the pleading brown eyes, the soft hair wildly blown by the sea wind.

'Now listen, Nicola, once and for all. From the very moment you were born – a squalling, noisy, very self-willed baby, I may say – you were my daughter, and have been ever since, so don't let me hear you say that again. Understand?'

'Yes, Pa.'

'Good. Now we'll go and find the car, and after that I'll buy you a cream tea.'

They were travelling first to the Ukraine to link up with Bart Malone's mission. It was a long and tedious journey beyond Kiev into the heart of the farming country where the peasants forcibly dispossessed of their little farms were dying like flies from hunger and disease. The mission consisted of a small group of nursing nuns from an American Irish order, three doctors and two voluntary helpers. From there Andy and Luke would travel to Moscow.

'You can't possibly go there under your own name,' said Bart when they discussed it with him. 'It's far too dangerous. The GPU would be on to you before you even stepped off the train. They've eyes in the backs of their heads, that lot. You'd better call yourself Joe Kinsale and borrow his papers and visas. Joe's work here takes him out and about among the villages, so it will be easy to find excuses if by chance they come sniffing round and asking inconvenient questions.' Andy opened his mouth to protest and Bart raised a quelling hand. 'Now don't start worrying. I've squared it with Joe and he has agreed with me. He's left everything ready for you. Now remember. You're Dr Joseph Kinsale, our one Russian-speaking operative, who is being sent to Moscow in the hope of drumming up more medical supplies. But for heaven's sake go carefully. We don't want poor old Joe to end his days banished to the arctic wastes of northern Siberia.'

It was September before they eventually reached Moscow, not having encountered any particular difficulties except the usual close scrutiny of passports, visas and every single item of luggage.

'We'll start at the beginning and try to follow in her footsteps,' said Andy, so they booked into the Hotel Metropol and for the first few days were at some pains to lie low and act like ordinary tourists on their way to some other destination.

To Andy in some strange way it was almost like coming home. He had no particular memories of Moscow, but the sights, sounds and smells, the language spoken all around him, swept him back to his childhood years.

To Luke it was a dream suddenly become reality. Here before his eyes was the Russia he had only heard about at second hand, the dark mysterious Kremlin, the oriental skyline of glorious domes and crenellated spires, the dark narrow streets of the old part of the city, the mingling of so many races in the streets, fair-haired

Slavs, slant-eyed Mongols, Tartars, Circassians, Kurds, even Chinese. He was endlessly fascinated.

At first, and purely by chance, they were successful, almost too much so. It should have warned them. It was Andy's fluent Russian that helped them. Nobody expected a foreigner to speak the language, so after a day or two of suspicion and guarded remarks he was accepted by guests and hotel staff alike and by keeping close, understanding a little and nodding wisely when he didn't, Luke came to be accepted as well.

That was how they found out what really happened on that terrible day in the Hotel Metropol. There were a couple of mining engineers up from the Urals, big, good-natured men called to Moscow for congratulations and reward on their exceptional work achievements, cheerfully cynical about it but fully prepared to celebrate the public acknowledgement and the medals. Andy and Luke were invited to join the party that night. They contributed two bottles of vodka to the general entertainment and everyone got gloriously drunk and confidential.

'Got to make the best of it while it lasts,' said one of them, eyeing Andy owlishly. Saw a nasty sight here last time I was up. About a couple of months ago it was, nice couple, well-dressed – you know, bit of class from the old days – and then pouf!' – he snapped his fingers – 'suddenly out of the blue it was all up with them.'

'How do you mean? Arrested?'

'Worse than that. Shot down like some damned mad dog. Saw them sneaking the body down the back stairs, quite turned my stomach, and the young woman, pretty little thing, marched off between a pair of those bloody guards. Half an hour later it was as if it had never happened. Gives you the shivers, I can tell you, leaves a nasty taste, no safety anywhere, no saying when the ground under your feet is going to split open and it's all up with you, but that's how it is. Come on comrade, you're not drinking,' and he slopped more vodka into Andy's glass.

So that was the picture. They faced it bleakly. Now the next step must be Anna Petrovna. They talked it over in their room that night. Somehow they must contact her, but it must be done discreetly. On the surface all was quiet, but Andy had an uneasy feeling that they might be watched, every movement noted. Again chance gave them the opportunity, and they were not to know that it was the last time for a great many weeks when it was to work in their favour.

While they were still wondering how they could approach her, there was some kind of army review held in Red Square. There were massed crowds watching soldiers marching by, cannons, tanks, bands playing, and with their engineer friends they found a good place wedged near the front of the mob. A row of high-ranking officials were standing along the usual balcony.

'Which one is Shukilov?' whispered Andy.

'There, at the far end. GPU don't often put in an appearance. They prefer to be faceless behind closed doors.' The engineer spat disgustedly.

Luke stared at the heavily handsome face. Behind those hooded eyes lay the information they needed so badly, and how was it going to be possible to force it out of him? Andy said, 'What about the wives? Don't they get a look-in on these occasions?'

The engineer grinned. 'Not often. Most of them are kept shut away – kitchen and kids, if you know what I mean. There are one or two, Shukilov's wife for instance, who like to cock a snook at their husbands. There she is. They say she can't stand the sight of him.'

He pointed to one side, not far from where they were standing. A small group of women herded together behind a barrier with a security guard at one side. So that was Anna Petrovna, a delicate-looking woman, youngish, her face pale as she stared blankly in front of her.

Then it happened. As a mounted contingent rode by, a dog in the massed crowd slipped its leash and ran out in front of them barking noisily. One of the horses reared. The rider strove to control it but it crashed into the barrier. In trying to avoid the flailing hooves Anna Petrovna tripped and fell almost in front of Andy, her head striking the edge of the kerb.

There was immediate confusion. The soldier had at last got his horse under control. People swarmed around the fallen woman and Andy seized his chance.

'Let me through,' he said urgently. 'Let me see her. I'm a doctor.'

Instinctively at the voice of authority they fell back. He knelt down beside her. He guessed that she was only temporarily stunned but he made the most of it.

'It could be concussion,' he said gravely. 'Where does the lady live?'

He lifted her up, and they made way for him as he carried her through the crowd and out of the square, closely followed by Luke, while the procession regained its momentum and moved on. The security guard had come hurrying after them and Andy turned to him.

'Can you find me a car? I had better see the lady home.'

The guard began to raise objections but was overruled. Within a few minutes one of the sleek black cars had drawn up. Anna had begun to recover by then and was protesting weakly at the fuss.

Andy was still supporting her. 'Don't distress yourself. I saw you fall. I will see you to your home, then you can send for your own physician.'

It was a handsome house at no great distance, and the room into which he insisted on carrying her was richly furnished. These top men certainly knew how to look after themselves, he thought cynically. He put her gently on the sofa, piled cushions behind her head, and ordered the maidservant to bring him a bowl of water and a towel. As he had thought, she had suffered nothing more than a bad bruise with a painful graze from the rough stone of the kerb. He cleansed it gently, made a brief examination, and then smiled down at her.

'You will probably suffer from a headache for a day or two,' he said, 'but it is not serious.'

'I am very grateful to you,' she said faintly. 'It was so stupid of me to fall like that. My husband will be angry with me for creating a disturbance and spoiling the procession. May I know the name of my rescuer?'

'In a moment. I have in fact been seeking an excuse to make your acquaintance.'

She frowned. 'Indeed, and for what reason? If you are seeking favours from my husband through me, then I regret that is is quite out of the question. I cannot help you.'

'No, it is nothing like that.'

She stared at him for a moment and then nodded to her maid.

369

'Katya, take the bowl of water and towel outside. Then you can make us some tea.'

When the door closed Andy said quickly, 'Thank you for that. My name is Aylsham, Andrei Aylsham.'

He knew he was taking a risk, but fate had thrown him the chance and he felt it was worth it.

Her eyes widened. 'Aylsham?' she breathed. 'Then you are . . .'

'Tanya's brother.' She drew a quick, startled breath and he went on. 'My father received the letter.'

'How did you know about me?'

'Your name was on the envelope. We must talk . . .'

'Not here, not now.' She looked around her fearfully. 'I can trust no one.'

The maid came back carrying a tray with glasses in silver holders, with sugar and lemon. She glanced at Andy curiously as she put the small table beside the sofa.

Anna sat up. 'Where are you staying, Doctor?'

'At the Hotel Metropol.'

'I will remember. I'm sure my husband will want to thank you for your kindness.'

'No thanks are needed. I was happy to be of assistance.'

'Will you take tea?'

'Thank you, no. My friends will be wondering what has become of me. I would advise you to rest today, take things easily.'

'I will, and thank you again.' She held out her hand, and as he bent over it he felt the slight pressure and heard the faint whisper intended for his ears alone. 'Tonight. I will come.'

He found Luke waiting impatiently in their room and told him what had happened.

'Do you think she will come?' Luke asked.

'I don't know. She seemed to be afraid of being spied on even in her own home.'

The afternoon passed very slowly. In the evening they dined with their engineer friends, who were making the most of their last day of freedom. Tomorrow they must return to the Urals.

They had almost given up hope when there came a gentle tap at the door. She had come up the servant's staircase, avoiding the watcher who dozed at the other end of the corridor and slipping into the room like a shadow in her long dark coat, a scarf tied round her head and partly concealing her face.

She looked at Luke questioningly and Andy said quickly, 'He is a close friend.'

'We will speak in English,' she whispered. 'It will be better in case someone listens.'

'Does anyone know that you are here?'

She shook her head. 'Tonight there is a banquet for men only. My husband will not return till very late. Now tell me quickly, why has Lord Aylsham done nothing to rescue his daughter?'

'We have done all we could but have drawn a blank. They will say no more than a flat statement that my sister and her husband left Moscow. We know now that it is a lie, that he was murdered and she was arrested. Is there anything more that you can tell us?'

'Very little. Sergei does not confide in me, but I do know he was angry because she would not sign the confession of guilt he had prepared. That is why it was hushed up and why they will admit nothing.'

'Was it your husband who shot Livinov himself?'

She turned away her face. 'Perhaps. I don't know. I don't want to believe it.'

'Do you know where my sister has been sent?'

'To a labour camp in Mariinsk.'

'Then we must go there. We must try to trace her.'

'It won't be easy. It is a vast network but it all goes through Sergei's hands, and prisoners are often moved arbitrarily from one camp to another.' She suddenly gripped Andy's arm. 'You must go quickly, you and your friend, leave Moscow as soon as possible. If he finds out you are here – and he will, you can be sure of that, there are spies everywhere – he will make sure that you *never* find her. Believe me, I know what I am talking about. It is not the first time.' She dug feverishly in her pocket and brought out a sheet of headed paper, stamped and signed. 'Take this.'

'What is it?'

'It is an order signed by Sergei himself giving the bearer permission to move from camp to camp. I took it from his desk. From time to time messengers are sent with orders and instructions. It may help, but use it carefully. Now I must go. I daren't be seen here.'

371

'Why don't you leave him?' asked Luke impulsively.

She looked at him sadly. 'I think of it often, but I have very few skills and I am afraid. That is the worst thing of all, to live in fear. Where would I go? What would I do in the Russia of today?'

'We are enormously grateful to you,' said Andy. He took her hand and then, moved to gratitude at what she had risked for them, he kissed her cheek. 'God go with you.'

She smiled faintly. 'I'd almost forgotten what that sounded like. Goodbye and good luck.'

Then she had gone as silently as she had come. Luke closed the door after her.

'Poor woman, married to a brute like Shukilov.'

'She enjoys all the privileges,' said Andy drily.

'But at what a price. Now what's the next move?'

'Start packing at once. If she's right, the first priority is to get out of Moscow as unobtrusively as possible. Then we can begin to plan our journey to Mariinsk and pray that Tanya has not yet been sent on to some further camp.'

'And after that?'

'God knows. We can only move one step at a time.'

They spent what remained of the night poring over maps. Mariinsk was in Western Siberia, a long and difficult journey, so the sooner they got started on it the better. What they did when they reached it depended on so many factors that they could make no plans. At first light they shouldered their packs and set off for their distant destination.

21

The little glade between the tall masts of the pines was carpeted with grass as soft as green velvet. Tanya had discovered it by chance one morning and it had become a retreat, a place of refuge from the wretchedness of camp life. The magnificent pine forests stretched up the mountain as far as the eye could see. The prisoners had each been allotted a part of the forest, their job being to collect the resinous sap dripping from the deep cuts in the bark, and the fuller the bucket, the bigger the ration of food at the end of the day.

The few minutes of peace and quiet away from the noisy, squabbling women, away from the crowded, foul-smelling horror of the hut where they lived and slept, were infinitely precious to her. She put the bucket down carefully. Once it had tipped over, the resin had poured out before she could save it, and the whole back-breaking task had to be done again if she was to be allowed a mouthful of the tasteless, porridge-like stew, the black bread and mug of tea which was their daily supper. At first she had rejected it in disgust, but if she did not eat she would die, and she would not give Sergei Shukilov that satisfaction.

She leaned back against the trunk of the tree, aching in every limb. The sun of late August was scorchingly hot, and she was grateful for the cool shade and the sweet, pine-scented breeze blowing through one of Dirk's striped shirts which had somehow got itself into her suitcase on that fatal day and for which she had been grateful. It was faded and torn now but better than the sackcloth skirt supplied by the camp overseer when her own had slowly disintegrated. She had draped a scarf round her shoulders to protect her neck from the stinging insects and huge spiders that fell from the trees and tormented everyone.

She had saved some bread from breakfast and took care to escape from her fellow workers at the short midday break. She broke off a small piece and put it on the grass. Presently as she lay very still she heard the chittering, the scuffle in the treetop, and the striped Siberian squirrel came sliding down the trunk and sat there, watching her with his bright eyes as he nibbled the bread in his paws. The slightest movement and he would be off like a flash.

Lying back with half-closed eyes she could dreamily imagine herself at Ravensley, riding beside her father in the early morning, punting with Luke through the backwaters of the marshes. Dear Luke, what would he think of her now? The two months behind her had been hell, but somehow she had come through them and surely that was what was important.

That first train journey crawling slowly across Russia had meant sixteen days of torment when she could not eat or sleep, when there was never enough water even to wipe her face, and since they were only let out of the train once a day at some suitable stop, a kind of primitive latrine had been set up in the corner in full view of everyone except for a two-foot board so that sometimes she would go through agony rather than use it. Worst of all were the lice, something she had never seen, scarcely knew existed, something you only read about with a shudder. The first time she saw them crawling up her arm and neck, infesting the seams of her blouse and skirt, she was sick with disgust. It was Maria who showed her how to deal with them, a more or less hopeless task when the whole coach crawled with them, and the other women laughed at her fastidiousness, resenting her fine clothes and eyeing the suitcase with greedy, envious eyes so that every day she expected to find it stolen.

She did not think she would have survived if it had not been for the anger, the fierce sense of injustice, the burning determination that she would somehow defeat the purpose of the man who had sent her there, and Maria helped. The sturdy peasant woman had taken Tanya under her wing, fighting for a ration of food for her and persuading her to eat as if she were a small child.

When the train arrived at Mariinsk she was so weak she could scarcely stand. The women stumbled out of the wagon, a motley group of scarecrows, and were taken to a *banio*, a huge stone bathhouse where at last she could pour water over herself, scrubbing away the sweat and the dirt, washing the dust and grit out of her hair, and afterwards putting on fresh clothes.

They spent the night miserably in a long barrack-like room with nothing between them and the stone floor but one thin blanket. The next day, clean and deloused, they were marched to the hospital, sloshing through the mud and the drizzling rain, for their medical examination. The doctor was brusque but not unkind. His thankless job was to sort out the prisoners according to physique and state of health and allot them to the various work teams. It was the lack of privacy that was so unbearable. To stand naked and shivering before watching hostile eyes made her feel humiliatingly vulnerable.

The doctor was looking at her and frowning. 'Light duties only,' he barked to the overseer, who assigned her to the ranks of the washerwomen.

She had no idea what it entailed till she stood in the courtyard and saw the enormous wooden tubs overflowing with filthy shirts, sackcloth trousers and stained underwear, she who had scarcely even washed out a handkerchief in that former life that was so rapidly receding. The two women with her, too old to work in the fields, took pity on her, told her where to fill the buckets with boiling water, how to pound the clothes with wooden sticks, how to rinse them, wring them and hang them out. The work was heavy and exhausting. She took off her jacket and rolled up the sleeves of her blouse, going at it with as much vigour as she could and then shrieking in sheer horror when she saw the lice come rushing up out of the water and crawling thickly up her bare arms and neck. There was nothing to be done but to strip and beat them off, to the intense amusement of a couple of guards, who lounged against the wall doubled up with laughter at her antics to rid herself of the pests. In a curious way the laughter helped by feeding her anger and sharpening her resolve not to be defeated.

Thankfully after a few weeks she was considered strong enough to be sent into the fields where the women were harvesting the flax and tying it into huge bundles. The heat was intense and there was no shade, her hands soon blistered and there were times when she was very close to collapse, but at least she could pause now and then and draw long breaths of fresh clean air.

The long, monotonous days merged into one another, and she could hardly remember the date or distinguish one from the other. She grew desperately thin and undernourished, but some inner strength of constitution kept her going while others dropped around her.

For a few desperate weeks when her period failed to appear she feared she might be pregnant, the result of that last night she had spent in Dirk's arms when they had loved so passionately, a night which she did not care to remember. Once she would have welcomed it, but now the very thought of bearing Dirk's child in these appalling conditions was unbearable. The fear was so great that when it came at last a month late she was almost glad of the pain and discomfort, so much worse than usual because of her weakness and exhaustion.

The flax harvested at last, they were moved on, not by train this time but marching four abreast for fifteen miles a day. She would never have believed she could do it, but in some ways it was more bearable than to be shut into a stinking wagon. There were men in the party, wild mountain men from the Caucasus, and as they marched they would sing, rollicking gypsy ballads or haunting laments for their homeland. One of them walked beside her for part of the way offering to carry her suitcase, and occasionally the women sang along with them. It helped to keep them marching. Then there was another train journey, in proper compartments this time, each one guarded by a soldier with a fixed bayonet. Why, for heaven's sake? Nothing was ever explained. Eventually, staring out of the window, she saw the mountains towering above them tipped with snow. Some of the women began to cheer, and she knew they had arrived at last.

From somewhere far off there was a long-drawn whistle and she sat up guiltily. She must have dozed off, and there were still hours of work to be got through. She began to put on her shoes woven out of the bark of the linden tree. Years ago as a small child at Dannskoye she had envied the peasant children racing across the fields in their *lapty* as they called them. Her leather high-heeled shoes would have been useless climbing over the steep ridges of the pine forests, and the bark shoes were light and comfortable even though her heels were blistered. She was tying the bark strips round her ankles when a voice spoke just behind her.

'Are they the only shoes you have?'

She looked up quickly. It was one of the work overseers, who were usually chosen from prisoners serving long sentences and were considered trustworthy. Dmitri Kurnov was older than most of them, in his late forties, very tall and thin. He smiled as he looked down at her, but she was wary of all those in authority.

'They are the best I have,' she answered curtly.

'They don't give much protection against the snakes and poisonous insects in these forests. I have a pair of boots in my office, old of course, left behind by someone. If they fit, you can have them. Come and see me when you return tonight. In the meantime hadn't you better make sure that bucket of yours is filled?'

'Yes, yes of course, I'm going now . . . and thank you.'

She watched him walk away and then climbed up to the ridge, going carefully as once she had blundered into an anthill and the result had been disastrous. Nothing for it but to strip naked and beat off the crawling millions. She thought about Kurnov's offer as she went from tree to tree. A prison camp was not the kind of place where anything, even a pair of old boots, was given for nothing, and she wondered what he would ask in return. But the thought of the boots for her blistered feet was tempting, so she plucked up her courage and knocked at the door of his little office that evening. He was working at a desk covered with papers. He looked up as she came in, and nodded to a corner of the room.

'The boots are over there. Try them on.'

They were ankle length in soft black leather and not too much worn. She wondered if the previous owner had been one of those who dropped dead at their work, which had already happened more than once.

He glanced across at her as she slipped them on. 'Well?'

'They're fine. A little big, but that's easily remedied.'

'Good. Take them. At least I shan't have to send you to the hospital with snake bite.'

'It's kind of you.'

'Best get back to your supper,' he said brusquely, with a dismissing gesture that sent one of the papers fluttering to the floor. She picked it up and saw with a flicker of interest that it was a British pamphlet on plant diseases.

He looked at her curiously. 'Do you read English?'

'Yes.'

'Easily?'

'I ought to. My father is English.'

377

'Is that so?' He took the paper from her. 'You might be of service to me. Could you translate something like this?'

'I think so if it is not too technical.'

He smiled wryly. 'I taught English once, but after twelve years in a labour camp one grows rusty. Could you spare a little time each evening and do some translating for me?'

It was the first time since she had been imprisoned that anyone had treated her as a human being with a mind, and she could not help responding to it.

'I could try.'

'Splendid. I'll fix a time. I would be grateful.'

It was the start of a kind of friendship. Up to now her only mental relaxation had been with Luke's novel. For some reason she could not now remember, she had put it in that hastily packed suitcase, and now she was deeply grateful. Starved as she was of real companionship and with no reading matter of any kind, it had proved a godsend. She still shut her mind against memories of Dirk. They were too mixed, too painful, too full of regrets, so whenever she could she buried herself in Luke's vivid picture of Wales in the last century and found so much of him in it, so much of what he had told her of his grandfather, his mother, his brother, that only now, she thought, did she really understand and value the young man whom she had often treated so flippantly. It was queer to feel that she was beginning to know a person simply from what he had written.

She told Kurnov about it once and he was immediately interested. He had once been a schoolmaster in Kiev and had lost his job and his liberty because he refused to alter his teaching to conform with the ideology of Lenin and the Bolsheviki.

They talked sometimes when the translating work was done, and she found it a relief and a pleasure. He was friendly but cool and never so much as touched her hand, but because she held herself so aloof from the rest of the camp she did not guess at the tales that grew and spread amongst the women. To them those few hours in the evening in the overseer's office meant only one thing and they were bitterly envious, not that she had received any favours except a bar of chocolate once that she shared with Maria, an occasional cup of coffee instead of the eternal tea. But in the inflamed imaginations of her companions she was revelling in all kinds of luxuries denied to them, and they took their revenge.

It was about three weeks later. She came back to the sleeping barracks, humming a little, happier then usual, and then stopped abruptly. On her narrow bunk bed lay her suitcase, everything in it tipped out, the few garments it still contained ripped to pieces, pages torn from Luke's took lay scattered across the floor, the satin-lined case which she thought she had hidden so successfully lay open and empty, the emerald and its gold chain gone. For a moment she just stared at the wilful destruction. She knew they were all there at her back waiting gleefully for her reaction, and a violent anger flooded through her.

She swung round on them, eyes blazing. 'Which one of you has done this? Which one?'

She had always been so quiet, hardly saying a word, never taking part in any of their many quarrels, that they were momentarily taken aback.

She advanced towards them and they drew back a little.

'Answer me, one of you, or are you afraid?'

Then the leader tossed back her long, greasy black hair and outfaced her.

'We all did it, share and share alike.' She took a step forward and spat at Tanya's feet. 'That's what we think of the traitor, that's for Kurnov's whore!'

Quite suddenly something in Tanya exploded, a fury that had been steadily growing in her for many weeks. She launched herself at her enemy. Within another five minutes the hut was filled with screaming women, clawing, biting, kicking, fighting with each other when they couldn't get at Tanya. One of them, more timid than the rest and terrified of the violence, sneaked out and ran for a guard. He came back with half a dozen others. They cuffed the women apart, butting at them brutally with their rifles. Panting, dishevelled, bleeding, they pointed at Tanya. She started it. She was the scapegoat. Two of the men gripped her between them, her hair wild, a long bloody gash on one cheek, her shirt torn off one shoulder, still unrepentant and shaking with rage.

They dragged her away and shut her into the punishment cell, a tiny airless box of a room where prisoners were kept in solitary confinement with black bread and a jug of water pushed through the door twice a day.

After a few hours, when the fury had died down, it became well nigh unendurable, calculated to quell any spirit no matter how fiery. Long, stifling days in semi-darkness followed by even longer nights. When she was let out after a week, she blinked painfully, scarcely able to stand. It was late evening and she stumbled across to the pump in the courtyard, splashing the ice-cold water over her face and neck. Then, damp and miserable, sick to her stomach, she walked through the hut to her bed in the far corner, her head held high, aware of the eyes that watched, and determined not to show weakness or give away one inch of her pride.

She found that someone had gathered up the torn clothes and rescued the pages of the book and had put them back in the battered case. She stretched herself wearily on the bed, and much later, when the lights had been turned out and the others slept, Maria crept towards her corner and knelt down beside her.

'I did what I could,' she whispered. Something hard and cold was pushed into Tanya's hand. 'I got the emerald back for you but not the chain.'

'Oh God, what can I say?' she murmured and pressed Maria's hand hard. It was only then that she turned her face to the wall and wept.

The next morning when they set out for the forest as usual she saw that Dmitri Kurnov had gone and another overseer, harsher, more brutal, had taken his place. He had not mentioned that he was leaving, and she wondered unhappily if it was the result of his kindness towards her. In any case the resinous sap was drying up, their buckets were only half full, and it was obvious that work in the forests was coming to an end. In another week they were all aware that the camp was to be split up and they would be sent on, but where no one yet knew.

The worst blow was parting from Maria. The big peasant woman with her rough and ready ways had been a stalwart friend through all the worst days, and Tanya would miss her horribly. She was being sent with a party into eastern Siberia while Tanya with the rest of the women would be travelling south.

'You'll soon be going home, little one,' said Maria, 'I'm sure of it. There'll be an order of release and you'll be going back to that

380

fine home in England and you'll forget all about clumsy old Maria.'

'Never, never,' said Tanya. 'Never so long as I live.'

She threw her arms round Maria, hugging her and kissing her on both cheeks.

She watched the train jolt forward with tears in her eyes, waving till it rounded a bend and disappeared from sight. The next day the rest of them were herded into a long coach guarded as usual by the armed soldiers, as if at any moment one of them would make a dash for freedom. And if they did, where would they run to? thought Tanya, settling herself uncomfortably on the hard wooden seat. The doors slammed and the train moved forward, leaving the clean pure air of the mountains behind and setting out on the long wearisome journey to the devastated famine areas of the farming south.

Tracing a prisoner through labour camps was both tortuous and time-consuming. Andy doubted if they would have got anywhere at all without the signed pass which Anna Petrovna had obtained for them. Hundreds of miles from Moscow, where communications were very slow and sometimes non-existent, it worked like magic. They were passed on from one official to another, and at last, after a slow and difficult journey, they arrived to Mariinsk, only to find that the prisoners had already been sent on much further into Siberia.

The camp supervisor was not inclined to be co-operative, but one of the doctors in the hospital, himself a prisoner with a fifteen-year sentence, was more sympathetic and actually remembered Tanya.

'Poor girl, she was different from the rest, too delicately reared for this kind of life. Pretty well knocked up already in my opinion. Some of them die, you know, quite suddenly like a candle blown out by the wind. What further crime has she been accused of?'

'None so far as we know,' said Andy cautiously, 'but there are certain directions for her future which I have been ordered to pass on, so it's important that we find her as soon as possible.'

'Someone high up with an axe to grind, eh?'

'Perhaps.'

'It's happened before,' said the doctor with cheerful cynicism. 'I seem to remember that particular group went on to Borovlianka, but you won't find it easy to reach there. The prisoners, poor devils, had a sixty-mile walk before they picked up the train. You will have to wait till transport goes up to the mountains.'

The frustrating days stretched into weeks, with the ever-present dread that back in Moscow Shukilov might find out what they were doing and track them down. It would be easy for him to have them arrested and deported. Andy spent the time in the hospital where he had struck up a professional friendship with the convict doctor. Luke explored the camp as far as he could without arousing suspicion, shocked and distressed at what he saw of the conditions. He had been disturbed by the doctor's comments. How had his lovely girl, his golden princess, survived in these frightful circumstances?

'For God's sake, be careful, say nothing,' warned Andy, 'and don't voice any criticism. You never know who is listening and will only be too pleased to report it.'

'Don't worry. I'll keep my mouth shut.' But all the same Luke was finding it desperately hard to contain his anger and his impatience at the long delay.

They joined a truck carrying supplies on the start of its long trek into the mountains only a couple of days before Tanya left for the south.

22

The field of cabbages seemed to stretch to the skyline. Tanya could scarcely see the end of it, and up to now the small team of women, despite working twelve hours a day, had made few inroads upon it. Their job was to chop off the huge white heads, which then went into the mincing machine to be salted, pickled and packed into barrels. The stems were thick and tough and very hard to saw through, and down here in the south the October sun was still hot at midday. The sweat trickled down Tanya's face and neck. She pushed back the scarf over her hair and sat back on her heels for a second. Hard as she tried she could never keep up with the other women.

'Not used to a little hard work, eh, comrade? Try putting your back into it next time.'

She saw the booted feet close beside her and knew it was the camp overseer. Viktor Trebov seemed to enjoy needling her. Not a day passed when he did not make some jibe about fancy ladies from Moscow with their lily white hands. She had borne it in silence for weeks, and now quite suddenly she lost her temper. She looked up at him.

'Since it's so easy, what about you showing me how to do it?'

No one ever answered him back. The other women paused, grinning happily, waiting to see what he would do. He was a young man, not yet thirty, and only recently appointed to his first position with a little power. He looked around him and knew he was being challenged.

He snatched the knife from Tanya and made a sweeping cut at the cabbage stalk but, old and leathery, it resisted the blunt knife, springing back again so that it took several hacking blows before the cabbage tumbled to the ground. The women fell about with laughter at his discomfiture. He glared round at them and then, red-faced and sweating, he threw down the knife and strode away.

'One up to you,' shouted the leader of the team. Tanya smiled, but guessed that she might have made an enemy.

This time the sleeping quarters for the team of farm workers were in what had once been a peasant's house, but it was so dirty, so crowded and bug-infested, that Tanya took refuge in a kind of shed attached to the house. It was draughty, there were gaping holes in the timbered walls, she would have to sleep on a hard straw-filled pallet bed, and the window didn't fit properly. It would be icily cold when the frosts came, but it was reasonably clean, no lice or bugs, and for the first time since she had been imprisoned she had a little privacy and could sleep in peace during the night. Her chief trial in the next few weeks was fending off the attentions of Viktor Trebov, which varied between hostile and overfriendly.

One day she found him in her sleeping quarters and demanded to know what he was doing there.

'It's part of my duties to see how the prisoners are lodged. Why are you sleeping outside the house?'

'Because I prefer to be alone.'

'The great lady, I suppose, looking down on us poor peasants.'

'You said it. I didn't.'

He had the habit of coming up behind her when she was drawing water from the pump to wash off the sweat of the day's work, making teasing remarks which she stubbornly refused to answer. Once she felt his hands run down her body. She stiffened, deliberately letting the water in the jug spill over and splash across his boots so that he stepped back hastily. Another time, tempted beyond endurance, he dropped a kiss on the nape of her neck where the golden hair curled into damp ringlets, and she swung round, giving him a stinging blow across the cheek. He caught at her hand and gripped it brutally.

'You'll pay for that,' he muttered thickly.

'How?' she asked boldly.

'There'll be a time,' he replied, and just for a second, nursing her bruised hand, she was frightened.

The days went by with agonizing slowness, the cabbages were cut at last, the weather grew colder, and they were put on sorting onions in long, dark, narrow sheds where the smell was so pungent that her nose never stopped running and her eyes were red and inflamed.

384

One day when she came stumbling out blinking in the light he was waiting and offered a sweet-smelling handkerchief.

'Here, take this, it will help,' he said.

'I'm all right, thank you.'

He seized her shoulder and swung her round angrily.

'Too proud, is that it, too bloody proud to accept anything from one of us.'

She wrenched herself free. She knew the other women were watching with a lively interest, and it made her furious.

'Can't you understand?' she said fiercely. 'I want nothing from you or from anyone like you. Why can't you leave me alone?'

But that was what he found impossible to do, and he couldn't explain why even to himself. In his way he was good-looking, tall and well built with a shock of dark curly hair, and he took a pride in keeping himself clean and smartly turned out, his boots polished, his uniform neatly pressed. There were one or two plump beauties among the women who would have welcomed his attentions, but he wanted none of them. His fancy had been caught by this young woman with her prickly pride, her slender body enticing him even in the ugly prison smock they were all obliged to wear. She was one of those women he had gazed at as a small boy in the great house where his mother slaved in the kitchens, one of those idle women, exquisite, aristocratic to their fingertips, and now here was one of them under his thumb, as it were. Useless women like that had had it easy for too long. It should have been satisfying, but it wasn't. Instead he found it disturbing. He had erotic dreams of possessing her, arousing her to passionate response, forcing her to submit. All nonsense, of course, in the broad light of day. There were stringent regulations about illicit relationships between prisoners and those in charge. Then one day something happened that brought it one step closer.

The fields where the prisoners worked were part of a huge collective farm like many others which had been established, driving the peasants out of their villages and swallowing up their tiny strips of land. Every sack of grain, every pail of milk from their cows, had to be delivered to the farm, and since the harvest had been poor that year, the yield had not been as much as was expected.

One morning Viktor was summoned to the office of the farm manager.

'Moscow is not satisfied,' he was told. 'They are convinced that the peasants are holding back their produce for their own use. It is necessary to make a new drive. We want you to make a circuit of the neighbouring villages, go into every house, every barn and shed, hunt out what they are hiding, force them to give up what they owe to the State.'

'And if they prove stubborn?' he asked doubtfully.

'You have a free hand. Use whatever measures you think suitable.'

'And what about my prisoners?'

'They will be taken care of. It's a post of responsibility, comrade, be glad you have been chosen for it. You'll need someone with you who can take notes when you are interrogating these stubborn wretches and undertaking the searches. We're short of staff here on the dairy side, is there anyone in the agricultural section who is suitable?'

Viktor saw his chance. 'One of the prisoners is an educated woman,' he said. 'Her record states that she worked as a translator in the office at Bovrelianka.'

'Very well, as long as she is trustworthy. Take her with you, but be careful. We don't want any trouble, nor do we want any attempt at an escape.'

'There'll be none, comrade. I'll make very sure of that.'

If it hadn't meant working with Viktor Trebov, Tanya would have been pleased. It would be a relief to be free of the heavy sweating work in the fields, to be given a uniform tunic and skirt instead of the hateful grey smock, to ride out into the country each day in a little two-wheeled cart with a brisk pony in the shafts. Had there once been a time when she lived in luxury, bathed every day in gloriously hot water, wore silk next to the skin, ate delicious food? Sometimes she dreamed of Betsy's roast beef, crisp baked potatoes, Yorkshire pudding that melted in the mouth. She lay on her uncomfortable straw mattress that night and smiled at herself. How absurd to be finding pleasure in the thought of being free of the camp for a few hours, with the promise of decent food because Viktor would make sure of that, and the only real disadvantage the plain fact that, just as with Sergei Shukilov, she was acutely aware that he desired her and that, alone with him, she would need to be on constant alert.

By now it was late October, and though the nights were growing much colder, the days were still fine and sunny. The woods they drove through on that first morning were turning to yellow and gold, the trees heavy with nuts and the scarlet berries, but any pleasure she felt vanished as soon as they reached the first village.

She had never witnessed famine, never imagined such terrifying conditions could exist. In those first few days she saw sights she would never forget, children with legs like sticks and horribly bloated bellies, women clutching spectral thin babies to dried-up breasts, old men like grey shadows, emaciated corpses piled up on carts ready for burial in the common pit. She was forced to wait in the cart while Viktor hammered on doors, demanding that they should be opened to the government representative, harrying the women, forcing them to give up their pitiful hidden stores.

They gathered around the cart watching her with haunted eyes. Everything she had suffered in the prison camps seemed as nothing compared with this silent tragedy.

Once, unbearably moved at the pitiful sight of the children who made no sound but whose eyes silently begged, she took the food, the bread and cheese and apples they had brought with them, and put it into their hands. They did not fall upon it like ravening wolves but instead stared at it unbelieving, then moved away, sharing it with minute care between them, no more than a mouthful each.

Viktor was furious with her when she had to confess what she had done. They argued violently about it, and she forgot that she was a prisoner whose opinions could never safely be expressed.

'How can you snatch every handful of flour, every cup of milk from them when their children are dying? It is the act of a savage, a barbarian.'

'I have my orders,' he replied sullenly.

'You should tell them in Moscow, you should make them understand how insane it is to expect a man to work in the fields when he is too weak to lift a harrow.'

'Shut your mouth,' he raged. 'It is not your concern, and neither is it mine.'

Of course she knew he could do nothing else. He was bound into the system just as much as she was, but she found it impossible to keep silent.

'Death and famine should be the concern of all of us,' she flung at him.

Another day she saw long lines of villagers, men, women and children, waiting in forlorn groups, clutching their pathetic bundles, one of them with a brightly coloured blanket, another with a cheap clock, a third with some treasured cooking pot, and as they piled into the waiting trucks, she asked Viktor where they were going.

He shrugged. 'To the mines in Siberia.'

This was what Leon had told them and, God forgive her, she had thought he exaggerated. She regretted now that she had not listened more carefully.

'But they're not miners,' she insisted, 'they're farmers. What will they do there?'

'Work if they want to eat. Don't look at me like that,' he burst out, 'don't accuse me. It's not my fault. I have to carry out my orders or I shall be punished, deported to some filthy labour camp worse even than this.'

Sometimes she was tempted to refuse to go with him, to return to any kind of work, no matter how hard, so that she could put the horror of what she had seen out of her mind. But she knew in her heart that it would be cowardice, and she could never forget so long as she lived, never, never! She must see it, all of it, so that one day, when she was free, she could tell the rest of the world.

One evening when they returned later than usual, he sent her to the dairy farm to deliver the lists of the day's takings. She had never been there before and was struck with its cleanliness and efficiency, all built, she thought cynically, on the starvation and death of the peasants. She lost her way among the various buildings and stopped by the packing sheds to ask for the manager's office. She was given the direction but not before she had seen the machines that sliced the butter into bars and wrapped it in paper. She could read the imprint quite clearly – *USSR Butter Export*.

How dare the newspapers boast of great Soviet achievements, how dare they export butter to the well-fed countries of the West, when millions of their own people were dying of hunger?

For the first time in her life she began to understand something of suffering, of injustice, of the sacrifice demanded by an uncaring State machine, and in her isolation it had the effect of drawing her closer to Luke, to deeper understanding of what he had written of his own country, to the realization that it was not just fiction but the sad bitter truth.

The very fact that she argued and quarrelled with Viktor in some strange way drew them closer together. They were no longer prisoner and guard but two diametrically opposed people forced into one another's company and obliged to make the best of it. She discovered that the bullying manner he so often assumed was a shield against his own insecurity, and her first wariness of him relaxed a little.

By common consent they would stop to eat their black bread and pickled cucumber at some country spot far away from the villages, and once or twice they even shared a laugh at the greedy birds that circled around them waiting to peck at the crumbs, and she told him about the squirrel that had shared her meagre ration in the pine forest.

One day he even went so far as to offer her one of the harsh brown cigarettes and lit it for her. The smoke curled up as he lay back watching her, the October sun turning the windblown hair to gold, the pure line of her cheek, still very thin but with a little more colour from the fresh air and the rest from back-breaking labour.

That morning a new order had arrived from Moscow, sent on from camp to camp and taking many weeks to reach them. He had been summoned to the Camp Supervisor's office. No one liked Comrade Kranchenko. He had a reputation for harshness not only towards the prisoners but even to his own subordinates.

'The prisoner von Richter is in your work team, I understand, Comrade Trebov,' he barked.

Viktor stood smartly to attention. 'She is at present working with me on the investigation of the peasants.'

The Supervisor gave him a sharp look. 'That will have to stop. A directive has come through from the GPU. She is to be sent with an armed guard to Yakutsk.'

'But that's in eastern Siberia,' he exclaimed, 'more than a thousand miles away.'

'Quite so.'

'May I ask why?'

Kranchenko smiled sourly. 'You may ask, but you will certainly not be informed. The order comes from the highest source. There can be no questioning of it.'

He knew then that it must have been issued from the Lubianka, from Sergei Shukilov himself, and was no doubt an act of private revenge sending her as far away as possible, preventing any remission of sentence, removing her effectively from those who might seek her release.

'I must have a little time,' he said, 'to find someone suitable who can take her place.'

'A week should be sufficient. Report to me when it is done so that further arrangements can be made.'

It had thrown him into a turmoil and he had not yet told her of the harsh decision. It was ridiculous to feel so disturbed at parting from her. It warred against all his most cherished beliefs. He had joined the Party before he was twenty, had worked loyally and devotedly for a future he believed in, and suddenly in the last few weeks all these firm beliefs, all these fine ideals, had been thrown to the winds because he had allowed himself to be tempted into love with this woman from another world about whom rumour said terrible things – she had been involved in conspiracy against the State, her husband had assassinated one of Russia's great leaders and had suffered the penalty for his crime. He had fought against it at first by deliberately attacking her, turning her into an object of derision, but it had not worked, and these last weeks, working side by side, she had only to smile at him, accidentally touch his hand, give her low, enchanting laugh at some triviality, and he was utterly lost. What was it about her? She lacked all the qualities he had once thought desirable in a woman, yet she possessed some damnable magic which he could not explain. He was caught in an enchantment from which he did not even want to escape. The decision as to what he was going to do about it still unresolved, he got up, throwing down his cigarette and grinding it angrily into the mossy ground.

'Come on,' he said roughly, 'back to work,' and he busied himself with untethering the horse.

It was during that afternoon that Tanya heard of the Red Cross mission. Viktor was on one of his fodder-hunting trips, forcing the unhappy farmer with his two emaciated horses to disgorge the hidden sack of oats. Tanya, waiting in the cart, noticed the woman crouched outside her hut, rocking the baby in her arms with such a look of despair that she climbed down and went across to her.

'What is wrong?' she asked gently.

The woman drew back from her almost as if expecting a blow. 'He is sick. I think he is going to die.'

'Let me see.'

She put back the blanket, saw the rash on the baby's face, and guessed that it was scurvy.

'That is caused by the lack of fruit and vegetables. It need not be serious. Isn't there a doctor?'

'Not for the likes of us,' said the woman bitterly. 'I wanted to take him to the Americans, but it is a long way and my husband is afraid. He will not let me go.'

'Americans?' echoed Tanya wonderingly.

She realized that the woman must be speaking of one of the Red Cross missions to the famine areas organized by the United States, and the thought excited her. It was not easy to make out the direction from the garbled description, but it was obviously some ten miles further away towards the south. She fetched the two withered apples from their midday food and put them into the woman's hands.

'Boil them and feed him the pap. It may help,' she said.

That night Viktor tossed in his bed, still undecided, his mind racing after crazy ideas of making a run for it, of asking to go with her, even of marrying her, all utterly absurd and certain to be forbidden.

At the same time Tanya was lying on her uncomfortable straw mattress and thinking about what she had found out that afternoon. Dare she think of escape? Could she find her way, and if she did would they welcome her? She remembered Andy saying once that missions of mercy were only accepted in Russia on sufferance, regarded with the utmost suspicion, and those in charge would certainly not jeopardize their difficult and delicate position by befriending an escaped prisoner except under the most exceptional circumstances. It was tempting, but it must remain a dream, impossible to fulfil.

* * *

Maybe it would never have happened if the weather had not taken a hand in it. The sunny autumnal days came to an abrupt end. It turned very much colder. The wind got up and Tanya shivered under her thin blanket as the icy draughts whistled through the gaps in the shed walls. The sky was dark and threatening on the morning that they set off for one of the more distant villages. Viktor had done his work well. All those immediately surrounding the farm had been investigated and purged. Only those too old or too sick to be deported remained to struggle through the winter months as best they could.

It proved to be a long, tiring and unproductive day. There had been some claps of thunder before they started on their return journey, and they still had a considerable distance to go when the storm broke in all its violence. The rain came lashing down and they pulled the old canvas cover over their heads. They were galloping through a copse of siler birch when the lightning blazed through the sky, followed by a crack of thunder so loud that the pony shied violently, nearly overturning the cart.

'We must get out from under these trees,' shouted Viktor above the uproar, the wet reins slipping through his hands as he strove to control the frightened horse. Out of the wood at last and in open country he saw the deserted forester's hut. It was derelict but it would provide shelter till the worst of the storm had passed. He pulled up.

There was some kind of lean-to, partly broken down but giving rough cover for the horse and cart. Viktor drove into it and then he and Tanya made a dash for the hut. It was better inside than they had expected. The rain leaked through, splashing on the floor here and there, but mainly it was dry enough. At some time it must have been used by the foresters because there were a number of short logs heaped in one corner and dry shavings had been piled together on a kind of stone slab, but it was cold, their clothes were damp from the rain and Tanya shivered.

'Why don't we light a fire?' she said suddenly.

'It is not allowed,' said Viktor conscientiously.

'Who's to know?' she replied. 'I'll do it.'

She knelt down, pushing the wood shavings together with some twigs, dried roots and straw, then building them carefully into a kind of cone. She held out her hand.

'Give me a match.'

'Isn't it dangerous?'

'Of course it isn't. I've done it before dozens of times.'

He handed them over reluctantly, and in a surprisingly short time the fire was burning quite merrily, and she lugged across one of the smaller logs and put it in the middle. It sparked and flared but the flames soon began to lick around it, and presently the air was filled with a pleasant aromatic smell of burning wood. It didn't give out much heat, but the glow gave an illusion of warmth and comfort.

Viktor stared down at her as she sat back on her heels holding out her thin hands to the blaze.

'Where did you learn how to do that?'

'My brother taught me when we were children. We used to pretend we were gypsies sitting round our camp fire,' she said dreamily.

'On those wonderful estates of yours in Britain, I suppose?'

'Oh, they're not so wonderful. Ravensley is quite small really, nothing like we had in Russia, but it's still hard to keep it going. We are really quite poor.'

He had heard all the gossip that circulated about her.

'Poor!' he repeated scornfully. 'Poor, when your father is some great lord.'

'He may have a title but he works very hard. He is a doctor.'

'Why hasn't he obtained your release?'

She was suddenly very still, staring blankly into the fire. 'I don't know, but he will. I'm sure he will.'

And now he couldn't keep it to himself any longer. She had to know. He dropped down beside her.

'I've got something to tell you.' She turned to look at him, the flames lighting her face to eager expectancy, and he went on hurriedly. 'It's bad news, I'm afraid. You are to be sent away, far away, to a mining labour camp near Yakutsk.'

'Yakutsk?' she repeated blankly.

'It's in eastern Siberia. It's where the old Tsars used to send their prisoners. It's a terrible place. Only very long-term prisoners are banished there.'

She frowned at him. 'Are we all to go?'

'No, only you.'

'But why, why?'

'I don't know why,' he said wretchedly. 'The order has come through from Moscow. Perhaps it is because of what your husband did.'

'But Dirk was innocent,' she said fiercely. 'He did nothing, nothing. They knew that, and yet they murdered him for it. Oh God, is this persecution never to end?'

The despair in her voice struck him to the heart. He knelt upright facing her.

'I've thought and thought about it ever since they told me. There is a way, a kind of a way – you could marry me.'

'Marry you? she repeated incredulously.

'It has been done more than once,' he went on eagerly. 'It won't be easy but it is not always forbidden, and once we were married you would be all Russian like me. Then you would be safe. They couldn't touch you any longer.'

'Marry you?' Oh, Viktor, it's so ridiculous. How could I possibly marry you?'

She began to laugh helplessly at the absurdity of it, at his innocence, his naïvety. Did he imagine such a stratagem would prevent Shukilov doing what he pleased with her? Did he think he would escape punishment for daring to oppose his will?

She did not mean it, but to his ears it sounded like the cruellest kind of mockery, and he seized her by the shoulders.

'Why is it so ridiculous? What is wrong with me? I love you, don't you understand? All these weeks I've thought only of you. Stop!' he was shouting at her. 'Stop laughing at me!'

But she couldn't stop. It was as if an accumulation of all the miseries, agonies and torments of the last few months had mounted into one huge hysterical reaction, not against him but at the whole crazy situation that had put her where she was. She struggled hard to free herself but it was too late. He was stifling her laughter with his kisses, his mouth on hers, the passion that he had suppressed battling with a furious anger at her mockery. The very fact that she fought against him, turning her face away, struggling to escape from his grip, only inflamed him further. If he took her now, if he possessed her wholly, then she would have to realize that he was right. She would belong to him. Outside, the storm still raged in one last violent assault on the sky and the earth, and it seemed to become part of the fire that burned within him.

She was like a wild bird fighting for its life, but he was a powerful young man and she had little strength after the months of hard labour and poor food. He had her pinned to the floor. One hand tore at her clothing. Her head swam, she felt herself weaken, and with a terrible despair she knew she could not escape. She shut her eyes to steel herself against the pain, the utter humiliation. She bit her lip till the blood came, trying to shrink within herself while her body, her treacherous body, betrayed her, responding to the physical assault which, try as she would, she could not prevent.

A flash of lightning lit up the whole hut, followed by an ear-splitting crash as a tree was struck and riven apart. It went up in a tower of flame that came luridly through the window and with it came the climax, then it was all over. She lay spent and exhausted with his weight crushing her to the hard earthen floor.

Presently he rolled away from her. The rage that had possessed him slowly died, leaving him deeply ashamed, hardly daring to look at her, bitterly regretting what he had done.

He stood up. 'I think that was the last attack of the storm,' he mumbled. 'The rain has stopped.'

She dragged herself painfully to her feet. In one blinding flash she knew she could not go back to the camp with him. After this she would be his possession. It would always be there between them, and she could not face it any more than she could face that other hideous threat. To be sent so far away, abandoned, forgotten, it would be like being buried alive.

Viktor had his back to her. He was kicking apart the half-burnt logs.

'I will put out the fire, then we must go,' he said.

It seemed as if someone else made up her mind for her. One of the smaller logs chopped into two-foot lengths had rolled close beside her. She picked it up. He turned to say something and she swung it with all her strength. By pure chance it struck him on the temple. She saw the astonishment on his face before he crumpled to his knees and fell forward in front of her.

She stood panting, filled with a horrible fear that she had killed him. When he did not stir, she went down on her knees beside him. There was blood on his forehead but he was not dead, only temporarily stunned. She must go quickly before he stirred. Where she could go, she hardly knew, but she was seized with a desperate anxiety to escape.

She crept to the door. He was right. The rain had stopped and the sky had brightened a little. Water dripped everywhere and the ground squelched under her feet. The tree blasted by the lightning still smouldered. The cart beneath its shelter was comparatively dry and the pony, shaken and unhappy, whinnied and rubbed its head against her. She thought of taking it out of the shafts and riding it, but that would take too long and Viktor might recover consciousness before she could get away. She took the old blanket that lay folded in the body of the cart. It might help if it began to rain again. Then she began to walk along the road which they had driven over a few hours earlier, her one hope to reach the American mission and throw herself on their mercy. She had only the name of the village and the sketchiest notion of how to get there, but anything, anything at all, was preferable to the fate that Shukilov and Viktor between them were planning for her. She walked steadily on in a southerly direction.

23

Tanya opened her eyes and wondered vaguely where she was. Instead of being icy cold, wet through and utterly miserable, she was cocooned in warm, rough blankets. She moved her head to look around her and sharp pain shot through it. She shut her eyes again and muzzily tried to think back. She remembered walking and walking. It had started to rain again and the blanket round her shoulders had become heavy and sodden. She remembered realizing she was hopelessly lost and asking the way and being given a lift by a peasant farmer who had bundled her into his cart among a pile of stinking sacks. There was the track stretching before them, the bony horse plodding wearily on and then a complete blank. What had happened? Had she fallen out? Had he thrown her out? Trying to think back made the pain in her head worse. She gave up and concentrated on the present. She was lying on a mattress in some kind of a barn. There was a murmur of sound but she could see nothing, because a blanket on a rough screen shut her off from it. Her eyes felt blurred and gummy. She raised a hand to rub them and felt it taken and held.

'Let me do that, my dear,' said a gentle voice, and it spoke in *English*. It wasn't possible. She must be dreaming.

Her eyes were wiped with something cool and sweet-smelling.

'Where am I?' she asked wonderingly.

'Don't be afraid. You're quite safe now. I think she's coming round, Doctor.'

'Good. That's splendid, Sister.'

Another figure, a man this time, loomed beside her, stocky, solid and reassuring. He knelt down beside the mattress.

'Sorry we can't come up with something better for you to lie on,' he said and his voice had the same lilt as Diana's Craig. American – that was it. Had she reached the mission after all?

397

'I'm going to give you something that will help you to sleep. After that we will know what to do for the best,' he went on.

Her arm was bared. She felt the prick of the needle, then the blankets were closely wrapped around her again. Someone was holding her hand with a gentle comforting pressure, and gradually a warm sweet drowsiness stole through her.

Luke tucked the hand he had been holding under the blanket and rose to his feet. Dr Bartholomew Malone looked from him to Andy.

'You're absolutely certain she's the one you've been searching for?'

'Of course I'm certain,' said Andy. 'Do you think I don't know my own sister?'

'I guess not. You two had better come along to my office.'

'Where was she picked up?' asked Luke when they were in the shack that was serving as headquarters for the famine relief mission, one of many which in the face of strong opposition and a great deal of frustration were managing to survive and bring food and medicines to the starving millions in the Ukraine. This one might only consist of three doctors and six nursing nuns, but at least they were helping the children even if they could do little for the old and the dying.

'Joe had taken some food out to a farm we'd been told of – six helpless kids all under twelve and the mother dead. On the way back he saw what he thought was a bundle of rags lying in the middle of the road. It turned out to be a young woman in the last stages of exhaustion, soaked through and bleeding from a nasty crack on the head. He brought her in, and Sister Clemency stripped off her wet clothes and sent for me. I'd say she had been robbed. She had nothing on her, no papers, no money, nothing to identify her but this, which her attacker must have somehow missed. She was holding it in her hand so tightly we had difficulty in loosening her fingers.'

It was the emerald on a piece of string. Andy took it and exchanged a look with Luke.

'It was her husband's wedding gift.'

'The few words she muttered were in English and not Russian, so we sent for you two as soon as you came in. We thought you had better have a look-see.'

It was like a miracle, thought Luke, an answer to his prayers after weeks of despair. It was a fortnight since he and Andy had returned to the mission oppressed with a wretched feeling of failure. They had reached the mountains only to find Tanya gone from Borovlianka. Whether deliberately or from ignorance, they never knew which, they had been sent on further into eastern Siberia only to discover after gruelling weeks of travel that they were hopelessly wrong, something they would never have known if it had not been for Maria. Strangers in a camp always aroused curiosity, and news filtered through as to whom they were seeking. She took pains to pass on a whispered message that her friend Tanya had gone south, probably to the Ukraine. They looked at one another in dismay. It was a vast area where they could search for a year and never find her.

'Bart Malone is our one hope now,' said Andy decisively. 'We'll go back to the mission. We may be able to find out something.'

Travel was desperately slow, involving many changes, and everywhere there were officials who demanded papers and looked at all foreigners with suspicion. Sometimes only Andy's fluent Russian saved them from weeks of detention, and once, fearing arrest, they hopped off the train at the first stop, trudged some thirty miles through wind and rain, and then were given a lift by a friendly farmer to the next station.

'There are teams of prisoners working at all the collective farms. We found that out today,' went on Andy.

'It looks as if she took it into her head to cut and run for it,' said Bart, 'and, by God, that must have taken some guts, but don't think they will let it rest. They'll be sending out search parties. They will want to find her, dead or alive. An escapee who gets away with it is a bad example for the rest. They could come here.'

'You'd surely not let them take her back?' exclaimed Luke.

'Not if I can help it, you can be darned sure of that, but we do have to move carefully. The least excuse and we're out on our ear, the whole lot of us. However, we'll cross that bridge when we come to it.'

'What's your opinion of her condition?' asked Andy a little jealously. Bart was head of the mission. It was not for him to interfere. 'She looks pretty sick to me.'

'Exhaustion mainly, and malnutrition of course. The ration

doled out to prisoners only just about keeps them alive with absolutely no margin. The chief danger is pneumonia from shock and exposure. If that sets in, I'm sorry, but I'd not give a lot for her chances. Take a look at her yourself. The very fact that you are here will give her fresh heart, and that's half the battle in these cases.'

For two days it was touch and go, then very slowly Tanya began to gather a little strength. To know herself safe, to wake from sleep and see Andy or Luke within reach, gave her such enormous comfort that she could close her mind to the horrors that were past. She tried not to think about what had happened in the hut with Viktor. The blow on the head with the temporary amnesia seemed to have put a distance between then and now, but she still could not control her dreams. She would wake shaken and trembling, with a terrible feeling that her body had been invaded, it no longer belonged to her, its identity had been lost. One night she cried out in a nightmare, fighting the blankets that covered her, and woke at last to find Luke beside her, his arms around her, holding her close against him.

'What is it?' he whispered. 'What frightened you?'

But she could not tell him or anyone. She turned away her head, but still clung to his hand as a lifeline to sanity as he eased her back against the pillow and wrapped the blankets round her again.

At first she accepted his being there without question, but when the pain in her head had receded, when she could think more clearly, she wondered about it. He brushed it aside lightly when she questioned him. It was not the moment to say he had come because he loved her, because he'd willingly give up everything to be near her when she needed him, because he'd never have forgiven himself if anything happened to her and he'd not tried to prevent it.

'Couldn't let old Andy do it all on his own, could I?' he said and grinned. 'Besides you all talked to me so much about Russia, I thought I'd take a look for myself, and just now I can't say I think all that much of it.'

She frowned. 'But you were just beginning to make such a big success.'

'Not so big, and anyway it'll still be there. It won't run away.'

'What do you do here?'

400

'Well, I'm not a doctor, and I'm not much of a hand with nursing, but I help out.'

And he did, climbing up on the roof and mending it where the rain trickled through, carrying in the big heavy pot of thick milky gruel which was all the famine victims could digest. She used to watch him ladling it into their bowls and stopping to feed those too weak to help themselves, and she felt comforted simply because he was there.

As soon as she was strong enough to travel, they would have to face the problem of getting her safely out of the country. They discussed it a dozen times, but before they had come to any satisfactory solution something more immediate put it out of their minds.

Joe Kinsale, whose work took him out far and wide, came rushing back with the alarming news that a couple of officials from the labour camp at the collective farm had been touring all the other missions determined to trace their escaped prisoner.

'I hoped they'd think she was dead,' said Bart gloomily.

'Don't you believe it! Those Reds don't give up so easily. You'd better get cracking. They could be here before the end of the day.'

Where in God's name could they hide her, and even if they did what about the other patients? Who could be sure what they might let out under questioning even if none of them knew Tanya's real identity.

It was Sister Clemency, who hid a steely courage and an astute mind under a deceptively gentle manner, who came up with a suggestion.

'Is your sister anything of an actress, Dr Aylsham?' she asked Andy. 'Could she play the part of Sister Mary Agnes?'

'Play a part? What do you mean?'

'It's very simple. Sister Mary Agnes was one of our team till six weeks ago. She was a delicate creature and should never really have come. She developed a fever and died rather suddenly, poor girl, and lies buried out there. Suppose we bring her to life? Suppose she is lying sick here in our hospital?'

'They'll never swallow that,' exclaimed Bart.

'Why won't they? You probably don't know, Doctor, but all nuns have their hair cropped short before they take the veil, and they never show their shorn heads to anyone, not even to a doctor.

You'd be surprised how a tight linen cap tied under the chin can alter a face. She will not of course understand one word of Russian, and must lie very quiet with downcast eyes as befits a nun in the presence of strangers.'

'It's an idea,' said Luke slowly.

'It's the best we've come up with so far,' said Bart. 'We can put the screen up again as an extra safeguard. With any luck they might not even ask to look behind it, but if they do we'll be prepared. Do you think Tanya is up to it?'

'I'm sure she is,' said Sister Clemency. 'Anything rather than go back to the hell she came from. I'll go and prepare her for it.'

Wearing the high-necked nightgown and with the close-fitting white linen bonnet tied tightly under the chin, the small pale face reminded Luke of a stone figure on a medieval tomb, only Tanya's eyes, large and frightened, belonged to his love.

Sister Clemency had explained exactly what she must do. She lay very still, her hands clasped together, a rosary twisted between her fingers, her stomach churning queasily. She heard them come in, two of them, their voices loud and peremptory. She heard Bart reply in his basic Russian, with Andy smoothly interpreting as the heavy footsteps paused by each bed. They reached the ramshackle screen and Andy explained that the patient was one of the nursing sisters who had been seriously ill and should not be disturbed, but they were not to be put off so easily. The screen was roughly pushed aside and the two men stood facing her. She guessed that one was the Camp Supervisor, whom she had never met; the other was Viktor Trebov.

She had not expected it, and for one startled moment her eyes met his before she modestly lowered them, stiff with terror, absolutely certain that he had recognized her. There were a few seconds that seemed to last an hour, then the Supervisor made an impatient movement.

'Well, comrade, is this the woman von Richter?'

'No,' said Viktor, his voice flat and colourless. 'No, she is not the one. She is nothing like her.'

'It seems we have been misinformed,' said his companion drily. 'Are you quite certain?'

'Quite certain.'

'I'm sorry we have been unable to help you,' said Bart smoothly.

'Will you come this way, gentlemen? The rest of our working team are outside if you wish to question them.'

She lay shaking as the voices died away. He had known her instantly, she was sure of it. There had been recognition in the eyes that met hers, and yet he had not denounced her. Why? She had struck him viciously, had left him to face the anger of his superiors, and yet he had not taken his revenge. He had cruelly abused her and now she could only feel deep gratitude.

The truck started up outside; they were going away. A few minutes later Bart came back with Andy and Luke, all three of them jubilant with relief.

'You did magnificently, my dear,' said Bart and patted her on the shoulder.

Luke had taken her hand. She tried to smile up at them while the tears ran helplessly down her cheeks.

Sister Clemency hustled them away.

'Go on, off with you. The poor child is worn out, and little wonder. All that nervous strain. Now you lie quiet, my dear, have a little nap. I'll fetch you something to drink.'

She bustled away while Luke still lingered.

'Why are you crying?' he said gently. 'Is anything wrong?'

'Silly, isn't it, when it's all over?' Then she couldn't keep it in any longer. 'He knew me, Luke, the younger of the two, Viktor Trebov. He knew who I was.'

'You must be mistaken.'

'No, I'm not. He knew. We'd worked together for several weeks. I waited for him to denounce me and he didn't. Why?'

'Well, even a Communist can have a heart,' he said lightly. 'He was probably sorry for you.'

'But you don't know what I did to him. They were going to send me away, far away, thousands of miles, to Yakutsk in eastern Siberia where there are labour camps for the mines. Viktor offered to marry me, to save me from it, and I laughed. It seemed so ridiculous, so impossible, but he meant to be kind, and all I did was to laugh . . .' She stopped abruptly.

'And then what?'

'We were sheltering from the storm in a forester's hut. He turned away and I hit him with one of the logs. It was terrible. I thought I'd killed him but he was only stunned, and then I ran away.'

403

'Was he in love with you?'

'I don't know. He said he was.'

It was the first time she had spoken of what had happened, and they had all assumed the blow on the head had resulted in a temporary amnesia, which often happens. He guessed that this was not the whole story, that she was keeping something back, but he did not want to press her.

He said soothingly, 'Don't let it worry you. If he wanted to help you, then accept it and be grateful.'

'But suppose he suffers for it?'

'Why should he?'

'You don't know what they're like. There is no trust. They suspect everyone.'

Then Sister Clemency was back with a cup of tea and an aspirin and shooed Luke away.

Tanya drank the tea obediently and tried to rest, but it wasn't possible. She had attempted to put the whole episode out of her mind, and now it all flooded back, she could not escape it. A new fear shot through her mind, something that had not struck her before when she was still sick and dazed by the injury to her head, but which now sprang into life, real and threatening. Suppose she was pregnant, suppose she was to bear Viktor's child? She cringed at the thought. It was too bizarre, too appalling to contemplate, but the possibility was there, and in the days that followed the fear began to grow into a feverish certainty. During the day, with returning health, she could dismiss it, but in the quiet hours of the night it haunted her, and yet she could not bear to confess it to anyone, not even Andy.

The success of their deception had given them an idea backed up by Sister Clemency and Dr Malone. She had played the part of Sister Mary Agnes once, why not continue with it? They had all the dead girl's papers, her passport, her visas. Dressed in the nun's grey habit she would simply be one of the nursing sisters whose health had broken down and who was being escorted back to England by a doctor and a fellow worker. Now suddenly it was as if she couldn't wait to get away. She was obsessed with an intense longing for Ravensley, for her father, for the ordinary things of home where she could hide herself, where she would be safe.

'Not so fast, my girl,' warned Bart when she insisted on getting

404

up, on walking up and down outside, testing her strength, trying to grow accustomed to the thick, enveloping folds of the long grey habit and the tight-fitting wimple and veil. 'You must keep calm and don't fret. You don't want to break down on the way, do you?'

'Andy will look after me.'

'You're a fortunate young woman to have two such devoted slaves,' he remarked drily.

It was late November when they set out after an emotional farewell. All the nuns embraced her in turn, with a special hug and blessing from Sister Clemency. Joe drove them in the truck to Dnepropetrovsk. From there they would go by train to Kharkov, on to Kiev, and then by a devious route overland to Poland, avoiding Moscow.

They reached the border safely and were congratulating themselves on their good luck when there was an unexpected delay. Then orders were shouted all along the platform and everyone was ordered off the train.

It had turned icily cold. A thin sleety snow was falling as the guards went up and down the long line of shivering passengers examining papers and staring closely into faces.

Tanya could not stop shaking. It carried her back to that dreadful day on the platform at Kiev when her mother had been murdered, the day that had given her so many childish nightmares. She thought she might have fallen if Luke had not held her arm firmly within his. The guard reached them, looked them over, all three of them, and barked an order. Despite Andy's strong protests they were shut into a cold waiting room for several hours, their nerves on edge, not knowing what was to happen to them.

Men and women eager to escape from Russia had fled out of the country in a variety of disguises. A grey nursing nun with a seemingly valid United States passport was new, but the man from the GPU was taking no chances.

Tanya was taken into an adjoining room and ordered to strip by a female guard who enjoyed being brutally humiliating. It was hard to maintain a look of innocence and non-comprehension at the abuse and coarse jests made at the expense of her nun's habit, the crucifix round her neck, the rosary at her girdle. Dressed again, she was subjected to a lengthy interrogation, laboriously interpreted by Andy. Once she came close to fainting and Luke, whose anger had been steadily growing, would have intervened if Andy

405

had not stopped him with a warning gesture. The last thing they wanted was an emotional involvement. They must at all costs remain calm and cool.

A glass of water was brought, they waited grimly for her to recover, and the questioning went on as they tried to trick her into some damaging admission. It became increasingly difficult to look merely bewildered when insults were hurled at her, and she was wondering why so much trouble was being taken when the reason suddenly became obvious.

Her interrogator glanced at a paper in his hand. 'Why do you persist in these stupid lies, Madame von Richter, when I hold here a confession signed by you in the Lubianka months ago? Don't you realize it can only be the worse for you?'

If he meant to shock her into indignant denial he very nearly succeeded. What had happened? Had Viktor's lie been detected? It was on the tip of her tongue to say furiously, 'Shukilov knows perfectly well I didn't sign his lying confession and would never sign it.'

Somehow she bit the words back. There was no need to simulate the tears that sprang to her eyes. She looked pleadingly at Andy, her fingers on the rosary at her waist, her lips moving.

'What does she say?' her tormentor asked irritably.

'She is praying that God will forgive your brutality towards her, as she does,' said Andy quietly.

'There is no God. We have abolished that superstition once and for all in Russia. It is the State that is important, not the mumbling of outworn prayers to a powerless idol.'

'I'm afraid, Comrade Commissar, that you have not yet succeeded in converting the whole world to your new belief,' said Andy ironically.

Baffled, he at last gave up. Their papers were returned and they were allowed to board the train. It was not until it had drawn out of the station and they were well into Poland that Tanya dared to look up, trembling between laughter and tears.

'Di used to tell me I was the worst actress she had ever had anything to do with. I wonder what she would think of me now.'

24

It was a grey December day when the cross-Channel steamer groped its way through a thick sea mist into Dover. It had been a long and wearisome journey broken only by an overnight stop in Paris to buy Tanya some clothes.

The girl in the thickly carpeted room in the elegant Paris salon had glanced with startled eyes at her grey nun's habit.

'What is it madame would like me to show her?' she had asked doubtfully.

'Everything,' Tanya had replied gaily. 'Everything from the feet up.'

It had been a relief to strip off the thick woollen skirts, the close-fitting wimple and veil, to bathe in hot scented water, to have her hair washed and cut, to put on new silk underwear, not to feel afraid any longer or on the defensive or sick with hunger and yet nauseated by unpalatable food, and yet the old carefree delight had vanished, perhaps for ever. She was impatient to be done with it. She longed only for home.

Andy had cabled his father, and Simon was on the quay waiting for her. She ran down the gangway into his arms, finding there comfort and solace as she had done so many times before. Then for the first time in her life she held out her hands to the stepmother she had hated, as if in some strange way what she had suffered had made them sisters instead of enemies. Galina hesitated and then put her arms round the girl, holding her close, feeling her tremble, aware of how desperately thin and vulnerable she was.

Walking with them to the car it was hard to believe that it was barely two years since she had defied them to marry Dirk, had gone from this very dock radiantly happy, sure of his love and her future. It seemed a lifetime ago, an age during which she had become a totally different person who had experienced intense happiness and pain, grief and bitter regret.

There were still days of trial to get through before she could get away to the peace of Ravensley. Mr Brown was there asking question after question, grudgingly obliged to admit that their unorthodox methods had succeeded where his efforts had failed. Aunt Hester arrived one morning saying what a pity it was that she had lost her looks and she had always known that marriage to that foreigner would end in disaster.

News leaked into the press. Reporters besieged Wimpole Street, cameras in hand, looking for a story, and were kept at bay by Andy refusing to give them anything but the barest facts. Luke didn't escape either. Since they could get so little from Andy or Simon they hung about James Tait's flat in Bayswater where he was staying, until he dreaded answering the telephone and was obliged to slip out of the house by the back door.

'And what's wrong with that, my dear chap?' said his publisher when he called on him at his office in Maiden Lane. 'Why not let it rip? You're the hero of the hour, so why not let them have it hot and strong? It'll give your sales no end of a boost. When are you going to marry the girl?'

'For God's sake,' exclaimed Luke. 'Who said anything about marriage? Her husband has only been dead for a few months.'

Hugh Carter looked at him with raised eyebrows. 'You're not telling me that you dashed off on that forlorn quest without being dotty about the young woman, are you? It would make a beautiful bit of publicity when we publish the new book. We held it up, you know, waiting for you, though I had a horrible feeling I was acting the fool and you'd end up in one of their damned penal settlements in Outer Mongolia.'

'Well, I didn't, and if you dare to use that marriage lark as a stunt, I'll never let you publish another book of mine.'

'Dear, dear, playing the great author now, are we, on the strength of a couple of books?' Hugh Carter grinned. 'All right, old man, we'll let it go if we can invite her to the party I intend to give to celebrate.'

Down in Tredegar where he had gone for Christmas, he met with a very similar reception. Of course his mother was overjoyed to see him return safely, but Dai took good care to spice his relief with a dose of sarcasm.

'Let's hope that's the last time you go off acting the giddy goat.

I should say you've been damned lucky. I only hope that Lord Aylsham is properly grateful to you for returning his daughter to him.'

'It wasn't what I did. If you really want to know, it was her brother, an American doctor and a bunch of Catholic nuns who came up with the solution, so shut up about it, will you, Dai? I've got other things to think about.'

'When are you going to marry your princess?' asked Megan, who had come to take tea with his mother and hear all the news.

'Now don't you start,' he said irritably. 'Why should everyone believe I did what I did because I was in love with her? If you want to know why I did it, it was because I hate injustice and owe a great deal to her father, and that's the end of it.'

But of course he had thought about it, more than once. How could he help it? He told himself over and over it was ridiculous, that she had been married to Dirk and still grieved for him, that he didn't want to catch her on the rebound, that she had lost the first dazzle of her enchanting beauty. None of it made any difference. She was the woman he had wanted ever since he had first seen her, and one day she would come to him. He had only to wait till she had recovered her health, till she was able to tell him what it was that tormented her, because he knew there was something. He had never told Andy about Viktor Trebov and what had happened in that forester's hut. She had spoken in confidence and it was not for him to speak of it, but somehow it had erected a barrier between them and he did not know why.

She had a curious dislike of any kind of physical contact, not only with him but with members of the family, whereas before she had always possessed a charming spontaneity. He mentioned it once to Andy, who showed a practical good sense about it.

'You've got to remember she's been through a pretty nasty experience. It can do all kinds of things to you. I did suggest she ought to see a doctor now she's home, or even let Pa look her over, but she refused absolutely, said she felt perfectly well, but I'm not so sure. It's not entirely physical, you know, there's a mental side to it.'

Andy was right, but he didn't guess the real reason. The obsession was like a monstrous growth inside her. She had missed her period when she was still at the mission, and tried to convince herself that it was the same as before when she had been first imprisoned. Then came the second missed period, and she stared at herself in the mirror, running her hands down her naked body, still pitifully thin.

'Eat little but often,' had been her father's advice. 'Then gradually the body will adjust.'

Diana had gone back to New York, otherwise she might have confided in her. Diana was so practical, so down to earth. As it was, she found it totally impossible to speak about it to anyone.

After the months of semi-starvation she was perpetually hungry and yet nauseated, which only added to the dread, and with it came a deep feeling of shame. Could she have prevented it? Was it all her own fault? Had she in some way encouraged him? It was like a nightmare which will not go away, not even in the clear light of day. She felt trapped as though, in spite of being home and free, she was still in prison.

Luke knew he was lucky. He had burned his boats behind him when he went off to Russia, but seemingly they were still there when he came back. Aberystwyth University had found his substitute unsatisfactory and the lectureship was still open to him. Something deeply Welsh inside him responded to it, but he was still hesitating when Hugh Carter rang him one morning with the dazzling proposition of a lecture tour in the United States.

'They can't want *me*,' he said incredulously. 'Is this one of your jokes?'

'Far from it, dear boy. Your American publisher is hot as mustard for you to accept. It's your knight errant stunt that's taken their fancy, coupled with good sales of *The Lost Leader*, and it'll boost the new book no end. You'll be the glamour boy to all the middle-aged ladies with their blue rinses in their teatime clubs from Manhattan to California. They'll be hanging on your words of wisdom. The money's good too, far better than the measly offer from Wales. What do you say?'

'I don't know. Perhaps.'

It was not the kind of thing he liked, and it would take him out of England for months, perhaps a year, and he was not sure that he wanted that. He was still undecided when he was invited down

410

to Ravensley. Tanya'a Uncle Niki and Aunt Sonia had come over from France for Christmas and were staying for the New Year. It was a crisply frosty morning in January when he arrived, and he was exuberantly welcomed by Nicola and promptly dragged off to inspect the new litter of pups.

'Jason is their father. Aren't they gorgeous?' She picked up one of the squealing, velvet-coated puppies and hugged it. 'They've a very good pedigree. Would you like one?'

'Very much, but I mustn't take him. I may be going to America.'

'Lucky old you. Are you going to lecture?'

'Perhaps. Don't breathe a word. It's still not settled.'

'Does Tanya know?'

'Not yet.'

She put down the puppy and said thoughtfully, 'Tanya will miss you. She likes you, you know, but she's been in a funny mood ever since she came home, all bottled up inside herself.' She glanced up at him. 'She's going to be quite rich. Did Andy tell you?'

'No.'

'Dirk's stepfather is insisting that everything he gave to Dirk should now go to her.'

Damn, damn, and damn again! The very last thing he wanted! To find her an heiress when he felt they might be on equal terms! He swallowed hard and managed a smile.

'Good for her after all she has been through. How's the vet business going?'

'Very well really. I've just got to get through Matric next year. Andy says it's even harder than studying for a doctor. He's going up to Edinburgh to work at the hospital there. He's made up his mind to specialize in brain surgery, did he tell you? He says I can go up in the hols and stay with him and he'll help me with it.'

Andy and Nicola, thought Luke; perhaps it was a solution after the unhappy affair with Diana. Now she was out of England and far away from him, maybe it would be easier to face the break. Andy was eleven years older than Nicola, but did that matter? The age difference would lessen with every month that passed. He felt a sharp pang of envy.

Dinner that evening was a lively affair. Niki and Sonia were good company, and Tanya, though she ate very little, was in high spirits. Too high, thought Luke, noticing how her father watched

411

her. Her voice was too brittle, her laughter too forced, as she told them about Leningrad and her visit to their old home at Dannskoye. Afterwards coffee was brought to the drawing room and Andy busied himself with the drinks tray.

'Brandy for you, Pa? What's your poison, Luke?'

He brought the glasses across and said casually, 'I ran into Bart Malone today. Actually he's on his way to the States to rustle up more money for the mission, but he told me something interesting. Remember those two chaps who came from the labour camp and luckily for us failed to recognize Tanya in her nun's get-up? Well, one of them, a fellow called Viktor something, has come to a very sticky end.'

'He's what?' Tanya, who had been sorting through gramophone records, had swung round. 'What do you mean, Andy?'

'Well, it seems he was accused of treason against the State and sentenced to *katorga*, which I gather means twelve years' hard labour in a penal settlement, which seems pretty drastic to me, and the poor fellow couldn't take it. When they went to the punishment cell he had hanged himself.'

The record fell from Tanya's hand and smashed on the floor.

'Oh no,' she said. 'Oh no, no, not that!'

She clapped her hand to her mouth and ran out of the room.

There was a momentary pause, then Simon said quietly, 'You might have kept that to yourself, Andy. You know how easily she is upset these days. I'd better go to her.'

'No,' said Galina. 'No, Simon, I'll go.'

Sonia stood up. 'Shall I come?'

'No, my dear, it's not necessary. It's only a few weeks since she came home and she's not quite herself yet. Luke, would you pick up the broken record? The dogs might cut their paws.'

She left a feeling of uneasiness behind her. Luke gathered up the pieces, and Andy rang for Alice, who came with brush and dustpan. Then Galina was back looking worried.

'She's not in her room, not anywhere in the house. Jake said he thought he saw her run out of the front door. He was coming to tell us.'

'On a freezing night like this? Whatever can she be thinking of? I'd better go after her.' Simon was already on his feet.

'We don't know where she has gone.'

'It can't be far,' said Andy. 'I'll come with you, Pa. Not you, Uncle Niki. We don't all need to go.'

They went out into the hall pulling on coats, and Luke went with them.

'We'll need torches,' said Andy. 'There are some in the garden room. I'll fetch them.

Outside, everything glittered in a white frost and the dark winter sky was blazing with stars.

'God knows which way she went. We'd better separate. I'll take the stables first,' said Simon.

'All right. Then I'll go through the gardens. What about you, Luke?'

'I'll go down to the river.'

He had remembered something that frightened him. That afternoon years ago when they were groping tentatively towards a friendship – the ruined mill and Tanya saying, 'I come here sometimes when I'm miserable and remember terrible things.' What terrible thing was she remembering now?

The water was black and smelled foul and dank. There was no boat and he followed a narrow path soggy with dead leaves. It was further than he remembered. He walked rapidly, lighting his way with the torch, and then suddenly it was before him, a gaunt ruin, grim and spectral against the night sky, and standing on the water's brink beneath it a wraith wrapped in a thick white shawl that trailed on the muddy ground behind her.

He moved slowly towards her, his feet making no sound on the soft earth. He put his hand gently on her shoulder and she swung round, her face very white in the pale light of the rising moon.

'I wanted to jump but I hadn't the courage,' she whispered and choked on a sob. She was shivering violently as he put his arm round her. 'It was what Andy said,' she went on. 'Viktor must have done it because of me. It's all been because of me, everything. I saw Dirk die, and I could do nothing to help him, nothing at all; and now Viktor, and I didn't even like him. I laughed at him . . . Oh God, if you knew how I have despised myself.'

'It was the shock,' he said gently. 'You'll feel better about it tomorrow.'

He was beginning to understand that she had reached some sort of crisis and the first necessity was to bring her back to warmth

413

and safety. She stumbled in her thin shoes and he guided her along the rough path. They reached the lawns and Simon, coming from the stables, hurried to meet them, taking her other arm, his voice quiet, bringing her back to normality.

'A fine fright you gave us running off like that, puss.'

'I'm sorry, Papa, I didn't mean to upset everyone.' She had mastered herself with a mighty effort. 'I felt rather sick. I had to get out into the air.'

Galina was there in the hall and took her from Luke.

'You're chilled through, my dear, and little wonder. The sooner we get you to bed the better. Ask Alice to bring a couple of hot water bottles, will you, Simon? And get yourself a hot drink, Luke. You look perished.'

Her level voice was absolutely right, bringing them down from high drama to ordinary practical needs. Luke watched Galina take Tanya up the stairs, then followed Simon into the drawing room.

When Tanya was in bed, the warm blankets tucked round her, hot water bottles at her side and by her feet, Galina drew up a chair.

'Now, my dear,' she said gently, 'you and I are going to have a little talk.'

'Not tonight.'

'Yes, now, tonight. This has gone on long enough. You've been walking about the house like a ghost all these past weeks. I want to know what is troubling you.'

'There is nothing.'

Galina had ordered a fire to be lit as soon as the men had gone into the gardens, and the bedroom was already filled with a warm glow.

She turned the averted face towards her. 'Don't lie to me, Tanya. I want to help, but how can I if you won't trust me? Would you rather I fetched your father?'

'No, not Papa, please not Papa.'

'Very well, but he loves you, Tanya, very much.'

'I know.'

'Is it the thought of Dirk that haunts you?'

'You were right about him, and yet in some ways terribly

414

wrong,' she said slowly. 'He did love me, Galina, and yet I couldn't save him. For weeks and weeks I couldn't bear to think of it, but at night I would dream. I'd see him fall, see the blood, feel his hand in mine before he died and they dragged me away. I didn't even know what they did with him.'

The man she had lived with, whose body had given her joy, whose child she might have borne. It was still unbearable. She shut her eyes against it for a moment.

'He was driven by something stronger than himself, something you were powerless to change. You must try to see it like that.'

The girl was staring in front of her, and after a moment's pause Galina went on. 'There is something else, isn't there?'

Suddenly Tanya sat up, her eyes fixed on her stepmother's face. 'How did *you* feel when that man, Igor Livinov, attacked you?'

So that was it. For a moment Galina hesitated. It was important to find the right words.

'Outraged, numb with horror, utterly ashamed. I couldn't talk of it to anyone, not even to my closest friend. You must remember that your father and I had been lovers, we were to be married in a few weeks, he was far away when I found I was pregnant. For a time it seemed like the end of my world and I ran away from it.'

'How did you live through all those months not knowing who was the father of your baby?'

'The awful fact is that, however desperate one is, life has to go on. I hoped, I prayed, and it was like a miracle when I knew that Andy was your father's child, but by then it was too late. He was already married to your mother. But all this is in the past, Tanya, why ask me about it now?'

'Because I believe I am pregnant.'

There was a long pause. Galina looked searchingly into her face.

'Is it that man whom Andy spoke of, this Russian who killed himself?'

'Yes.'

'Tell me about it. Were you in love with him?'

'Oh no, no, never!' Then it all poured out, the life of the camp, the work she had done with Viktor, how in some strange way it had drawn them together, the storm and the forester's hut, his coming to the mission afterwards.

'He knew me, Galina, he had only to admit it and they would

415

have taken me back and sent me away, far away, I could still be there now; but he didn't denounce me and he has suffered for it. They must have suspected that he lied. He was a good Party member, he believed in what was being done, we used to argue about it. He must have felt that he had betrayed his own ideals, and in some terrible way his death is all my fault.'

'No, Tanya, you mustn't go on believing that. He made his own choice, a generous one. It is sad that he has suffered so cruelly for it, but you did not ask it from him. Each person makes their own life. Why do you believe you are pregnant?'

'It began there, the fear, the anxiety, and then I missed my period, and again since I've been home. You see I was pregnant once before in Germany, so I do know something about it.'

'Missing a period does not necessarily mean you are with child. There are other causes, anaemia from malnutrition, anxiety, abnormal conditions to which the body has been exposed – all these things can be causes.'

'I wish I could believe that.'

'My dear, you forget that I am also a doctor.'

'But supposing it is true?'

'Then we will find some way round it. Now let us be practical. You must tell your father.'

'I can't. He will think so badly of me.'

'Don't you know him better than that? If you would prefer it, I will tell him. He will see that you have every possible test. Why didn't you confide in us before and save yourself weeks of misery?'

'I couldn't. I was so terribly ashamed, so sure everyone would believe that I had brought it upon myself, and perhaps in a way, without meaning it, I did.'

'Everyone has something to be ashamed of. We wouldn't be human beings if we didn't. It is what makes us real, gives us character, helps us to be considerate towards others. If any good has come out of this,' went on Galina wryly, 'it is that at least it has brought us closer together. I've waited a very long time for that.' She leaned forward and kissed Tanya's cheek. 'Now try and rest.' She smiled, putting back the tousled hair with a gentle hand. 'There's been enough soul-searching for one evening. I'll send Alice up with a hot drink for you.'

She lay quietly when Galina had gone. Nothing had materially changed, yet she felt relieved, almost as if a poisoned dart had been withdrawn from deep within her and a healing process could begin.

When the door opened it was not Alice but her father who came in with a hot milky drink on a tray.

'I've been instructed to bring you this and stand over you till you drink it.'

'Oh, Papa, I'm not still a child.'

'Aren't you? You look about ten sitting up like that.' He put the tray down on the table. 'There are a couple of pills to help you sleep.'

'Has Galina told you?' she whispered.

He sat down on the bed beside her and took her hand.

'Listen, my pet. I'm a very old hand at this kind of thing. Do you think I wouldn't have guessed by now? In my opinion you're not nursing a pregnancy but a huge great guilt complex.'

'Are you sure?'

'So sure that I'd wager the fortune I don't possess on it, but we'll prove it scientifically just as soon as you feel you can stand it.'

'Tomorrow?'

'Tomorrow it is. You can drive up to London with me. Now drink your milk and swallow the pills and go to sleep like a good girl.'

He got up and she caught at his hand.

'Papa, I do love you.'

For a moment she was poignantly like Nina, so like her dead mother whose consuming love he had never been able to return, that he couldn't speak. Then he bent and kissed her forehead.

'Go to sleep, puss,' he said huskily and went quickly from the room.

The party which was being held in the Albany, where Hugh Carter's colleague had a bachelor apartment, was in full swing. The two rooms were crowded. A motley collection of writers, publishers, agents, critics, with a sprinkling of theatre folk, all talking at the tops of their voices while waiters moved discreetly among them with trays of drinks, of canapés and lobster patties, of sausage rolls, crab vol-au-vents and cheese fondue. Egos fought egos, those perched precariously on top of the ladder were being besieged by those still at the bottom in the vain hope that a little of their good fortune might brush off, and all of it was spiced with charm and jealousy, with good humour and a hint of malice.

Luke, at the centre, was not at all sure he liked any of it. Something deeply Welsh and independent, highly suspicious of the pretentious and the bogus, rebelled against the flattery, the congratulations tinged with envy, the women who crowded around him, not one of whom had read *The Lost Leader* or showed any real interest in the new book they were celebrating. They were far more intrigued by his trip to Russia and what he was going to do about it now he had come back. It was all very far from Dai's sarcastic comment.

'For the Lord's sake, boyo, when are you going to stop scribbling those old books of yours and settle down to a real job of work?' he had demanded.

Luke could see Hugh Carter holding forth to an elite group with accomplished ease. He gave him a significant glance above the head of the *Times* literary editor and it stopped Luke in his tracks. He had been about to do a vanishing trick now that the first rush was over, sure that he wouldn't be missed, but Hugh had gone to considerable trouble and expense on his behalf. He couldn't in all decency back out of it now.

He braced himself to answer more of the questions being fired at him. 'Why did he choose to write about Wales? Weren't there wider political issues? Wasn't he just producing pap for the millions?'

'I write about people, not political propoganda,' he snapped, and then stopped abruptly as he saw her come in.

Tanya was standing in the doorway, no longer the waif who had sobbed helplessly in his arms at the mission, no longer the shivering, distraught girl he had rescued from the ruined mill. She was poised, superbly sure of herself, looking incredibly lovely in a simple black dress with a silver thread that glittered in the light, her hair burnished to gold. Her face, thinned by grief and privation, had achieved a mature beauty, the emerald on a new gold chain glowed on the white neck. So she still grieved for Dirk, and it struck Luke painfully that all that had happened in the last

418

few months to bring them so close together meant nothing. She was still the princess, still as far out of his reach as she had ever been.

There was a momentary hush as heads turned to look, then Hugh Carter went to greet her and she was immediately swallowed up in a buzz of talk and speculation.

In actual fact Luke didn't realize how much courage it had needed to bring her there that evening. It was barely a week since she had come away from the hospital feeling light as air, the burden lifted, but still uncertain of herself.

'What did I tell you?' her father had said. 'You may be suffering from a variety of minor ills, but you're certainly not pregnant. Be off with you now, have some fun, buy yourself something pretty and charge it to me.'

So she had done just that, and with the stifling weight lifted she began to believe she could at last accept what had happened to her and begin to live again.

As Galina had said out of her own experience, life has to go on, and the grief and regret, even the shame and the guilt, become part of you and only serve to strengthen you to meet new challenges.

The invitation had come from Hugh Carter with a little personal note.

'You are, I understand, Luke's inspiration. Don't disappoint him.'

Was it true? She owed him a great deal. In the darkest days of her imprisonment she had grown very close to him in a desperate attempt to remain sane. At the mission he had become a rock to which she had clung, but how much had he guessed about her and Viktor? What must he be thinking? How he must despise her. She had not seem him since that painful Sunday night, and it had opened a chasm between them she found it difficult to cross.

She wished Andy had been there to go to the party with her but he had gone to Edinburgh to discuss his future. She had not ventured to go out anywhere since she had come home. It was stupid to be so nervous about it, and yet she was. In the end, realizing suddenly how late she was, she had dressed very hurriedly, putting on a light make-up, snatching up the fur coat her father had given her to replace the one lost in Russia, and running down the stairs to find a taxi.

Once there it was easier than she had expected. Glass in hand she regained a certain social poise, could talk lightly about nothing at all, answering questions and giving little away, and all the time she was edging closer to Luke. She could see him in animated conversation with a handsome woman whose powerful personality seemed to turn all those near to her into nonentities. She had taken his arm, he was listening intently, and Tanya's insecurely held self-confidence began to drain away. He had his own life to lead, he was on the way up. Why should he any longer concern himself with a tiresome young woman whom he had rescued from a disastrous situation of her own making?

She was suddenly sick of the idle talk around her. She put down her glass, resolved to leave now quickly before he noticed her. But she was too late. Luke's companion laughed, patted his cheek familiarly, and pounced on her next victim.

Luke turned, caught Tanya's eye, and smiled disarmingly.

'I thought she'd never stop. She is one of the top agents and was doing her damnedest to lure me away from Hugh – as if I would . . .' He was talking at random. They might have been alone in the crowded room.

'How very beautiful you look,' he whispered.

'I can't think why.' She was suddenly shy. 'I haven't a thing to wear that isn't years and years old.'

The party was beginning to thin out and now he didn't care. He was going to make a bid for her. He'd earned the right. If she was going to be rich, well, that was just the hell of it. Perhaps he could persuade her to give it all to a dogs' home!

'Tanya,' he said urgently, 'shall we escape?'

She gave a quick look around her. 'Should you?'

'Why not? I've given of my best. Come on.'

He grabbed her hand and moved through the guests, with a smile and a nod here and there till they reached the hall. They paused for him to collect a coat and then they were out in the courtyard.

'Shall we make a run for it?'

Hand in hand they raced under the archway and into Piccadilly. It was icily cold, the wind swirled around them, and they stopped breathless while he helped her into the short fur coat and struggled into his own overcoat.

'I'm hungry, aren't you? Let's go and find something solid to eat instead of all those fripperies.' He had taken her arm and was hurrying her along. 'Where would you like to go? The Savoy?'

'Oh no, no, not there.' The Savoy was Dirk. She thought she'd never willingly go there again. 'I'd rather it was somewhere quiet and cosy.'

'Right.'

He hailed a taxi and took her to Soho. It was early for Bertorelli's and they had a choice of tables. The handsome old Italian was there with his basket of roses even if it was winter outside.

'Beauty is but a flower,' he said. 'For you, madame. Welcome home.' And he laid a white rose beside Tanya's plate.

She picked it up and smiled her thanks. Here they had come in those early days, not often because money had been tight, but it carried her back to that close companionship before she had met Dirk and everything had changed.

They did not speak of anything vital to them both till the meal was almost done and she asked him when he was leaving for America.

'I'm not going,' he said flatly.

'But you must. Hugh Carter was saying what a wonderful experience it will be and how profitable.'

'It's an experience I can do without, and money means a lot but it isn't everything. I made up my mind quite suddenly tonight when that woman was holding out all kinds of golden promises and I discovered I didn't want any of them. He paused. Her eyes were on his face. He had caught her interest. It was now or never. He took a deep breath and went on. 'Before he died my father said, "Never forget what you owe to Wales," so I'm going to Aberystwyth. I'm going back there to try and repay a debt. Give something to kids who like me are bursting to get away from the valleys. Does that sound daft?'

She shook her head. 'Go on.'

'I shall rent a little house just outside the town not far from the mountains. I shall ask my mother to come and housekeep for me, and buy a bicycle so that I can research my next book. I'm going to write the story of the struggle in which my great-great-grand-father was hanged. No one has done it properly yet: the battle against the English ironmasters who chained five-year-old children to their wagons and employed pregnant women, forcing them to work on and on till they gave birth to their babies down in the pits under the black earth; the story of whole families who worked and died so that others might live. It all came to me in a rush. I knew exactly what I wanted to do.'

He was spreading it all before her, the life he was planning for himself, independent at last, take it or leave it, and it appealed to her greatly. Something to work for, something to achieve, but she had learnt a great deal in the past few months. You can't grab at things, you must earn them.

'I'm talking too much as usual,' he went on, smiling a little shamefacedly. 'Once a Welshman gets started, he'll never stop. He'll drown you in words. What are your plans, Tanya, now that you are going to be rich?'

'With Dirk's money?' She looked away. 'I don't know yet. First I have to go to Zurich. I have to see the Baron, tell him all I know, stay with him for a while, try to comfort him. He's old and sick and very lonely. I'm not looking forward to it, but that's my debt. I owe it to Dirk and I must pay it. He loved his stepfather.'

'And afterwards?'

She looked at him across the table, colour creeping into her pale cheeks.

'Luke, you know what happened, don't you, between me and Viktor?'

'I think I guessed when you first told me. It doesn't make any difference. You are you, it doesn't change you in any way. This is what really matters, isn't it?' and he leaned forward to touch the emerald on its gold chain.

She was staring down at her clasped hands. 'It's strange. At first I tried to shut Dirk out because the pain was so great, and now it has all come flooding back. I feel only half a person.'

'Are you still in love with him?'

'Yes and no. I wish I had given him more. It was only at the end that I really knew him, and then it was too late. One day perhaps I will be able to tell you about Dirk, but not yet.' Her hand touched the jewel. 'I fought to keep this. When it was stolen,